SLAUGHTERED GODS

SLAUGHTERED
GODS

PART THREE OF THE HANGED GOD TRILOGY

THILDE KOLD HOLDT

SOLARIS

First published 2022 by Solaris
an imprint of Rebellion Publishing Ltd,
Riverside House, Osney Mead,
Oxford, OX2 0ES, UK

www.solarisbooks.com

ISBN: 978 1 78618 745 1

Designed & typeset by Rebellion Publishing

Printed in Denmark

To the ones we shall never cease mourning,

THE STORY SO FAR

Northern Wrath
Chapters One to Sixty-Eight

AFTER THE FALL of the town of Ash-hill, the surviving warriors, including Einer and Finn, travel south to attack Magadoborg, to send a message to the Christian Southerners. A last stand to protect their own lands and beliefs.

Meanwhile, Hilda—another survivor of Ash-hill—joins the warriors in the south, having followed the mysterious whispers in the wind she calls the Runes, and her snow fox fylgja. She has walked through a passage grave into another world and had her eyes burned by a fire demon from Muspelheim. She has even gained an Ulfberht sword and axe. Yet, after she offers the sword to the chieftain—Einer's father, Vigmer—he is still reluctant to let her join their raids. Hilda's and Einer's childhood friend Sigismund steps forth to offer her a place on his crew.

Hilda drips blood into her eyes to soothe the pain. The other warriors call her a draugr and whisper in fear. As they should: a fire demon lurks inside her, waiting to possess her.

9

The warriors continue their journey south, but Einer's father dies in an early battle and their unity is threatened. Finn and Einer face each other in a deadly single combat to decide who of them will become the next chieftain. Finn is discovered to have taken the dead chief's sword—the Ulfberht given him by Hilda—and Einer ends the duel in a rage. He orders Finn to become his thrall, bound to him as a servant until the debt is repaid.

Hilda's father, Ragnar, former skald of Ash-hill, has passed away, but instead of waking up in Valhalla or Helheim in the afterlife, he is stuck in Darkness. Killed anew whenever he makes himself heard, Ragnar finds a way to look through the veil of the worlds and sees Loki lying in a cave. Next, he sees Ragnarok, the fall of his gods and realises that he can influence the gods to do what he wants with his own thoughts. But how will it help him escape this terrible Darkness?

Einer's mother Siv and Tyra, a girl of the village, have also survived the battle of Ash-hill. Siv saved Tyra at the battle by hiding her in the mysterious Darkness inside their sacred ash tree. Siv is a giant, whose true name is Glumbruck, and she knows that the nine worlds are drifting apart. Her brother, Buntrugg, tasks her with strengthening the old beliefs in Midgard. With that goal in mind, Siv travels to King Harald Bluetan in Jelling and impersonates his new wife, adopting Tyra officially as their daughter, hoping to turn Harald away from his new Christian faith.

In turn, Buntrugg is tasked with closing the furnace Hilda has opened. The task brings him far through the nine worlds: reviving a dwarf called Bafir, meeting with young Tyra and finally passing through the dark of a leaking passage grave to the furnace where fire demons rage. Buntrugg slams the furnace shut with the aid of his forefathers, but he is severely burned and falls into the water surrounding the forge, thinking his life forfeit.

As the distant furnace closes, the fire demon waiting inside Hilda gains enough strength to emerge. At the battle at Magadoborg, it burns Hilda's snow fox fylgja to escape.

Desperate to save her dead fylgja, Hilda recites the runes, not caring about the consequences. She feels different when the snow fox comes back to life. Her eyes are not burning anymore, and she can see better than ever before. She rushes back to the fight.

Einer too has left the heat of the battle to search for Hilda, who did not come back when she promised. Out there, on the fields, he sees her dead body. Angry at the gods for taking her so soon, Einer welcomes the ancient rage of the forefathers within him and launches himself at the enemy.

Hilda, not realising she is dead, follows the whispers in the wind to leave Magadoborg with the warriors. From afar, she sees Einer's white bear fylgja battle in the southern town.

Shackled Fates
Chapters Sixty-Nine to One Hundred and Thirty-Three

BUNTRUGG HAS BEEN nursed to health in Valhalla. The Alfather tries to convince him to take over from his master, Surt, but Buntrugg knows that when Ragnarok comes, the giants will only rally behind the ancient giant.

Buntrugg brings Einer to Asgard. Even standing in Valhalla, in the presence of the grand Alfather, Einer only has one thought: Where is Hilda?

In the Darkness, Ragnar accidentally frees Loki from his chains, and suddenly, the Runes stop whispering to Hilda. Searching for the voices, Hilda stumbles across Loki, in Midgard. She steals the god's falcon skin and flies away with her snow fox into Asgard, where she is captured by the goddess Freya. Hilda is brought into the goddesses' lavish lifestyle, but they offer her no help.

In Midgard, Finn is sent to negotiate with Harald Bluetan. Thanks to Siv's influence, Finn, still a thrall, returns to Ash-hill in triumph and becomes its chieftain. In return, Finn promises to care for Harald's son Svend. Hoping to save Tyra from the Alfather's claws which claimed her sons, Siv decides to finally face the old god.

Siv's arrival in Asgard has all of the gods and goddesses hunting for her, for Glumbruck used to live among them. Odin also leaves Einer's side to hunt, after having introduced Einer to his bench-mates in Valhalla, all of them Glumbruck's sons—Einer's half-brothers.

Einer fights his way across Ida's bloody plain to clash with the giants. Responding directly to Einer's thoughts, the giants say that they will bring him home. Einer is propelled across the Jotun Sea to Niflheim's icy shores, where his grandmother fetches him.

Meanwhile Buntrugg has reported to Surt and been tasked with a new quest: to close *all* of the passage graves in the nine worlds, because time is slipping, faster and faster, and the passage graves are leaking.

Hilda goes to Valhalla to win her rightful place among the Alfather's warriors, but the hall lays abandoned. Odin has left his warriors to rot on Ida's plain, while he hunts Glumbruck. Loki arrives and reveals that he is the one who has been whispering to Hilda in the wind. He wanted her to use the Ulfberht axe to release him from his chains. Instead, he was liberated by someone hiding in Darkness, and give Hilda a new quest: discover who hides in dark. In order to do so, Loki says, they will need to speak to a slain giant; and he can guide her to one.

In the Hall of Fates, Siv and Tyra are brought to their own destiny threads by the three nornir, when they are interrupted by valkyries in crow skins and the Alfather himself. Siv makes Tyra flee, and Siv faces off against Odin, begging for Tyra's safety, as she cuts her own destiny thread. She would rather die than be captured by the Alfather, for Glumbruck knows what happens to those who are shackled by him.

Alone in Asgard, Tyra uses a debt owed to her by Bafir the dwarf. She gains a bleeding dagger, which is said to bleed until Ragnarok, and which will permit her to travel through the passage graves and return to Midgard. Time flies by faster and faster; Tyra becomes a young woman, plotting the murder of her fire-demon-possessed husband, Styrbjorn.

Meanwhile, Hilda accidentally cuts a hole into Yggdrasil's root. She looks inside, into Darkness. Her father, Ragnar, stares back.

Someone else joins Ragnar's Darkness: Siv. For the Darkness is Siv's afterlife, and the shadow warriors who slay Ragnar over and over are the forefathers of the giants. She calls Ragnar "the story-maker" and "fate itself."

In Jotunheim, Einer thinks of Hilda, who was not in Valhalla where she belongs. She must have ended up on Niflheim's icy coast. So he goes searching. His grandmother tells him not to disturb the ice, but Einer finds a corpse that he knows: not Hilda, but his old friend Sigismund, who drowned but was refused entry to Ran's and Aegir's afterlife in the sea. Einer frees Sigismund from the ice, points him to Helheim and, to protect him, gives him his magical bracteate, which has saved him more than once.

An ice mist rises and Einer is captured by giants, who place him on trial. For, by disturbing the ice, Einer has provoked the three-year winter that precedes Ragnarok.

Whispering through the wind, Loki brings Hilda to a funeral where the gods have gathered. Ordered about like a simple thrall, Hilda is sent into the Hall of Fates. There she sees that the funeral is for Siv. In the Darkness, Ragnar opens the veil into Asgard to witness the same funeral.

Loki leads Hilda further into the Hall of Fates, where the nornir ambush her. From her blood they spin a new destiny thread for Glumbruck. To revive a dead giant, they need the blood of a norn, and Hilda's skill with Runes proves her lineage.

On top of the pyre, Siv wakes suddenly from death. She

grabs onto runes to hold Ragnar in place, for she knows that he is there, watching her funeral, and of him—of fate itself— she asks a favour: "Unshackle me." Her blood-drenched new destiny thread ties itself into place in the nornir's hall.

As the three nornir spin with Hilda's blood to revive Siv, Hilda's own destiny is undone. All memories of her are erased from the nine worlds. Even the spinning nornir no longer recall who she is, but they can see that she is a norn like them and they resolve to care for her as a sister.

Across the nine worlds, in Jotunheim, Einer no longer remembers who he was searching for when he disturbed the ice and brought on the snowstorm which announces Ragnarok.

EINER

Chapter One Hundred and Thirty-Four

THE BLOOD OF a giant stained the snow at Einer's feet. Red, it dripped from the tip of his Ulfberht sword. This time, Einer had not been lost to the rage. This time, he knew exactly where he was, and what had happened.

The giant pressed a palm to his left ribs where Einer had cut him with the Ulfberht blade, and then took a step forward. The jotun's feet crunched over the thick snow, and in a moment, the storm covered his shoes. Red blood dripped from his wound down over his legs and onto the fresh white coat of snow.

'Stay away,' Einer warned. Despite the howl of the northern wind, the giant's blood still dripped hot from his sword.

This was not the first time Einer had fought off a giant, and he knew that it would not be the last either, for Ragnarok was coming, and soon he would fight and die on Ida's plain.

'On whose side will you fight at Ragnarok?' asked the bleeding giant. His voice was comforting like that of a storyteller or a chanter, and he forced a snicker to cover for his obvious pain. Despite his wound, he had not defended himself, or even drawn a weapon, as Einer had. Whoever this giant was, he was not like the others who had come searching.

During the three long winters since his trial, many had come to kill Einer, and his body carried the scars of their encounters. This jotun was not lost to the rage of the forefathers as the others had been, and he was not consumed in anger, or stumbling through the snow. He was calm, and composed, and Einer knew at once that it had been a mistake to strike first.

An insolent smile spread across the giant's chapped lips. 'So...' said he. 'When the final battle comes, will you fight for your gods or for your kinsmen?'

The northern wind pushed at his back for an answer, but Einer had none. He knew that his father would stand on the battleground with one of Valhalla's golden shields in hand, protecting the gods. All Einer's friends would fight under the same colours, and Einer had always thought that he, too, would fight for his gods, but the choice was no longer as easy as it had been.

He knew now that his mother was a giant, although she had always shunned her lineage, and Einer did not know where his mother would have stood on the eve of the final battle, had she been alive. And he did not know where he ought to stand himself.

'Your grandparents assume that you will fight with them,' said the giant, and he was right. Einer's grandparents had sheltered him for three long, harsh winters. They had taught him the way of Jotunheim, and they had taught him about his lineage, and yet the more they taught him, the less Einer knew where he belonged in the final battle.

'When you stand on Ida's plain again, you will know,' said the bleeding jotun, who could not possibly have known that Einer had already fought on Ida's plain once and killed in Odin's name.

'Who are you?' asked Einer. His breath came out white as the falling snow. He clenched his father's sword, feeling the grip through his thick wool gloves, and readied his stance. His heart was beating fast in confusion and warning, as it hadn't done in years.

'You know who I am,' said the giant. 'You know my name, as I know yours, Einer Vigmerson.'

Einer gaped at the jotun. It had been years since anyone had said his father's name. He doubted his grandparents even knew who his father had been. It was a name that belonged in Midgard, not here, among giants.

The jotun removed his hand from the wound Einer had inflicted and stroked the snow and ice out of his beard with bloodied fingers. The heat of runes within him melted the snow right off. His thin coat flapped open and revealed the light summer colours he wore beneath. Einer had never before seen one so powerful, and he had met many giants. This was the third of the last three winters before Ragnarok. So deep into winter it took strength and attention to keep warm with runes.

'You dress like a valley jotun,' said the giant, as if it surprised him. 'Wrapped in wool and furs. I don't know how you keep warm.' His tone was light, but Einer recognised it as a threat.

He swallowed the spit that had accumulated in his mouth. Once more, he cursed himself for having struck first.

His grandparents had tried to teach him to stay warm, but Einer had no skill with the runes. All they had been able to teach him was how to steer his thoughts away from getting him into trouble and to not think as loudly as he had used to do.

'This isn't loud?' mocked the giant, combing his bloody hand through his long hair. His hair had no tangles, although the northern wind had played with it and braided white snowflakes into the red and black strands. He had the appearance of a god. Although his size was not much larger than that of Einer, he was clearly a giant. His grasp on runes came with a jotun's gentle touch, and his protruding chin and sharp jaw marked his lineage at first glance, although his closely trimmed beard tried to shield his giant build.

'Who are you?' asked Einer again.

'You know,' answered the jotun, although they had never met. 'I am Ragnarok itself, and I call upon you, Einer Vigmerson.'

The superior smile of the giant widened, and no matter how Einer thought of it, in all the nine worlds, he knew the name of only one giant who was known to have such a wicked and stable smile.

'Why have *you* come for me?'

'Despite how you look, I knew you weren't a stupid valley giant,' praised Loki, giant among gods, and blood-brother of the Alfather himself.

'Why have you come?' asked Einer again, although he knew. Ragnarok was close, and that was why Loki was here, standing in front of Einer. He was on his way to Helheim to rally the short-lived to fight for him in the final battle, and after the long winter all the beings of the nine worlds had suffered through, it would not be a difficult task.

'You have a pendant,' said Loki, quite simply, and it was not the answer Einer had expected. 'A gold coin neck-ring. You know the one.'

'A pendant?' asked Einer, desperate not to think about the gold bracteate his mother had given him or what had happened to it.

'What happened to it?' Loki asked, knowing exactly how to steer Einer's thoughts where they were not supposed to go.

'Nothing,' said Einer, repeating the word loud in his mind, over and over again, as his grandparents had taught him to do to keep his thoughts hidden.

'We both know that isn't true,' said Loki.

They also both knew that the famed giant could force the truth out of Einer in an instant with his runes, yet he did not.

'I suppose my blood-brother would have done exactly that,' said Loki. 'He would have skipped past all of the fun and *made* you give up the truth, and then been on his way again.'

The northern wind howled between them, making Einer shiver under his bear skin and nine-layered wools.

Another wicked smile flared across Loki's lips. 'But unlike my blood-brother, I would much rather have you *choose* to tell me where the pendant is and what happened to it. For someday… you will want to help me.'

Einer doubted that was true. He could not imagine ever helping Loki, especially not giving up what he knew of the bracteate and willingly putting his friend in danger, but Loki's certainty made Einer doubt himself. Even the gods were frequently tricked by the cunning giant.

Loki crouched into the thick snow. He lowered his bloody hands to the ice at their feet, melting it, and washed his hands clean of blood in the water. He stared down at his wound.

'It would seem that you owe me. So, I shall gladly accept your hospitality,' Loki said, although Einer had offered nothing at all. 'A warm meal and slumber in a warm jotun house will do me good.'

With those words he rose and began to walk. Before Einer could even think to stop him, Loki had already taken a good ten steps into the thick snowstorm.

Einer hurried to follow, and somehow, despite the thick snow that made it impossible to see ahead, and only allowed those more than familiar with these lands to navigate through them, Loki headed straight towards the home of Einer's grandparents.

'So,' said the famed giant, as they trampled through the snowstorm, leaving a fine trail of red blood behind. 'Tell me, Einer, when Skoll swallows the sun and Thor's thunder rumbles over Ida's plain, will you fight with me, or do you still blindly trust your gods?'

DARKNESS

Death, pain, and fear.

Alone in the dark, Ragnar slumped to the hard ground and buried his face in his hands. No matter how he tried, he could not prevent Ragnarok. He had tried, and he had suffered horrid deaths for his attempts, but in the end, the Alfather always died, and Ragnarok always happened, exactly as he had made it happen when he first walked through the veil onto Ida's plain.

Nothing he had done since that first time had prevented Ragnarok from happening and his gods from dying.

The Darkness had almost begun to feel welcoming. It felt like Ragnar had spent an eternity roaming around the dark, and he had long lost count of how many deaths he had suffered and how many times he had gone through the veil he summoned with his distaff. The count was a long way beyond a thousand.

In the end, it was all futile. Ragnarok *would* happen. His gods *would* die. Everyone he had ever known would die in the bloody battle and there was nothing Ragnar could do about it. He had doomed them all without meaning to, and himself, too, for he knew that he would never get out of the Darkness unless he prevented Ragnarok, perhaps not even then. An eternity of silence and darkness and dread—such was his fate.

Time after time, Ragnar had tried saving the Alfather and steering him away from the battlefield, but never had he succeeded. He had tried everything in all the nine worlds to save his god.

The silence and darkness seemed to press on him the one idea that had formed there many hundred deaths ago. He had tried to save his god a thousand different ways, but there was one other way to prevent Ragnarok: he could kill the Alfather before the final battle. If Odin was not alive, then Ragnarok would never happen, and his god would not die on the battlefield, as Ragnar had made it happen. All of his mistakes would be undone.

All Ragnar had to do was kill his god.

HILDA

Chapter One Hundred and Thirty-Five

THE FUTURE FLASHED before Hilda's eyes, neither for the first nor last time. She knew it was the future, for she was fighting in it—a battle she had yet to fight. All she knew was its name. A name that struck fear into giants and gods alike: Ragnarok.

Soon that future would become the present. That was how the nornir spoke of Ragnarok, and how Hilda, too, had come to think of it. The third winter stretched on. Soon it would end, and all knew about the deadly battle that followed the third long winter. No god or giant would escape its grasp. They would die at each other's hands, exactly as Hilda's visions of the future continued to show.

Blood will splash over her face. Her feet will wade through a pool of dark blood. A giant will roar at her, a mountain of corpses at his back. Her sword will strike the giant's ankle. He will plummet to his knees. The sky will be black. Thunder will strike in the distance.

The northern wind howled past, and gone was the vision.

Hilda stood breathless outside the Hall of Fates. It had been more than a mere vision; it had been a vision of her own future. She hadn't been hovering above or at a distance. She had been *in* the vision, fighting.

At last, she had a future.

With the whispers in the wind at her back, Hilda darted up the snowy hill. Her snow fox came tumbling out of the snow that spilled into the Hall of Fates. Its fur coat had turned white and puffy. Happily, it shook snow off its snout and stared up at Hilda. Their steps echoed into the cold hall.

What happened? asked Verthandi, who always knew when something did. Her voice came in the wind, like the visions.

The nornir had told her that she had no present or future either, but Hilda knew better. She was alive, so she had a present, and her visions showed her fighting at Ragnarok, so she had a future too.

She shivered from the cold as she ran deeper into the hall, before she answered Verthandi. She had yet to master speaking through runes and wind.

'Ragnarok is near,' said Hilda. She slowed to a walk to savour the moment.

At last, it was time. Hilda so longed for battle, though not in the way she used to before Ash-hill had been attacked; no longer did she crave the blood and rush. But she craved a fight all the same. Her whole life she had fought. Even if none of the people she had known in life knew her anymore, fighting would always feel like home.

'You can crave it all you want, but Ragnarok is a battle in which you have no place.' Skuld's voice echoed out from the darkest corner of the hall.

'Then how do you explain my vision?' Hilda responded. 'I'm fighting in the future.'

The quiet noises of drumming threads and the nornir's hummed songs stopped all at once. All three of them walked out of the dark corners of their hall where they worked, and into the light that shone in from the snowy landscape outside.

Urd, who had much to see and little to do, came out in her apron, for while her eyes were focused on the long past of all the nine worlds, she cooked for them with the meat Hilda brought home from days spent in the snow. Urd's hedgehog fylgja slept on her shoulder.

Verthandi's blonde hair had turned as white as the snow. Her appearance reflected the present of the nine worlds, robed in snow and doom.

Skuld, ever hopeful about the future that she saw, had gained deep lines of worry on her forehead, for to her, and to them all, the only future ahead now was Ragnarok.

'It can't be *your* future,' the three nornir decided through one unified voice.

Verthandi's seagull fylgja screeched. Skuld's rat came out from behind two pillars. Even Urd's hedgehog woke from its slumber. They were all alert.

'Look at it,' said Verthandi in her motherly voice, and all of them stared up at the ceiling. The norn's seagull fylgja was flying around the threads up there.

For the past three years of winter while Hilda had lived with them, the nornir had been busy untying threads and hanging them high in the hall, into a tight cluster of a web that they called Ragnarok.

'We have tied so many of them up,' said Urd.

'And when we are done, there will be no room for your thread,' said Skuld. 'There will be no room in the future for anything at all.'

Hilda had been given the speech before, but she wouldn't let them dismiss what she had seen. 'Then make me a destiny thread and I shall cut straight through that ugly tangle up there.'

It was not the first time she had asked to be given a destiny, but it was the last time that she would, for she knew now that she *had* a future, no matter if the nornir spun her one or not.

No one bothered to answer her request.

'I saw my own future,' said Hilda and watched the three nornir's focus dissolve into visions of the future. They were searching for hers. Their eyes went blank, their voices faint mumbles, and in a heartbeat, it was done.

'Nothing,' said Urd.

'Nothing,' said Verthandi.

'You have no future,' completed Skuld.

Their certainty hit Hilda right in the heart, where new hope glimmered, but she quickly swallowed her doubts. She knew what she had seen. 'I saw it clearly,' she insisted. 'I was fighting at Ragnarok.'

'How do you know it was you?' asked the nornir, as if they thought she couldn't tell.

'I saw the vision through my own eyes.'

The three sisters diverted their stares from Hilda, and she knew that something was amiss. She had expected that revelation to force them to re-examine the future for any sight of her, but they didn't even bother to try. They were as certain as they had always been that she had no future.

'Were you fighting with your axe?' Verthandi eventually asked.

'Nej...' Hilda had been fighting with a sword, although she had never fought with a sword in her life, not truly. A few times during practice a long time ago in Ash-hill, she had borrowed Einer's sword, but it wasn't her sort of weapon. She couldn't imagine that she would choose to pick up a sword on Ragnarok's battlefield.

'Was your snow fox with you?' asked Verthandi, though she didn't need to ask anything more.

Hilda turned away from the three nornir without answering. Her snow fox darted ahead towards the thick snow outside, and Hilda followed in a slow march. She heard the three sisters walk back into the depths of their hall, to resume their busy tasks.

Her hope shattered, she slid her feet through the snow, while her fylgja hopped all around and buried itself in it.

It was not the destiny Hilda had wanted. To have none at all. She always liked the idea of being pulled along by her destiny thread. Of having choices given to her by Fate itself. Instead, she had nothing at all. No destiny and no past. No one knew her or knew of her. Not as they had. All she dreamed of these days was finding a place where she belonged. Home.

The nornir knew her, but only what she told them. Hilda didn't tell them much, and the little she had said, they didn't believe. If the nornir didn't believe her existence, then no one else would either. Three years without a destiny had stalled her in place. She had learned visions and runes, for there had been nothing else to do, but none of it mattered. If Hilda had no destiny, she had no purpose in the nine worlds. She needed her destiny back.

For a moment she stared out over the plains outside the Hall of Fates, coated in snow and mist. Her hands stroked an old burned carving of Freya that she picked up in Midgard such a long time ago. A carving Tyra had made for her, back when Hilda had a home, and a family, too. Absentmindedly, she caressed it, longing to find that again: a proper home with people who knew her and cared.

Yggdrasil's large roots waved up and down the hills. Every day the roots needed to be watered, and as the youngest norn, it was Hilda's task to do so. A task she had willingly taken upon herself for the past three years of winter while the nornir had taught her all about the runes and the whispers in the wind, which carried the voices of all with norn blood who had trained in runes. Once, Loki had whispered to Hilda in the wind, but since he had left her bleeding in the Hall of Fates, and since Hilda's past, present and future had been robbed of her, she no longer heard him. The nornir said it was because he didn't know her. He didn't remember. No one remembered Hilda anymore.

She had gone to Valhalla after it had happened, but the Alfather hadn't known who she was. She had found Ash-hill's benches and seen her neighbours and kinsmen, and all those who had died at Magadoborg. None of them had known her. They had sailed together and fought together, shield to shield, but none of them knew who she was. No one in the nine worlds knew who Hilda was or who she had been.

Except perhaps for Einer, Hilda told herself. He hadn't been seated in Valhalla, and Einer *had* to know her, but it was a hope that she kept to herself, because she knew the nornir wouldn't agree.

'What now?' Hilda asked the wind, her snow fox, and the nine worlds. The wind caressed her hair. It felt both reassuring and strange to know what the whispers in the wind truly were, now that she knew they were not the Runes, and they were not just Loki either.

What she knew as the Runes was gone, and in their place was something new: over winter, Hilda had sharpened her ears to hear *all* of the nornir's whispers. She heard the future, and she heard the past. Sometimes she even heard the present, and not only did she hear, for when the wind pushed harshly at her back, the words turned into visions, and in those moments, she saw what *they* saw. All of the nornir. The past, the present, and the future.

And none of them saw her.

Absentmindedly, Hilda stroked her sharp axe. The fox barked, and the wind pushed against Hilda's face and reminded her of her past, that only she knew and remembered.

Not knowing her destiny had never hindered her before.

Back in Midgard, she had looked directly at a fire demon and been condemned to Muspel sight, and yet that hadn't hindered her. Without hesitation, she had stumbled through her fiery sight and raided and fought at Magadoborg, exactly as she had set out to do.

Hilda had always trusted in her destiny, but now that she didn't have one, she had been sitting around for too long, wondering what the point of an afterlife was if no one knew the renown she had gained in life.

'I'm done waiting for my future to find me,' Hilda muttered and trailed into the untouched snow. The snow fox yelped contentedly and darted down the hill to lead the way.

'Takka,' Hilda whispered. The last three winters had been peaceful in the nornir's presence, and she had learned much about the Runes, both those in the wind and the ones she could use.

She had learned much about herself, too. There was no reason to doubt her place in the nine worlds anymore. If no one had made a place for her at Ragnarok, or in the nine worlds, then Hilda would make a place for herself.

You can't leave! the three nornir yelled after her. Their voices chased her down the snowy hill in the wind. They sensed her leaving, as they sensed so many things. *You don't have a future. You don't have a destiny!*

Hilda sped up and smiled wickedly, as she imagined what Loki would have said, and what her old Runes would have told her. 'If I don't have a destiny, then no one will see me coming.'

EINER

Chapter One Hundred and Thirty-Six

'BY THE WILL of the nine worlds,' exclaimed Einer's grandmother when she saw the company Einer reluctantly kept. 'How long has it been?'

'At least a few hundred winters,' Loki said, and they both laughed at that as she ushered him into the warmth of the house.

'You haven't aged at all.'

As easily as he kept warm, Loki made himself larger to match her size as they walked into the warm room. He let her fuss around him, giving him pillows and blankets and dragging the honour seat in the house out to sit by the fire where it was warm. Einer's sleeping furs were hastily tossed aside to accommodate the famed giant, while Einer stood back alone, by the door, removing one layer of wool after another. His fingers were frozen from the cold outside, but no one fussed around him, or pulled out a seat for him to sit by the oven and get warm.

Loki lowered himself into the intricately carved chair and thanked Einer's grandmother for the pillows and attention.

He was welcomed like a long-lost son, and out in the thick snowstorm, he had known the way to the house without asking Einer for directions, or halting to think, even for a heartbeat. Perhaps he *was* a son? Einer thought. Perhaps Einer had more than one uncle.

'I'm much too old to be your uncle,' Loki said over his shoulder in response to Einer's loud thought. 'But I could have been family. Isn't that right, Grythak?'

Einer halted his doing and stared at his grandmother as she rushed around, cleaning the house to make it fit for Loki. Never had Einer heard anyone call his grandmother by name, not even his grandfather.

'You should have been,' his grandmother replied, blushing.

At the sound of commotion, Einer's grandfather emerged from his private room, and he was smiling. Einer could hardly believe the sight of it. Not once during the three cold winters Einer had stayed in this house had he seen his grandfather smile, not even during the mead festival two years past.

Loki rose from the seat of honour, and with happy grumbles the two men embraced each other.

'I thought we would never see you again,' said Einer's grandfather. His voice broke with emotion, and Loki tapped him reassuringly on the back. 'Especially after everything.'

'Everything happened as it should,' Loki reassured and tapped the old jotun on the shoulders. 'If it had happened any differently, I wouldn't be here, today.'

Across from Loki, Einer's grandfather seemed like a child, despite the wrinkles on his forehead. Although Loki looked young, aided by the golden apples eaten in Asgard, he was not as young as he appeared to be. He was of similar age to the Alfather, Einer had to remind himself—almost as old as the nine worlds. Hundreds, perhaps thousands of years old, although he carried himself like a young man, and talked like one, too.

Blood dripped from Loki's wound onto the stone floor. It splashed over the smooth trodden floor, and Loki clenched his teeth in pain and held a hand to his bleeding ribs. In his grandparents' infantile happiness, even Einer had forgotten the events that had led Loki to their home, but wounds did not forget their maker.

Einer's grandmother gasped at the dark blood. His grandfather urged Loki to sit again, so as not to use any unnecessary strength. Once more, Einer cursed himself at having attacked first, and he turned away as he unravelled the thick scarf from around his neck.

'I didn't announce myself to your grandson,' Loki explained at his back. 'And the snowstorm was thick.'

Although that was not quite how it had happened, and despite the stares Einer's grandparents sent his way, Einer was thankful to Loki for phrasing it as he did.

'It's nothing much,' Loki dismissed, and it almost felt like he was answering Einer's thoughts, although he was speaking to the two jotnar in the house. Already Einer's grandmother was off to fetch bandages and clean water, and his grandfather had made his way to their most expensive mead barrel.

For three long winters, Einer's grandfather had taken a hornful of mead with each meal, and slowly one barrel after the other had been emptied. It had been three moons since he had run out of mead, save for that last barrel, reserved for the eve of Ragnarok.

So, the time had come.

Grinning, Einer's grandfather rolled out the barrel and placed it by Loki's seat. He fetched his expensive clear glass horns, handed Loki one and kept the other for himself.

Meanwhile, Einer's grandmother arrived from the back room, a basket of bandages and ointments in one hand, and a bowl of apples in the other. 'They aren't golden,' she said as she placed the apples next to the mead. 'But they will fill you up. Now, let's look at this.'

By Loki's seat, she crouched down, and lifted his bloody tunic to examine the damage Einer's Ulfberht had caused.

Baffled into silence, Einer watched his grandparents run around their house to accommodate sneaky Loki. Staring, Einer removed his gloves and boots and leg wrappers, and hung everything by the door to drip dry. He had never seen them so excited before, and so full of life, not even during the Yule feasts, where he had seen them dancing.

Despite how Loki was welcomed, Einer strapped on his weapon belt with its two swords, for Ash-hill's skald, Ragnar, had often told stories of Loki's trickery, and in spite of his grandparents' reaction, Einer did not trust Loki.

He felt somewhat unwelcome as he crossed the room, cautious not to get in his grandparents' way. At last, he placed himself across from Loki, back against the oven, and felt his fingers and toes prickle to life again. His wet socks began to warm.

'They've been looking for you,' said Einer's grandmother as she cleaned Loki's wound with her healing ointments.

Since the beginning of winter, aesir and vanir had chased Loki through the nine worlds. In the local tavern, it was all people talked about: the end of the nine worlds and the great hunt for Loki.

'Have they been here, yet?' asked the famed giant.

'The Alfather wouldn't dare,' Einer's grandfather replied. He came in holding his axe and pried open the mead barrel.

'Thor might be stupid enough,' Loki said with a snicker.

'Ja, but he wouldn't be smart enough to come looking here.'

For a moment all three of them laughed at great Thor as Einer's grandfather handed out drinks, and Einer, too, found himself smiling. His grandparents had calmed, now that the house was in order, and Loki had mead in his hands and apples at his feet, and pillows at his back.

Despite how he had injured Loki, Einer was even handed a small cup of mead, although in his hands even the smallest cup in the house was much too large.

'I miss her stew,' Loki said, after they had been sitting there and sipping on their mead for a long time, while the fire snapped and Einer's grandmother mended his wound. 'She made the best hare stew in all of Jotunheim.'

Tightly, Einer's grandmother wrapped up Loki's wound with one last white strip of cloth. 'In all the nine worlds,' she corrected.

Einer stared at them. He could not interrupt to ask about who they meant, but deep down he already knew. His mother's hare stew had been the best in all of Midgard.

'Have you heard?' asked Loki. He watched Einer as he said it, but Einer was well aware that the question was not addressed to him.

His grandmother glanced up at her husband, who was suddenly much too focused on the glass horn of mead in his hands to answer. He twirled the contents and licked his lips for a good moment before he said anything. 'Do you have news?'

'Three-winter-old news,' said Loki. 'I saw her. Not long after my chains fell off. In Asgard.'

Einer's grandmother tied off the last bandage and rose from Loki's side. Taking the basket with ointments and strips of cloths, she left them sitting by the warm oven. Einer watched her leave and knew that she wouldn't be back for a while. She still cried whenever someone mentioned Einer's mother, and so no one ever did.

'I watched her funeral pyre burn,' Loki said, staring into the fire of the oven. 'It burned for days. At night you could see it, all the way across Asgard's lands.'

'So, she *is* dead,' said Einer's grandfather in a conclusive tone, and emptied his glass in one draught. Loudly, and eager to think on other matters, he poured himself another drink, and filled Loki's glass at the same occasion.

Loki sighed longingly and tapped the side of his horned glass in a song-like rhythm.

'How did she pass away?' asked Einer, for no one else did.

'She went to Asgard,' Loki said, as if that explained everything. 'And the Alfather caught up.' He stared into his horn of mead as he spoke, still tapping his fingers in that entrancing rhythm.

'He offered her shackles as if they were some great gift, as he offers everything, even death. But your mother... Glumbruck was never a beast to be tamed.'

'How did she die?' Einer persisted.

'She killed herself,' said Loki.

The statement drifted in the hot air, and Einer struggled to make sense of what he heard. It went against everything he knew and loved about his mother. To him, she had mostly been comfort and warmth and a true mother, but she had also been strong. All his life he had looked to her for guidance; even with a chieftain as father, he knew that the true strength came from his mother, and he could not in a thousand winters imagine that she might give up—on anything.

'Oh, she didn't give up,' Loki agreed. 'Glumbruck would never give up. She made a choice to save you. A choice to save the nine worlds.'

'How would her death save—?'

Einer never got to finish his question.

His grandfather's expensive glass horn shattered. He rose to his feet, not minding the mead and shattered glass spilling out over the floor.

'Loki,' he whispered and gestured to his private room. Quick as a fox, Loki was on his feet, shoes grinding the glass as he ran to the room at the back of the house.

'You too, Einer,' his grandfather whispered, so softly that Einer found himself doubting if he had said anything at all, and then Einer, too, heard the commotion from outside, of animals howling and the crunch of snow.

His grandfather went cautiously to the door, in a trancelike state, while Loki fumbled to open the closed back door. The last thing Einer saw, as Loki grabbed his wrist and pulled him away, was his grandmother walking in with red puffy eyes, and his grandfather opening the door. Then he was swept away inside his grandfather's back room, into which he had never been allowed before.

The door closed behind him and shut out all light but for a small candle in a glass burning on a table.

Einer heard the door in the main room being kicked open.

'What is this?' his grandfather bellowed. 'What are you doing?'

Mumbled voices responded and Einer's grandmother screamed. Meanwhile Loki was crawling on the floor in the dark of the room.

'Don't lie to me. I know he was here,' a voice growled in the other room. 'The hounds followed the trail of his blood to your doorstep.' Einer heard a struggle, and then a creak as the door to the house opened further. 'Blood, on your honour chair. Blood on the floor. Where have you hidden him?'

Loki tugged on Einer's tunic, urging him away from the door. There was a stone passage in the corner of the room that looked like an old unused oven. Loki had crawled inside to hide, but the space was hardly wide enough to fit both of them.

'My son was injured,' lied Einer's grandfather in the other room. 'He left already.'

'Then whose thoughts are those?'

Einer's thoughts had been too loud again, and he knew at once why his grandparents had urged him to leave with Loki. He would get them into trouble by staying there.

Loki swept Einer into the dark of the oven passage, and it was deeper, much deeper than Einer could ever have imagined.

'Don't stand in my way, jotun!' yelled the voice outside.

A stone rolled down behind Loki, and Einer hoped and wished it would be thick enough to shield his thoughts so he wouldn't accidentally betray his grandparents, as he had almost betrayed Sigismund when Loki had asked him about the bracteate.

'You will die for this!'

Just as the stone finally closed the passage, Einer heard the gathering rumble of thunder, and the last thing he saw before the stone rolled back into place was a flash of lightning. It could only have been conjured by Thor.

'Come,' Loki hissed at Einer. 'Before that dimwit figures out where we are.'

He crawled away, and Einer heard his fast steps echo as if they were not inside an old oven at all, but a vast hall.

'Wha—?'

'They're dead,' Loki interrupted in an emotionless tone, his voice further away with every step. 'Your grandparents have joined the forefathers, and if you don't come with me now, then soon we, too, will be crushed under Thor's hammer.'

TYRA

Chapter One Hundred and Thirty-Seven

A THOR'S HAMMER hung from the neck of Tyra's new husband-to-be, and indicated that he was no Christian, like most chiefs and kings, but a proud man of Odin. His smile reached every wrinkle on his face.

Burisleif was old, but his calm demeanour was reassuring. Tyra supposed that she could come to love it, and him, or at the very least appreciate him. His hall was soothing in its familiarity, with images of heroes and gods carved into the beams. The wedding preparations too reminded her of a safe home, long forgotten. Not since her childhood in Ash-hill had Tyra seen a week of drinking and laughter quite like this one, which had already lasted eight long days.

Tomorrow she would be married, anew, with the gods as her witness, and unlike her last husband, her new match was a kind man.

Tyra smiled back at Burisleif, but her heart was not in it.

For more than ten years she had fought the tyranny of her last husband, Styrbjorn the Strong with his eyes of fire, and such memories were difficult to forget. Even if she tried not to think about the past, her body remembered, and she recoiled when her future husband's wrinkled hand touched hers.

His hand was cold, not burning as Styrbjorn's had been, and his eyes were not lined with fire as those of her last husband, and yet Tyra felt her heart speed with worry, and she was glad to have her blood-dripping dagger fastened to her belt. The same dagger she had stabbed her old husband with, before she had made her escape with her brother Svend.

At the opposite end of the hall, Svend was seated with his future wife, for tomorrow both of them would be married: Tyra to King Burisleif, and Svend to Burisleif's daughter. The matches had been arranged and agreed upon by Svend himself, on his father's behalf, and he was well content with his success.

Tyra had not wanted to get married at all, but Svend had insisted that this would be better. He had dragged her along with promises that Burisleif was old, so she wouldn't have to be married for long, and that he himself would marry the king's daughter so he would never have to leave Tyra's side, but Tyra knew that was not how it would be.

Burisleif *was* old, but he was healthy. He seemed kind, but Tyra's last husband too had seemed kind before their wedding night. And Svend's plan to stay at her side was doomed: sooner or later his father would call for him and he would leave. Or some great war would start somewhere, and he would leave. She doubted he would even stay the winter out; he had never known how to settle. But she appreciated his resolve, even if she didn't have his optimism.

Across the hall, Svend rose from his seat. His cheeks were flushed red from the foreign wine they had been drinking, and his future wife was just as invigorated. Svend swung her to her feet and shouted for the musicians to play louder as he launched into a stomping dance.

'I'll be back,' Tyra whispered to her future husband, before he too could get the idea to dance.

She stepped gingerly; the floor was sticky where she had spilled the wine she had pretended to drink. The feasting crowd was too loud and tight for anyone to notice Tyra slipping through their midst and out of the hall into the night.

Outside, some men and women had made a fire. Accompanied by the music from inside, they sat around the bonfire, laughing and telling stories.

'If it isn't the bride,' one of the men yelled to Tyra. 'Come and join us, my queen,' he added, with particular care not to slur his words. 'It's warm by the fire.'

'I don't need any more warmth, after all that wine,' Tyra said, to excuse herself. 'My cheeks are red as a pig's bum.'

That made them laugh, and they were still laughing as she passed them by. In truth, she hadn't been drinking at all tonight, only plotted her escape.

She didn't encounter anyone else as she rushed to the inlet and pushed the rowing boat into the water. The night was clouded, and she struggled to see anything as she climbed into the small rowing boat and untied it from its post.

'Where are you going?' someone asked as Tyra was readying her oars. 'Why are you leaving?'

It was Svend. She had thought him too drunk and content to notice her leaving, but of course he had. No matter how close or far away Svend was, he had always kept one eye on Tyra, and made certain she was safe.

'I can't stay here,' she told him. 'I can't do this.'

'Do what?' His words were slurred with drink, and she knew that his thoughts would be too. 'Marry a good man and live a happy life?'

'I can't pretend that I feel safe here,' Tyra said. 'We're not safe. I can't ignore what's happening everywhere else in Midgard.' For many moons she had tried to tell him as much, but it was difficult for Svend to understand and accept that *safe* did not mean to her what it did to him.

'Why not?' he asked.

Tyra's boat began to float out into the inlet, and she had to stroke the oars once to stay close enough to speak to Svend so others wouldn't hear.

'Why not?' Svend pressed. 'Why can't you just be happy?'

'Siv...'

'Siv is dead,' he said flatly. His voice was harsh, but Tyra knew that was not his intent. The strong drink that had filled his stomach made it come out as such. 'Forgive,' he said.

'She can't be dead,' Tyra insisted as she always did, despite the more than a dozen years that had passed since she and Siv had parted ways. 'In the afterlife I will meet her. She promised, so I have to make good on my promise too, so that in the afterlife, I can look into her eyes and know that I did exactly what she asked of me.'

'Can't this be enough?' asked Svend. 'We could be happy here.'

'I'm not twelve anymore, Svend,' she said, in the kindest voice she could muster. 'My happiness doesn't come from closing my eyes to the world we live in. I can't sit and laugh in that hall for all eternity and pretend to be blind to how Midgard is burning. I won't stick my fingers in my ears and pretend that I don't hear my kinsmen scream in my dreams as they're burned alive on Christian pyres. All over the north people like us are dying, Svend. Do you realise?'

Svend didn't answer immediately, and the night was too dark for Tyra to see him properly.

'Don't you see what it means?'

'The end is coming,' he obliged.

Tyra nodded, although she doubted Svend would be able to see her. 'The fire demons are here,' she said. 'Their pyres are burning all over these lands, and I *must* stop them. Even if it's the last thing I do, I must. So that in the afterlife, at least, *we* can be happy.' She didn't just mean her and Svend, but also Siv, and her parents, and her sisters, and everyone she had known and loved in this life, and everyone she yearned to see again in the afterlife. 'Will you come with me?'

Svend took a long time to answer, and in the gloom his silence seemed all the longer. 'If you had wanted me to come, you would have asked me before you left,' he decided.

'I didn't think you would listen,' Tyra admitted. 'So, I'm asking you now that you *are* listening.'

'If the end is truly here…' Svend began instead of answering her request, 'then there won't be time for happiness in the afterlife.'

'That's precisely why I can't get married tomorrow. I can't afford to sit here and waste time, Svend. Soon there won't be anything left of Midgard to save.'

The distant sound of song and laughter echoed out onto the inlet, and for a moment they both halted to listen to the raucous joy echoing from the feast.

'What is the point of saving this world, when you don't want to live in it?' Svend asked, and then Tyra heard his steps through the foliage, leaving her alone in her rowing boat.

'Because *you* want to live here,' said Tyra although Svend was already gone. 'And if I don't do something, then even *this* place won't be safe much longer.'

BUNTRUGG

Chapter One Hundred and Thirty-Eight

'OUR TASK IS done,' said Buntrugg into the dark of the last passage grave before he left. The svartalvar who worked for him gave no answer, but he knew they were there.

He exited into cold Jotunheim with a sigh, now that his task was finally done. All the passage graves in the nine worlds had been closed. For longer than Buntrugg could keep track of, he had travelled in the dark of night with svartalvar at his back to close leaking passages. In the end, *all* the ancient passages had been leaking, and he had closed them all. Some he had closed at one end; some, he and the svartalvar had been forced to collapse altogether.

Buntrugg shuddered. Jotunheim was cold as Niflheim, and the road thick with ice. The Muspel flame he had captured out of Muspelheim played around in his right palm, and he used its heat to keep warm.

Travelling through passageways as often as he had, Buntrugg had lost all sense of time, but he knew he had been working to this end for at least thirty moons. During those thirty moons, every time he had come home to Jotunheim, it had been thick with a snowstorm that seemed to never end. No matter where he arrived in Jotunheim, thick ice lined the plains. Here, by his childhood home, as well. It had been winter in Jotunheim for much too long. The last winter was upon them.

The end was coming, and Buntrugg had just closed off all the popular passages between the worlds. There would be no easy escape from the terrors to come. Only the old rifts could be used to travel between the nine worlds now, and it had been many centuries since people had used those. Not since the jotunar had opened the first passage graves, a few thousand years back.

Apart from the old rifts there was only Bifrost, the aesir's rainbow bridge, left. No one but the aesir had easy access to travel between the worlds anymore.

Since the beginning of his latest task, Buntrugg had only been home once, for a visit so short he had barely managed a hello to his father. For many moons he had looked forward to coming home, properly, and sitting by the warm oven as his mother knitted at his side and his father watched the fire burn with his daily cup of mead in hand.

At last, Buntrugg returned.

He trailed through the last of the snowstorm towards his parents' home with a grin as he thought of it. He had overcome all those long, quiet days and nights because he knew that once his task was complete, he could enjoy the comforts of home again, as he had not done for decades. Buntrugg wondered if his sister's son was still with them, or if Einer had left at the beginning of winter. He had been looking for something, or someone, although Buntrugg no longer remembered whom, or what.

Buntrugg blew on the small Muspel flame in his right hand. Bright yellow fire raged through the snowstorm and melted away both snow and ice so Buntrugg might see his parents' house.

The longhouse was blackened, and the roof had caved in. Fires danced around the blackened pillars. It was not Buntrugg and his flame who had started these fires.

Someone was standing in the midst of the destruction. A man who flaunted long red hair and a bright blue coat embellished with gold. An aesir in Jotunheim.

Alerted by Buntrugg's blazing entrance, the aesir faced him, and Buntrugg swallowed, for he knew that face. Thor's red and murderous eyes stared at Buntrugg from afar. The god's red beard was frost-rimed and his short-shafted hammer was in his hand. Thor had done this.

A growl challenged the storm. The Alfather's son was not alone. Three jotnar had been bound on leashes, like hounds. Three jotnar lost to the rage of the forefathers, too far gone to be helped. They howled and roared at the scent of Buntrugg. Within himself, Buntrugg felt the forefathers stir in reply.

Buntrugg's own weapon belt was light and empty, but even so, he continued his walk towards his family home and towards the aesir known as Giant-killer.

He tried, but failed not to let his emotions show. His eyes shook with tears and rage as he took in the burning pillars of his home. The dining table around which they had talked and laughed was burning. The far wall upon which his parents had measured his height for the first half a century of life had been blackened beyond recognition.

The forefathers' rage was fuelled by Buntrugg's memories. Tears rolled down his scarred cheeks as he approached the famous aesir who had burned his home to the ground.

Thor was laughing, or at least his white teeth were showing. The jotnar hounds battled each other to get to Buntrugg and make him release the forefathers as they had, but Buntrugg knew the forefathers better than anyone, and their rage did not frighten him.

'What are you doing here?' Buntrugg said through gritted teeth when he was close enough to be heard over the storm, yet far enough away that the lost jotnar could not reach him on their tight leashes.

'Where has he gone?' asked Thor in a calm tone. He casually combed his long red hair out of his face with his free hand. His hammer hung loose, but pointedly in his right. 'I know he was here.'

'If he's not here, I don't know where my father is,' answered Buntrugg. At least his parents weren't there. They must have been out. At least they hadn't been struck by Thor's lightning strike and burned with the house.

'I don't care who your father is,' said the famed aesir in a bored tone. 'I'm looking for Loki.'

'What happened here?' asked Buntrugg, fearing to know. He clenched his teeth and his fists and tried to suppress the anger. The forefathers were loud with demands of blood and revenge.

The three jotnar hounds felt it too. All three of them roared like bears, and to Buntrugg's satisfaction Thor flinched away from them. He held their leashes in his hammer-hand, but no one was in control of a jotun lost to the forefathers.

'What happened here?' Buntrugg once more demanded to know. He took three steps closer to his burning childhood home to show that he was not afraid of the beastly jotnar, although any wise giant should have been. 'Where are my parents?'

Thor's red eyes dropped to the ground. Only for half a heartbeat, but long enough for Buntrugg to notice and follow the aesir's gaze. Next to the grand oak table, mostly hidden under the roof that had caved in, were bloody bones that could only have belonged to a giant.

Buntrugg's eyes opened wide in horror, and before he had time to think or reflect, he lifted his hot Muspel flame to his mouth and spat fire at Thor. It fed the flames on the house, burned the angry jotnar and licked Thor's protective blue coat.

It was not with the forefathers' rage that Buntrugg attacked, but with his own. Even the angry forefathers within seemed unprepared for his ferocity. Tears spilled from his eyes and blurred his vision as he spat fire at Thor. The aesir was yelling, swinging his deadly hammer over his head, and thunder rumbled above, but Buntrugg barely heard it. With runes he fed heat to his fire. Red flames turned to hot blue fire, which cut through snow and wood, all the way to the lightning god.

The grand aesir and giant-killer squealed. Buntrugg took a deep breath and blew harder. His eyes were fixed on the spot under the ceiling where his parents' burned bones had been sticking out, although he couldn't see them for tears. With all the strength of his runes and his Muspel flame, Buntrugg attacked the murderous aesir in front of him.

'*Why?*' was all the self-control he had left to scream, when his lungs filled with air again, but it came out as a roar.

The forefathers and the three lost jotnar howled it with him, and even the wind seemed to listen to their unified roar of pain. Rain fell over Buntrugg. His Muspel flame soared around him, burning everything. The snow melted and dripped over his burning home.

Loud thunder gathered above. Thor had regained his calm and was swinging his hammer again, but Buntrugg didn't try to evade the blow. He saw no reason to.

Buntrugg should already have died, a long time ago, and he had finished every task given to him, for the sake of the aesir. This was how they repaid him.

'*Why?*' Buntrugg cried anew and his voice rivalled even Thor's echoing thunder. His eyes cleared of tears and through tall blue flames he saw the blood-eyed aesir clearly. Fear stained Thor's face, but only for a heartbeat, before anger returned and his great hammer left his grip.

Screaming, Buntrugg blasted heat and fire at the hammer, although nothing would melt it or slow its deadly flight.

A strong wind knocked him over. Thor's hammer smashed through Buntrugg's left elbow, and he slumped into the snow, his severed arm falling on top of him. His mouth was open wide, but no scream came; the pain had silenced him. His stump of an arm splattered blood, and the cold numbed him. Ice stung the edges of his wound. A new flesh pain he had never known.

Thor's hammer swished overhead, back to its master's hand.

Despite the pain, Buntrugg pushed himself to his knees with one arm. His severed arm flopped into the puddle of melted snow at his feet. Buntrugg readied his Muspel flame to burn everything in sight, but Thor and his hammer were gone.

The three rage-lost jotnar howled into the night. Buntrugg felt the forefathers loudly demand his attention, but the pain that rang through his entire body drowned their voices.

Buntrugg clenched what was left of his arm. Blood mixed with melting snow at his feet and ran over his leather shoes. With his Muspel flame, he burned the wound, to halt the gushing blood.

His roar echoed into the nine worlds. Had it not been for the anger that burned within him, he would have tumbled unconscious onto the snow, but anger—his own anger, that had not been fostered by the forefathers—burned hot and kept him on his knees.

The cowardly aesir would be back, and when he *did* come back, Thor would not be alone. They would all come, all the powerful aesir, and they would all tread over the home of Buntrugg's parents, and they would spit on his parents' bones, and they would insult every last memory of them.

Buntrugg fostered his anger carefully so it would sustain him through the pain. The forefathers' rage roared through the mouths of the three jotnar Thor had bound as hounds. Without a second thought, the aesir had abandoned them to the murderous rage of another giant. Such was the loyalty of gods.

Buntrugg knew what he had to do. Despite the pain in his head and body, and despite the anger that made him shake, he knew what he had to do.

All his life he had known the danger of the forefathers and the cost of using their anger. His uncle had been like these three jotnar: lost to the rage, nude in the snow and like a wild beast, roaring all day and night. With grim steps, Buntrugg approached the first of the three lost jotnar, preparing his strength, as he thought about how his father had once had to do this same deed for his own brother.

Without hesitation, Buntrugg raised his hot Muspel flame and made it tear through the first jotun. He guided the fire into the beast's mouth and lungs and out through his entire being. Buntrugg could think of no worse way to die, but he had no other weapon, so he made his fire swift.

The two other jotnar roared louder at their companion's death, but easily Buntrugg directed his fire at them. The pain had taken away his reservations.

Before long, it was done, and all three of them had suffered the same horrid death at the hands of a kinsman. Ignoring the scorched sight of them, Buntrugg moved past their hot bodies to his childhood home. His eyes fixed on the bones he could see beneath the rubble.

The meat on his parents' bones had been burned crisp like a pig's. Clearly Buntrugg saw the birthmark on his mother's right leg, and he recognised the shape of his father's large skull. There was no mistake. Buntrugg tumbled to his knees in the midst of the torn limbs of his parents' corpses.

'Why me?' he cried over his parents' burned bones. His father was dead, his mother was dead. Even his sister had passed on. His entire family had been turned to forefathers and only Buntrugg was left. He had survived, despite his destiny to die down in that dwarf forge years ago, burned to death by fire demons. 'Why am I alive?' he sobbed.

'Because the nine worlds need you to be.' Surt's burned voice came to him from behind. It scraped Buntrugg's ears like burning nails, but he had been burned more than once in his short life and it was a pain he had learned to live through.

The cold sorrow in his chest, however, was new, and he did not know how to mend it, or if it could be mended. It felt like ice and heat all mixed together around his heart, and it hurt more than the pains of the flesh that had left his body in scars. Blood rushed over the melting snow all around him from his stump. The pain had hindered him from sealing the wound properly, and it was not an even burn. His blood mixed with his parents' blood in the ashes of their home.

Silently Surt stood at his back, and the fire giant's presence alone was enough to melt the snow and ice all around them.

It's time to leave, Trugg, said Surt's voice inside Buntrugg's head. *Before the dimwit returns. The nine worlds demand it.*

'Why did the nine worlds have to choose me?' asked Buntrugg between sobs. He had been through worse than anyone, and yet Surt, and the Alfather, and the forefathers, and the nine worlds always insisted that he survived, no matter the pain. This time it was too much. His parents had not deserved a worthless death at the hands of a filthy aesir.

'You've taken everything from me,' Buntrugg cried. 'Everything! What more do you want?'

As ever, the nine worlds yielded no answer.

DARKNESS

KILLING THE ALFATHER was the only possible solution.

Ragnar's thoughts wandered to Ragnarok and the sight of the Alfather being torn apart by the great wolf, Fenrir. The memory of his god's brains being torn out of his skull made Ragnar gag. If only he could find within himself a wolf-like strength to kill the Alfather. At the very least, he had to try. He owed it to his family, and the nine worlds, and the gods themselves.

Tap, tap, said Ragnar in his mind. A thread surged out from his distaff with the sharp shriek of metal scraping against glass. It ripped open a veil into another world, and Ragnar passed through.

He did not arrive in the Alfather's presence as he had expected to do.

He stood alone in a hall, bisected by a long, narrow fire. The walls and the floor were made from flat sand-coloured stone, so smooth they reflected the flames, like mirrors. He knew that hall. On that floor, the Alfather had died at Ragnarok, at

Ragnar's own commands. The great wolf Fenrir had torn him apart, limb by limb.

Voices and steps resonated down the hall. Something sharp like claws scraped against the smooth floor.

Kauna, Ragnar thought, so his distaff pushed the Darkness far away and he could see thirty arm-lengths around. He stared down the hallway, terrified at the thought that the wolf would come for him, as it had once done.

Out of the Darkness arrived the Alfather at a brisk walk, and behind him the great wolf. Fenrir was quick at the Alfather's back, his steps scratching over the floor.

Ragnar barely dared to breathe.

The Alfather strode past him, followed by the great wolf, and then, to Ragnar's relief, Thor walked out of the Darkness, hammer in hand, face wreathed in a mean scowl.

It was not the end, Ragnar reminded himself. It was not Ragnarok. That was over, and he could never go back to witness the Alfather's death. This was some other time, although he still trembled at the thought of the wolf being so close.

It took him a while to remember why he was there. He had to kill the Alfather before Ragnarok. This had to be before Ragnarok, and he knew that Fenrir was more than capable of killing Odin. All Ragnar had to do was provoke the wolf to attack.

Before he could will himself to move, two more gods arrived out of the edge of the Darkness.

Tyr came next, a true warrior, ready for war, in chainmail so bright that it could only have been made from silver; then Thor's golden-haired wife Sif, with a frown that matched that of her husband. With them walked the two twins: Frey who farmers prayed to all year around, and Freya who ruled over spring. They were like mirror images of each other, yet entirely different. Together they were a perfect carving of what a man and woman ought to be. They looked healthy and strong; walked with their backs erect and their long, bright hair almost reached their hips.

Mesmerised, Ragnar stared at his gods as they passed him by, and then he saw who followed them. The creatures behind them were neither vanir nor aesir, but monsters.

A worm the size of Yggdrasil's roots slimed its way across the floor, its mouth a terrifying maw filled with teeth. Ragnar had thought that Fenrir was the most terrifying beast in the nine worlds, but the huge worm was worse. Its yellow eyes were hollow, so it was impossible to see where it was looking, and the entire time it wormed past him, Ragnar was convinced it was staring directly at him.

Yet what followed the worm was an even more frightening sight: a small naked girl who was neither a god, nor any creature Ragnar knew, and he knew them all. Nothing could describe her but the word *monster*. Half of her was bright pink, like the skin of a new-born, with long dark greasy hair, and the other half of her was like ashes, with no hair and skin scorched and peeled, like a darkened skeleton.

A wolf, a worm, and a little girl. They were Loki's three monstrous children.

Fenrir would kill the Alfather at Ragnarok, but perhaps, with all three monsters together, they could kill the Alfather before then. Now was his chance. All Ragnar had to do was to influence the three monsters to attack the Alfather and kill him. Even the gods would not be able to save the Alfather from Fenrir, Hel, and the Midgard Worm.

HILDA

Chapter One Hundred and Thirty-Nine

CONFIDENT THAT SHE would get her way, Hilda marched towards Valhalla. Her father had taught her all about the Alfather. She knew all his sayings by heart. For days of travel she had argued with Odin in her mind, and she was confident now that she could get her way.

Light shone out of the grand hall, through the tree-trunk-thick spear and axe handles that marked the outer walls of Valhalla. The night was bright with snow, and voices echoed from outside the hall. A snowball fight had broken out by the gates, and warriors ran around squealing like children.

Amused, Hilda marched through the crowd without minding the snowballs flying around her. Three years of winter had passed and although the winter had been long, Hilda hadn't done any of the usual things of snow and winter. The nornir weren't really ones to start a snowball fight, and they certainly didn't have skating bones lying around, or a sled.

Back in Ash-hill, Torstein had owned a sled, Hilda remembered. Thick snow was rare, but whenever there *was* snow, all the kids had fought over who got to use Torstein's sled. Of course, Einer had usually won that fight, and always ensured that everyone got to ride it.

The wind pushed at Hilda's back with whispers and visions of past and future, all of which Hilda ignored. She had spent too long dwelling on the nornir's whispers. Confident, she marched up the twisted arm-ring steps to Valhalla. The snow had been trodden to brown slush and the steps were slippery. Her snow fox bounded up in three great leaps and disappeared into the tangle of warriors inside the hall.

The crowd was thick. Some were seated, but many were moving around, and none of them stopped to question why Hilda was there. She looked like a shieldmaiden, and she fit right in. It was good to be back among true fighters.

There were too many fires and too much smoke to see far down the hall, so Hilda stared up at the ceiling of gold shields, held up by the long branches of Valhalla's oak tree. The branches grew thicker to her right, which meant that the oak tree and the Alfather's high tables were that way. Hilda and her snow fox set out towards it.

She had only been inside Valhalla twice before—once when it had been empty, and once right after the start of winter to demand a seat in the great hall—but it was a place that felt familiar in every way. It felt right.

The smell of roasted meat and honeyed stew mingled with the smoke from the fires and the stench of thousands. All about her, Odin's chosen combatants were laughing and enjoying this night. As she passed them by, Hilda caught conversations about battles, sailing trips and women. The same sort of conversations she might have overheard in the tavern at home. From now on and until the end came, she decided, this would be her home.

The night stretched on as Hilda marched towards the great oak tree under which the Alfather and the best of his warriors feasted.

She saw the Alfather's two ravens before she saw him. The ravens swirled over the crowd and right over Hilda. One of them cocked its head at her, and she knew that her arrival had been announced.

With that assurance, she walked on.

The Alfather's high tables spanned the width of the hall, to mark the status of those seated there. With the puffy snow fox at her side, Hilda marched out of the crowd and down the length of the high tables until she found the Alfather.

His single eye was fixed on her from afar. Her approach had indeed been announced, exactly as she had thought. Yet the Alfather didn't meet her halfway, as Freya once had; he waited for her to come all the way up to him.

He was seated on a bench with his supporters, listening to their stories, but his single eye did not stray from Hilda. The ends of his long blue robes lay bundled on the floor behind him, but even the corners were sparkling perfect, as if they had been washed a heartbeat ago.

Hilda stopped by the Alfather. Even seated, he was taller than her. Her eyes were level with his neck, around which a loose gold ring hung.

The warriors at the Alfather's table fell silent and turned to look at Hilda. They expected her to speak and tell them why she was there, but Hilda said nothing. Since she had entered Asgard, she had learned to appreciate the wisdom of her father's lessons. Her father had always advised her to let others speak first. That way their motives lay bare.

With runes Hilda protected her own mind and thoughts from the Alfather, so that he had to ask if he wanted to know why she was there. Her runes made her thoughts blank to him.

'The girl with bloody tears,' the Alfather eventually mused, when the silence had stretched long enough for half the warriors at his table to turn back to their horns of mead. 'You've been here before. At the beginning of the three-year winter. You wanted a seat in my hall.'

'That was then,' said Hilda. 'Now I won't settle for so little.'

The Alfather burst out laughing, a warm laughter that felt like home in the same way his grand hall did. It did not feel like mockery, but praise.

Again, Hilda waited for him to speak first. She expected him to ask her what she wanted, then, if it was not merely a seat in his hall, but that was not his first question. 'Who are you?'

'A warrior fighting for your cause,' answered Hilda, for she had learned that the truth wouldn't be trusted. Not when she had no destiny to confirm her story.

'Then I shall have your name and lineage,' demanded the Alfather.

She had to answer, but she could not give her father's name: the threads of destinies in the nornir's hall made it clear that Ragnar Erikson had only ever had a son. 'I am Hilda,' she said. 'And I have no lineage.'

One of Odin's two ravens flapped down to sit on his shoulder. It was a terrifyingly big bird, and its black eyes seemed to look straight into Hilda's heart and recognise that she spoke the truth, or at least a version of it.

'Yet, without kinsmen at your side who can speak for you and attest your worth, you come to demand a seat in my hall.'

'Nej,' said Hilda. 'I don't just want a seat in your hall, I want a seat at your high table.'

Fierce fighters all around them began to laugh. They thought her presumptuous and unworthy, but they didn't know anything about her, and Hilda knew where she belonged.

The Alfather didn't laugh with his warriors. Any hint of a smile had disappeared from his thin lips, half-hidden behind his silver beard. 'You left before you could prove your worth last time,' the Alfather correctly remembered.

Hilda smiled wickedly. '*Cattle know when it's time to go home, and then they leave the pasture,*' she quoted. They were the Alfather's own words, a speech delivered centuries ago and famed through all of Midgard.

The Alfather mused on that for a moment. A simpler man might have stroked his long beard as he mused, but the Alfather was a god and he looked wiser by doing nothing at all. For his beard was perfectly combed silver as it was, and his single eye only needed to narrow to show his guarded interest. 'Why have you returned to the pasture now?'

'To demand my rightful place. Right there.' Hilda pointed to the bench at Odin's right side.

'Why should I give you anything at all?' the Alfather asked, and he seemed amused. Easily he could have dismissed her, but he didn't. The mystery of her was enough to keep him asking, as she had hoped.

'*No man is so good that he has no blemishes, and none so bad that he has no use.*' Once more Hilda used the Alfather's own famed words against him.

Odin matched her smile. The longer Hilda was allowed to stand in his presence, the more confident she felt that the Alfather might decide to keep her around; if for nothing else, then for her wits.

'Yet…' the Alfather began, the smile on his lips spreading. 'A bad man may only be useful at the dark corner of my hall. I have no reason to seat him at my side.'

'Then I will gladly prove my worth.'

The Alfather chuckled, a long growl of a sound that reminded Hilda of wolves, telling her that despite his grey beard and hair, and the perfect wrinkles on his face, the Alfather was perhaps the most dangerous being in all the nine worlds.

'*Often, when he comes among the wise, the greedy man's stomach is laughed at.*' Odin too knew how to quote his own words.

Before Hilda could find the right response, Odin pushed away from the table and rose to his feet. At his full height, his perfection was devastating. Lesser warriors would have stumbled over their words at the sight of him, but Hilda knew her own worth. She pushed the intimidation to the back of her mind and focused on the task ahead.

'Let me fight on Ida's plain tomorrow and you will see that I am worthy,' Hilda pleaded.

'There is only one way to prove that,' the Alfather said dismissively. 'Follow me.'

The Alfather had not yet granted her what she wanted, yet even this honour made her dizzy. The Alfather was considering her request, and he had asked her to follow him.

His strides were long, and Hilda struggled to follow his pace down the width of the hall. Warriors and shieldmaiden stared and parted for them as they passed by. All the way to the nearest gate, they rushed. It felt like they walked for half the night.

The Alfather neither looked over his shoulder to make certain that Hilda followed, nor said anything more. He exited the hall, down the nine arm-ring steps into the crisp snow outside. It had stopped snowing while Hilda had been inside, and the air was all the colder for it. The ground was slippery too. Even Hilda's snow fox was struggling, but the Alfather never slowed his walk.

At their backs, warriors stared out of the hall after them.

Dawn was near. The horizon had begun to brighten. Soon the day's battle would begin.

A few good strides from Valhalla's gates, the Alfather finally stopped. Hilda hurried to catch up the last of the way. 'How do I prove my worth?' she asked.

Before the Alfather could answer, a loud horn was blown inside Valhalla. Hilda twirled around to look at the bright hall. The walls were made from huge weapons, and the thick branches of Valhalla's oak tree stretched out over it all. A loud crash and roar followed, and birds took flight from the roof of Valhalla. The first sunlight hit the top of the gates, and then came the rumble.

Shoulder to shoulder came nine hundred and ninety-nine fighters out of each gate. Gold shields in hands, roaring for blood and murder, and headed straight for Hilda.

'It's simple,' the Alfather told Hilda. 'Kill nine hundred and ninety-nine of my best and you will have earned a seat at my side, with them.'

Warriors were rushing at her, gold shields raised. Men and women twice her size, who had fought for centuries before Hilda had even been born.

Hilda clenched her teeth hard and brought out her axe. Her heart beat fast in her chest as she raised the axe in both hands. She had no helmet and no shield to protect herself. She hadn't trained all winter, not like she had used to do, and she had never had to fight such fierce foes either, but she would win. She would prove her worth as she had always dreamt of doing. Finally, the day had come.

The Alfather might have given her an impossible task, but if this was what it would take to accomplish her dreams, then Hilda had no other choice but to succeed.

'For a seat at the high table,' Hilda said to confirm. She glanced over her shoulder at Odin, but the Alfather had disappeared.

Alone with her snow fox, Hilda stood on Ida's snowy plain, with Valhalla's fiercest defenders rushing at her. Her knuckles were white where she clenched her axe. Her snow fox howled.

'*Shieldmaiden die, and snow foxes die,*' Hilda sang to her fox and to the nornir through the wind.

The song calmed her speeding heart, reminded her to breathe, and reminded her of her training. She could do this. She knew that she could.

The whole of Asgard seemed to slow.

The warriors bounded closer. Their chainmail rang in the wind.

'They must die likewise.
I know one thing that will never die.
Our glory in the Alfather's eye.'

EINER

Chapter One Hundred and Forty

'WHAT IS THIS place?' asked Einer as he and Loki rushed up never-ending steps in complete darkness.

'A passage grave to another world,' replied the giant. 'And we're finally at the top.' He stopped walking, and Einer bumped into him.

The grave was so dark that Einer had stumbled more than once as he rushed up the stone steps, and yet Loki had not conjured a flame to better see, as Einer knew jotun familiar with the runes were capable of doing.

'A flame might give us away if Thor was to open the passage at the other end of the grave,' Loki replied to Einer's thoughts.

He was fumbling with something. Obediently, Einer waited at Loki's back in the dark, and looked down beneath where it was equally dark, with a sudden worry that Thor and his lightning might stride up the steps after them.

Loki let out a long sigh. 'The passage is blocked.'

'Then what do we do?' asked Einer, eyes still fixed on the stairs they had walked up, although he could not see a single step.

'We go back down, and we face Thor and his lightning.'

'But you said we would die.'

'I don't intend to die.' Loki shuffled past Einer and started down the steps, and this time he *did* conjure a flame. Einer had never seen one so at ease with the runes. Loki did not even have to say the name of the rune of fire to conjure a flame to float in front of him. He truly was an ancient being, and a powerful one.

'I was hoping we would both get out of this alive,' said Loki, with a smile on his lips that meant he had most definitely heard Einer's thoughts again. 'I know Thor. I know how to provoke him and escape the swing of his hammer. But I don't know how *you* might survive that encounter.'

'I've stood across from Thor on a battlefield before,' said Einer aloud, so Loki wouldn't respond to his thoughts. On the practice field of Ragnarok, Einer had looked straight into Thor's red eyes, and nearly been crushed by the weight of the aesir's hammer, and then he had almost suffocated under the consequent rain of corpses, but he had survived then, and he would survive again.

'The pendant protected you, then,' Loki correctly guessed. 'You won't survive without it, so where is it now? You obviously don't have it anymore.'

With a sigh, Einer gave in to his curiosity, because no matter what, he doubted that he could shield his inner thoughts from Loki, certainly not inside this passage where there was nothing else for the giant to focus on. 'Why are you looking for it?'

A few steps down, Loki turned to look at him. The flame at his back cast deep shadows over his sharp face. Without a word, the giant brought his hands to his neck. Hidden under his tunic was a neck-ring; he tugged on the chain to produce the pendant that hung from it.

Eyes narrowed, Einer walked down three more steps to better see. Loki's gold neck-ring twinkled in the dim light. It was a bracteate, a gold coin neck-ring, like the one Einer's mother had given him at Ragnar's funeral, so long ago. It bore the intricate image of the tree of life, exactly as his own had, and as Einer stared at it, he knew at once that it was not just similar, but the same.

'You already have it,' Einer muttered, and at once his heart raced with worry. He hoped Sigismund had made it all the way to Helheim's shore and to safety before Loki had stripped him of the bracteate.

Loki's smile spread wickedly across his lips. 'I already have *one*,' he corrected.

Einer choked on his own spit and coughed. There was more than one, and what Loki held was not the one Einer's mother had given him. Unwittingly Einer had revealed where his own neck-ring had disappeared to. His loud thoughts put Sigismund in danger, although he had not meant to say anything or endanger his friend.

'Take it,' said Loki. He lifted the neck-ring off over his head and held it out to Einer.

The gesture was more than kindness: it put Loki in danger. But it also ensured that Einer had a chance of surviving their inevitable clash with Thor.

'Why would you risk it? You know where mine is now.'

Loki took a few rapid heartbeats to answer, as if, for a moment, he considered not giving an answer at all, but then he did. 'You're her son.' With those words he dropped the bracteate into Einer's hands and resumed his walk down the steep passageway.

Einer knew better than to ask again. He brought the ring over his head and felt the familiar weight of the bracteate hanging from his neck. With the gold neck-ring, he felt safe.

'How did you know my mother?' Einer asked.

'Once, I taught her runes. I used to visit often, on my travels home. Grythak and Fraktir lived right at the edge of Niflheim. It was a good place to stop for a glass of mead.'

Einer took a moment to realise that the names were those of his grandparents.

Loki held a dramatic pause and then went on, as a skilled skald would have.

'I used to bring them tokens from my travels whenever I went home to see my own mother. Fraktir's glass cups I brought from Vanaheim, Grythak's bronze hairpin was from Alfheim. But little Glumbruck never cared for the things I brought. She wanted to learn the runes. So, whenever I came by, I gifted her a set of runes, and by the time I came again, she had mastered them.'

'My mother was talented with the runes?' asked Einer.

'It wasn't talent,' Loki said and laughed at that for a moment before he embellished. 'If she really wanted to learn something, no matter if she could do it or not, Glumbruck just kept trying, over and over, until she mastered the craft.'

Einer's mother had always been good at everything she did. Even her runic staves were perfect when she sometimes carved words into wood. Einer had never known anyone who could carve staves so straight and true, but it had never occurred to him that it was a result of constant practice.

'The only thing she never learned was how to quit,' Loki reflected. 'Or maybe she did, in the end.'

After spending so long in the company of his grandparents, who had always refused to speak of Einer's mother, it was exhilarating to hear about her, especially from someone who had known her well.

'Why did she settle in Midgard?' Beyond all other questions, it was the one Einer could not solve. Everything he had learned about his mother after first setting foot outside Midgard brought into question what he knew about her, and he found it difficult to understand how one so powerful with runes and so feared and respected in the other worlds would ever choose to live a simple life in Midgard.

'I suppose...' Loki began as he resumed walking.

Their steps echoed up and down the passageway and they walked in silence thereafter for so long that Einer thought

Loki had fallen into a trance and forgotten all about their conversation before the giant went on.

'...she wanted to learn how to live. In Asgard and Jotunheim, she merely survived. I suppose she wanted to learn to live.'

Einer mused on those words for many steps.

For three years he had lived among giants, and their world certainly was different. Giants had no reason to rush or hurry because their lives were so long. There was always tomorrow, and next year.

'Oh, they *have* been rushing, these past three years,' Loki interjected. 'They have been busy.'

Einer blurted a laugh, because the thought had not even occurred to him that the slow way of life he had observed these past three years had seemed rushed to the giants themselves. At last, he understood why his grandparents had given such loud sighs whenever they came home from a Ting or a gathering, declaring that they would refuse to leave again for at least a moon. What he had witnessed *had* been a busy giant life.

'No one lives more intensely than short-lived,' Loki said, and it felt like the opening line to an ancient story. 'Everything happens so fast in Midgard. It's impossible to keep up. Even old Odin struggles, despite how keen an eye he keeps on Midgard. It's why Glumbruck could disappear there.'

'Disappear?' Einer asked, hoping to learn more. Loki knew so much about his mother that Einer could never have guessed or known otherwise.

'Do you know *anything* about your mother?'

'Not much,' Einer admitted. What he did know: the feel of her soft hands stroking his hair, how no one's praises had felt warmer in the chest, and how her smile felt when she looked into your eyes—all of it seemed so trivial now that he had found out who she had been to so many people.

'No matter who she was to us, she will always be your mother,' said Loki and as easy as that, the tale ended.

They walked the rest of the way down the passage in heavy silence, although Einer was well aware that it probably did not feel like silence to Loki, who was forced to listen to Einer's every little thought. Knowing that people were listening sometimes made weird thoughts spring forth. Sometimes it even felt like he had less control over his thoughts from the mere knowledge that someone was listening.

'So, the last one is in Helheim,' Loki muttered after a long while.

Einer sighed loudly at the idea that perhaps Loki had been too focused on his own thoughts to listen to Einer's.

'How many bracteates like it are there?' asked Einer. There was his own, that he had given to Sigismund to save him and help him to a peaceful afterlife in Helheim. Then there was the one that Loki had given Einer. In Asgard, Einer had seen one more. The Alfather wore a neck-ring with a near identical gold bracteate. Unless Loki had stolen his one from the Alfather.

'Those are the three,' Loki answered. 'Yours, mine and that of the Alfather.'

'What do they do?' asked Einer, for he had been in mortal danger enough times to know that they were not simple decoration.

'Anything and everything,' answered Loki, although that did not make Einer feel any wiser. 'They steer the Ginnungagap.'

'Why are you looking for them?'

Loki had risked a great deal by approaching Einer as he had in the snow, especially considering how the aesir were chasing him through the nine worlds.

'I need them to be able to end Ragnarok,' said Loki.

'I thought you wanted to *start* Ragnarok?'

'It needs to be started to be ended,' Loki said in a bored tone. 'Unless I gather the bracteates, it'll be a useless fight that will leave all giants dead and the Alfather to rule unbothered for the rest of eternity.'

It all began to make sense to Einer. He knew the strength of the bracteate. His own had once healed a mortal wound that Finn had inflicted upon him, and it had steadied him in fights and made certain he survived the slaughter on Ida's plain.

The Alfather's own would ensure that the god survived even Ragnarok.

If Loki gathered them all, only those *he* deemed worthy would survive the final battle. Einer felt the weight of the bracteate around his neck, and he knew that it was only on temporary loan until they escaped Thor's grip. Once they were safe, he would have to give it up. 'Who will you give them to?'

Loki laughed. 'That was the Alfather's plan. Three bracteates, three survivors. My Ragnarok won't be like that.'

'You won't give them to anyone?'

'Those pendants should never have been made. They need to be destroyed.' Loki's voice echoed around the dark. 'It's time the nine worlds got their way. Let the shackles fall and let the Darkness consume us, as it was always meant to do.'

The giant's voice was so deep and hollow that Einer swallowed his other questions. He did not dare ask anymore of Loki, lest he wake a murderous rage within the giant. Einer felt his own blood beat with more strength and the familiar anger of the forefathers tried to trickle up his arm.

'Don't waver,' warned Loki. 'Thor won't be alone. Get away as soon as you can.'

They had reached the end of the passageway. A large rock closed them in. On the other side of that rock lay Einer's grandfather's private room and his grandparents' house.

'I'll find you in Helheim.'

So that was where they were headed, after they escaped Thor: Helheim. Of course. That was where Sigismund had gone with the bracteate.

Loki stroked a hand over his wound and touched his bloody palm to the rock.

The whole passage began to shake as the rock rolled apart.

Bright light from outside blinded them. Einer's heart beat loud in his chest and mind. The bracteate warmed his skin, and he made sure it hung under his tunic so it wasn't easily visible.

Stone dust and the smell of burning wood entered the passage as the stone rolled aside. Fire crackled nearby and fresh snow was falling. Loki took a loud breath before he slipped through the passageway ahead of Einer.

'Were you waiting for me?' asked Loki in a singsong voice as he elegantly jumped through flames and black cinders.

Einer crawled out of the passage after the giant, but stayed low, heeding Loki's warnings. A quick glance around revealed that Loki had been right. Red Thor was not alone.

There were a dozen war-clad warriors, and although he did not know their faces, Einer still thought that he knew them. If they hunted with Thor, then they had to be famed aesir, and escaping from them would be difficult—perhaps impossible.

Their eyes were all fixed on Loki as the giant advanced towards them, away from the passage. The aesir fanned out and circled the giant. Einer counted ten of them, with Thor standing back as commander.

Loki walked on casually, drawing further away to give Einer a chance to escape into the thick snowstorm. None of the aesir had laid eyes on Einer yet. This was his chance.

Einer was about to slip out behind Loki and leave him there, but then he remembered. The bracteate burned hot on his chest and kept him warm despite the lack of a coat to guard against the snowstorm. His socks were wet from snow already, but his feet were not cold. Loki had nothing but runes with which to protect himself, not just against the cold of Jotunheim, but against Thor and the other aesir. He might be skilled with the runes, but eleven aesir were far too many.

Einer's grandparents had believed in Loki, and they had died to protect him.

Einer rose to his feet behind Loki and unsheathed his two swords, his own sword in his left hand and his father's Ulfberht in his right. He was a trained warrior, and unwise as it was to stand up to Red Thor, Einer was not a coward, and he would not run away.

'I have decided,' he said aloud to Loki, 'on which side I shall stand at Ragnarok.'

For a moment, the aesir's eyes all flicked to Einer, and a moment was all Loki needed.

The giant wielded runes like blades. The falling snow solidified into ice shards that rained hard over the gods. They wore gold and silver armour, and now their shields were above them to protect them from Loki's ice.

Without a blink of hesitation, Einer lunged ahead, wielding his two swords. His own he used in place of a shield, and with the Ulfberht he attacked. The sword cut through shining armour and tunics, coming back with a blooded tip. The first aesir grunted from the pain and pawed at his wound while Einer slammed into the next.

The bracteate hammered hot against Einer's chest, keeping him aware, and alive.

The next aesir had no shield, but a thick helmet protected him. His eyes were fixed on Einer and his spear fought off ice shards as they fell. The aesir aimed his golden spear head, but Einer parried the thrust and attacked with the blooded Ulfberht. His sword went through empty armour where there ought to have been a right arm. The blow landed by the aesir's hip before Einer could retrieve it.

Einer's eyes went wide. A god with no right hand, clad like a great hero. It was Tyr, god of war and strategy, his hand chewed off by the terrible wolf Fenrir. Tears pressed into Einer's eyes as he hurried out of Tyr's reach and carried on.

So many times, he had offered riches to Tyr before a fight. So many times, he had asked the god for help and protection, and now, Einer had wounded his own god.

Roaring for the forefathers to help him, Einer fought against his gods. His heart felt tight as his father's Ulfberht blade clanged against their weapons, and where it cut, left gashes and wounds that would never quite heal.

'Einer!' yelled Loki above the clatter of Einer's swords, the ice shards crashing against metal shields.

The giant was no longer in the midst of the gods, as Einer was. Loki was running away, and Einer had been too busy swinging his swords and worrying about his gods to realise.

Trusting Loki, and the bracteate to protect him, Einer launched into a run. His gaze was fixed on Tyr as he ran away from his gods to follow the trickster giant no one ought to trust.

Tyr did not easily allow Einer to escape. The great god of war launched his spear, and Einer cast himself aside. The point missed his head but sliced through his side and made him double over himself as he hurried into the blizzard. Hot blood splashed over the snow. The bracteate burned itself into Einer's flesh and core. It kept him warm and guarded him against the cold of the ice mist.

Crashes and yells echoed at Einer's back as he ran with all his might after Loki. The snow grew thicker the further away from the burned pillars of his grandparents' house he went, and Einer tried his best not to think about what used to be there, and how he had spent the whole winter in the warmth of that house.

Loki was a mere shadow in the blizzard.

All of Ragnar's old stories of Loki and the gods made it clear that no one should trust Loki, for Loki only worked for himself, and helped others to help himself, yet Einer followed the giant willingly. He knew it to be foolish, but he trusted Loki not to lead him astray.

He sheathed his swords and raised his knees to run through the snow and follow Loki's fast pace. A harsh wind blew around them. It lifted the snow off the ground to shield them from the aesir on their trace. At last, Einer understood how Loki could have escaped the aesir for so long. He was not just *skilled* with runes, he was exceptional, although in close combat there was no doubt that the aesir could win in nine heartbeats.

Loki made himself large, larger than a giant's usual size, and with a frustrated sigh, he picked Einer up. His fingers closed around Einer, crushing his chest so he could hardly breathe. The bracteate thumped against his heart and burned. Focusing on breathing and clenching his teeth to suppress the pain of the heat was all Einer could do as he was swung through the cold air in Loki's tight grip.

They rushed through the snowstorm as the wind howled, and Einer felt like he was being lulled to sleep by the sound and warmth on his chest, when at last, Loki came to a stop.

A loud crash rumbled down over them. Einer tried to turn and see, but locked as he was in Loki's grip it was difficult. The blood flowed to his head as he was dangled upside down. There was another loud crash. Einer knew the sound well: the waves striking Niflheim's coast.

Once, the treacherous waves had crashed at his back as he had freed Sigismund from the ice on the beach and released the blizzard upon the nine worlds. Trusting Einer, Sigismund had cast himself into the high waves to swim to Helheim. Despite how the Midgard Worm guarded these waters, and despite the venom that Einer knew the ocean was full of, and despite the waves that had nearly killed Einer when he had first journeyed to Jotunheim. Sigismund had trusted him.

The reality of what was about to happen hit Einer like Thor's hammer. They were going to swim to Helheim. His stomach was already in uproar from how he was dangled in the giant's grip, but Loki did not stop for long.

Before he had the strength to protest, Einer was lifted as easily as a pebble and thrown through the air, straight towards the treacherous waves. Einer only had a heartbeat to take a deep breath before his head hit the cold waters.

DARKNESS

RAGNAR WOULD SUCCEED. He would truly kill the Alfather, and no one would know that it was him who had done it, hiding in the Darkness. They would blame Loki and his three monstrous children. The gods always ended up blaming Loki for their problems.

Loki's terrifying children slithered past Ragnar, and behind them came one last god: Heimdall, with his gold horn fastened to his back. The Gjallar-horn was entirely made of gold, and on it was the swirling image of the great battle that would someday be fought, unless Ragnar could prevent it.

With low grunts, Heimdall urged the naked girl along after her monstrous brothers, ignoring her tears.

Reluctantly, Ragnar followed both gods and young monsters into a room down the hallway, entering just before Heimdall shut the gates at his back. There were more gods inside the hall.

The Alfather filled the high seat, and his wife Frigg sat at his side. Next to Frigg, the twins, Frey and Freya, had placed themselves. Their father, Njord, who barely ever left his home by the sea, seemed wind-blown at their side. His silver neck-ring was in the shape of a monstrous fish that barely reached around his thick neck.

At Njord's side sat Idun, with a plump face like that of a young girl and her eyes big and full of curiosity. Her hand was wrapped around her husband's, the gods' skald, with his mouth hanging open to show his runic carved tongue. Every rune had once been carved into Bragi's tongue to make his words smooth. At the sight of him, Ragnar felt unworthy to ever have called himself a skald. Every ring and bracteate that Bragi wore—and he wore many—seemed to tell a story of its own.

The other gods had placed themselves at the Alfather's other side, and among them were two that Ragnar had thought he would never see, although he recognised them immediately. Blind Höd wore a dark blue tunic and silver rings, while Baldur was dressed in white, both tunic and loose trousers, and his arms were covered in thick gold rings. They were night and day, the two of them, and Ragnar's eyes were fixed on them. He had never thought he might see them alive, for they had both died so long before Ragnarok.

Höd had a hand on his brother's arm for support, and just like the stories described him, Baldur was perfect in every way. It almost seemed as though his skin shone. He would have been a worthy successor to the Alfather, had he lived.

The thought made Ragnar's resolve grow. If he killed the Alfather now, while Baldur was still alive, then Baldur would take Odin's place, and all would be well in the nine worlds.

The gods had formed a horseshoe formation around Loki's three monster children. No chains bound the great wolf. The Midgard Worm was out of the waters, and not nearly large enough to surround all of Midgard. Hel was only a small girl. They were young, and they had not yet been sentenced.

Ragnar glanced to the great god of war. Tyr still had his right hand, which meant that Fenrir had not yet been bound by the gods, and his sister and brother had not yet been sentenced to their endless tasks. If Ragnar succeeded, they never would be. The Midgard Worm would never guard the oceans and Hel would never have a realm to rule. There would be no Helheim, and nowhere but Ragnarok and the icy shores of Niflheim for people to pass on into.

Ragnar's wife and son would have nowhere to go in the afterlife. Nor would he, if he ever escaped this Darkness. Yet Ragnar did not think that he would get a better chance, or that he even had a choice. The Alfather had to die, or they would all die.

The gods had begun talking over each other about what to do with Loki's three monsters. They were shouting and insulting each other, as people did at Tings, although hearing such words from the mouths of gods felt different. It felt right. The Alfather's one eye moved around the room quickly, not missing a single argument.

Suddenly the doors at Ragnar's back were thrust open. In stormed Loki.

The heated conversation was replaced by an icy silence when Loki made his entrance. He puffed and his cheeks were red like his tunic that hung sloppily over his belt as if there had been no time to make himself decent. Loki had dressed in a hurry; even his hair, which was only a little longer than his shoulders, clung close to the back of his neck under his gold neck-ring, slung on hastily.

Then Ragnar's eyes fell on Loki's calves, wrapped in an embroidered strip of yellow fabric up to his knees. Bands like those took a long time to bind with the perfection that Loki's had been. The giant had not truly dressed in a hurry, he simply wanted to appear as though he had.

'What are you doing here?' Loki hissed.

'Discussing what to—' Odin began, but Loki interrupted the Alfather.

'Not you, blood-brother,' he spat, and instead twisted around to look at the three monsters in the room. 'I told you to stay away.'

The first of the three to turn to the giant was the girl. Her right eye was completely black and almost hollow. On that side of her face, her lips resembled scars. The pink side of her was swollen in comparison, her normal eye barely visible from her full cheek. Ragnar did not know which side of her was worse to look upon.

Tears flowed from both her eyes and although she opened her mouth, she said nothing. Fenrir also faced Loki. The huge wolf, the eldest of Loki's three children, had sharper and longer teeth than any Ragnar had ever seen before. They glistened and seemed to be calling for blood to be spilt, and his fur was so coarse and sharp it seemed as though each hair was a tiny grey dagger.

'I told you never to come in here,' Loki hissed, when the silence had hung in the air long enough.

'But, Father,' the wolf muttered. Ragnar shuddered when he saw the throat behind the sharp teeth.

'Never!' Loki shouted. He took a pause and lowered his voice before he continued with disgust in his tone. 'Never call me that. I don't raise monsters like you for children.'

Wretched sobbing joined the girl's tears.

'Back to Jotunheim,' Loki hissed.

His monstrous children did not move.

'*Now!*' Loki yelled in such a loud voice that the fires dimmed, and the room darkened.

The wolf snarled, but moved nonetheless. His two siblings joined in close behind. First the girl, and then the worm who was the slowest of the three.

Ragnar's breath caught in his throat. They couldn't leave yet. *Attack*, Ragnar thought loud in his mind, staring at Fenrir's spiky fur. *Kill the Alfather.*

The wolf glanced over its shoulder to the Alfather, but it continued to move out of the room after its father and siblings.

The Alfather wants you dead, Ragnar thought, to try to convince the creature. *Kill him.* But the wolf did not follow his command. Ragnar needed more time. Desperately, he looked to the Alfather. *Stop,* he commanded, and as ever, Odin listened.

'Wait!' The Alfather had risen from his high seat, one foot still on the wooden footrest and the other on the stone floor.

The three monsters stopped their beaten march halfway towards Loki and the door.

'We're only discussing what's best for them,' Odin said.

'And you couldn't do this with me around?' Loki growled with such force that it came as no surprise that he could have fathered a wolf. 'Well, well, high Odin,' he mocked. 'I never thought you'd treat your own blood-brother like this.' Not wasting a single breath, he swirled around, readying himself to leave the hall with his three monstrous children.

Refusing to give up, Ragnar watched the Alfather, and with all the strength in him, he wished that Odin would listen to him once more and keep Loki and his three children from leaving this hall.

'I had to. Believe me, brother,' Odin begged. His stance was hunched, not healthy and perfect like that of the vanir twins to his left. 'I had to.'

It was only because Loki now directly faced him that Ragnar noticed the giant's wicked smile.

'The veulve... She has made a premonition,' the Alfather added. Ragnar shuddered at the mention of the veulve, remembering how she had made him burn and how she had grabbed him.

Loki rid himself of the smile and slowly turned, as though to say that a premonition changed everything, and as he did, the gods' tense stares seemed to relax, if only slightly. 'And what does this premonition have to do with these three—*monsters?*' Loki asked.

This was all just another of Loki's games. A small part of a bigger ploy, as all things seemed to be when Loki was involved.

Someone else spoke: not the Alfather, but the little naked girl that Ragnar could barely make himself look at. 'They say, someday, we'll be the ruin of all, both gods and giants,' she muttered, and as though her appearance was not bad enough, she had also been gifted with a hoarse voice that seemed to swallow all the bright things in the nine worlds and replace them with despair.

'Who could *you* possibly ruin, Hel?' Loki asked scornfully.

Ashamed, she diverted her eyes from her father to the stone floor.

Hel's wormy brother wheezed in her stead: 'We're only children now, but perhaps someday, Fenrir, Hel and I might do what they say we will.'

Not someday, thought Ragnar, loud for the three monsters to hear. *Today. The Alfather must die, or he will kill you.*

None of Loki's three monsters looked as though they had heard, although the runes on Ragnar's distaff shone. Again, he thought the words: *We have to kill Odin.*

No one reacted. The three monsters were beasts, and while Ragnar could sway the minds of gods, he could not influence beasts.

Ragnar turned his thoughts to Loki, whom he knew he could influence. Loki could make his children do it, or maybe even do it himself. He was capable of it, and he had always been a good scapegoat for the gods.

The Alfather must die, Ragnar thought as loud as he could, focusing on the giant in the room.

'I have no reason to kill the old man,' Loki muttered, so quietly that only Ragnar could hear, and as easily as that, Ragnar's commands were ignored. 'Everything is going according to plan.'

Perhaps it was, for Loki, but not for Ragnar. He shivered from fear, for he knew what this meant. There would be no scapegoat. Even Loki and his three monstrous children could not do it for him. The death of the Alfather was such a terrible deed, and such a difficult one, that Ragnar had to accomplish it on his own. He stared at his own hands, clenched onto the distaff. No one would kill the Alfather for him. Ragnar had to do it himself, with runes, and his own bare hands.

HILDA

Chapter One Hundred and Forty-One

WARRIORS STORMED TOWARDS Hilda. Snow was cast around them. The day's first light broke above Valhalla and hit Hilda right in the eyes.

Of course, Valhalla had been built so that its combatants would have the sun at their backs and any attackers would be blinded by the light of morning. But Hilda had fought before without being able to see either weapons or shields. She had raided with Muspel sight. A little sunlight didn't scare her. Besides, at Ragnarok, there would be no sun to blind. It wasn't an advantage that they would have for long, and she wouldn't allow it to be an advantage today either.

The warriors were rushing out to fight their daily battle, and as the only person standing on the battlefield, Hilda became their first target.

Hilda narrowed her eyes, drove her feet through the snow so she knew the terrain underneath, and calmed her racing heart. Her snow fox yelped and reminded her of what her goddess had once said. The two of them were connected. Hilda might survive, if the snow fox did, and she might die if the fox did.

'Run,' she told the fox. 'Run and hide in the snow.'

She would need all the advantage she could get against Odin's most skilled champions if she wanted to join their ranks. They would not be easy to beat. Not a single one of them, and certainly not nine hundred and ninety-nine of them.

The warriors bounded towards Hilda, yelling and grunting so loud it felt like the ground might break around her. They were tall, like half-giants. Their shields were as large as Hilda.

Battle-axe ready to strike, she reminded herself of all the runes. They tingled around her hands as she thought of them. The nornir had taught her all of them; they had not trained her to fight with runes in hand, but Hilda knew how to fight. She didn't need anyone to teach her.

The northern wind whisked in at her back with whispers of pasts, presents and futures.

'Show me their past,' Hilda whispered to the wind, as she stared at the men running at her. The first of them were all men. All much larger than her, too. 'Show me their deaths.'

The wind abided.

Green eyes had been stabbed with a spear-tip. Blood had rushed from a stomach wound. A man had been trampled to death. Hundreds of images of the past flashed before Hilda's mind, but a few endured. *Red hair had flicked in the wind. A hand had grabbed the red lock. A dagger through the throat.*

The warriors had nearly reached her. Hilda brought herself out of the visions. With a quick glance to the side, she checked that her snow fox was gone. Its track had been covered by the wind which made snow rise and she couldn't see it anymore.

Hilda brought her axe up to her own face and slashed open the skin above her eyebrows. Fresh blood trickled over her cheeks as it had when she had died in Magadoborg. It dripped to her lips and blooded her teeth. There was no greater weapon in battle than fear in an enemy's heart.

One had broken free of the crowd. He was faster than the

others, decked in armour and helmet, a sword in hand and his large gold shield covering him. The first warrior lurched forward with his sword. Hilda twisted out of the way of his blade. His move had exposed his left shoulder and, axe head to the fore, Hilda attacked. Long red hair hung free from the helmet at his back as he swung out of her reach.

Red hair had flicked in the wind, the Runes reminded Hilda. *A hand had grabbed the red lock. A dagger through the throat.* That was how he had died in life. Hilda smirked, for now she knew how to kill him. Fear was her greatest weapon.

The red-haired warrior attacked. Hilda ducked out of the blow and sprang forward. He lifted his shield, and Hilda hooked her axe on it. His sword rose at her back. Hilda barely evaded the blow.

The man danced to the side to free his shield of her axe. Hilda held on and unclasped one hand. The man's long red braid of hair slapped to the side as he struggled. Hilda grabbed his hair as she released his shield, and his eyes widened in surprise and horror. He recognised his first death. *There* was that brilliant fear of death.

Hilda pulled hard on the red braid, slamming him down into the snow. His sword cut her left arm as he fell. With a grunt, Hilda lifted her axe and chopped his neck. The blood splashed up her wool-covered legs. Her axe wrenched off a piece of flesh as she pulled it free.

More foes rushed at her, and Hilda backed away from her first kill. She didn't have time to snatch up the man's large shield. Besides, it was too large for her. His helmet too.

'One,' she shouted. Odin's two dark-winged ravens circled above, and she knew they would hear. They were watching, and counting the kills, with her.

Three warriors came at her at once. At their back others clashed, giving Hilda a few heartbeats of opportunity before she was drowned in a larger crowd.

'Laguz,' Hilda shouted, calling upon the runes. Out of

nothing, she conjured water with the command. It came much easier to her than conjuring fire; the snow helped to make it happen. Water appeared exactly where she willed it to—at the feet of the three nearest attackers. The icy air froze the water as it appeared. One after the other, they slipped over her freshly made ice, falling to their knees. One after the other, she hacked into their backs as they glided within axe reach.

'Four!'

More warriors rushed at her. They slipped over her ice, straight to Hilda's feet. She chopped off heads and hacked through armour, killing them all. She searched for a helmet she might use.

'Twelve!'

The pile of corpses at her feet put her in danger. Warm corpses were easier to march atop than slippery ice and snow. Hilda wrenched a helmet off one enemy. A shadow moved at her back.

'Iwaz,' called Hilda, not a heartbeat too soon. A spear was thrust at her, and the rune of defence deflected the hit, so the point only scraped the side of her face. Hilda swung towards a shieldless spearman. She hooked her axe under his spear to lift it up and away and glided close to him. He tried to break free, but she was already too close. Horror flashed across his face as he looked into her bloodied eyes, as dark and unforgiving as those of Thor himself. Hilda swung the helmet into his. A blow with the Ulfberht axe and he fell down dead.

'Thirteen!'

Others had advanced at the spearman's back.

'Laguz!' called Hilda and forced the helmet over her head. In a large circle around her, water splashed out and froze, forming an ice barrier between her and the warriors. The first of them were too close and eager to stop before their feet slipped over the fresh ice.

With her Ulfberht axe, Hila smashed through helmetless skulls and sliced necks.

'Fifteen! Sixteen! Seventeen!'

Fighters fell at her feet, but more came. They formed a wide circle around her, tiptoeing at the edge of the ice. Many had taken up the Alfather's unnamed challenge to kill her, for she was worthy, and with her death they would prove their own worth. She had walked with the Alfather. Odin had spoken to her, and acknowledged her, and that came at a price on Valhalla's battlefield. They had all seen her, and that made her the day's target.

A shieldmaiden cautiously tried to walk over her ice. Hilda darted ahead and swung her axe. Missed, but it didn't matter. The woman stumbled back. Out of her reach.

The day darkened. Birds had gathered in great masses above Hilda and the warriors. It was no longer just Odin's two ravens. The attention would draw more eager fighters to her.

Hilda noticed the looks her opponents gave each other. They were coordinating an attack, and Hilda stood alone, with warriors all around her. She needed to disappear into the fighting crowd for a chance to survive and complete the Alfather's task.

'Algiz, algiz, algiz,' chanted Hilda. The rune of opportunity might provide a chance to escape. Somehow. Before the warriors launched a coordinated attack she couldn't evade. 'Algiz, algiz, algiz.'

Dark wings swooped down. Birds attacked all around her. Hilda had called upon their service with the runes. Gold shields shot up to form a ceiling. Spears and swords changed targets.

For a moment, no one looked at Hilda.

It was like back in Ash-hill, her first fight. When Einer's bear had come and fought to let her out. Maybe she had used runes back then too, without realising it. The nornir said it was her blood that gave her such ease with runes. She had always heard whispers in the wind. Maybe she had always used runes, too.

An eagle shrieked. Its call wrenched Hilda back to the cold present. Her chance was now.

'Kauna,' she whispered to melt the slippery ice she had formed. She trampled through melting ice at the warriors' backs. Hacked and sliced through every exposed neck and back knee that she saw, as she ran through the crowd to get away and disappear.

'Twenty-one, twenty-two, twenty-three!' Her Ulfberht always cut true.

She was short compared to these half-giants, but that made it easier to hide in their midst. The crowd was tight, like a midsummer feast. Without a shield getting caught everywhere, Hilda more easily slipped away from the murderous crowd and disappeared into the regular fight of Ida's plain.

The battle was like a thousand different fights in one. Hilda chanted the rune of success as she slipped away and made enemies fall by kicking the back of their knees and slicing their necks.

'Thirty-six, thirty-seven,' she counted and between each few counts she repeated her runic chant to keep safe and successful.

There were battles in shield-walls and there were close Holmgang-like combats. There were warriors who fought fair and warriors who didn't. Hilda rushed through their midst, never halting long enough to truly be challenged again, and avoiding the shield-walls. She needed to kill too many to trust the numbers in a shield-wall.

Her ears were sharpened for the high-pitched yelps of her snow fox, but her fylgja was long gone. It made her uneasy to be apart from her fox, but Hilda reminded herself that being apart gave them both a better chance of surviving.

The wind howled with the past of her attackers and dried her bloody tears into her cheeks. *A stab to the eye. A spear through the back.*

Each time Hilda recognised one foe from the visions in the wind, she ensured a kill that matched the death from Midgard. Odin's battlers were easier to kill when they were petrified with fear.

The Runes made Hilda tingle with strength.

'One hundred and six,' she yelled to Odin's two ravens, and she felt more powerful than ever before. Even Odin's best were no match for Hilda, who had more than just an axe in hand: she had the nornir's visions and she had the Runes.

A pain stabbed through Hilda's heart. She gasped for air and looked down at herself. There was no weapon and no blood.

Someone attacked at her back and Hilda ducked out of the way. She examined herself. She wasn't bleeding. Yet the pain in her heart persisted.

Her snow fox was hurt. Hilda felt it at her core. Maybe it was dead, surviving only on Hilda's life. Her body began to cool. She felt hungry and hurt. The scrapes she had suffered burned with pain. Her muscles were sore. She was surviving, alone, for the both of them.

A shieldmaiden slammed his shield into Hilda's face. She stumbled backwards. Her nose was blocked and bleeding. Hilda swallowed her instincts to never back away from a fight and clenched her axe tighter. Puffed for breath and scrambled away fast until she could fill her lungs.

The shieldmaiden chased her through the crowd. She fought with shield and axe. The reach of her axe was greater than that of Hilda's who struggled for breath. It felt like she was drowning. Her lungs were weak.

The other lunged ahead. Hilda cast herself out of her way, reached after her with her axe. She cut through fingers. The shieldmaiden screamed in pain until Hilda planted the Ulfberht axe in her face.

'One hundred and seven!'

Her mind and body pulsed and ached as the shieldmaiden fell away. Her snow fox was hurt, and Hilda felt like she was dying.

The breath was pushed out of her to make place for pain. A spear tip wrenched through her stomach. The pain screamed through her body, and then worsened. The spear drew out of her gut. It was real, this time.

Hilda collapsed forward, gasping for air. Struggling and worming to get up. She rolled onto her back. Her stomach seemed to close in on itself with pain. Everything felt both warm and cold, like down in the forge where she had seen the fire demons. Her thoughts were slipping.

'One hundred and seven, one hundred and seven,' she muttered and tried to remember the runes that might heal her, but her mind kept slipping. She was bleeding out, feeling cold all the way to her bones as the northern wind howled around her. For what felt like a long time, she lay and tried to blink herself awake with the little strength she had left.

One man stepped on her chest, using her body as a foothold as he fought above her. Hilda couldn't breathe. The warrior stepped back. She took a deep breath, and then the boot came down hard on her face.

Death, pain, and wrath.

HILDA BLINKED AWAKE, anger coursing through her, eager to fight and claim her seat in Valhalla. The battlefield stank of rot and shit, but there were no clashes anymore; she had woken too late. Her chest no longer ached where she had taken the spear-blow. Her snow fox stared down at her. Its white fur was bloodied, and its breath was as foul as the battlefield.

Her wounds had been healed, much more completely than the wound Freya had once inflicted upon her, though this had been a deeper wound. A mortal wound.

With her axe-hand, Hilda felt her stomach where she had been speared. There was a scar there, but it was not like the scars she had suffered in life. The ones that had left a permanent streak of bloody tears on her cheeks, or the one in her thigh from Ash-hill, or the one from her encounter with the goddess Freya. Wounds didn't heal this quickly, except when one passed on into the afterlife. She had died, then.

Blurry faces stared down at her, above the snow fox. All

Hilda's limbs ached as she pushed up to sit. The battle was long over. Night had set. All Hilda had done was survive the morning. She had only killed a portion of the warriors the Alfather had demanded of her. One hundred and seven, she eventually recalled. It felt like her head needed more time to recover from death than the rest of her.

Valkyries were staring at her, and they were not impressed. They leaned on their spears, and their fylgjur—all crows—sat on their shoulders. Small fires dangled in the air and lit their bloodied faces, and at their backs stood someone else.

He lent against his famed spear, and even though he stood on corpses and even though all the valkyries were drenched in blood, Odin looked like he had walked straight out of a bath. Only his shoes carried bloodstains. In her dazed state, Hilda couldn't understand at all, how he could have walked through such a bloody battlefield, and look so perfect? His two wolves roamed around his feet.

Hilda's snow fox licked her bloody arm, bringing her to her senses.

The Alfather was there, watching her waking from death on his battlefield.

She might not have succeeded in the task he had given her, but she had killed more opponents than she ever had in life. She had only fought in Ash-hill, Hammaborg and Magadoborg. Three battles she had lived through before she had died, while the foes she had fought on this snowy plain had fought thousands of battles.

None of the warriors at the Alfather's high table would have succeeded in the task he had given her. None of them would have been able to kill nine hundred and ninety-nine of their bench-mates. Most of them likely wouldn't have been able to kill even as many as Hilda had.

Although she thought it, and knew it to be true, Hilda didn't say it aloud. For she also knew that she was better than any of them. She wouldn't put herself on the same foot as them, for they were not her equals. She was above them, in every way.

'I win,' she told the great Alfather, instead. 'They're all dead. All of them lie dead at my feet. More than nine hundred and ninety-nine warriors delivered to you dead. I win.'

'But you are one of them. Dead along with them.'

'You didn't say that I wasn't allowed to die. You merely said I had to kill nine hundred and ninety-nine of them, and I have.' Her voice screamed with the pain of death and the pain of being woken, too, and she could hardly think. 'They are dead.'

'Not all at your hand.'

'Enough at my hand.'

'That is not for you to say.' He was right, of course—Odin was always right—but Hilda knew that she had done well and proven her worth, and she knew that she belonged in Valhalla. So close to Ragnarok and the end of all things, all Hilda wanted was to find somewhere she belonged.

'I might have died today,' Hilda admitted, 'but I will *not* die tomorrow.'

'Everyone dies at Ragnarok,' answered the Alfather.

She didn't know if he meant that Ragnarok was tomorrow, or merely that no one was spared from death for long. Either way, Hilda had to think of a response, and fast, while she still had the Alfather's full attention.

'I thought you wise,' she said. Her wits had impressed the Alfather before, enough for him to entertain the thought of her joining his ranks. She closed her eyes and made a show of listening to the wind that blew around her. 'The nornir tend to whisper as if you are,' she muttered, to remind him of what he would lose by deciding not to grant her a place in his hall.

That got the Alfather's attention. 'So, you do hear them, and you know how to use them.' It was not a question. He was intrigued. None other in his hall who could hear the nornir's whispers and visions. She would be of value to him.

Hilda opened her eyes again and stared straight into Odin's single eye. 'A seat at your high table,' she demanded again.

'The greedy merchant sells little,' answered the Alfather, and at that he began to walk away into the night. A single flame dangled behind him, following him away.

Hilda watched him leave, and then it hit her. She had failed her task, so the Alfather had had no reason to watch her be woken on the battlefield. The valkyries could have simply relayed his message. Odin had only one reason to come all this way himself: he *wanted* to invite her in. Hilda merely had to give him a good reason, and she had prepared the perfect one.

As she watched the Alfather walk away, his shadows thrown long, with his two ravens circling close above and his wolves at his side, Hilda knew exactly what to say.

'There is one more reason you ought to grant me a seat at your high table.'

The Alfather looked over his shoulder to Hilda.

She held her silence and waited for him to speak. She had time. She could sacrifice her entire afterlife, but the Alfather only had until Ragnarok. His time was a lot more precious than hers. The wind howled full of visions and whispers as she waited for the Alfather to finally ask: 'Why?'

'Because I can grant you something no one else can. I can ensure that you survive Ragnarok.'

TYRA

Chapter One Hundred and Forty-Two

TYRA GLIDED AFTER the guards along the path to the king's hall, smiling as she went, as she had once seen Siv do. She had learned how to seduce and how to tickle the ambitions of powerful men so that they couldn't resist her. She had learned how to whisper into their ears and convince, and she had learned to remain cautious.

Her racing heart reminded her of the danger, and she calmed it with a warrior's calculated breaths. She knew of no one in Midgard more dangerous than King Olaf. That was why she had come, bearing no gifts but herself, hair neatly combed and braided, eyelids and lips coloured, gold rings hanging from her arms and fingers.

The king who burned the Alfather's followers alive would be her next husband. His ear would be for her lips to rest and whisper into, and his hands would be hers to steer. She would have to speak foul words to make it a reality, for she knew the stories of King Olaf and how much he hated any follower of Odin.

King Olaf's hall was large like Jomsborg, and somehow it felt like Tyra's old husband, Styrbjorn, was still alive and she was on her way to meet him, although she knew King Olaf was much worse.

The guards opened the outer door. Loud talk escaped the king's hall. There were two dozen people inside and they were feasting on meat and delicacies. A hunting feast, like she remembered them from back in Ash-hill, so long ago. Although this was different: the feasters were all men and all Christian, and clearly, they had not yet drowned themselves in mead.

'Tyra Haraldsdóttir,' announced the guard who'd led her into the feasting hall, before backing away to grant Tyra audience in the middle of the hall.

The hunters were seated around the feast table, eating and talking, but when Tyra entered, the talk died. King Olaf was seated at the far left end of the table. Most chiefs placed themselves in the middle, but the king had no need to, for even Tyra, who had never met him before, knew exactly which of the men was King Olaf. All of the Christian men in the hall glanced at him to gain his approval and waited for him to speak.

The king was the only one who hadn't even glanced up at Tyra. His eyes remained focused on the piece of meat in his hands.

'You're Bluetan's daughter,' he mused between bites. A few bloody scraps had settled in his brown beard.

'Ja,' Tyra confirmed. 'I am the daughter of Harald Gormsson, King of Danes and Jutes, who unified Denmark and rules over their lands.'

King Olaf took another large bite and narrowed his slim eyes at her as he chewed.

'May I join you? It has been a long journey.' Truly, it was not her place to ask, but Tyra had usually found that raiders and murderers, like Olaf, admired a woman who spoke out of turn, as long as she had something to say and knew how to flatter them.

The king gestured for her to sit, and the company he kept moved down the bench opposite Olaf to make room for Tyra. She approached, lifted her skirts enough to show her knees, but no further, and stepped over the bench to sit.

'Takka,' she said to King Olaf, making certain not to match his stare for too long before she focused on the food. She felt his gaze on her as she reached for bread and meat.

'I heard you were getting married,' he said, eyes taking in all of her. 'To my old father-in-law.' Despite his age, which was not so much greater than Tyra's own, King Olaf was widowed twice over. Neither of his previous wives had died in childbirth. Tyra had not arrived in ignorance, and she knew everything told about Olaf, good and bad.

'I was,' Tyra answered simply as she dripped a dark red sauce over her meat. 'I never met Geira,' she added, to show that she knew the name of the king's first wife, who had been the eldest daughter of Tyra's last marriage match.

'I met Styrbjorn,' said Olaf, to show that he too knew who she was and knew about *her* first husband. 'On the blooded battlefield that claimed his life.'

'You fought at Uppsala?'

'I would have, if I had been told that there would be a battle,' he said, and the way he phrased it made Tyra think, just for a heartbeat, that he knew how the ambush at Uppsala had been arranged, and that it was her who had set it up.

'I arrived later,' Olaf explained. 'The corpses still hadn't been dragged away. I had expected to see yours there.' King Olaf knew. He definitely knew. Tyra felt it all the way down in her core. For a moment the fear overwhelmed her, but then she remembered how Siv had sometimes said that fear was what made things a reality. "Show no fear, and there will be nothing to fear," Siv had once said.

'I had expected to be there too,' Tyra said coolly, as if she was bitter about her fate. 'My brother dragged me away before the battle.' She took a ragged breath, as if she was struggling not to cry. 'He betrayed me. Betrayed *us*. And then he told me to marry a heathen.' She scoffed at the thought of it and bit into the tender meat. It came apart like butter on her tongue.

Her unconcern forced him to ask: 'So, are you? Married?'

'Not to old Burisleif,' Tyra said as if the mere suggestion offended her.

'If not to Burisleif, then to whom are you married?'

'God,' answered Tyra, fully matching the king's stare for the first time since she had entered his hall. She leaned in and glanced down the table as if to tell him a great secret. 'I could never marry a heathen.'

He smiled at that, as she had known he would. 'Last summer, I was keen to marry Sigrid, leader of the Swedes.'

'A fair match,' Tyra praised, for it would have been the most dangerous marriage in the Norse lands had it happened. Together they would have ruled over everything but the Dane and Jute lands, and with their combined armies, they would easily have taken those from Harald and Svend.

'So I thought,' said King Olaf. 'But she was heathen like no other woman I have ever met. She refused to give up her faith. I couldn't possibly marry her after that revelation.'

Tyra allowed herself to smile, genuinely, at the idea of Sigrid of the Swedes protecting her own faith and that of her followers at the peril of making a mortal enemy of Olaf Tryggvason.

She resumed her meal, and for a while there was silence and only the occasional exchanged glances. The conversation further down the table got loud before Tyra spoke again.

'That's why I came here,' she said. 'I knew I would be safe here. And...' She trailed off, pretending that she wasn't sure if she should tell or not, what she was truly thinking.

Olaf leaned forward in his seat. His eyes were fixed on her, but Tyra barely granted him a glance and didn't allow her eyes to linger. As a woman it was always best to be looked at than to look.

'I've heard the tales,' Tyra flattered. She took a big bite of meat and bread and sauce and chewed it long and well before she said more. 'The skalds sing of your childhood with the Rus and of your raids in Gotland. And I have also heard that it was you who sailed around the Danevirke fortifications about a dozen summers back and burned your way up through Jutland.'

She needed to know if the songs about King Olaf were true, and if he had truly led the attack that had killed her parents and sisters.

Olaf's lips wrenched into a wide smile. 'It was my father-in-law at the time, none other than Burisleif, who found the post for me,' he confirmed. 'A wretched summer, that was.' He laughed at the old memory of it.

Tyra forced a smile, although a rage burned inside. Olaf had been in Ash-hill.

He had slaughtered in the name of the Christian god. He had been standing on the other side of the shield-wall. He had murdered her sisters and her parents.

Under the table, Tyra clenched a handful of her skirt to suppress the anger shaking her. Olaf had slaughtered everyone she had cared for, had ripped her from her life—her good life. She would make sure he died for it.

'Then I have you to thank for my father becoming Christian,' she said with a sweet smile, as her insides burned to pull out her Ragnarok dagger and plunge it into the king's heart.

'Does Harald keep the faith?' Olaf wanted to know.

'He does,' Tyra confirmed. 'I was raised Christian thanks to you and that summer's raids.'

Olaf was more dangerous than anyone she had ever met before. More despicable and worse than anyone. Worse than her last husband. Worse than Harald. If Siv had been there, Siv would have dealt with him, but Siv wasn't there, and she hadn't been for many years. The task fell to Tyra. At last, she would take revenge for the slaughter of her parents.

'We, too, would make a fine match,' said King Olaf, as she had hoped he would.

Tyra smiled, as if she agreed. She clutched the skirt of her dress with one hand as Olaf reached over the table to take her other hand and profess his intentions for them to marry. His fingers clasped over hers, warm as fire. Tyra's heart skipped a beat. His hand was as warm as her first husband's had been.

Fearing the worst, Tyra snapped out of her anger. Slowly, she lifted her chin and looked deep into King Olaf's eyes, and there, deep within, she saw fire. Whatever had been inside her husband, she saw it in Olaf too. Flames, of a sort. His hands were warm, but not sweaty as they ought to be. They were steady and hot like a burning fire. Like Styrbjorn's had used to be.

His fiery eyes told her everything she needed to know. King Olaf was even more dangerous than Tyra had feared.

A fire demon lived under his skin.

MUSPELDÓTTIR

Chapter One Hundred and Forty-Three

ONE, TWO, THREE, four, five, six, seven, eight, nine.

Muspeldóttir snickered contentedly. She stared out of the eyes of her host. Little Tyra sat in front of her. Small Tyra who had tried to kill her. Muspeldóttir knew to be wary. This time she wouldn't be defeated. This time Muspeldóttir would triumph. Finally, her brothers would be freed.

One, two, three, four, five, six, seven, eight, nine.

She had picked her third host with great care. Many, she had allowed to walk past, before King Olaf had come along. Weakened, waiting for the perfect host, she had hovered above Styrbjorn's corpse. When at last Olaf had come, she'd pounced, and dug herself deep into his eyes. So now, her flames burned strong and steady.

One, two, three, four, five, six, seven, eight, nine.

Although Styrbjorn had been a good host, none was more perfect than King Olaf. She steered him easily with flamed pain. He worshipped her in the name of God, and feared Muspeldóttir's hellish fire. More loyal a servant, never seen.

He rejoiced, executing her will. Burn them all, she said, and burn he did. Worshippers of Odin, set aflame.

One, two, three, four, five, six, seven, eight, nine.

More would burn to satisfy Muspel. With the flamed shrieks of dying fylgjur, Muspeldóttir would free her brothers. Out of Muspelheim, they would arrive, their flames raging through all of Midgard. At last, escaped, Midgard would be theirs. Together, they would burn and destroy. Together, they would scorch, melt, and laugh.

One, two, three, four, five, six, seven, eight, nine.

BUNTRUGG

Chapter One Hundred and Forty-Four

'WHAT DO THE nine worlds need of me?' Buntrugg asked Surt as they walked up the mountainside. His tears had long dried onto his puffy cheeks.

Your allegiance, answered Surt. Even in his thoughts, Surt's voice was like a chisel against a rock.

Buntrugg sighed and lifted his arm to rub his burned head, but his arm and hand did not listen. There was no hand or arm, he reminded himself, as he had many times already. Surt had tended to Buntrugg's wound with fire and runes and clean cloths, wrapping it so tight that the bandage had begun to hurt more than the wound.

It still felt like he was supposed to be able to move his fingers, his hand, his arm. Never before had Buntrugg appreciated the comforts of having all his limbs. His right shoulder had begun to itch, but his right hand could not reach and there was no other hand to scratch it with, so he was left wriggling his shoulders, hoping his tunic would hit the right spot. His left hand had given him balance as he walked over uneven ground;

it was a hand he could always catch himself with, if he felt he was about to fall. His left arm had had so many purposes that Buntrugg had never thought about, until now.

The pain had numbed his mind, along with the soup Surt had fed him. Buntrugg could not even hold a spoon anymore. His right hand was enclosed within the Muspel flame, so he couldn't use wooden spoons. Everything was so much more difficult than it had been, even eating, and walking.

'What do the nine worlds need my allegiance for?' he asked. There were so many other beings in the nine worlds, yet they had chosen *him*, of all beings, and they had killed his sister and they had killed his parents and they had taken his arm and they had burned his skin. They had taken everything. 'What for?'

His feet splashed through the melting snow that ran down the mountainside.

The nine worlds didn't choose you, Surt huffed. With every step, his body puffed with heat that lit up the night. Fire spluttered from the black creases on his arms and at his neck. He was burned so completely from his years in Muspelheim that his skin had become crisp, and his insides were all fire. His voice alone, spoken aloud, made lesser giants combust. It was why all of Jotunheim would follow him to war, when at last Ragnarok was to be fought.

'But they did,' Buntrugg protested. 'I am here, because the nine worlds chose me to be.' Even before he was born, he had been selected to grow up with Surt as a fosterer. To live in a home so cold that he might freeze to death at night, and with a giant so powerful and hot that the mere sight of him had left Buntrugg with burns more than once. That had been his destiny—the nine worlds *had* selected him for this life.

Your sister stole from me. A long time ago, Surt loudly thought. Smoke rose from his forehead. *Your parents chose to pay her debt to me with your life. You are here, alive, because your sister is a thief and your parents sold you like a thrall.*

Buntrugg shook his head. Already his eyes were tearing up

again, although he had been so certain that he had already spent all the tears he was allowed until Ragnarok. It was not fair to say such things, now that all of them were dead and no one could deny it. His life had been promised to Surt before he had been born, and his sister had stolen from the most dangerous giant in the nine worlds, but it was not like that. It was not fair to disgrace Buntrugg's memory of his parents and his sister.

'Nej,' he decided. 'Nej.'

Surt did not insist or try to convince, and that was worse, for it meant that the truth had been given. His parents and sister had doomed him and abandoned him, in life and in death alike.

'Is that why Glumbruck was put on trial? Because she stole from you?' Buntrugg asked. Now that they were all gone, only Surt could provide the answers to Buntrugg's many questions.

She was banished from Jotunheim long before she stole from me.

Buntrugg nodded, trying to piece it together. Tonight, especially, the questions were important. They distracted Buntrugg from the terrors he had lived through. They distracted him from the crunching pain he felt in the arm he had lost.

'How do you know that it was her?'

I wasn't sleeping, merely resting my eyes when she tiptoed into my house.

'You *let* her steal from you?'

I knew what she wanted, and it was better in her hands. I never asked for it to begin with.

Surt had never been a generous being. Buntrugg could not for a heartbeat imagine that he might have *allowed* someone to steal from him, or even enter his home unannounced.

The first night Buntrugg recalled sleeping in Surt's stone-cold home, he had heard a crash outside. An argument that had quickly ended. Outside the house, Surt had been standing over the corpse of a giant, killed with fire and not with steel. "What did he do?" Buntrugg had asked, and soft as a whisper Surt had placed the terrifying answer into Buntrugg's mind. *He was in my way.* Before that night, Buntrugg had thought Surt's house was the coldest place in all of Jotunheim, but after that night, he knew that the hard, icy ground outside was much colder. All night he had dug through it with his bare hands to bury the giant, as Surt had silently asked of him.

Yet, the same fiery giant who had forced Buntrugg to dig more jotun graves than he knew how to count, had known that Glumbruck was in his house, and he had allowed her to steal from him?

'What did Glumbruck steal?' Buntrugg finally asked.

A neck-ring that the Alfather plucked from the corpse of his brother to hand me. There was disdain in the thought. It was not a proud tale, as Buntrugg was certain the Alfather would have made it to be. It was a tale full of anger and regret. That was why Surt had allowed Glumbruck to steal from him: he had wanted to be rid of the neck-ring.

'Did you make her steal it too?' asked Buntrugg. The thought nagged him. It was too convenient that his sister would have known that Surt had something of value just when Surt wanted something stolen. No jotun was dumb enough to try to steal from Surt, and Buntrugg's sister had been anything but dumb.

I planted an idea in someone's mind, Surt confessed. He had put Glumbruck up to it. Surt himself had made Buntrugg's sister steal from him and had allowed her to succeed, and then, after all of that, he had demanded payment from Buntrugg's parents. He had demanded Buntrugg's life.

Buntrugg had only one question left. One question that no matter how he thought of it, he could not find the answer to. 'Why would you want *me* as payment?'

Surt did not answer, in thought or otherwise.

He placed a burning hand on a large rock. Fire from the core of him flowed over the rock and granted him passage. They had reached the cave. It was not a passage grave, not truly, but it served as one. A place to travel through the veil between worlds.

With old rage and strength, the rock rolled away to reveal the cave beyond. Buntrugg entered behind Surt, and the rock closed after them. The cave was not pitch-black, as once it had been, but bright with fire that escaped from the crevasses of the rock at the other end of the cave. The threshold between Jotunheim and Muspelheim.

'May your thoughts be filled with ice,' Buntrugg said, as he always had when Surt went off to fight fire demons. The cave was always where they parted ways when Surt had to work and keep peace in Muspelheim. The heat of the fire world was too strong for Buntrugg to survive.

Once it was, Surt conceded. His voice scratched inside Buntrugg's head like he was scraping his skull with a knife. *But now you carry a Muspel flame in your hand. It is comfortable in your palm. A flame of Muspel.*

Although Buntrugg had grown accustomed to the Muspel flame in his right hand, he was not comfortable with fire. Demons had burned all the skin off him and left him to die. They had scratched his ears and eyes. The crackle of fire still terrified Buntrugg, although he had needed fire to stay warm during winter. In the nights, he often woke in a sweat at the snap of flames consuming wood. All over his body he felt the pain of being burned alive.

Yet you survived, thought Surt, although surviving had not been Buntrugg's choice. *You tamed a flame.* He had done what he had needed to do to accomplish the tasks Surt had set him, but he had not done so willingly. The svartalvar had demanded fear in exchange for their help undoing the passage graves through the nine worlds, so Buntrugg had showed them Muspel's own flames.

Despite how it looked, Buntrugg had not survived due to courage. He had not conquered his fears and fire itself, as Surt had.

No one conquers Muspel's sons, Surt's thoughts sighed. His voice was worn like the nine worlds. Heat and smoke puffed from every fissure of his body. He had all but melted into fire from centuries spent fighting flames. *The only way to fight fire is to isolate it. Keep Muspel's children locked away. Give them a home and let them roam and burn all of Muspelheim, but nowhere else.*

They sounded like words of caution that had once been sung, or orders passed down from mouth to mouth, becoming simpler each time they were said aloud.

The old man was not entirely wrong. Only old sacred beings like Surt and the veulve who remembered a time before the nine worlds called the Alfather an "old man".

'Not wrong about what?' asked Buntrugg. His heart was beating loud in his chest from a mixture of pain and fear. Never before had Surt faltered before he went into Muspelheim. Never before had they exchanged so many words in this cave.

About you.

The Alfather had said much to Buntrugg when he had been in Valhalla, recovering from his burns. So many things Odin had said, and implied, about Glumbruck and Buntrugg himself. So much flattery and so many threats, all in an attempt to get Buntrugg to rebel against Surt, take over, and doom all giants. For at Ragnarok, it was Surt who would unite them all to fight in Asgard. Without Surt, Ragnarok would be a simple slaughter of jotnar led by murderous Thor.

Ragnarok is upon us. May your thoughts be filled with ice, Surt thought. The same words Buntrugg had always uttered when the fire giant was about to walk into the world of fire.

Surt put a hot flaming hand to the rock through which they had entered. In silence, he left the cave.

So, that was what Surt meant by the Alfather being right. Odin had said that Buntrugg could take over the task, and Surt and the nine worlds had agreed. Ragnarok had to be fought, and when Surt left, there was no one to protect the other eight worlds from Muspelheim's rage. That was why Surt had wanted Buntrugg as payment for that which was stolen from him. It was why he had sent Buntrugg off to burn and die in that forge. It was why the forefathers had refused to let Buntrugg join them. Why Buntrugg had closed passage graves throughout the nine worlds, both to isolate the terrors of Ragnarok and to hinder the fire demons. The nine worlds had needed a guardian who could survive Muspel's flames.

The thoughts became so clear in Buntrugg's mind. Everything made sense to him. His entire life. All the tragedy had led him to this very moment. To the beginning of Ragnarok, when he would have to take on Surt's eternal task and keep the other eight worlds from being consumed by fire.

The passage closed behind Surt. Alone, Buntrugg stood in the cave that flickered with that terrible light. His breathing was loud in his ears as he approached the far end of the cave. His body tingled with heat the closer he came.

He was shaking with fear as he pressed his hand with its Muspel flame to the far wall of the cave. Despite what the forefathers, the Alfather, Surt and the nine worlds thought him capable of, Buntrugg knew that he was not strong like Surt. He would not survive. Yet he held his ground as the rock rolled away to reveal the murderous flames of Muspelheim, raging beyond the bright veil of the passage. After all the pain and grief Buntrugg had suffered in life, death would be a relief.

With that thought burning in his mind, Buntrugg passed through the only active passage into the world of fire.

DARKNESS

'So, you want to kill them now and be done?' Somehow it felt like Loki was speaking to Ragnar as much as he was addressing the crowd of gods, and for a heartbeat, Ragnar forgot that Loki was not talking about the Alfather, but about his three monstrous children.

'Kill Loki's children and all will be well?' said Loki in a mocking voice.

Odin's white-haired, perfect son, Baldur, cut in. 'Nej, that's not—'

'That's *exactly* what's going on here,' Loki interrupted.

'It really—' Baldur attempted again.

'Do you hate me so much you have to kill my small monsters? *My* monsters,' Loki emphasised. 'You have no right. I've done everything for you. Greedy aesir, filthy vanir,' he spat at them. 'Who do you crawl to every time you get yourself into trouble? "Oh, Loki, Loki, it's all your fault, you have to do something." And who answers your every call? That's right: me!'

Every single aesir and vanir attempted to intervene, but Loki's voice outshouted them and he left no room to be interrupted at all.

'You call yourself fair and you call yourself gods,' he hissed. 'Well, let me tell you: to be gods you must earn the name, and there is *nothing* fair about this. What have you done to deserve your glory? Only my blood-brother has ever achieved anything, but even he's lost his way now.'

'You—' Thor yelled louder than any had before, but still Loki's voice drowned him out.

'Ja, what have you done, Thor? Other than go and kill giants for your own amusement? You never listen to anyone but yourself, and see how easy you anger, you—'

'Shut your ass!' Thor thundered so the floor shook, and Loki's solitary talk ended. In Thor's right hand he clenched great Mjölnir, menacingly. 'These'—Thor gestured towards the three monsters, struggling to come up with a suitable name for them—'these *creatures*. They'll kill us, if we don't do anything.'

'So, you don't want to kill them,' Loki said. The gods eagerly nodded, relieved that at last the giant believed them. 'You want to be good to them, so they'll see your goodness and not want to kill you.'

Thor cleared his throat and smoothed his long red hair back. 'Ja, exactly,' he said, and it was obvious to all that the original plan had been quite different.

'We called them here to see what they might be able to do, how they could be useful,' Odin said with confidence, a better liar than his son. 'They're your children, after all, and a useful creature is a grateful creature.'

Loki gestured for the three monsters to approach the gods. 'Well, show the kind aesir and vanir how useful you can be.'

The big wolf, Fenrir, glanced back at his father, who gave him an encouraging nod. 'I'm strong. Stronger than any other *creature*,' he snarled the last word with reproach.

'He's so strong I'm sure he could break both wood and metal,'

Loki eagerly supplied. 'My young wolf is too modest, just like his father.'

Fenrir's ears were erect, and his tail curled up with the praise. He showed off his teeth. A useful wolf is a grateful wolf, Ragnar thought.

'Can you truly break metal?' Ironically it was Tyr who asked. The war-happy god who still had his right hand, although some day, and Ragnar was certain that would be soon, he would lose it to the very wolf he was now addressing.

'Ja,' Fenrir snarled.

The gods nodded approvingly, and Ragnar imagined that this was also how they would nod when they successfully tied Fenrir with a chain that he could not break and told him that he was unworthy to serve them and Asgard.

'I'll send for the dwarves to make the strongest chain they can, and if you can break it, then we'll know you're worthy to help us,' said the Alfather in a pensive tone. Already, he was plotting how to tie Fenrir up so the wolf could not kill him at Ragnarok, although Ragnar knew that was how Odin's life would end. Unless he could find a way to end it sooner.

No one listened to his commands when he tried to plant the thought of killing the Alfather in their minds. Not Loki, not his three monsters, and not a single one of the gods, for Ragnar had tried them all. He would have to do it on his own.

Fenrir wagged his tail, glancing back to his father again for another approving smile, but Loki was already focused on the next of his children. 'Go on,' he whispered to the slimy creature who wriggled his way back into the room and settled next to his brother.

'So, *worm*, what can you do?' Thor asked, always eager to take control, just as Ragnar had imagined him to be.

'I can breathe both air and water and I grow bigger and longer every day,' the Midgard Worm hissed. The beast's voice made goosebumps rise across Ragnar's body.

Although Loki's second child was still young, and not so

long as the tales told, he would soon be able to surround all of Midgard and still bite his own tail.

'He grows so much that soon he'll be able to surround all of Midgard and still bite his own tail,' Loki said. So, the giant *did* listen to Ragnar's thoughts. Somehow, killing the Alfather was just a leap too far.

Ragnar stood back and watched, thinking about what to say and how to convince these three beasts, or Loki, or anyone to kill someone so powerful and so loved as the Alfather.

'We need someone to protect Midgard,' Odin mused, and leaned back in his seat to consider the matter. 'Who better to protect Midgard than a frightening creature long enough to surround it?'

Affirmative murmurs rang around the room as the aesir and vanir agreed that the worm could be useful, and at that it was decided. The slimy creature no one liked to look at would be thrown into the ocean and grow and grow until it surrounded all the lands in the sea and could bite its own tail.

With Fenrir and the Midgard Worm's fates decided, Hel walked forward. Tears rolled down her face, and for three whole breaths Ragnar forgot all her ugliness. All he saw was a small fragile girl, walking into the middle of a room filled with gods who would decide her fate.

'What can *you* do?' Odin asked expectantly, a smile on his lips, heady from his successes so far.

No answer was given. There was only silence, and the girl's quiet whimpering. She faced her brothers, not the gods, and Ragnar could clearly see the pink, swollen side of her face.

'She can cry,' Frey remarked, and they all howled with laughter; High Odin and blind Höd, even Loki laughed. All but Hel and her two brothers, and Ragnar, who knew better than to make himself heard.

'Nothing,' she wept. 'I'm not like my brothers, I can't do anything.' Her wail made Ragnar remember the pain in his chest, and the many deaths he had suffered in the Darkness, and every moment of terror he had ever known. 'Nothing.' She repeated the word again and again as she cried, and no one broke in. Even Loki could think of nothing Hel might be good for.

Ragnar's chest tightened, and when Hel shrieked, he collapsed on the stone floor, remembering all his sorrows. His last conversation with his wife. His son, Leif, paling as he lay dying.

Ragnar clasped his ears to keep the wail out and the sorrow away, but Hel's cry went right through and into his ears.

Stop it, he wanted to yell at her. But he did not, for her squealing also made him remember the many times he had been killed in the Darkness, and never did he want to suffer such pains again.

Finally, someone spoke, and Hel's wail faded.

'She sure knows how to get attention,' Odin said pensively. 'Hel,' he called, to make the girl look at him. 'I have an offer for you. We have a problem, you see, and I think you might solve it for us.'

The girl stopped crying, though she did not dry her tears or the yellow-green snot that ran from the red side of her nose.

'When the brave die in battle, I take them to Valhalla to feast with me,' Odin explained slowly. 'But there are many who die of illness or old age, or simply do not earn the glory of Valhalla. These dead folk have nowhere to go, so they end up in Niflheim, in the misty world of frost.'

The gods all smiled and nodded in agreement, understanding what Odin wanted the youngest monster to do. Loki's smile was broadest of all. It was almost a proud smile, like a father might wear when his children prove their worth. Almost.

'The corpses wander around out there, confused and without a home, until they get trapped in the ice. I've tried, but they don't listen to me. They listen to no one. But I believe they'll listen to you.'

Hel beamed and the tears rolled down her swollen pink cheek

again, but they were different from before; they were tears of relief. 'I'll make them listen,' she choked. 'And I'll build them homes so they'll never be alone.'

Thor broke in before she could say more, eager to get the three monsters out of the hall. 'It's decided, then,' he said and cleared his throat meaningfully.

No other words were needed to make the three monsters walk back out. First Hel, followed by her brother Fenrir, who took tiny steps to match his sister's pace, and finally the Midgard Worm wriggling around to follow them.

Ragnar stared up at his gods. The Alfather leaned back in his seat with a satisfied grin. The gold rim on his coat twinkled, as did the rings on his neck and arms. His smile was consoling, and looking up at the great Alfather, Ragnar understood that he would never be able to convince anyone to kill such a perfect being. He could hardly even convince himself.

Yet it had to be done. Somehow, Ragnar had to find the strength to kill the Alfather with his own bare hands. No one would do it for him.

Something slimy dripped on Ragnar's shoulder and stung like venom. Ragnar swung around. The Midgard Worm was behind him. Its sharp teeth glistened with venom. Ragnar yelped, and tried to get away, but even he knew that it was too late. The Midgard Worm opened its round mouth wide and clasped Ragnar's head.

The sharp teeth tore into his skin. His cheeks were torn open, his eyelids ripped off. The venom burned his face as the Midgard Worm swallowed him whole.

Death, pain, and fear.

EINER

Chapter One Hundred and Forty-Five

THE FREEZING WATERS slapped against Einer's cheeks and thrilled the back of his neck. The bracteate thumped hard against his chest, keeping him steady.

Water crept up Einer's nose, and he flailed his arms. He knew which way Helheim was, but with the waves casting him aside, it was difficult to tell if he was swimming the right way—or if he was swimming at all.

He struggled to reach the surface and breathe. A cough was building up.

Einer kicked his legs, and at last, his head broke the surface. He coughed for air and kicked all he could to stay afloat. A wave splashed over him mid-cough and sent him spiralling back into the depths of the sea.

Refusing to give up, Einer kicked and kicked until his head rose out of the waters again, atop a great wave. He filled his lungs and struggled to see Helheim's coast.

Using all the strength left in him, Einer swam on. The icy waters bubbled with the bracteate's heat around him and kept him warm. He used every last burst of strength to kick ahead.

He had no other thoughts in mind but the next stroke, and the next, and the hope of reaching Helheim before he drowned. He was getting seasick and his arms were failing.

So, this was how corpses ended up sealed into the ice on Niflheim's coast, thought Einer. Captured during their hopeful escape, knocked back by the waves of the Midgard Worm's tail. Had it not been for the bracteate that burned itself into his chest, Einer was well aware that he would already have frozen to death.

He swam so long that he could hardly keep his eyes open and his head above water. His swords, his tunic and clothes dragged him down. His arms had fallen still, and he barely even kicked with his feet anymore. Still, the coast was far away.

A wave crashed over Einer, dragging him into the depths of the current, although he tried to resist and swim back up. The waters were clear, due to the icy weather. Einer thought he saw something move ahead of him, further into the sea: a tree-trunk, swishing past underwater. Or the terrifying slither of a tail.

The Midgard Worm.

In all the seas of the nine worlds, there was no beast more dangerous.

Now, Einer found the energy to struggle again. He beat his arms to drive himself to the surface. Something swished underneath him, and Einer stared down: there, below him, the long body of the Midgard Worm swept past.

An eel-like body thick as a tree-trunk, and so long Einer could see neither its face nor its tail, but he was in no doubt as to what it was. Spears stuck out from its slimy green skin. Many had tried to kill the great beast, but none had succeeded.

Einer fixed his eyes on the glittering surface and swam away. Just as he thought he had managed to escape, an undercurrent caught his left leg and pulled him back into the depths—down towards the worm. The gold bracteate burned through his skin.

Bubbles rose around Einer as he was dragged down and down into the cold sea. His lungs emptied faster from the shock.

Something scratched against his leg and caught in his weapon belt. Einer was dragged through the waters. A spear-end had grabbed Einer and pulled him along with the deadly serpent who would someday, soon, kill the great god Thor.

He was being dragged along too fast to pull his swords from their scabbards and ease his weight. Besides, he would need his weapons, for Ragnarok was coming. Without his weapons, Einer couldn't fight in the final battle with the giants as he had promised Loki he would. Against his gods.

'Godsss,' hissed a voice. There was no one but himself and the Midgard Worm. 'Godssss will die.'

Fear caught in Einer's throat. The Midgard Worm could hear his thoughts. It knew he was there. It would find him and bite him so he died from its venom as Thor would.

Einer's lungs were screaming for air. It felt like his insides were being pressed together. And then, at last, the Midgard Worm cast him aside. Einer floated away, struggling to reach the surface. He thought he might faint, but closed his eyes and struggled through it. His head thrust into the icy air.

Einer coughed up water and gulped down fresh air. The waves were tall all around him, and he struggled to stay at the surface. A wave lifted him to the top.

Helheim was no longer as far away as it had been. He could see a bare coast lined with ice, but not covered in it. It was close enough that he thought he might even reach it, although he was long out of strength. To Einer's left, a huge tail splashed out of the water. The tip had been sliced off and blood and salt water sprayed all around. The tail slammed onto the ocean bed; waves rose up, large as mountains. Einer turned to Helheim's coast and swam all he could to get ahead and not be crushed under the weight of the great waves.

The gold bracteate drove heat into his very core. His vision pulsed. He was lifted to the top of a wave and pushed along with it. The wave began to foam and break under him. Einer took a deep breath. The wave swallowed him. He was flipped upside down and carried along.

The wave let him go, not gently as he had hoped, but smacking him hard onto the sand.

Einer clambered to his feet and ran up the beach before the next wave could crash over him. He had thought he would drown. He had thought the Midgard Worm would swallow him whole. His heart pounded fast, and his stomach was in uproar as his feet slipped over the wet sand.

He ran until he heard the next wave crash at his back, and at last, let himself fall knees-first into the wet sand. The remains of his breakfast rushed into his mouth. Einer coughed them up and rolled into the sand, away from the vomit.

Emptily, he stared out towards the raging sea, and wondered if Loki's journey across the waters would be as perilous. Einer had truly thought that the ocean would be the death of him, but terrifying as it had been, the Midgard Worm had not killed him. Instead, it had helped him on his way.

The Midgard Worm was Loki's child. Perhaps that was why. Einer could not have swum the distance on his own, and as he stared out to sea, he worried that perhaps sending Sigismund off had been a mistake. The bracteate alone would not have been enough. Perhaps his friend had drowned out there.

Even the bracteate burning on his chest could hardly keep him warm any longer. His extremities were freezing. He did not know where Loki was. The waves were too tall and wild to spot anyone out there. Perhaps Loki would not swim but fly across the ocean in his famous falcon skin.

The giant had said he would find Einer in Helheim, and Einer was much too cold and exhausted to wait on this beach. He pushed himself up from the ground. The sand around him was wet, even though the waves did not reach so far up the beach. Einer's palms stung where he had touched the sand. He was quick to wipe them on his wet trousers. He tried to drain some of the water from the edge of his tunic and his trousers. His tunic hung sloppily off his shoulders; had it not been for the belt, his trousers would already have fallen down.

There was movement on the beach. Einer jerked his head around. His heart beat fast as he looked for what it was.

A body lay in the sand a few arm-lengths to his right, and another a little further ahead. The corpses were not lifeless; they were attempting to crawl out to the deadly sea. Whatever lay inland was worse than the dangers of the icy ocean and the Midgard Worm.

Einer clenched a hand around the Ulfberht's pommel as he turned inland.

Beyond the beach was a clearing at the edge of a dark spruce forest. There, in the clearing, was a longhouse that seemed to wriggle and crawl as he looked at it. The walls were not solid, but swayed, as though the house was built of living wood that was trying to get away, like the corpses.

The house stood on its own, and the clearing that surrounded it was too perfect to be natural. It had been man-made, somehow. Hand on the sword, Einer approached the house. The trees had not been cut down to form the clearing; they had fallen. Pine and spruce had simply risen from the earth and fallen. The trees were sick and dead. Even the earth looked as though it was ready to give up and part.

At throwing distance, Einer stopped and stared at the longhouse, and as he did, it all made sense, for the longhouse was not made from living wood as he had initially thought, but from woven snakes. They were long and slippery, curving around each other to form the walls and ceiling of the longhouse. Their venom dripped from their fangs, streaking over their kin to the ground. That had to be what had killed the trees and sickened the earth.

Einer had not been cast onto just any shore in Helheim. He had arrived on Corpse-shore. He remembered Ragnar's tales of the criminals who ended up being outlawed to Corpse-shore to have their nails ripped out before they were sent to Niflheim to roam in all eternity. Although Einer had been to Niflheim, and he knew that no corpses roamed free there. They were all locked in a thick layer of ice.

Warily, Einer cornered the snake house, keeping an eye fixed on it, and disappeared into the spruce forest away from the beach. Never had he thought he might find himself in Helheim someday. It had always been Valhalla for Einer, where the Alfather had saved him a seat at his high table. The seat was still there to claim, if Einer wanted it, and that thought was both comforting and terrible.

The air in the spruce forest was cool, and in his dripping wet tunic the wind cut through Einer, but the bracteate beat at his chest with faint heat. For a long time he walked, talking shelter from the wind among pine and spruce trees, before he saw another house. This one did not move, and was not built from snakes, but from greyed wood left uncoloured.

Warily, Einer approached the front door and knocked. 'Hei!' he yelled. 'Is anyone home?'

No one answered his call, and the door was locked.

Einer rested his back against the side of the house. His stomach grumbled with hunger, and despite the bracteate, he had begun to shake from the cold.

Once more, he set off, further into the last of the nine worlds.

So, this was Helheim.

Houses were scarce, and each one he encountered lay abandoned. The space between them was filled both with fields and dark forests. It was much like Midgard. This was close to how he had imagined Hel's realm, though it was not as grim as he had expected it to be, and Einer was almost certain those squeals echoing in the distance were the laughter of children.

At last, Einer exited another pine forest, and this time, he did not arrive to silence and abandoned houses, but to a town that was both living and alive.

Children chased each other around tables. There was a feast

going on. Perhaps that was why no one had been home in all the lonely houses he had passed on the way. A group of corpses were singing and stomping around a fire. Adults and children alike.

Feast tables filled the town, although the meal was mostly over, and most of the people who were still seated only nibbled at the food.

Einer saw his chance and grabbed it. He approached with smiles and plopped himself down by a table a little way from a larger group. They were not like people in Midgard; their skin had paled, and he could see the veins almost pop out on some of their faces.

Eagerly he reached across the table for a bread bun. His stomach growled from his swim. He needed to fill it with food, and he needed to get warm. He swallowed the first bun quickly, grabbed another and approached the fire, but at a safe distance from getting pulled into song and dance.

He began to feel his fingers, legs, and even his toes again, as he stood and munched on the bread and nodded along to the song.

'Tall new stranger,' a woman said, approaching from behind. 'Who are you?' She batted her long eyelids at him. Her skin was almost blue, as if she had been left outside in the cold for a little too long before her body had been burned and her spirit sent into the next world.

'Einer Glumbruckson,' he said with a smile.

'Glumbruck?' she inquired. 'That's a strange name.'

Einer gave her a brief smile, but no answer, and focused back on the fire and dance, and his bread.

The woman stepped closer. Her blonde hair reached her lower back, and she was pretty. In a different life—or rather, a different afterlife—he might have entertained the thought of spending the night with her, perhaps even more than one night.

She mimicked him, tilted her head to the side and watched the fire burn. Einer's clothes had almost dried from the heat, even his wool tunic. He no longer smelled of burning flesh either. The bracteate did not burn as it had when he had arrived on Corpse-shore.

'I'm looking for someone,' Einer eventually said. He was about to say Sigismund, but then his thoughts drifted to someone else in Helheim, someone he had not seen in a long time, and another name slipped from his lips. 'Leif Ragnarson of Ash-hill.'

'Was he grand in life?' she asked, and her wording felt off and ancient. She must have died a long time ago, although the style of her dress was modern.

'Nej,' Einer admitted. Leif had not been preceded by a grand reputation in the afterlife. He had died so young. That was why he had ended up in Helheim and not Valhalla, which is where they had both been certain they would meet in the afterlife.

'Someone you knew in life, then? A son?'

'A friend,' answered Einer.

'Leif Ragnarson,' the woman mused. 'Of Ash-hill? Where and when is that?' She smiled up at Einer, eager to make a good impression.

'Jutland,' answered Einer. 'When?'

'When did he die?'

'A good ten winters ago,' said Einer. It had to be longer, now, but time did not feel the same in Jotunheim where he had spent the last three winters, and he was not sure it passed the same way either.

'What are you doing all the way out here, then? You're looking for the young settlers. New arrival?'

'I arrived today,' Einer admitted, but at once he knew that he had said something wrong, for the woman's smile faltered momentarily. A heartbeat later her smile was back, but it was no longer eager to flirt and impress.

Her eyes dropped to look at Einer's fingers. His fingernails were long, like no fingernails of any corpse were supposed to be. He had not cut them for half a moon. Corpses had their nails trimmed short before they were burned so the nails could not be ripped from their fingers in the afterlife.

The woman's stare was fixed on Einer's long fingernails. She thought he was a criminal and outlaw, Einer realised, for he had come from the direction of Corpse-shore, but he still had his fingernails, and they were too long. Any corpse who came into the afterlife with fingernails such as these could not have been respected and loved by anyone in life.

'I'm not a criminal,' Einer said, although he had been convicted of a crime in Jotuheim's court and sentenced to death for releasing the blizzard which still ravaged through the nine worlds.

The woman must have sensed the hesitation in his voice. 'Who are you, really?' She backed away, slowly, her eyes fixed on Einer's hands.

'I still have my nails,' he told her, and took a step forward. 'See?'

The woman jumped away from him. Her hand flickered to her belt and at once she held a knife. 'Stay back,' she warned.

Einer could easily have overpowered her and taken the knife, but instead he showed the empty palms of his hands.

The singing stopped and the dancers stared. Even the corpses gathered around the feast table were staring, as if it were a competition.

'Does anyone know this man?' the woman yelled. 'Has anyone seen where he came from?'

'He came from the forest by Corpse-shore,' announced a helpful corpse from one of the feast tables.

'Just as I thought,' the woman said.

'I'm not a criminal,' Einer insisted. They all watched him as if he were.

Knives and axes were pulled out, and Einer slowly backed away, hands in the air.

A few of the men who had clearly been fighters in life lined up, as if they carried shields, and advanced towards Einer.

He continued to back away. His right hand reached for the Ulfberht blade, but then he stopped himself.

With the Ulfberht he could kill them all, without even seeking the strength of the forefathers. Yet this was not Midgard; killing a corpse in Helheim was different from killing in Midgard or slaughtering murderous giants. Folk in Midgard died and passed on into their afterlife, and giants became forefathers, but when a corpse in Helheim died, it stayed dead. A murder in Helheim was the worst of crimes.

Einer unclasped his hand from the hilt of his father's Ulfberht and backed away from the advancing men. One, two, three steps, and then he turned and broke into a full run.

Roaring, the men followed him.

Einer darted through a town he did not know. He heard footsteps behind him, catching up. One of his pursuers was faster than the others.

His mind made up, Einer ran back towards the man chasing him. Before the pursuer could lift his knife or fully stop, Einer punched him in the face, so hard that the man fell into the mud at their feet. Einer waved the pain out of his knuckles as he started running again, sprinting for the edge of the next forest that he could see at the end of the street.

Villagers were shouting after him. They wouldn't let him disappear. Even when he reached the forest, Einer did not slow down.

Not only had he talked himself into trouble, he had been tired and foolish enough to give his real name and lineage, and that of Leif too. They knew where he would go now, and they did not look likely to let him leave. They would chase him, even after they stopped running. They would chase him all the way through Helheim. Einer *had* to find Leif, before these corpses did.

HILDA

Chapter One Hundred and Forty-Six

THE ALFATHER LEANED in over the table towards Hilda. Although they sat across from each other at one of his high tables, the Alfather had made it clear that Hilda hadn't yet earned her place among the best of his warriors. For now, he merely tolerated her presence.

'How will you ensure my victory at Ragnarok?' asked Odin in a raspy voice.

At last, the Alfather wanted to resume the conversation that had begun out on Ida's blooded plain when the valkyries had woken Hilda. In Asgard even simple conversations seemed to be carried out over the span of days. All night, they had feasted at his high tables where he had granted her a temporary seat. Yet in all that time, the Alfather had not spoken a word to Hilda. Until now.

'I will ensure your victory in any way you want,' Hilda replied.

The Alfather leaned away, ready to drop the conversation, and leave, or chase her from his hall. She could see it in his eyes, even though he guarded his thoughts well. He wanted her to see how close he was to abandoning her. He had waited a while to have the conversation. He expected a clean answer.

'On Ragnarok's battlefield, I am an unmarked piece of tafl,' she explained. 'I have no destiny.'

All winter, in the nornir's Hall of Fates, she had used to think it the most unfortunate thing. At last, seated in front of the Alfather, she understood that having no destiny was the biggest advantage in the nine worlds. 'No one knows I'll be there,' she told him. 'No one can predict it.'

The Alfather did not so much as narrow his eye or lean in further as she spoke. He showed no response to what she told him.

'I have seen the nornir spin their fates,' Hilda continued. 'They have been tying Ragnarok knots for three long winters. They bind their fates, thinking that they know everything to come, but they can't see my present. They don't know my past. They can't predict my future.'

Still the Alfather did not respond, and Hilda felt a pain in her chest and in her throat. It was a terrible feeling to be ignored by the Alfather, when he was sitting right there.

She was desperate to please. 'I can even kill Fenrir for you,' she volunteered.

The high table went quiet. Hilda had spoken in a much louder voice than she had meant to. The warriors stared down the lengths of their tables at Hilda and the Alfather.

Odin rose to his full height. The light from the fires at his back obscured his face, so only his glossy eye shone. He looked like a grand shadow about to swallow Asgard whole.

'I shall say this only once,' the Alfather announced. He had not raised his voice, like Hilda, but he was clearly addressing *all* of those seated in his hall. After he left, his words would be passed down the hall in whispers. 'I eagerly await the day when the giants walk across Bifrost. For on that day, *I* shall finally kill that... beast, who has so dishonoured my reputation.'

His warriors clamoured their approval.

'You think a simple shieldmaiden like you can kill Fenrir?' The Alfather's tone was rewarded with laughter.

At once, Hilda remembered why she had followed Loki into the nornir's hall, three winters past. In all the Alfather's glory, she had forgotten how easily he had dismissed her back then.

'If you *do* kill Fenrir before the last battle begins,' the Alfather continued, 'then truly, you will have earned your place among us.' He placed his hands on the table, and leaned in close, so Hilda could see his face. 'And my respect,' he added. He was smiling. Secretly, the Alfather was smiling at her.

He was showing off to the crowd. Made sure everyone knew that he was not weak, and that he was not afraid. But he approved of the proposal. If anyone could kill Fenrir before he devoured the Alfather, he knew that it was her. He had given her a mission, and if Hilda succeeded, no one in all of Valhalla would be honoured more. She would be the Alfather's favourite for the rest of their eternity together.

At his side, she would fight at Ragnarok, as in life she had always known she would. With Fenrir dead before the final battle, they would both survive.

There was laughter all over the hall. The mere suggestion that someone could kill the great wolf that would someday devour the Alfather was absurd.

The Alfather pushed up from the bench. Once more, his face was obscured by shadows, and then he turned away. His blue coat flicked elegantly as he turned, and with long strides the Alfather left Hilda and his warriors alone in Valhalla.

The laughter spread like echoes down the hall as the tale of what had been said was passed from mouth to mouth and table to table.

Through the mockery, Hilda smiled. They would all regret laughing at her. When she returned to Valhalla, swinging the severed head of the great wolf they all so feared, they would beg for mercy and forgiveness. And Hilda didn't forgive.

THORA

Chapter One Hundred and Forty-Seven

THORA'S SON CARRIED her through the busy marketplace. She clung onto him and stared around. There were all sorts of people here, even affluent. Thora spotted a wealthy woman in a dark red dress and matching coat walk into the market from out by the stables. Bulky guards flanked her on each side, crosses clearly visible on their neck-rings. Wealthy Christians like her were the reason things continued to get worse. They were the reason Thora couldn't walk around with a proud Thor's hammer around her neck. Anyone who dared to do that would undoubtedly be burned at the pyre.

'Are you getting cold?' asked Thora's son. She had begun to shake from the cold, although she hardly noticed. 'You want to go back down to the ship?' She hugged him all the tighter, for although her son spoke the local tongue, he had always pronounced the word *ship* like she did, like a true Jute.

'That might be good,' she agreed. They had already been to the smith and Thora was not as interested in what else the market had to offer. 'For you too. You must be tired from carrying your old mother around.'

'I'm fine, Ma,' he assured her, as he always did, and always had. 'It's good training for this summer.' He shifted her higher up on his back and flexed his muscles as if to demonstrate.

His daughter giggled at his joke and tried to hang onto his lower arm as he squeezed it.

'That's what *I'm* supposed to tell *you*,' Thora said and clapped Halfdan on the arm so he would stop pressing against her legs.

Her legs had not been the same since Magadoborg. All the spears and arrows they had taken and the fall from top of the barricade. She had been told stories of it, but she had been too far gone in her berserker rage to remember much, other than blood and yelling. All Thora truly remembered was waking up in pain, and the months of pregnancy that had followed. How she had unsuccessfully tried to get on her feet again, and how she had stopped trying.

'Shall we take you down to the ship?' Halfdan asked again as he uncurled little Ida's claws from around his arm and set her on the ground.

'Ja.' They still had things to buy, but the pain had returned in Thora's back where a southern arrowhead no one had been able to remove remained lodged. The pain of it had begun to spread from being carried so long, and the cold was creeping in, too. Besides, she wanted Halfdan and Ida to have some time alone as father and daughter.

Leaving the market, they headed to the harbour, laughing about the people and things they had seen.

They passed the Christian cross on the harbour where the tall carved figures of the gods had stood before Olaf had declared himself king. Now there were only crosses—everywhere. Everything Thora had fought to prevent. She spat at the cross as they passed.

'Someday you'll get in trouble for that,' her son warned her.

'Who's going to kick an old cripple like me?' she retorted. 'Give me a spear, point me their way, and I'll colour their crosses red.' She glanced down at Ida, who had sharpened her ears to hear what her father and grandmother were talking about. Thora stopped herself from voicing what else she would do to anyone who complained, not that Ida hadn't heard worse.

'I don't think you have enough wrinkles to be considered old,' her son said.

'Ah, watch out, Halfdan, I don't think Ida agrees with that,' Thora replied. 'Do you, Ida?'

'What is *conseared*?' asked little Ida, exactly as she had been taught to do.

'*Considered*,' her father corrected. 'To think carefully about something. So, consider this: does your grandmother look old?'

Ida looked up at Thora and thought carefully about that. 'Ja,' she decided and all three of them laughed, Ida most of all. She was the prettiest girl in all the nine worlds when she laughed, and even when she didn't. She understood so much for her age. 'But not like the other grandmothers,' Ida kindly added as they walked down the pier towards their ship.

None of the crew had arrived yet. Thorgald was usually early, but they had agreed to meet at midday and it was still morning. At least Thora would be on the ship as she waited for the crew to gather. She loved just sitting there and watching her ship, and the sea, too.

'Wait here,' Halfdan told Ida in front of the ship. He let go of Thora's right leg, which fell to his side, and Thora clung firmer onto him as he carefully stepped from the pier onto the ship with her on his back. He carried her all the way to the back of the ship, lifting his legs high so as not to trip on any of the rowing benches. Thora kissed him on the cheek in thanks as he set her onto the helmsman bench.

'Do you need to pee before we go?' he asked in a lowered voice, crouching in front of her, as he packed her legs into a wool blanket. He knew that she hated it when he asked, but still he did.

Thora shook her head.

'Are you sure? I won't be back for a while.'

Thora waved him off and busied herself scooting further back on the helmsman bench, dragging her legs and feet into place and strapping herself in, so she could sit upright.

Finally, Halfdan nodded and walked down the ship and onto the pier again where little Ida waited.

Thora watched them leave. Halfdan was as kind as his father had been. He tickled his daughter and lifted her up to sit on his shoulders mid-giggle. The sight made Thora smile fondly. Sigismund too would have made a good father, if he had lived long enough to see his son be born.

Sometimes she liked to imagine what could have been if Ran and Aegir had not claimed him after that bloodied winter in Magadoborg. Sometimes, when she was out sailing, she wished for them to claim her too. Most of the time she was just happy that the gods had at least spared Halfdan. It had been good that Sigismund had agreed to let them sail on separate ships back then. Thanks to that decision, Halfdan had been able to grow up in Midgard and live a life.

The wealthy woman from the marketplace walked past Halfdan and Ida, in her red wool dress with silk strips. The large guards were no longer at her flank.

The rich woman eyed the large cross as she passed. Thora prepared herself for what was to come. Her son was right; finally, Thora would pay for the many times she had spat at that Christian cross by the harbour side.

The woman walked down the pier, and with her long, elegant legs, stepped right onto Thora's ship.

'I did not invite you aboard,' Thora said in a strict voice that left no room for compromise, but the woman did not listen, and Thora was in no position to grab her silk clothes and carry the woman off the ship by force.

'Do you know who I am?' asked the woman as she came closer, balancing on top of the rowing benches.

'Nej,' answered Thora, but there was something strangely

familiar about the woman. While most Christian women liked to keep their hair shorter, rarely ever braided, this woman's long brown hair was braided in an old style that few still knew. Back in Ash-hill, Vigmer's wife Siv had used to wear her hair that way. It had highlighted her elegance, as it highlighted this woman's beauty.

The woman stared at Thora's legs, unsurprised and unflinching, as few people were at Thora's old injuries. 'You are Thora of Ash-hill, aren't you?'

'Not anymore,' said Thora instead of asking the woman how *she* knew. 'But this is still my ship, and you're not welcome.'

The pain in Thora's lower back was getting worse and she just wanted to be left alone until her son and their crew came back from the market.

'It might be your ship, but the harbour is mine,' said the woman with a smile. She was not just any rich Christian then, she was the king's wife.

Thora gulped down the worry at what would happen to her for treating the wife of King Olaf as she had and frowned again. 'Then you can stand on the pier for as long as you want. This is *my* ship.'

'You won't even allow an old friend to come aboard?' asked the woman.

'I don't have any old friends here,' said Thora, but then she took another look at the woman, and there was so much that was familiar about her. Maybe they had raided together, in a past long gone, although the woman seemed much too young for that. Brown hair and eyes like hers were rare to see so far north, though, and her hair was not just in a similar style to the one Siv had always worn back in Ash-hill, it was the exact same. The strong shape of her jaw, too, felt familiar. Few women had jaws like that, like Gunna, whom Thora had sailed with on her first few raids.

'You're Gunna's daughter, aren't you?'

'Tyra,' said the woman and nodded.

Thora opened her arms wide, and Tyra willingly leaned into the hug. 'Little Tyra,' Thora muttered as she stroked Tyra's hair. Once, so long ago, she had raided with Tyra's elder sisters, and she had thought that someday she might raid with Tyra too, and show her the ways, but then the southerners had attacked and their lives had never been the same. 'We thought you died in Ash-hill.'

'And I thought you died in Magadoborg,' Tyra said, pulling back from their hug.

Thora smiled. *She* had thought herself dead, considering all the wounds she had taken before she had collapsed. The berserker mushrooms had done their deed. She had charged without any thought of consequence, roaring for blood. In the oddest of moments, she still remembered what it was like to be invincible.

'How did you know it was me?' Thora asked. She never would have recognised Tyra, if she had not come to her as she had. It had been so long ago, and Tyra had been so young.

'We crossed paths two nights ago. I heard that little girl say your name. I was hoping you would still be here, and I heard you speak. Your accent is the same.'

'Our last day in town,' Thora said. 'We sail out at midday.'

'Perfect,' said Tyra and twisted away. Clearly, she had not come to reminiscence about old days. Something was amiss, and not just the fact that she was wearing silk-decorated clothes, owned the pier, and had guards following her.

'How are you here...?' Thora asked warily. Perhaps this was some new scheme designed by King Olaf to catch more of the Alfather's loyal followers to burn on his pyres. Yet the woman in front of Thora was most definitely Tyra Gunnasdóttir. There was no doubt. She looked so much like her parents and her sisters.

'It's a long story, but I'm here, married, because Siv trusted me to make a change for the better.'

'Siv is alive?' asked Thora. Neither of their bodies had been found in the remains of Ash-hill, but many others also hadn't been found, and many pieces of corpses had no known owner. Both of them had been presumed dead.

'Siv isn't around anymore.' Tyra took a deep sigh and looked at the pier. 'I can't be gone too long,' she said as if to steer them towards a different sort of talk. 'Or the guards will suspect I didn't go to the wool trader as I told them I would. They can't find us together.'

'Then tell me why you've come,' Thora said. No more formalities were needed. They were both from Ash-hill, they were as good as kin, and Thora had never let a kinsman down.

'My husband is getting suspicious. He knows I work for the Alfather. He is trying to force me into a confession so he can burn me like the rest of our kinsmen, and I can't let him.'

It felt like a trap, but at the same time, Thora knew that she could not afford to think of it as such. No matter what clothes Tyra wore and no matter who she was married to now and what faith she truly kept in her heart, she was as good as a kinsman.

'I can't keep anything un-Christian with me anymore.' She reached for a dagger in her belt.

Thora was ready to defend herself, but the dagger was already dripping with blood. Tyra's silk skirts were darkened from it. 'You're bleeding.'

'The nine worlds are bleeding,' answered Tyra, and then she smiled. 'Finally, I have found a fresh cloth to bind the wound.'

'I hope you don't mean me, because I'm hardly fresh,' Thora said to make them both laugh. 'Although I do know my binding knots.' All she gained from Tyra was a brief smile.

Tyra held the dagger out in both hands as if it were an offering before the gods. 'I need to get this to Svend Haraldson,' she said. 'Tell him it's from his sister, and he will know what to do.'

'His sister?' asked Thora as she took the blade into her own hands. The blood wasn't from a wound the dagger had inflicted—it seemed to come from *inside* the metal. Blood oozed from it and dripped along the length of the short blade.

'After the battle, Siv married Harald of Jelling,' Tyra explained. 'They adopted me.'

Thora gaped up at Tyra. That explained the elegant dresses, and her braided hair and just about everything else. So, this was Tyra Haraldsdóttir she heard such gossip about. Little Tyra from Ash-hill. How far she had come.

'You must come visit us sometime,' said Thora, trusting that their shared past would have prompted Tyra not to lie. 'For Winter Nights.' No Christian celebrated Winter Nights anymore.

'I heard you once sacrificed southerners in Magadoborg for Winter Nights,' Tyra said. It truly was her. 'It would be an honour to feast with you again, someday.'

They both smiled at the knowledge, and the promise, and their secret exchange. Tyra rose from the bench and with a final smile to Thora returned to the pier. Thora watched her walk away, but not once did Tyra glance back.

She was no longer the girl Thora remembered from Ash-hill. Tyra had become a woman, and although she carried no weapons anymore, not even a dagger, she was clearly a warrior.

SIGISMUND

Chapter One Hundred and Forty-Eight

THE TREK UP the mountain towards Hel's home was as miserable as it was every time. The rain poured over Sigismund, and he had mud up to his knees. His walking stick was completely muddied, too. It always rained on Hel's mountain. That was why the dead called her house Rain-soaked, for no one arrived at the top until even their socks and breeches were soaked through by the rough weather.

When Sigismund had first been appointed chief in his village in Helheim, he had thought it a great honour. He had only lived there for a few moons before they had entrusted him with their afterlives. Only after the first Ting, when he had to deliver the outcome to Hel, did he realise why he had truly been chosen.

No one wanted to trek up through the eternal rain to Hel's home, and more to the point, everyone was terrified of Hel. Once, Sigismund had been called to her mountain with half a hundred other chiefs, and only Sigismund had dared speak in her presence.

Since, he had been Helheim's designated spokesman. Corpses knew that if they had a serious concern to raise with their realm's ruler, they needed Sigismund to argue on their behalf. So, Sigismund made a good living off his bravery. Although he had begun the afterlife in Helheim as a smith, he no longer smithed for riches, only for his own enjoyment. He had plenty of riches to provide for his wife of two years and her entire household, and still he was able to buy a round of mead at the tavern for his friends and the future warriors he trained.

At last, Hel's terrifying home came into sight. The wooden walls of her grand hall were darkened so that the whole house looked like a shadow. Sigismund barely halted to look before he continued his journey. His inner layer of clothes was still dry, and he smiled at his small victory: he had never come so close to Hel's home and still been dry. His idea to tar his outer layers of clothes had been the key, and right as he thought that, he felt water trickle in at the shoulders and down over his chest, and gone was his smile. Another failure.

At least the gold bracteate around his neck ensured that Sigismund did not feel cold. Not once had he fallen sick from a visit to Rain-soaked. The same could not be said about any of the other chiefs.

A large foot plopped down next to Sigismund, and mud splashed all the way up his outer tunic. Sigismund gaped up at the giant who came to a halt next to him. More baffling than the fact that a giant was there, next to him in Helheim, was the fact that the giant was dry. Even his socks looked like they had never trodden through the mud puddles.

'Have you tried wax?' the giant asked as he stopped next to Sigismund. He wore a red tunic and fully embroidered blue wool trousers, and none of it was wet. Not even his black and red hair looked like it was wet. He had pushed it away from his face with grease.

'Your outer layer is too heavy,' said the giant as he leaned in to examine Sigismund's clothes. 'It's coming apart at the seams.' His size decreased as he leaned closer, slowly and subtly, so that when Sigismund blinked, he almost thought he had dreamt it all.

'May I?' the giant asked and pulled forth a slim dagger. His eyes were fixed on the seams at Sigismund's shoulders.

'Sure,' Sigismund agreed. He was already soaked, so he didn't think it could get much worse.

The giant brought his dagger up to Sigismund's shoulder and carefully sliced open the seams, and then placed a warm hand on top. Heat spread across Sigismund's right shoulder. The giant mended the fabric with runes.

'You're one of her chiefs,' said the giant as he examined his work.

'Sigismund Karson.'

The giant did not give his name in return, he simply walked around Sigismund to examine the seams on his left shoulder. Their heights were the same now, and it was all too strange for Sigismund to wrap his head around.

Deftly, the giant begun to undo the seams at Sigismund's left shoulder with his dagger, as he had done with the right side. Sigismund felt a sting at his neck. He grunted.

'Forgive,' the giant said, and he seemed to mean it. The dagger was bloody at the tip. The giant pulled Sigismund's tunic out a little to examine the cut. Rainwater trickled down Sigismund's back.

'Is it bad?' asked Sigismund. It stung, but not a lot.

'Nej,' the giant said. 'You won't need to bind it.' He placed his warm hand on Sigismund's shoulder and used runes to close the fabric. 'I really did not mean to...'

'It's fine. Takka for mending my tunic.' Already, the rain had stopped dripping down over his torso, and Sigismund began to feel warmer for it.

'Glad I could help,' said the giant, and took a step away from Sigismund now that his task was done. 'Sigismund, Sigismund, what a pleasing name,' the giant muttered. 'What a pleasing name.' He stroked the length of his dagger, rubbing the blood off it. At the tip was a darkening of the blade.

Sigismund's eyes opened wide at the sight of it. The giant's dagger had collected his blood. Exactly like an Ulfberht axe he had seen once that he could hardly recall, and Einer's Ulfberht sword, too.

'So, it's you... the smith,' the giant said as he stroked his dagger where it had collected Sigismund's blood. He spoke as if he knew Sigismund. 'Isn't fate wonderful, at times? I always knew, deep down, that fate was on my side.'

'How did you know I'm a smith?' Sigismund asked. He resumed the walk up the steep mountainside again, and the giant followed easily, despite his lack of a walking stick.

'You've got the shoulders and hands of a smith,' said the giant, whatever that meant.

Together they ascended the last of the rocky mountainside to Rain-soaked, both puffing from their efforts when they reached the top.

A threshold with no door led into Hel's home. A fire burned somewhere inside the house. In this moment, as it was every time Sigismund reached Rain-soaked, he could think of nothing that felt more inviting than sitting in front of a fire to dry his wet socks. Yet he knew that Hel's home was cold. All the warmth from the fire escaped out of the open door. Besides, even Sigismund didn't dare stay inside Rain-soaked long enough to get dry by the fire.

'You can go first,' said the giant at his back.

Sigismund was used to that. Rarely did he come to Hel's home with another without being the first one ushered through the door.

Sigismund stared at the threshold with dread as he approached the open door. He attempted to hop over it into the hall. The wooden threshold rose quickly and made him trip. Sigismund dropped to his knees. His palms hit the floor. Everyone who entered Hel's home kneeled to her as they did so. She was the true ruler of Helheim, and she demanded respect and fear.

The giant stayed outside, so Sigismund proceeded on his own. The great wooden hall was nearly bare. A fire had been built in the middle, large as a funeral pyre, and it lit every wall and every corner of the room, but Sigismund felt even colder than he had outside in the rain.

At one end of the room was a single chair standing by a lone table on which the plate called Hunger and the knife called Famine had been laid out. At the other end of the room was Hel's bed, named Sickbed, surrounded by a dark veil that they called Nightmare. Back in Midgard, Sigismund had often been told stories of Hel and her home in Helheim, but the actual sight of the loneliness attached to this place was sadder than any of the stories he had ever heard. No matter how many times he saw it, it still saddened him.

'Sigismund,' said Hel's wail of a voice. She walked out from behind the funeral pyre where she had been standing. She was as tall as the pyre and as tall as the giant out in the rain had first been.

Every time Sigismund entered her home, he thought he was better prepared for the sight of Hel, but all the same he winced when his eyes fell upon her face. One side of her was dark as ashes and the other bright pink like a sunburn that had recently peeled off. She towered over Sigismund, and he quickly diverted his eyes from the horror of her face so as not to be stunned into silence.

'It's not a Tings-day. What news do you bring?' Her dark robes flowed off her shoulders, and if he only avoided looking at her face and skin, she seemed to have a certain elegance.

'A corpse has escaped Corpse-shore,' Sigismund told her. All of Helheim was shouting for justice and searching for the escaped criminal. 'A tall male corpse with long, uncut nails.'

'Abandoned by his kin in life, a criminal in the afterlife,' said Hel. 'What is his name?'

'Einar Glumbukson,' Sigismund told her. It was the strangest of names.

'Glumbukson... Glumbruck?' Hel asked. Clearly, she knew who he was, and what he had done.

Sigismund took a deep breath to build up the courage to look at Hel's terrifying face. Her lips were curled upwards, like a crooked scar torn across her face. Hel was smiling. A smile so terrifying that Sigismund was certain it could kill. Quickly, he diverted his eyes, and looked down at his feet where a puddle of rainwater had formed.

'You *must* find him,' said Hel. Her voice felt like it sucked all the strength out of Sigismund. 'Bring him to me, this Einar Glumbruckson.'

Sigismund nodded his understanding, for he could hardly force a single word more in Hel's presence. He submitted to her will, backing away towards the open door.

He had begun to shiver from the cold inside Hel's home, and from Hel's presence. In here, the bracteate did not feel warm as it usually did. Sigismund reached a hand to his neck. It was bare. 'The giant,' Sigismund muttered like a curse.

At once he turned to the open door and stumbled over the threshold. He fell into the mud outside, and quickly rose to his feet.

The giant was still out there. He hadn't had the sense to run. Sigismund found his foothold in the mud. He had no weapons, but he had his walking stick. He flicked it up and held it in both hands like a blunt spear. 'You robbed me! You stole my neck-ring.'

'Borrowed,' the giant said, as if that made all the difference.

'You didn't borrow it. You didn't ask, and I didn't agree.'

'Well, I couldn't risk you saying nej.'

'Give it back,' Sigismund said.

'Nej,' the giant replied. 'I need it more than you.'

'How do you know you need it more than me?' he asked, dumbfounded.

The giant scoffed as if it were a stupid question. 'Ragnarok is so close, you won't need to go to Rain-soaked more than three times. At most,' he said dismissively, as if he were not lightly discussing the end of the nine worlds.

'Not the nine worlds,' the giant replied, directly to Sigismund's thoughts. 'Merely the end of gods and giants and afterlives.'

Successfully the giant had steered the conversation away from his thieving.

'The bracteate is mine,' said Sigismund. He took a secure step closer, readying to use his walking stick as a spear. Einer had given him that neck-ring, and it had saved his afterlife, more than once. 'It doesn't matter why you stole it.'

'Nej, it doesn't matter,' the giant agreed, to Sigismund's surprise. 'What matters is why I'm still here.' And with those words he made Sigismund wonder. 'I could easily have left after taking it. By the time you realised, I would be worlds away.'

'So why are you here?'

A superior smile crossed the giant's thin lips, and he combed his fingers through his mixture of red and black hair. 'I'm glad you asked,' he said. 'I'm in need of a smith. I'll trade you the gold neck-ring for your smithing services.'

For a moment, Sigismund's resolve to fight for the bracteate retreated. It would be easier just to smith something for this giant and be done. Then Sigismund remembered where he was standing. Hel's home was at his back, so all he truly had to do was walk back inside, over the tripping threshold and declare that a giant had stolen from him. Theft was a high crime in Helheim, and Hel herself took care of such matters.

'Great idea,' said the giant with a widening smile that made Sigismund halt a mere step away from Hel's tripping threshold. 'Let's go inside.'

A sneaky, well-spoken giant freely walking around in Helheim. Sigismund stared back at the giant, and his expensive clothes. He was so perfect, in every way, like a god, and of course he would have been. He was exactly as Sigismund had always imagined he would be.

'Loki...' Sigismund muttered.

'At last,' Loki sighed. 'If I hadn't smelled the iron in your blood, Sigismund, I wouldn't trust the sharpness of your knives.' He pushed past Sigismund and walked through the door to Hel's home. The threshold made him trip and fall to his knees.

'Hel!' he called loudly as he rose to his feet again.

Sigismund hurried after Loki, back into Rain-soaked. His hands knocked hard against the wooden floor, and it took him a few heartbeats to get up and see Hel's shadow tower over her father.

'How are you here?' she asked, and she was still smiling, as she had been when Sigismund had told her about the escaped corpse from Corpse-shore.

'I've spoken with Worm,' said Loki, as he made himself large like her. 'It's time to release your brother.'

Sigismund stood back by the open door, gaping at the two of them. Hel was turned to her father so Sigismund could only see the swollen part of her face, but Loki was laughing. The pyre flamed tall at their backs, as father and daughter embraced each other in a chilling hug.

'So that is why Glumbruck's son is here,' wailed Hel as they parted from their embrace.

Her father stroked her hair, pushing it lovingly behind her ears. 'Let me know when you find him,' said Loki. 'He borrowed something of mine, and I'd like it back, before the end.'

At once, Sigismund knew why Loki had been so bold and stayed behind. Sigismund had already lost. Never would he get Einer's bracteate back. Even so, he had to try, for the neck-ring was too precious and he owed it to Einer to keep it safe until they met again.

Sigismund cleared his throat. 'I would like to report a robbery,' he announced to Hel, but before he could tell her what had been stolen and by whom, Loki explained in his convincing voice and phrasing.

'I took his neck-ring,' Loki told his daughter. 'And I offered him work, but he seems to have misunderstood me.' His gaze moved from Hel to Sigismund, and in the tone of a parent scolding his child said, 'You shouldn't trust everything you hear about me.'

Sigismund was humbled into silence. Hel and Loki towered above him, and their faces were obscured by the shadows from the funeral pyre at their backs. Hel was Sigismund's ruler and goddess in this afterlife, and her father, Loki, was almost a god himself. He had lived in Asgard with the gods. Dined with them, travelled with them, feasted with them.

In the face of one so powerful—of *two* so powerful—Sigismund could do nothing but submit.

Loki approached Sigismund, who still had not dared move further into Hel's hall, and began to tell a story, skilled like a famed skald. 'A long time ago, the dwarves came together to forge this.'

Loki held up the gold bracteate that he had stolen. The very one Einer had given Sigismund on the icy shore when he had helped Sigismund escape an eternity trapped in ice. The round bracteate had swelled with Loki's own height, until it was as large as Sigismund's face.

'It was the only time they all worked together,' Loki continued. 'Each dwarf gave it a hammer stroke, so that none of them could ever undo it. The vanir sowed their seeds. The alvar sang, and to the dwarves' hammer strokes, Yggdrasil grew. Out of the nothing it grew, and soon it encompassed all of the nothing, its growth controlled and preserved by the thick dwarf-made bracteate.'

It felt like a tale of the creation of the nine worlds. A tale too wild to be believed, and yet... So wild that one could do nothing *but* believe.

'The bracteate was too heavy a burden to be carried, so they split it into three. One for each brother. One for Vile, one for Ve and one for Odin. They ruled the nine worlds, the three of them. Until… Odin grew tired of his brothers and murdered them.'

Sigismund's heartbeat caught in his throat. He nearly forgot to breathe, listening to Loki's grim tale. The stories in Midgard could never quite agree on what had happened to old Vile and Ve, but all knew that they were no longer around and that only the youngest of the three brothers, Odin, ruled in Asgard now.

'I may have helped,' Loki admitted. 'Foolishly. I didn't know better, then.' It sounded like something those tricked by Loki might say about him.

Sigismund too was being tricked by Loki and his splendour, lulled by the pleasing sounds of his words and stories. Yet he did not have the strength to resist, nor did he know if he ought to. Hel was his goddess and she agreed with her father. As a mere mortal, and already a corpse, it was Sigismund's duty to submit to her will.

'With the bracteates at the necks of his chosen ones, the old man ruled freely,' Loki continued his skilled tale. 'When it became too much, there was no one to undo the damage. Every single dwarf had delivered a hammer stroke. None of them could take it back. Except…'

As such, Loki's tale ended, unfinished.

'Except…?' Sigismund summoned his courage to repeat. He yearned to hear the end of the story, and to understand.

Loki walked closer to Sigismund, a wicked smile on his lips. He leaned in close, so close that Sigismund could see their cold breaths mix in the air.

'You marked three dwarf blades, and they marked you,' whispered Loki in a raw voice. 'Three dwarf blades designated you to do what they never could.'

With that Sigismund understood. He understood why he had been denied entrance into Ran's and Aegir's hall under the sea. He understood why he had been found in the ice, and why Einer had given him the bracteate to escape. He understood why Loki had come to steal it from him, and why he had stayed too, when his dagger had been marked by Sigismund's blood. The nine worlds had designated him to do what no dwarf could.

'Undo the three bracteates,' Sigismund whispered.

DARKNESS

DEATH, PAIN, AND fear.

Ragnar came alive in the Darkness again, shaking from the memory of being devoured by the Midgard Worm. The memory of what he needed to do dawned on him. To willingly kill his own god with his own hands was not something Ragnar thought he would ever have to do, and yet he had tried everything else, and nothing had succeeded. There was no other option.

Only one person in all the nine worlds could talk Ragnar out of killing the Alfather—or, perhaps worse, talk him into it.

Ragnar tapped his wrought distaff in the Darkness and made the sounds in his head. *Tap. Tap.* The squeal of metal scraping against glass made his skin prickle with goosebumps. Light shone from the hollow part of Ragnar's distaff and with the horrid squeal, a white thread carved through the dark and opened a veiled entrance into another world.

Despite the squeal, Ragnar did not hurry towards the light, as he had used to do. Even that horrid sound had begun to feel comforting, for it meant that he was going somewhere else;

somewhere that wasn't the pitch-black Darkness in which he was stuck for all eternity.

Ragnar passed through the veil and blinked furiously to better see the world beyond.

The familiar hall came into focus, although to call it a hall was to embellish. It was the vapour room of a large alf bathhouse, although the ceiling was not shallow as those of the bathhouses Ragnar had known in life. The ceiling was high and that was what gave it the feel of a hall. The wooden walls had been painted white as the bark of a birch, and shadow-like figures had been drawn onto them. Sometimes, when the oven got really warm, and someone opened it to pour water for steam, Ragnar thought he saw the shadows move.

Often, he had come here, for company and for comfort. Although he himself could not speak, not directly, not using his own throat and voice, he had found a way to communicate, and when he sat in that hall, and when finally *she* came to him, it no longer felt like he was all alone in the Darkness. It didn't feel as much like he was doomed, although he was. Someday, there would be no future or past of hers for him to visit anymore, for never could Ragnar go back to a time and place he had already been. Someday, he would have visited every part of her life, and then, Ragnar truly would be all alone in the dark.

'What troubles you?' asked *she,* as she entered the hall in her flowing dark robes. 'I could hear you think from outside.' She was not dressed in white and bright colours, like the alvar who owned the hall. Here, she always wore dark clothes to highlight her outline. Her real features were faded. She was like a shadow, but a bright shadow in dark robes. Her gold-coloured hair was braided in the ancient style all the way to her hips, as it had always been, in this life, and in the previous one.

I have tried everything and failed. I must kill him before he reaches the battlefield. One of the shining runes carved around the top of Ragnar's distaff changed its colour from blue to red. Odin's rune, the rune of the messenger, and with its use Ragnar's loud thought was delivered.

'Then that is what you must do,' she replied simply, as he had known she would. Still, hearing her say it was soothing. He had her blessing, and since Ragnar couldn't have the Alfather's blessing, he was glad to at least have Siv's.

SIV

Chapter One Hundred and Forty-Nine

THE FOREFATHERS DRUMMED loud in Siv's head. She hummed in a low voice to force them into silence and remind herself of who she was.

'Glumbruck, Glumbruck,' she hummed, and then she began to recite the names of her children, although remembering was becoming increasingly difficult. 'Tyra, Einer, Troels, Viggo, Jary, Ove, Frode...' She knew many names were missing, and she knew that they were not all in the right order either, but she said their names over and over as she approached the bathhouse.

The forefathers gradually retreated from her mind and allowed her to be a little bit more than a forefather herself—almost a person. Her skin was translucent and only hard to the touch when she remembered to use runes to solidify her hold on the nine worlds.

She was not much more than an ancient jotun draugar, lost to the collective forefathers and without any grave or passage to guard.

She sealed her thoughts and readied her runes. Ragnar would be inside the alvar bathhouse, as he always was. It was the one place she had allowed him to visit. She didn't care for her life to be stalked by Ragnar Erikson, whom everyone knew as Fate. Her life—in Jotunheim, Asgard and Midgard—already seemed to have been ruled by fate and destiny, from what she still remembered of it. Even so, Ragnar was a good reminder of home, and of who she was, or rather, who she had been, when she had been alive.

Siv entered the steam-filled room. There was no one else there but her and Ragnar, who was always waiting there for her to come, so that he would not be alone in the Ginnungagap with Siv's forefathers.

'What have you come to discuss today, Ragnar?' asked Siv as she entered. Her talks with Ragnar were the most normal conversations she had these days, so close to the end of time, where every last being in the nine worlds was panicking at the thought of the end.

I have come to say goodbye, replied her own thoughts. A thought that Ragnar had put there with runes. She had helped him practise and refine the skill. It was strange to teach one who travelled in time, for the basics were not the first thing she had taught him.

'Have you found a way to leave the Darkness?' she asked as she made her way to the white painted wall and settled on a bench. She made herself comfortable underneath one of the shadows that the alvar had painted onto the wall after Siv had arrived to stay with them. They said that shadow was hers. It was bigger than all the others, and it consumed them all. Sometimes, she even thought that she saw it move, although it was merely painted on, not conjured with runes, as many things were in Alfheim.

I was foolish to ever think I could leave, answered Ragnar through Siv's own thoughts. *You were right, after all. I doomed myself to this fate. To be Fate itself.*

'Perhaps it wasn't so much you, as it was the nine worlds,' Siv suggested, for if Ragnar had come to say goodbye, and this truly was his last visit, then he would have to roam alone in the Darkness for the rest of eternity, well beyond Ragnarok, when the rest of them expected to die. If that was the case, then, at the very least, she wanted him to go with some comfort.

Ragnar did not reply, so Siv continued, in the hope of giving him something to keep him warm in the cold Darkness, and to keep him company in the loneliness.

'You were destined for this life, at birth,' said Siv, for although she had never laid eyes on Ragnar Erikson's destiny thread, at least not that she could recall, she believed it to be true. Even Fate himself had a fate. 'Your bloodline designated you, as it designates us all. You can only do so much to escape the pull of your bloodline, for without the blood in your veins, you wouldn't be alive, not even in the afterlife.'

Siv felt a faint pulse in her translucent arm, her neck, at her forehead. For although she was dead, somehow, she was also alive, and living, as if the nornir had spun a new destiny thread for her without her approval.

'We all are who we were born to be,' said Siv. Even she was who she had been supposed to be. In the end, after centuries spent in Midgard, she had been pulled back towards her bloodline and the life that had once been destined for her. Even if it was in the afterlife, she was required to serve her full purpose before the nine worlds would let go of their pull on her.

Ragnar was no longer with her. No thoughts were inserted into her mind in answer, and regardless of where he had ended up in his afterlife, Ragnar was not naturally inclined towards silence. He had said his final goodbyes, but although it would be the last time he saw her, Siv was well aware that a younger Ragnar would soon appear at her side.

Exactly as she thought it, she sensed someone use the runes in front of her. They tingled playfully on her skin. She felt them more strongly than she felt anything else: her sense of touch was reduced in her draugar form, but her grasp on runes and the Ginnungagap was stronger for it.

'Why have you come now?' she asked.

I did it, Ragnar said through Siv's thoughts. *I killed the Alfather. I stopped Ragnarok.*

Siv glanced warily at the ground in front of her, where she supposed Ragnar was standing. A long time ago, soon after the three-year winter had begun, Ragnar had come to her and told her that he knew how to stop Ragnarok. All he had to do was kill the Alfather, and with all the anger of having been burned on a funeral pyre in Asgard, killed by the Alfather's hand, she had told Ragnar to do it.

Never had she thought he might succeed.

'Wait here,' she told him, and stormed out of the bathhouse.

If Ragnar truly had killed the Alfather before Ragnarok, then the three winters ought to have lifted, and the snow would be melting. But outside, snow was still falling thick over the alvar village deep in Alfheim where Siv had taken refuge.

Her heart tightened with disappointment. She had tried not to hope, because hope was a dangerous thing, but all her life she had carried hope, and in death it was difficult to let go. Despite herself, she had hoped that Ragnar might succeed, so that Siv too might be released from the demands of her destiny. Although she shouldn't have, she had hoped that at last the nine worlds would be forced to let her go. As once the Alfather had been forced to let her go, when she had died at his feet.

Siv walked back into the steaming bathhouse where she still felt the light tingle of Ragnar's runes.

'Whatever you did, it changed nothing for me,' she told him. 'Ragnarok is closing in.'

But I killed him. He was dead. He was dying.

'Dead and dying are not the same thing, Ragnar. You should know that.' Once, he had pulled her off her own funeral pyre, right before it was set aflame. She had been dead, but now, instead, she was dying. Somehow, the nornir had revived her, but they had done so too late. She was neither truly dead nor alive, she was just dying, all over again.

He was dead, Ragnar decided. *He was dead.*

'Then even *his* death could not stop the will of the nine worlds.'

Although she could neither hear nor feel it, Siv knew that Ragnar was crying. His bloodline had a strength with the runes that even Siv, who had learned the runes well, envied, but he had never been strong of heart. They could not have been further apart from each other, the two of them.

That was why she told him what she would never have told herself.

'It's time to give up, Ragnar. Accept your fate and assume your role. Let the nine worlds have their way. You will never win.'

She felt the runes stir for a moment and then they were gone, and she knew that Ragnar had been killed by her forefathers and passed on into the Darkness again.

As soon as he was gone, Siv hurried out of the bathhouse, before Ragnar could come back with more worries and more talk. Today had not been one of their usual nice talks of the past that reminded her of who she was. There was enough worry in the nine worlds to occupy Siv's mind; she did not need to carry Ragnar's burdens, too.

A moment before, there had been no one, but now the streets outside the bathhouse were beginning to fill with alvar. Their clothes were white and their skin translucent, although not like Siv's own. Their skin radiated heat and light that made it entrancing to look at them.

Commotion was rising outside the assembly hall, and a terror travelled through the alvar. Perhaps Siv had spoken too soon, perhaps Ragnar really had changed something by killing the Alfather, but although Siv had once urged Ragnar to do it, she was not so certain that the Alfather's murder would result in good things for the nine worlds. If she had ever thought that to be true, she would have tried to kill Odin a long time ago, before she had fled to Midgard. The nine worlds needed their Alfather, as much as jotnar needed Ragnarok.

Siv joined the alvar outside the assembly hall. Even at her reduced height, she towered over them, and the crowd parted for her, as it always did. The alvar were terrified of her, and rightfully so. Even Siv did not fully know what she was anymore, nor what the point of living was, when she was already dead. She had never asked to be revived. She only ever asked to die, but even that, the nine worlds robbed from her.

Siv entered the alvar assembly hall. It was filled with people, and yet it was nearly as cold as it was outside, and that was unusual. At all times, the alvar kept their halls warm with runes, but today their minds were too busy.

Many times, Siv had been in here to discuss the fate of the nine worlds after Ragnarok with the alvar and dwarves who were all preparing for the end of gods and giants when the nine worlds would be yielded to those who chose not to fight.

Alvar were hitting the drums that hung far up under the glass ceiling. The thick layer of snow that had settled on top of the glass roof was shaken off with each drumbeat. No one was singing, not yet, and that, too, was strange. There was always music in alvar halls.

Their leaders were gathered in the middle of the hall, right under the coloured glass ceiling that had not let light through since the beginning of winter. They were not talking, but staring up at the ceiling far above, as the drums throbbed around them like heartbeats.

The snow was gliding off the roof from the drumming, but where before new snowflakes had come and settled in their place, now the sun shone through, as it had not done in three winters.

Sunlight hit the coloured glass and lit the alvar hall up like Siv had never seen it before. Images from the coloured glass danced around the many faces of the alvar, following the music of the drums that no one danced to.

Siv forced through the crowd towards the middle of the hall where the alvar leaders were gathered. Even them she towered over, although they were taller than all other alvar. The northern alvar leader was the tallest of them, and as a result they listened to her, whenever she spoke.

The woman's worried gaze turned to an expression of urgency when she saw Siv advancing on them. 'What does it mean?' she shouted in her sing-song voice. The others echoed the question, eager to turn their gazes away from the intruding sunlight.

They asked not because they did not know, but because they did not want to believe that the time had come.

'It means that my kinsmen will go to war,' said Siv. 'And die.'

'And we...'

'Will live,' Siv completed.

'Alone.'

Their gazes turned back to the clearing skies above. The sky was blue. The ice mist had lifted. The three-year-long winter had ended, and that could only mean that Ragnarok was upon them, for everyone knew what came after the three-year winter.

'Then it is time for you to go home, giantess,' the leader demanded.

To go home meant to die along with all the other giants. To Siv, it was a comforting thought, for dying was what she had meant to do three winters ago.

'Go release your sons,' said the northern leader. Her bright eyes stared straight at Siv.

'My sons?' asked Siv, trying to remember all their names. There was Einer, and Troels, and Jary, and Viggo, and Ove. There were so many, and Odin had claimed them all. Did the alvar mean for her to fight for the Alfather's cause instead of that of the forefathers shouting loudly within her? Or did they mean for her to turn her sons against their Alfather, so close to the end?

'Your name is Glumbruck,' the alvar leaders reminded her in a unified echo, not for the first time, but perhaps for the last. 'You have many sons.'

Siv nodded, for although she no longer remembered all their names, she knew that she had more sons than she could remember. All her life she had tried to keep them safe from Ragnarok.

'It is too late to ask them to fight for me and not their Alfather,' said Siv, for it was.

'You have other sons, too,' revealed the northern alvar leader, although Siv no longer remembered. 'You have sons who are not in Valhalla. Centuries ago, you left your firstborns in Iron-woods, and they have been howling for your return, ever since.'

She had. The words rang in her head and tried to dig up the memories. She had. She remembered giving birth. She remembered kisses and nestling into warm fur. She remembered the dark sky above Iron-woods, and the smell of blood. They were there, her firstborns.

'The time has come,' Siv agreed, and with those words she exited the hall.

No alvar followed her out. They were all staring up at the sunlight that hit their glass ceiling and cast images across the hall, entranced by the dance of light, as short-lived were entranced by the dances of alvar.

Outside, Siv stared up at the brightening sky. She was dazed by it all: the light, the memory of her firstborns, and Ragnar's words, too. So quickly it had happened. So quickly winter had begun, and so quickly it ended. Perhaps it wasn't what they all feared, for no famed visions spoke of the three-year winter ending before the last battle. Siv's eyes fell on the bathhouse. Ragnar had been right to say goodbye, then, for even she would never see him again. And perhaps he had been right about something else, too.

The sun danced over Siv's skin and through it, like glass, all the way to reflect off the snow on the ground. The ice at her feet was beginning to melt in the sun.

Siv allowed hope to flood her for the last time. Perhaps Ragnar truly had stopped Ragnarok.

FINN

Chapter One Hundred and Fifty

VICTORIOUS, BUT WITH no strength to sing of their victory, they rode back to Jelling. It had been a long journey; after summers spent fighting at Svend's side, Finn was less jittery on horseback, but it was only during this war that he had finally learned to sleep while riding.

For so long had they fought that Finn had learned to fall asleep as they chased southerners all the way from Hedeby to Danevirke, and even amidst war and corpses, his back to a barricade, or at a decent distance with his shield at his back. For weeks they had fought. For weeks shield mates had fallen at his side. For weeks their corpses had rotted at his feet. For weeks he had smelled them and watched their decaying bodies and slept in their midst.

Then, after the battle had ended, after the fortification had been secured, and the port city of Hedeby, too, there had come the long task of burning the fallen and honouring their sacrifices. It had not been a happy summer, and it had not been a good battle.

They were all exhausted, even Svend who had kept going when no one else had the strength to fight. Svend was well versed in war. Had it not been for him, they never would have won, and so many of them never would have survived. Finn knew battlefields and raids, but wars of this scale belonged to kings, and although Svend was not a king, he was the son of one, and he fought in his father's stead.

'I saved you another share,' Svend said with a smile. His beard had grown so long and wild that when he smiled, which was often, the strands of his beard parted in two opposite directions.

Svend reached into his bag and pulled out a money pouch, which he tossed to Finn.

Finn caught it, though not as effortlessly as Svend had cast it. He let go of his reins, letting the horse lead, and checked the content. Nine silver coins.

'Consider it an advance on our next conquest,' Svend said. 'It's time. It's time for you to shed your calling name, Finn the Nameless. Or shall I say Finn the Grey?'

Many wars and battles ago, Finn's beard had begun to grey, but this summer he had seen his last coloured hair turn grey as well, and his bones ached now, not just from battles and effort, but from age.

He stared down into the pouch. Nine coins. Finn gazed emptily at them. He could hardly believe it. Although they never spoke of it, Svend had kept count, and as carefully as Finn had. After this summer's war, the weight of nine silver coins more was all Finn needed to buy his freedom.

For twenty summers, he had set aside riches to buy his freedom from King Harald and regain his family name. For twenty summers he had slaved for that man with only the distant hope of someday being able to buy his name and honour back. He had been forced into battles and wars with no say of his own, at the peril of dying before he could regain his name, of never reaching Valhalla in the afterlife. He had been forced to build houses and fortresses, and Christian churches, with no right to refuse.

No more. There, in his grasp, were the last coins that he needed.

Finn swallowed the lump in his throat, stuffed the nine coins into his bag with the others and took the reins again, and in silence they rode on. Finn, with the last nine silver coins secure in his bag, and Svend at his side. Svend rode both at Finn's side and in front and at the back, always laughing about something, and entertaining hundreds of tired fighters. Someday, he would make a good king. A king who could move his people to willingly follow him, for he was a fair man, and a good friend.

When, at last, the sun indicated midday, Jelling's outer walls greeted them. The sun beamed over them and rewarded their victory as they dismounted their sweaty horses and moved into Jelling, to announce their victory to the king.

Warriors went off to find taverns and set up their tents, while Svend and a dozen of his closest supporters proceeded deeper into Jelling to Harald's halls. Naturally, Finn was among them. He was always among them, right at Svend's side.

'Are you happy with your advance?' Svend asked Finn.

'Rascal. That's why you were smiling the entire way home.' Finn leaned in and ruffled Svend's long hair as only he was allowed to do. Svend fought him off as he always did, and they both laughed.

As a thrall Finn had never been given permission to marry again and raise a family, although he had always wanted sons. Finn had begun to imagine that what Svend and him had together was much the same as what fathers and sons did.

His fingers played with the nine coins in his bag as they passed the inner barricade to Harald's lands. The time had come. Finn's beard and hair were grey, and he was much too old to father a dozen sons and raise them as he would have liked, but he was not yet dead. Even without a name and lineage to attach it to, he had gained much honour and respect in life. Once he had his name back, the honour he would attach to it would be certain to welcome him into Valhalla in the afterlife. His bones ached for a feast.

The weather was warm, out of the shade of the town. Finn was sweating, but he did not have the strength to take off his armour and carry it.

By the Christian church behind Gorm the Sleepy's grand gravemound, guards had gathered, and with them was Harald Bluetan, as ever robed in expensive blue. The sound of their approach caught Harald's ears, and he swung towards them.

Their armour was darkened with blood. They had washed in Hedeby, but their faces and hair were still scaled with the stuff. They arrived before Harald with fresh wounds clearly visible, and other wounds, felt but not seen, from the smells and sights they had survived to regain Hedeby and Danevirke for him.

'You arrived just in time,' the king exclaimed when he saw them. No enquiries about the success of the war. No concern for their bloodied appearance. With a bright smile he waved them over to the church where he was standing, delightedly watching something.

In a tired march Finn and Svend approached, the eleven chiefs who fought at Svend's side with them, while Harald impatiently tried to hurry them along.

He was standing by a large, brightly coloured runestone: Gorm the Sleepy's memorial stone. They had truly toiled to find that huge rock, the perfect runestone. While they had been away at war, the stone had been painted and something more had been carved into it.

Finn walked closer. His eyesight was not as clear as it had been as a young man.

The beautiful memorial stone for Gorm the Sleepy that they had carried across Jutland with such difficulty to place here, not five summers ago, had been corrupted. The carved memorial runes were there, but below them more runic staves had been added, and not in Gorm's honour.

'That Harald who won all of Denmark...' Finn read aloud. He glanced up at Harald. With their efforts down south in Hedeby, pushing the southerners back to Danevirke, all the lands that had once been Dane lands were now ruled by Harald. That was why he had added to the runestone now, to brag of his own accomplishments, although the battlefield had not seen even a drop of his own sweat or blood.

Even if he had been there, it made little difference. Good men did not brag of their own deeds on runestones. Good men raised good sons who in turn raised runestones in their father's honour.

On the other sides of the stone, images had been carved. A terrific lynx-like beast that Finn did not know the meaning of had been carved and coloured, and below the beast were more runic staves.

'And Norway,' Finn read aloud carefully, one stave at a time. All of Norway did not belong to Harald: there was King Olaf in Norway, and there were others who ruled over land up there. But Harald had begun his conquest of those lands, and he supposed these runic staves were a sort of threat to the north. He intended to possess it all.

Arrogantly, Harald stood back and nodded as he watched the chiefs in their blooded armours examine his work.

Finn walked around to the last side of the huge runestone. He was a slow reader, so it took him longer than the others. Svend and the others had stopped there, by the last side of the runestone. They were staring at it with the same empty looks as yesterday, when they had stared down at the corpses of their comrades.

Finn gasped when he saw it. His heart raced with shock.

Into the large stone that had been raised in the honour of Gorm the Sleepy, White Christ had been carved and coloured. Worst of all, into the memorial stone of that true man of Odin, and below the image of White Christ, were more runic staves about Harald's own grand deeds, carved into his father's memorial stone.

Finn muttered, reading aloud the full new addition of runic staves. 'That Harald who won for himself Denmark... And all of Norway... And made the Danes Christian.'

'You've defaced it,' Svend blurted. 'You took him out of his grave. You put a Christian cross on it. And now...'

'Isn't it beautiful?' said Harald, oblivious to his son's disapproval. He was proud. He was an old proud man, who had forgotten all about the perilous war he had sent them on, simply because the bright colours of the stone in front of him were fairer to look upon than bloodied armours.

Svend turned his back to his father and the stone. Tears were streaming down his face as he stared up at his grandfather's tall gravemound. A gravemound that had been empty for many years, ever since Harald had dragged his father's bones out of the grave to give him a Christian burial.

Harald was oblivious. Finn's jaw was tight trying not to say what they were all thinking, about Harald and the work he had done while they had been away risking their life so he could scribble words over his father's memorial.

The blood pounded loud through his veins as Finn unstrapped his bag from his belt. All the riches he had won for himself over summer were inside, along with the nine silver coins that Svend had given him.

Eager to be free from a master of such despicable actions, Finn handed Harald his money pouch.

The king took it, for he was fond of gifts. He ripped open the leather clasp with no regard for the bag itself and peered inside. 'Is this all?' asked Harald.

'That is my share,' said Finn. 'My *last* share.'

'Why would I need to take your share? Didn't you win me any riches down south?'

'This is the last of what I owe you,' Finn announced. 'With this, my debt to you is paid in full.'

At last.

Occasionally, Finn's slippery tongue had managed to talk

him out of dreaded obligations, but for the most part he was entirely at Harald Bluetan's mercy, and Harald had never been a merciful master. At last, he would be free. At last, he could fight without restraint, for with a name and lineage, he would be allowed to pass on into Valhalla in the afterlife. Most importantly, his name would no longer be linked to a man who thought it decent to dishonour his own father's memory. At last, he would be a freeman again.

'I demand my name back,' Finn announced. The chiefs at his side tore their eyes away from the defaced runestone to Finn and they were smiling, although none as brightly as Svend. They all knew how hard Finn had fought to be free. They used to say that he would never succeed, and a lesser man never would have, but Finn had been determined not to greet the afterlife as a debt-thrall.

'A name?' Harald scoffed. 'You're my thrall. I have no intention of freeing you.' He tossed Finn's bag into the grass at his feet and settled his sight back on the runestone in front of them.

'You have to,' Finn blurted. 'It's the law.' He had not expected Harald to be happy about it, but he had expected him to at least follow his own law. 'I'm a debt-thrall. I've come to pay the last of my debt owed to you. I demand freedom.'

'Demand? You watch your tongue, thrall, or I might have it cut out,' Harald said.

To be freed was Finn's right, but Harald was a king, and he could, and would, do whatever he pleased.

'He has earned his freedom,' Svend hissed.

'He's a thrall, he has no say.' Easily, Harald dismissed both Svend and Finn. His eyes were fixed back on his father's memorial stone, now defaced with Christian images and declarations of Bluetan's own grandeur. He could hardly tear his eyes from it.

'You will grant Finn his freedom and follow the law,' Svend insisted.

'I don't care what the law says,' Harald boldly declared.

At once, Svend's sword was out.

Guards and chiefs were petrified in shock. None of them had seen it coming, least of all Harald, but Finn had known it would only be a question of time. Immediately, he drew his own battle-axe. The other chiefs followed Svend's and Finn's lead.

Harald's guards rushed in. There were more of them than there were of Svend's people, but Finn was glad to stand with Svend. Even if he died, right there, without ever regaining his name, it would be worth it.

Together, they charged, armour bloodied from the summer's war and no shields in their hands.

Finn bumped into a young guard with little resolve. They both stumbled ahead, and Finn was quick to reverse their positions.

Harald was hiding behind his precious stone, but Svend was coming for him. He had knocked down two guards and launched after his father.

Finn's guard attacked. Finn barely evaded the spear, and the guard had the sense to stop his charge before Finn could get in close enough to land a blow with his battle-axe. The guard kept at bay; in skirmishes like this, spears were the perfect weapon. Svend, too, had abandoned his sword in favour of a spear.

'Kill them,' Harald was yelling loud above the clamour. 'Kill him!' Not content with dishonouring his father, the king was calling for the murder of his own son.

Finn's young opponent took a step forward, urged by his king's yell, but he was scared, and Finn no longer was. This summer had stripped him of any fear of battle and death. Finn pushed past the spear point before his opponent could react and slammed his axe-head into the guard's helmet. The warrior stumbled from the hard blow, his helmet dented, and with a push he fell. Finn bent down to pick up the spear, but before he could, another foe darted at him.

This guard moved in much quicker than the first, a Dane axe

in hand. A weapon somewhat between a spear and an axe, and much deadlier than either. Its reach was wide, its head sharp.

Finn stepped backwards. His back hit the coloured runestone. The guard swung his grand axe, and Finn hopped to the side, but not fast enough. The tip of the axe cut across his padded armour at the stomach. Finn backed away behind the stone to regain his footing.

His back bumped into a person this time. Finn swung around, but fingers clasped his arms before he could strike. Harald's eyes widened in horror. 'Kill him, thrall,' he ordered. His fingers dug into Finn's arms. Finn glanced over his shoulder to the guard with the Dane axe, but the man had moved on to other skirmishes.

Harald swung Finn around. 'Kill him, thrall,' he ordered again. There was no doubt about who he meant. Svend was being held away by three guards, and Harald was locked in by skirmishes on all sides, with no weapon of his own and nowhere to run.

Finn clenched his teeth in anger. He wanted to retort that he was no thrall, but that would give his intentions away, and Harald would flee before Finn could kill him.

Harald's fingers were firm on his arms.

'I can finish this,' he told Harald. 'Let me go.'

Despite all his skill, Svend struggled to hold up against three guards. He was getting pushed back. He had taken wounds to the left shoulder and his waist.

The skirmishes were moving away from the coloured stone, allowing an opening for Harald to flee. The time was now. Harald, too, saw it. He loosened his grip around Finn's arms.

At last, Finn was free to strike the king, as he had dreamt about for twenty winters and summers, but straight in front of him, Svend was being overmanned. One of the three guards readied a fatal stroke. He lifted a Dane axe back, as the others sparred with Svend to keep him exposed.

'Ja!' Harald cheered at Finn's back, and then, the king began to run.

Desperate to protect Svend, Finn launched, swinging his battle-axe with a grunt. It struck into the neck of the man with the Dane axe, who fell. Finn wrenched his axe free and approached the next guard. Svend was at his knees. Finn roared to be heard and seen and feared, and the two guards hovering over Svend turned to him in horror. They struggled to keep their weapons both on Finn and Svend. Now they were equal numbers. Svend smiled, as only he could, through pain and blood. He staggered to his feet, recovering from the blow he had taken to the hand. He was bleeding, but he was on his feet and still had a spear-pole in hand, although the sharp head had been chopped off.

Finn glanced at their back. Harald was running. Screaming and yelling for guards to come and protect him. 'Left!' Svend yelled to Finn.

The guard to Finn's left swung towards him, but Svend and Finn had fought together for so long that they had developed their own fighting language, where left meant right.

The man to Finn's right had turned to Svend, exposing himself to Finn. Finn hammered his axe into his back and pulled away, and as the warrior stumbled forward, turning to defend himself, Finn drove the axe head into his face. The warrior collapsed at his feet. Svend had finished off the other guard. He was crouched down by the body and had cast the broken spear aside.

Battle-axe raised, Finn stood at Svend's back to protect him, should anyone charge. With bow in hand, and five arrows, Svend rose to his feet. Calmly, he nocked the first arrow, watching his father flee across the grassy grounds, bound for the outer wall.

The chiefs were still fighting. Asbjörn had fallen, but he was merely wounded, not yet dead.

With the first arrow nocked, and the rest in hand, Svend rushed up the side of his grandfather's huge gravemound to gain a better line of sight. Harald neared the gates; once he was through, there would be no hope of striking him down.

Svend took a deep breath and felt the wind. He had always been a good archer, and a fast one.

A guard launched after Svend. Finn kicked the man back. It was easier from the high ground of the gravemound. When he looked back again, Svend had sent off all five arrows. All it had taken was a few heartbeats.

A loud squeal announced that at least one of them had hit its target, but Harald was carried out of sight before they could confirm the damage.

Svend darted past Finn down the side of the gravemound to join the remaining skirmishes. There were eight chiefs still standing and twelve guards. Finn joined too, although his bones were aching already. He had not yet recovered from their warfare in the south.

Reluctantly, Finn clashed against a guard. They faced each other. Finn evaded a blow, and the guard dodged two of his. Finn was not as fast as he had been as a young raider, but the guard who fought against him did not fight with full strength. The guard was holding back.

'Asmund, do you truly want to fight me?' Svend bellowed loud enough for all the skirmishes to halt, even Finn's. 'Because I do not wish to kill *you*.' At Svend's words, the guard called Asmund lowered his spear.

The guard opposite Finn still had his spear pointed at Finn's chest, and others also hadn't lowered their weapons. The chiefs stepped carefully backwards out of reach before lowering their weapons. Finn, too, lowered his battle-axe, but only enough to show that he would prefer not to fight, but that if he had to, he would still use his axe to kill.

'Who do you fight for?' Svend bellowed to those guards who still had their weapons pointed at his most trusted followers. 'Where is your king?' His voice echoed between the wall of the Christian church and the tall gravemound of his grandfather.

The guards looked around at those words. Their king had abandoned them without a second thought.

'He has left you,' Svend said. 'He flees from me, he flees from you, and he flees from these lands. Will you follow him, or will you follow me?'

Spears and axes were lowered. Even the spearman opposite Finn conceded. At the end of the day, these were people who had chosen to become guards instead of warriors, and they had no reason to die without a king to die for.

Patiently, Svend waited for all of them to make their choice. Not a single guard chose Harald. He nodded.

'What do we do with this?' asked one of the chiefs, eyes fixed on the defaced runestone.

Svend took a deep sigh. He could hardly look at it. Neither could Finn. It was such a stain on the old town of Jelling. This had used to be the fine town of Gorm the Sleepy, a man of Odin. Now the memory of Gorm had been ruined by his son's self-praise.

'We leave it where it is,' Svend decided. 'My father dishonoured my grandfather's belief. Dishonoured his way of life and his memory. I will not do the same. Let my father meet his White Christ. I'll be feasting with Odin.'

With his decision made, he walked back up the side of his grandfather's empty gravemound and invited them to join him. Together they climbed all the way to the top, where they could see beyond the barricade. See the town of Jelling and the fields where farmers were busy.

'I am the King of Danes now,' Svend yelled loud for all to hear. 'I, Svend, am the King of Denmark.' Faces out on the fields and far into town, who had no idea what the clashes from inside Harald's walls had meant, peered up at Svend and his first followers.

Some of the warriors who had stayed in town heard the message and roared in approval, and when their roar ended a chant picked up.

The word would spread now, and what would follow would be a long campaign through Jute and Dane lands to gain the favour of the chiefs who had once given their allegiance to Harald. Finn did not think it would be a difficult task, but it would take time.

They were all smiling at yet another victory, and a brighter future, as they descended the gravemound. 'Tonight, we shall drink at my expense,' Svend announced on their way down.

That promise had them all excited to heal the pains of their wounds with mead.

'As king, it seems that I own you, and your debts, Finn the Nameless,' said Svend when they reached the bottom of the gravemound. He stopped and the chiefs and guards turned to look at him. In a loud, reliable voice, Svend said the promised words—words Finn had longed to hear for over twenty summers. 'And *I* declare that your debt has been paid. I return your lineage to you, Finn, son of Rolf. You are free.'

Svend spread his arms and they joined in a tight hug. Never before had they hugged as equals. Never before had they stood on the same ground, and yet even now that Finn had regained his freedom, they were not equal, for Svend was a king now, and Finn knew what that meant.

They parted from their hug, and Finn looked deep into Svend's bright eyes when he said his first words as a freeman. 'Then, as a freeman, I shall ally my battle-axe with yours, King Svend.'

EINER

Chapter One Hundred and Fifty-One

THE BRACTEATE HAMMERED loud and hot against Einer's chest. Einer crouched to make himself small and disappear into the crowd at the city market.

The dead were roaring his name and shouting for him to halt. 'Keep hiding and you might not survive all the way back to Corpse-shore!'

Einer did his best to look nonchalant and merely busy, so as not to rouse suspicion among the people he passed. Five nights of fleeing from angry corpses and Loki still had not come to find Einer, as he had promised to do. Einer had not dared to stop. On most nights he slept in the cold woods with only the bracteate to warm him.

Last night he had finally found the town where his childhood friend, Leif, lived. It had not been as easy as he had hoped, for Helheim was as vast as Midgard.

When he was certain that the corpses chasing him were far enough back not to notice, Einer left the main road. Houses lined the wood-covered streets and there was no outer barricade to the city. None of the towns Einer had passed had needed barricades, for no wars were carried on into Helheim.

The city was larger than any Einer had ever seen before. It had taken him half a day's brisk walk to reach the inner city from the outskirts. The dead called it Jutland, for mainly Jutes settled there, even though it looked nothing like the Jutland that Einer knew from life in Midgard. There were none of the soft hills of Jutland. The city had been built between two mountains and spanned as far as Einer could see, in any direction, even up the slopes of both mountains.

Einer passed countless houses, all kinds of houses; small huts and longhouses where feasts were hosted by ancient chieftains and jarls who must not have died with enough worth to go to Valhalla. Had Einer not been rushing from town to town, to find Leif before those corpses did, he might have enjoyed his time in Helheim. For apart from the cold and dark, the ninth world almost looked the same as Midgard. Children happily ran around, while men and women roared with laughter. There were fights and trades and gossip, work to be done but still time to enjoy the afterlife.

Outside one of the jarl feasts, Einer stopped and tested his luck. The feast had spilled into the streets, where drunk Jutes stumbled around with horns of ale in hand.

Keeping a wary eye on the way he had come, Einer approached a small group of elderly men whose tunics made them look like they had died a long time ago. Farmers in life, no doubt.

'Hei,' he greeted, to gain their attention. All five turned to him, their laughter forgotten. 'I'm looking for Leif Ragnarson of Ash-hill.'

They stared blankly at him.

'You mean Signe's kid?' asked a corpse who stood nearby. 'Little blond one? Blue eyes?'

Einer turned to the man and nodded enthusiastically. That was the Leif he knew. Einer couldn't remember Signe, but she had been in Helheim a lot longer than Leif and Ragnar, so naturally she was the one people knew.

'Oh, Signe's kid?' the five farmers exclaimed. 'Ja, ja, ja.'

'They live out by the mill,' one of the corpses said.

Many more corpses stopped to join the conversation. Half a dozen of them surrounded Einer, all eager to help and examine the newly arrived. Einer looked around at their faces, trying to see if any one of them was among those chasing him. At any moment now, one of them might recognise him, or casually mention the rumour of a tall criminal escaped from Corpse-shore.

'You're a warrior,' the corpses realised, then. Their eyes settled on the two swords hanging from Einer's weapon belt.

Their own belts were weapon-free, only holding empty cup holders and money pouches.

'In Midgard, I was,' Einer said to dismiss it. 'And the mill is this way?' He pointed down the street, the way he had been heading.

The corpses laughed and pointed the opposite way, back where Einer had fled from.

'It's on the eastern bank,' one of them said.

'Five streets off the high road,' another supplied.

'Takka,' Einer said and hurried to shuffle out of their midst. They all stared after him as he broke into a run up the street he had come from. His breaths were short, and his heart pumped at the thought of being discovered.

He heard loud voices up the street, and hid in the shadows between two houses, until the voices passed, and then he headed up the road again, and crossed the busy main street, hoping and wishing that no one would notice him.

'Get him!' someone yelled.

Einer ran again. The voice was a lot closer than he would have liked. Steps on the wooden roads thundered around him. Einer sprinted to the other side of the high road and ran down a slim road.

He needed to get to Leif. Five streets off the high road, the feasting men had said.

They were fast on Einer's trail, yelling for reinforcements. Two roads ahead of Einer, three corpses turned down the road and raced towards him. He took the first street to the left, but they were coming at him there too, and at the back as well. He was surrounded.

His swords dangled at his side, begging to be used, but Einer did not draw his weapons. His swords were deadly—the Ulfberht blade could cut through anything and anyone—but he did not want to rob any of them of an afterlife with family and friends.

There were too many to attempt to get away. Thick rows formed around him, as if it were a performance and Einer was a fire breather. All their hard stares were fixed on him. Perhaps they would let him go if he explained what had happened and gained these corpses' trust.

'Whoever you're looking for, it's not me!' Einer exclaimed and held his palms out to the side for the crowd to see that he had not picked up any weapons.

'It's him,' one of the dead said, sure of himself. 'He walked up from Corpse-shore. Long-nails, and said he had arrived in Hel's realm that same morning. Einer Glumbruckson.'

All of it was true. 'It's not me!'

More and more corpses stopped on the street to have a look at the curious stranger and the spectacle. It had been a bad idea to come into town. Perhaps if Einer had stayed out on the plains and climbed a forested mountain instead, he wouldn't have been caught.

'If it's not you, then what's your name?' someone asked.

'Vigmer,' Einer blurted. 'Vigmer Ragnarson.' It was the first two names he could think of: his father's, and that of Ragnar who had been as good as a father to him for many summers while his own had been away on raids. 'It's not me you're looking for.'

'Ja, ja, sure,' one of the corpses said. 'You think we don't recognise you from down by the lake? We nearly captured you there.'

They had surrounded him then, too, but there had not been nearly as many of them, and Einer had been able to push one of them into the lake and swim to the other shore.

'That was me,' Einer admitted. He had never been a very good liar. 'But I'm not a criminal.'

'You killed Ingmar out by the corpse road,' one of them accused, an older man with a dishevelled beard in dire need of trimming.

'I didn't kill any corpses.'

The corpse with the wild beard walked out of the crowd, closer to Einer. 'You punched my friend, Ingmar, in the face,' he said, and he looked like he wanted to do the same to Einer. 'And now Ingmar is dead.'

He *had* punched a corpse in the face in the first town he had escaped from, but he had never meant to kill the man. He had been forced to defend himself to get away with his life intact. If what this man said was true, then there was no way that he could talk himself out of trouble. And yet, he had to try, for it was his only hope.

'I'm not who you say I am,' Einer maintained. He looked the old man straight in the eyes. 'My fingernails are short. See?'

'You cut them,' the old man correctly reasoned before he even glanced down at Einer's nails. 'They're not cut neatly like a corpse honoured in life.'

'Do I look dead to you?'

The old man laughed, but then their eyes met again, and the old man took him in, truly. Einer's skin that wasn't pale like theirs, no visible veins or darkened eyes. No signs of rot or decay.

'You've just got southern blood in you,' the old man decided. 'That's why your skin is darker. Don't listen to him,' the old corpse warned the others. 'He will say anything to go free.' He backed away from Einer. 'Where is Osvald?' he asked over his shoulder in an annoyed tone.

'He's coming,' someone volunteered.

Einer made a run for it. While the corpses were looking over their shoulders to find Osvald, he raced towards them and tried to force through. He punched and kicked, but the crowd was too thick. Einer was thrown back into the middle of the circle.

The angry mob turned on him. He did not stand a chance of escaping this time, and they did not want to listen to him. His only hope was that once they had tied him up, he might make his escape, then. Or that perhaps Loki would finally come to free him.

'Tie him up,' the bearded elder ordered.

Einer turned around himself. The corpses were advancing towards him, and there was murder in their eyes. There were too many for him to overcome unless he fought to kill, but even if he did, there was no guarantee that he would escape the town alive.

Dozens of hands were on him; Einer tried to shoulder and kick them away, but there were too many of them. They tied him up, hands behind his back, and rope around his legs, and then someone undid his weapon belt clasp. Einer felt bare without the weight of the swords at his hips.

'Where did you steal these?' asked the old man, holding up Einer's weapon belt to examine the swords.

'They're mine,' Einer said. 'I didn't steal them. I'm not a criminal.'

'We'll give them to Sigismund,' the old man decided, and handed Einer's precious weapon belt and swords off to a corpse in the crowd.

'Sigismund?' Einer asked, hopeful all of a sudden. 'Sigismund Karson? I know him.'

'Everyone knows Sigismund,' the old corpse dismissed with a laugh.

'In life, I knew him in life,' Einer desperately said. If only they would take him to Sigismund, all would be well.

'Ja, ja,' the old man dismissed, and he was laughing again. 'You truly will say anything.'

'Are you taking me to Sigismund?' All his troubles seemed lifted. Even if they did not bring him directly to Sigismund, Sigismund would know that he was there and soon enough Einer would be freed. Because, if nothing else, his father's Ulfberht sword would make its way to Sigismund, and he knew whose sword that was. Sigismund had attached the pommel and guard himself.

'We're taking you to Hel,' one said. That was good too. Hel was Loki's daughter. She would help Einer as the Midgard Worm had.

'To Hel?' the old corpse in charge questioned, raising his eyebrows high at the last who had spoken. 'Will *you* bring him up to Rain-soaked? How are you going to get him there? The horse won't go, so are you going to carry him?'

The corpse had no answer to that, and no one else did either.

'I can walk,' Einer volunteered.

The old man scoffed at the suggestion. 'Will someone bind his tongue?'

Before Einer could protest and say that there was no need, a long piece of cloth was forced into his mouth and bound at the back of his head.

A horse was coming up the road with a carriage at the back, led by the corpse called Osvald. Einer was lifted and loaded into the back and his ropes were checked again and again, and he was tied to both sides of the carriage so that he could not wriggle himself off the edge.

The old man with the wild beard stared down at Einer with hatred in his eyes. 'We're delivering you where you belong,' he told Einer. 'We're taking you back to Corpse-shore, so we can watch your perfect skin be etched away by the venom.'

HILDA

Chapter One Hundred and Fifty-Two

THE WIND WAS eager with visions and whispers.

'Fenrir, Fenrir,' Hilda whispered into the wind, and the visions obliged.

A young wolf howled eagerly. 'Can you break the chain?' someone asked. *'I can break anything,' growled the wolf.* Hilda searched through the vision to sharpen it. She was becoming better at it, each time she tried. *A wolf led the way. Tail up. Shining gods followed. They travelled through the dark forest. Yggdrasil stretched above them.*

The breeze passed, and with it the vision. Hilda blinked herself back to see Asgard unfold before her. Yggdrasil branched above her. In the eternal shadow of its bare branches, she would need to travel to find Fenrir. Her visions showed the way. Hilda needed no other guide.

The edge of the night-clinging forest was nearby. The air was cooler the closer she walked, and the forest thicker. The nornir had told Hilda of that eternal shade. They had told her all about Yggdrasil and where its roots and shade stretched across Asgard.

Hilda knew the dangers that lay ahead. She knew how the svartalvar hiding in the forest would bring out her worst fears and feed on them, though she couldn't guess what she might see. She had done so much and the Alfather was ready to honour her with the highest seat in his hall. She had no fears, Hilda told herself. But with every step closer to Yggdrasil's eternal shade, she doubted those words more.

Fenrir was so big. Even in the visions, where he was only a young wolf; he must have grown since then. But fighting the big wolf did not frighten Hilda as maybe it ought to do. Pain didn't frighten Hilda; death didn't scare her. She had died, she had been killed, she had been hurt and she had been stabbed in the back. Such things didn't scare her, but maybe, deep down, something else did.

Another breeze swished through the trees, pushed snow off high branches, and lifted Hilda's hair from her shoulders. Hilda focused on Fenrir, and the time he had been so eager to show his worth. Before the gods had shackled him.

A god in mail steered ahead. Tyr, war-clad and with both of his hands. The young wolf whimpered and growled, but followed. Gods cast runes off into the dark, warding themselves against svartalvar.

Through the vision Hilda searched for the path to take through the dark forest.

The darkness of the forest hung close. No stars above. No sunlight. 'Follow the sounds of the stream to the lake,' Tyr reminded them. Water rippled nearby. The wolf no longer howled.

Hilda blinked herself back to the present. Visions were difficult to shake off. The border between present, past and future became all fuzzy and blurred in visions.

At least she knew how to find the path through the dark. There was a river in Yggdrasil's eternal shade. If Hilda found it, she could follow it through the terrifying dark, all the way to where Fenrir was tied up.

Her snow fox looked up at her. She nodded to give it permission. It knew what she knew, she could feel it in her heart. They were so closely bonded, the two of them, that no spoken words were necessary.

The snow fox darted into the forest ahead of them. There was no snow in there to light up the dark. The foliage was too thick to let even a single snowflake through. In winter, the nights in Asgard had not felt truly dark, for snow covered the lands and lit up even the nights. But in Yggdrasil's shade there was pure black darkness. It seemed as if darkness swam out of Yggdrasil, where Hilda knew it resided. Within the great ash-tree, she had seen the black mass of Ginnungagap.

At the edge of the forest Hilda took a deep breath. Assured herself that she had no fears, before following her snow fox into the blackness.

'Kauna,' Hilda said to summon a flame. As ever, the rune of fire was fickle: no flame came. She had mastered many runes but not that one.

Into the complete dark she proceeded, hands in front of her, one slow step at a time. Before long, she had walked so far that even when she looked over her shoulder, she saw no light at all.

Her ears were sharp, listening for the sound of water. She heard her snow fox's soft steps, and the creak of wood, but no water. The forest seemed to wrap around her. Whispers danced by her ears, but not in the wind. There was no breeze in this, the tightest forest in the nine worlds. There was no light and no breeze, only darkness and fears. Although Hilda had none. No fears, she kept repeating over and over in her mind, calling on the runes and her own resolve to make the statement true.

She had to believe it to be true. For she was alone in the forest. It could swallow her whole and no one would ever know. No one would miss her. No one knew who she was. No one had memories of her. Even the nornir, whom she had spent three winters with, didn't know her. When they looked to the past, they saw nothing. They did not know who Hilda was.

A shiver travelled through her at the thought. She was all alone in the nine worlds. The dark woods enrobed her and hid her, but even when she stood in direct sunlight, she was hidden. She had no place in the nine worlds, nowhere to call home.

'Eihwaz, eihwaz,' Hilda chanted. The svartalvar were conjuring fears she shouldn't have.

She wasn't scared to be alone. It was calming to travel alone, Hilda told herself. She had travelled alone for so long in Midgard. Through Jutland, into the dwarf forge and across southern lands to reach the raiders. It was nice to travel alone; and besides, Hilda wasn't truly alone.

There was always her snow fox. Although she could not see or hear it anymore in the depths of the forest. There were the Runes too, whispering in the wind, although here, the forest was so tight that no wind blew.

She needed their whispers. They couldn't abandon her now. The wind was always silent when she most needed its whispers.

'Find the water, find the water,' Hilda said aloud, and tried to focus just on her hearing and not her thoughts. But the dark made it difficult not to think, and even harder to keep moving into it.

There could be a cliff right in front of her, and she wouldn't know. Hilda wasn't afraid of death, but as the fears crept up, she realised that she was afraid of *something*. Of being forgotten, as she already was. Of being no one, as she already was. Most of all, though, she was scared of not belonging.

Always was that nagging voice. Not the ones in the wind, but a voice inside that told her that she didn't belong. That she wasn't home.

She missed Ash-hill, and her father, and her uncle and aunt, and little Tyra whom she had taught to fight with a seax and shield; but more than anything, she missed Einer. She missed having a friend.

Alone, she would die here, her fears told her. In this forest, known to none, and forgotten by all.

Hilda wandered aimlessly ahead. Forced herself to push on, aided by her knowledge of the runes, alone in all the nine worlds. Even her own destiny did not know her. Even the nine worlds had let her go.

'Eihwaz.' Hilda chanted the rune of defence strong in her mind, to guard herself against the dark thoughts. 'Eihwaz.' Then, right then, as she said the word again, she heard water ripple over rock. A faint sound, but in the silent gloom, where there was only the occasional snap of a branch or the creak of trees, she didn't know how she had missed it.

"Follow the sounds of the stream," Tyr had said, and so she did, as once young Fenrir had.

Her fears crumbled away as she focused on the sound of the river and rushed towards it. Her control of the runes protected her from the fears creeping out of the shadows. The hair on her arms stood up and her skin was coated in gooseflesh. Still she chanted the runes she knew could help, over and over, and focused on that sound of running water.

It was much more than just a stream, like it had sounded in her vision. It seemed like a raging river. Hilda stumbled towards it, until her feet splashed into ice cold water. She took a step back.

The stream was loud. The water was so very cold. Ice, almost, although it moved too fast and steadily to form an icy crust at the top. The winter had been long in Asgard, but when Hilda had started walking towards Yggdrasil, sunshine had peeked through the snow-clouds. There were no mountains nearby, but there was Yggdrasil.

The river had to have been formed by snow melting off Yggdrasil, running down the bark and through the forest. The winter had been long. The layer of snow was thick and hard. The river was wilder for it.

Hilda crouched down and touched the river with a bare hand. The water was icy, but she kept her hand in long enough to be certain which way it was flowing, despite the fear and doubt in her heart.

Downstream she followed the river. Through the dark it would take her, all the way to the lake the gods called Lake Pitch-black. Out onto that lake they had sailed with young Fenrir. Out there, on the island Lyngvi, he was tied with the strongest chain in the nine worlds.

Refusing to listen to any sound other than that of the river and her own chanting of runes, Hilda rushed ahead. She accompanied the river endlessly downstream, stopping frequently to check she was still headed the right way. Her fears kept her questioning herself, despite her grasp on the runes.

For so long she travelled that she forgot why she was there. Habit forced her to keep going. Still she walked on, until at last the fear retreated and something else took its place.

Hilda laid eyes on tree-roots, and on the trunks around her, and the ground itself. She was out of Yggdrasil's eternal shadow, though the great ash-tree still stretched above her. Up there, through Yggdrasil's branches, she saw stars and a sliver of the moon. She was out of the shadows, and as if to reward her for her success, a fierce wind swept towards her, loud with whispers and visions.

The gods rowed onto the lake. Lake Pitch-black was bathed in shadows and as dark as its name. The weight of the wolf made the row-boat sway.

Hilda tried to look around in her vision, but there was not much to see. No directions to follow. Onwards she searched, scouring through visions of the past.

'I can break any chain,' announced the wolf. Its sharp fur bristled with pride. Its paws were clasped in heather, resting on a thick, broken chain. 'Any chain?' asked the Alfather. His single eye was fixed on the wolf. 'How about this?' In Tyr's hands lay a chain much greater than the first. Much thicker. Much stronger. 'Any chain,' Fenrir declared.

Hilda shook herself out of visions. It took a moment for her to see anything again. Though she was out of the eternal shade of Yggdrasil, it was night. Only the slim moonlight that escaped through Yggdrasil's thinning branches overhead showed the way.

It was easier to follow the large river now that she could see the ripple of its current. The glittering reflection of the slivered moon on the moving water kept her company. Before long, though, she was greeted by the perfect, unmoving reflection of the moon on the still waters of a frozen lake.

The river spilled out into Lake Pitch-black, where ice had frozen across the surface. Hilda followed the edge of the lake far enough away from the river to see the ice thicken. She crouched down and knocked against it, as if she were knocking on a door. The ice was solid, but if she walked out on it, in this night, it would be difficult to know if it was thick enough to carry her.

She couldn't wait until sunrise and risk the sun melting the ice.

'Show me the way,' she whispered to the wind, inviting its visions.

Two large chains lay broken in the heather by Fenrir's paws. Twice the wolf had broken his chains. Twice he succeeded, but the gods were ever eager. Forth now they brought a chain so fine it hardly deserved the name.

Hilda recognised the delicate look of it. She had seen it before. She had held it. She had bound her own fylgja with a chain like that, an act that ought to be as impossible as the chain itself. A chain made from impossible things: from the sound of a cat's paw fall, from the spittle of a bird, the sinew of a bear, the beard of a woman, the breath of a fish, and the roots of a mountain.

Often Hilda's father had told the story of Fenrir's bragging, and the ribbon-slender chain that bound him until Ragnarok. Hilda grabbed the light chain that she had twisted around her belt, no longer binding her fylgja, and let the wind flood her with visions.

The young wolf stared at Thor's wild eyes and knew. 'It looks no thicker than cloth,' Fenrir declared. 'There is no challenge in breaking such a chain.'

*The gods approached to bind the wolf to his lonely destiny.
'Then show us,' they demanded.*

*'There is no honour in it,' the wolf said. Fenrir backed away,
but his refusal was refused.*

*'Just try,' said the one-eyed god. 'I bet you can't break this
one.'*

Hilda struggled to force herself to see beyond the wolf and
the gods. The task was difficult and all she saw was the heather
on the ground and the blue sky above.

'I want no trickery,' said the wolf.

'No trickery,' the gods repeated.

'I need assurance,' said the wolf.

'What assurance?' asked they.

'A hand to bite down on.'

*The gods' leather-clad shoes hesitated on the lilac heather,
but the warrior never hesitated. Tyr stepped forward, unafraid
of suffering. Unafraid of pain. He offered his hand, willingly.
'There is no trickery,' he lied.*

*The wolf's dagger teeth clenched over the war god's hand.
'Then bind me with the ribbon.'*

The wind howled past Hilda. Her vision settled back on Lake
Pitch-black. There was no way for her to know exactly where
to head, but she would need to go far from the coast to find
the island where Fenrir was trapped. There was only one thing
to do.

Hilda stepped onto the ice. It crunched threateningly under
her weight. She couldn't see how thick the ice was and she
didn't fully know where she was going, yet she didn't hesitate.

She knelt onto the squeaky ice, and on all fours crawled forth.
She had to reach the island, wherever it was on that lake. And
if she couldn't row, and if she couldn't swim there, she would
have to crawl.

The night breeze was loud with whispers. Visions of Fenrir
flooded Hilda's mind, but now that she had seen his past, they
were all the same. *The wolf howls. The wolf howls,* was all

the wind whispered to her, and all the visions showed. A wolf bound alone, endlessly howling for the death of gods. She saw only the blue sky. Yggdrasil's branches too, and an island surrounded by an endless lake. She would have to crawl far to reach Fenrir, but he was somewhere out there, on the lake.

Through the night she crawled, strengthened by the whispers and visions of the wind. Morning came and the sun beamed over her. Her knees were wet with melting ice, yet Hilda persisted, and then, far out on the iced lake, she saw the dot of land. The heather island, Lyngvi.

A wolf howled. So deep and dark was the sound that it seemed to swallow the sun. Although she no longer travelled in night and the eternal shade of Yggdrasil, a shiver shot through Hilda, and fear shook her. Fenrir. She had found the great wolf, and Fenrir was still angry.

THORA

Chapter One Hundred and Fifty-Three

THE DAGGER WAS bleeding over Thora's palms. Tyra's dagger was always bleeding, like only something from another world might. Outside, the Winter Night celebrations were loud. With all the lights that were lit in the evening, Winter Night were Thora's favourite celebrations, although they hurt the most too, for that was when the memories came of a Winter Night spent slaughtering southerners in Magadoborg.

That had been the first winter she had fought for her family, not for a glorious afterlife, and she had never stopped fighting for them since. Especially not after Halfdan had been born.

Thora stroked a finger across the bloody edge of the dagger. Tyra hadn't come on this Winter Night, as they had agreed, and in a way that was good, for Thora still had not been given a chance to deliver the dagger to Svend Haraldson, as she had promised to do.

The door to Thora's house swung open. In came Ida, running straight into Thora's arms, and then her father, Halfdan, chuckling at the sight of them. Thora put the bleeding dagger away in her weapon belt and lifted Ida to her lap.

'Ready to go?' Halfdan asked. 'Ida picked you a good spot.'

'The best,' Ida bragged. 'And I plucked flowers for you too.' She handed Thora a handful of weeds that she had hidden behind her back.

'Takka, Ida,' Thora said and kissed the top of her head. 'They're beautiful.'

Someone screamed outside. A loud crash echoed in through the open door. Not the sounds of a feast. Halfdan and Thora exchanged a concerned look.

'Ida, stay here with Grandma,' Halfdan instructed and then he headed out again, closing the door behind him.

Someone squealed indistinctly.

Thora hugged Ida and asked her all about what she had been up to before the evening's feast and if she was looking forward to dancing and going to sleep really, really late. Outside, the yells were getting louder.

'Do you smell that?' Thora asked and took a sniff. She smelled smoke, and Ida smelled it too. It wasn't the kind of smoke that rose from a normal oak fire, like the ones they lit for Winter Night. It smelled like a funeral. Roasting skin, and reeds too.

Frey's-fiord was being attacked.

With a patient breath, Thora focused herself and set Ida down on the floor. Thora had raided enough towns to know how it went. If they could smell smoke, and so soon after the screams had started, then the attackers were already here. There would be no defence to mount. Undoubtedly, the attackers, whoever they were, were setting fire to the thatched roofs, to let them all burn. Thora's house had a thatched roof. The screams had come from the direction of the feast, and if attackers were moving out in groups, it wouldn't take long before Thora's roof was set aflame. And then, afterwards, the attackers would come to finish the task and kill any survivors.

Little Ida was looking up at her for answers.

Thora raced through the possibilities. They couldn't stay here. Before long, her roof would be burning. The feast hall didn't have a thatched roof, but that wasn't safe. The shipbuilders' shed didn't have a thatched roof either, and it was worthless; likely, the attackers wouldn't even bother trying to set it aflame. They would check the shed for survivors, but it was their best chance.

'Ida,' Thora said in a calm voice and with a smile so as not to alarm the little girl. 'We are going to play a game of hiding.'

'I don't want to play,' Ida said, much too loud. Her eyes were wide, like those of a horse at an offering. She was scared, and she couldn't afford to be. Not now, when they were already under attack.

Thora glanced to the closed door and spoke calmly and quietly. 'You don't have a choice. Sometimes we have to do things we don't want to, right?'

'Like chores?'

'Like chores,' Thora agreed. 'Now, it's not going to be much fun to hide in here, so we need to sneak around back to the work shed.'

'What about the naust?' Ida asked.

The children all loved to hide inside the ships in the naust, but Thora knew how raids went. The ships would not only be checked, but likely taken. They couldn't risk it.

'The work shed is better,' Thora insisted. 'No one ever thinks to look in there.'

Ida nodded enthusiastically like she agreed with that. 'Who are we hiding from?' she asked.

'Everyone,' said Thora. 'Your father, your mother, me, and you are together. We're hiding from everyone else.'

'It's a family game?' asked Ida. She was beginning to like the idea of it, so Thora confirmed with a warm smile as she gave instructions.

'You're a lot faster than me,' Thora said, and Ida giggled at that. 'So, you need to run first, and you close the door and hide really well. I will come there. You only come out when you hear *me* say your name, ja?'

Again, Ida nodded, and she was about to head off to the work shed, but Thora managed to grab the skirt of her yellow dress, just in time.

Thora drew the bleeding dagger Tyra had given her out of her weapon belt. She had no other weapons on hand. Her axe and swords and tools were all at Halfdan's house. Thora placed the bleeding dagger into Ida's reluctant hand.

'If anyone comes for you, and they see you, you stab them with this. In the foot, or in the crotch. And then you run. And you take the knife with you.'

'Why is it bleeding?' Ida asked.

'It's a very important dagger,' Thora said. 'It's very powerful, so it will protect you. But it's not mine. I need to deliver it to Svend Haraldson of Denmark. It's from his sister.' She made sure to speak slowly and clearly so that Ida would hear it and remember. The dagger needed to be delivered. Thora knew it in her heart, and if she could not do it herself, she had to ensure that someone else would, once Ida escaped. Ida *would* escape. She had to.

'Can you repeat that for me?' Thora asked to make certain she had been heard and understood. Ida was a smart girl, but she was still so young.

Ida's attention had drifted. She was gaping at something behind Thora.

Thora glanced over her shoulder. The door was still closed, but smoke was dragging in, and flames were spreading. The roof was burning.

'Ida. Ida, look at me.' The little girl's sight finally settled back on Thora. 'I need to hear you say it,' Thora insisted. 'Whose dagger is this?' The little girl shook her head, so Thora told her again, calmly, and asked the same question. 'Whose dagger is it?'

'Svend.'

'Son of...?'

'Harald.'

'And who is it from?'

'From his sister.'

'Good. Now, where do you need to go?'

'The work shed.'

'And what do you do when you get there?'

Again, Ida was gaping up at the burning ceiling. The fire was spreading fast. Thora saw it at the corner of her eyes, but made sure not to show any signs of fear although her heart was speeding.

'What do you do when you get there?' Thora repeated without raising her voice.

'Hide,' said Ida.

'And do you come out when you hear someone yell your name?'

'Ja!'

'Nej. You only come out when you hear *me* say your name. Or your father, or your mother.'

Ida nodded. Her eyes were still fixed on the fires that spread quickly above them. The smoke was getting thick, and Thora wanted to cough, but she held it in. She pushed a lock of blonde hair behind Ida's left ear. 'Thank you for the flowers, Ida,' she took the time to say. 'Now off with you. Back door.'

Ida hesitated to leave, but Thora planted her nose in the weeds Ida had picked for her, smelled them and smiled patiently at Ida. 'I'll be right there,' she assured the little girl.

At that Ida spun away and darted off, her blonde curly locks bumping against her shoulders. The door slammed shut behind her. Immediately, Thora secured the flowers Ida had given her in her belt and began to cough. She brought a hand up to cover her mouth.

Her house was small, so she could more easily get around, but with the smoke filling the room, and the roof in flames above her, it seemed much too large. Thora reached for her crutches and lifted herself up from her chair. Fire raged above her. Flaming bundles of straw were blowing down.

There were still yells from outside, and squeals, and Halfdan was out there, at the front, where the fire had been set. Thora stared at the front door. There were flames all around, but even on crutches she could make it there. She had promised Ida to get to the shed, however, and she could not leave Ida alone, not in this chaos.

Leaning on her crutches, with only her left leg capable of providing some support, Thora set out towards the back door. Her house was falling apart at her back, but she didn't halt to look at her belongings burning. Only Halfdan and Ida mattered.

Cautiously she opened the back door and peered outside. No one on the back street. Thora made her escape from the burning house and closed the door behind her to give the attackers no clues as to her and Ida's escape.

Down the narrow road, she went. Four houses down was the work shed. Thora went fast, but the back road wasn't laid with wood, and she needed a good hold for her crutches to carry her weight. Yells were ringing around town and the smoke was thick.

Thora heard the slap of heavy footsteps behind her.

A warrior raged down the slim road, long axe brandished.

Thora sped up as much as she dared, passing the work shed down the road and to the left. To lead the warrior off course. Around the corner, Thora thrust herself to the ground, still holding onto her crutches. She crashed against the side of a house and knocked onto the hard ground. Thora lifted her right crutch and prepared her swing.

The man with the axe came around the corner, and Thora knocked him hard in the head with her crutch. The wood splintered, but the man didn't go down. He raised the axe. Thora thrust her splintered crutch at his neck. The axe fell out of his grip and he fell backwards, her crutch stuck through his bleeding neck.

Supported by the wall at her back, Thora pulled herself up. She felt like a berserker again, on this Winter Night. Invincible in her rage. The blood coursed through her. Her breaths were loud. She calmed her racing heart.

Anyone who found the dead attacker would assume that any survivors had gone in the direction of the naust. Thora hoped that none had.

A hand on the house wall, she picked up the attacker's axe. She tested its weight and used its long shaft to hold her weight. With the axe serving as a missing crutch, she made her way around the corner of the house, across the road and two houses up until she reached the work shed.

Quickly she entered, closing the door behind her. The shed was dark. No Winter Night lights shone inside, but her eyes adjusted fast, and she could see Ida's blonde locks of hair moving behind the toolboxes to the right.

'I'm here, Ida,' she said. 'You can come out.'

The little girl came rushing out and hugged Thora tight. She was sobbing and crying. Thora rubbed Ida's small shoulders and shushed her to silence.

'It'll be alright, Ida, but we're not finished.'

The shed was small, but it was packed. Shelves full of things that went all the way to the tall roof. On the top shelf there was barely anything, just some old ropes and the broken boat tarpaulin from last season. It looked so sparse. No one would think to look up there.

Thora stared up at the tall shelf and knew she couldn't make that climb. Her arms were strong and could carry her full weight, but her legs couldn't. Only her left leg could even act as a support, and she wouldn't be able to reach from shelf to shelf using only her arms. Besides, the top shelf wouldn't take both her and Ida's weights. The broken tarpaulin wouldn't cover them both, either.

'We're not finished yet, Ida,' Thora said, and she wanted to kneel down and hug Ida tight, but her legs wouldn't allow. She settled for ruffling the girl's hair and giving a reassuring smile. 'You have to climb up to that top shelf, all the way up there,' she said and pointed. 'And hide up there.'

'But Dad said…'

'I know you're a good climber,' Thora interrupted. 'I won't tell him. You won't get in trouble, but only if you stay really quiet up there.'

She could see the fear in Ida's eyes, and Thora too was scared, but they needed to act quickly. She had already killed one warrior on the slim back street. It wouldn't take long for more to follow.

Thora removed her belt. The flowers Ida had picked for her fell to the floor. She strapped the belt around Ida and took the bleeding dagger out of the girl's hands to place it into the belt. At last, she swept up the flowers to show Ida that all was well.

The girl turned towards the tall shelf, and readied for the climb, but all was not well.

'Ida, come here.' Thora leaned down and kissed Ida on the forehead. 'I love you. I will always love you.' She kissed the top of her head, once and twice, and three times, and hugged Ida tight, and then she let go, knowing that it would likely be for the last time.

'I need you to climb up, now. And hide really well.' She managed to get the words out without her voice breaking.

At her instructions, Ida began to climb. Thora stood beneath her, leaning on one crutch, the axe at her feet, ready to catch her should she fall, but Ida was a good climber. She reached all the way to the top and rummaged around to hide.

Thora glanced around the shed. She would have to hide herself elsewhere, and hope that no one came inside.

Ida stopped moving on her shelf.

'That's good,' Thora praised, although she could still see Ida's feet. 'Pull those ropes on top of you and cover your feet with the boat tarpaulin.'

Ida did exactly as she was asked. She had always been a sweet kid. She was completely hidden from down here, and no one would climb that high up. There was nothing of value on the top few shelves. All it looked like was a holed tarpaulin and a ragged rope, which was all it had been a moment earlier.

'Be quiet. No matter what you hear, Ida. Don't peek,' Thora reminded her as she hopped across to the other shelf where they kept the tools. The axe was too long to fight with inside the shed, and Thora wouldn't go down without fighting. She was a warrior before anything else.

'You stay up there until your father comes to get you, or until morning. Until you don't hear anyone, and then you run straight to Gertrud's farm. Remember what you do if anyone else sees you. Foot. Crotch.'

Ida didn't answer, and that was good. She understood that the game had already begun.

Thora picked out a large hammer that she could swing with one arm. She wasn't going to get the proper swing she needed on her crutches. She hobbled to the door and slid down to sit next to it. There was nowhere else for her to hide.

She leaned her crutches and the axe next to her, so she could reach them both, and so they weren't as glaringly obvious.

Squeals and screams echoed around in the valley outside. Smoke entered through the gaps under the door. Everything smelled of burning flesh, but Thora had been right. The attackers hadn't yet come to burn the work shed. The roof above her did not burst into flames as her home had, and the screams were far enough away for Thora to hope that they would be forgotten, Ida and her.

She heard no steps outside on the back road, and she began to wonder if they should try to run, but neither of them was fast enough to get far. There were only two ways in and out of the valley, which didn't involve the mountains Thora was unable to traverse, and the attackers would certainly have posted guards on both roads. There was the inlet too, but the boats and ships were on land and would have to be pushed out to water, and Thora didn't think the naust would be safe either.

Even if they could have run, there was nowhere to run to. They would never make it out of Frey's-fiord. It was better to stay put and hope no one would come.

She heard voices outside. Urgent, but loud enough that Thora knew they belonged to raiders and not villagers. Thora clenched onto the hammer in her hands. To protect Ida, no matter what, that was her duty. No matter what.

Steps came closer. Doors were slammed open and there were screams and yells, and then the steps came closer, again.

Thora took short rapid breaths to calm herself. She remembered how once, on a Winter Night so long ago, she had sat with her back against a wall, chewing on berserker caps and waiting for the right moment to attack. She tried to remember the feeling of the caps influencing her mind. How everything had slowed, and nothing had seemed a threat.

The steps stopped outside the shed. Thora took a deep breath and raised the hammer.

The door swung open, and a man came inside. His leather shoes thumped down right in front of her. He would see her. If only he looked to the side.

Thora slammed her hammer over his toes. The man howled as Thora swung the hammer again. This time, she aimed for his crotch. Breathless, he buckled over himself, so she gave him a good slam on the helmet, which sent him straight to the ground.

Two others were at his back, and they were alert now. Thora got a good hammer stroke into the first one's thigh, narrowly missing his crotch. She prepared her next swing, but the second man was on her before she could put in her full force.

She ducked away from his axe, trying to wriggle to the side as she prepared another hammer blow, but she was on the ground with no way out, and it was only a matter of time. Thora cast her hammer at the first man as if she were Thor, and then she reached for the long axe at her side.

She swung the axe at them, cutting across their shins so their trousers were bloodied, but nowhere deep enough. The men stumbled back and out of her reach and Thora pointed the long axe at them.

They observed her, just out of her grasp. They hadn't expected to be attacked like that, and Thora was far from done. They were dressed like those guards who had followed Tyra out of the marketplace some moons ago: King Olaf's men.

'Don't be scared,' one of them said to the other and pointed to Thora's crutch. 'She's a cripple.'

Thora readied her grip on the axe. They would most definitely underestimate her if that was all they thought of her.

One of the two crouched to pick up the hammer she had thrown at him. Thora aimed her axe to slice him up once he came into her reach, but he didn't. He took aim and threw the hammer, as she had.

The hammer crushed through her right arm, and her bones snapped loudly. She lost hold on the axe. She fiddled after it with her left hand, but the men were on her before she could get a grip.

She was dragged out by the legs. Out onto the street. Her dress slid up at her back.

'Let me go!' Thora squealed. She didn't so much as glance back to the shed where Ida was hiding. She didn't tell the men not to go inside, although she wanted to scream the words. She acted as if her only concern was her own life. 'Let go!'

The second man was still inside the shed.

Thora squealed like she was being skinned alive and tried to wriggle free. If only she could kick. Her left leg was clasped tight and her right flailed helplessly to the side. Thora tried to turn around so she could drag herself away with the force of her upper body, but she couldn't.

The second attacker came out of the shed. 'Just the cripple,' he concluded.

Thora continued to fight for her life as if she hadn't heard. She grunted and tried to wrestle free.

The second man grabbed Thora's right leg and together they dragged her across the hard ground. Stones and rocks scraped at her back and Thora groped with her left hand, trying to find something to hold onto or something to throw, but they were dragging her too fast for her to grasp anything at all.

She was hauled away from the shed. The sound of screams rang loud as they came around the corner. Screams and yells and the roaring sound of fire consuming the town. The men dragged her onto the road at mid-town. Thora grabbed the edge of the wooden road and held on. One of the men let go of her left leg, which knocked hard against the road. The shock went through her body, but Thora held on. The man stepped on her fingers, hard, until she let go, and then the other towed her ahead so she couldn't grab on to anything at all, although she tried.

She didn't stop trying, never. Not as they hauled her down the road. Not as they dragged her past a bloody corpse, or when they yanked her around the next corner into the square where the Winter Night pyre had been built, but then, the men stopped dragging her, and Thora heard whose screams were the loudest in the square. Her Halfdan was screaming.

One of the men planted a foot at her back. Frantically, Thora tried to move and see her son, to see why he was screaming. How she could help him. Save him. She turned just far enough to see the Winter Night's fire, and there he was, her son. On top of the burning pyre.

He squealed and roared, and tried to fight his way off the pyre, but the men were holding him there at spear point. Burned corpses at his feet. Eight spears were pointed at him, piercing his skin as he struffled for his life.

'Halfdan,' Thora squealed.

Her little boy. She had fought so that this would never happen. Two dozen winters ago, she had taken berserker caps in Magadoborg so her family would be safe. She had sacrificed herself, taken irreparable wounds to her legs, so that Halfdan would never have to. So that he could grow up well and live a long life, and not fear for his family. Yet, there he was, in the end. The sweetest boy, *her* boy, burning on their Winter Night pyre.

His eyes found her as she screamed his name. His wide, searching eyes. He was looking for his daughter and hoping not to see her. Thora gave him a subtle nod. One single nod, that no one but him would notice. His daughter was safe.

Ida was safe.

His eyes stopped searching and his body let go. Thora watched him collapse on top of the flames, his life abandoned. Her boy. He had held out for his daughter, but fire consumed all. Thora roared for her son to wake. 'Halfdan!'

They lifted her. Hands groped her arms so she couldn't get away, and then they threw her onto the pyre. On top of her son's fresh corpse. She rolled off him, to the side. A spear was thrust through her left shoulder and forced her back up. Thora growled in pain and tried to wrestle free, but she couldn't. The spearman forced her onto her son's back.

She tried to push him off, but Halfdan was too big and heavy for her, and the spears were closing in on Thora, and the pyre was too hot. The smoke rose around her so she couldn't see anything but spear points and flames.

She couldn't move him. She couldn't move Halfdan. She let herself fall onto his back and hugged him as tight as she could. Her hands and arms were thrust into the burning embers and Thora screamed from the pain. Her burning skin and the pain in her heart. 'Halfdan.' She pressed herself into his back and wished that it was all a dream. That he would wake and he would be fine. 'Halfdan!' He wasn't moving. There was not even a breath or a heartbeat left. His beautiful face was burned, staring into the embers. He was gone already. Thora coughed from all the smoke around her and tried to stay there. Spear tips pressed into her skin.

Her son was dead. It wasn't his time. He wasn't supposed

to go. Ever. Not before her. Sigismund had died, but *they* had survived. This wasn't why. As Thora's skin melted and the pain made her collapse, only one thought kept her fighting for life:

Ida was still out there, alone.

BUNTRUGG

Chapter One Hundred and Fifty-Four

FIRE MELTED THE ice off Buntrugg's skin. He tried to keep cool with runes, but the fires of Muspelheim were beyond anything Buntrugg had ever felt.

Fires consume, the fire demons hissed. *Fylgjur burn.* They were laughing. Someone was burning short-lived alive, and the fire demons were revelling in the heat of their burning fylgjur.

The danger dawned on Buntrugg. They could leave Muspelheim. Through burning fylgjur, which burned somewhere *between* the worlds, the demons might escape from Muspelheim.

He rushed through the world of fire, knowing not where he should go. Red and blue flamed past Buntrugg. Heat bore into him. Steam rose from his own body. Demons were laughing and chanting. *Fylgjur burn. Fylgjur burn.*

They flickered past him, laughing at their victory.

In Surt's presence, they never would have dared, but it was just Buntrugg now. Flames of all colours raged above and below and all around. Everything in Muspelheim had been burned long ago. Now the flames fed on each other, and on wood burned in the other eight worlds. Everything looked the same to Buntrugg, but somewhere in this world, the demons were gathering in a thick crowd, chanting, hoping to escape their confines through a passage between the worlds, opened by burning fylgjur.

Buntrugg had closed all direct passages between the nine worlds, but there were still ways to travel. Surt had taught him all about it. Some things lived neither in this world nor another. Some things lived between the worlds, like the fylgjur. If fylgjur were burning, perhaps, just maybe, the fire demons could push through them and leave Muspelheim.

'Isa, isa, isa,' Buntrugg chanted as he pressed through the laughing flames. His runes had become stronger during the past three winters, and they kept him from combusting, yet the pain itched through his entire body as he moved further into Muspelheim, towards the most devastating heat in the nine worlds.

Fire demons were gathering, up ahead. Buntrugg's legs were wrapped in such tight flames that he could no longer see his feet. Pain rose all over his body. Buntrugg clenched his teeth tight and persisted. His face began to sting with new burns. The flames grew hotter and fiercer the further he walked, and their voices were overwhelming. *Burn, burn, open, open.*

They were chanting it together. Buntrugg struggled to see through the flames, but suddenly he felt the wind. The rush of fresh air from another world. Demons skipped ahead, towards an opening.

Buntrugg reached out with his Muspel flame to wrap around them and keep them here. He named and conjured all the runes he could think of. Ice and fire, defence and messengers. His runes wrapped around the demons and held them back. The wind gained intensity, and now Buntrugg too could see the opening. The flames, and the woods and houses beyond. Another world, ready to burn.

Demons struggled against Buntrugg and his runes. One, two, three, four, five, six, seven, eight of them slipped out of his grip, laughing.

The passage shut.

Buntrugg panted for breath and cool air. Eight demons had escaped.

Eight demons had travelled through burning fylgjur. Eight demons had left Muspelheim, and from within the world of fire, there was nothing Buntrugg could do about it.

Midgard would have to protect itself.

TYRA

Chapter One Hundred and Fifty-Five

THE WARRIORS WHO had returned from raids in the north were not the same. There was fire behind their eyes. There was more than one fire demon in Midgard now, and Tyra knew that even the one she already knew would be difficult to kill.

Including her husband, there were nine men with flames in their eyes, and burning hands. From the way they looked at her, eyes narrowed and watchful, she knew that they were plotting her death, for only *she* knew what they truly were.

She spent her days plotting too, and making sure she was never alone with any of them.

Inga came in behind Tyra and linked their arms. Tyra laughed in surprise and eyed the men as they passed each other's paths. These days, Tyra always kept company, and it couldn't just be any company either. She had to surround herself with people of influence that even a fire demon knew not to kill. Tyra smiled at Inga, and together they skipped ahead as if they were young, unmarried women, although neither one of them was unmarried and Inga no longer that young.

She was a wicked woman, Inga, with a hand in every pocket in the harbour city. Every day, the two of them ate together in Olaf's hall, and walked arm in arm through marketplaces, and spoke Christian phrases. Tyra had done well to befriend Inga, the wife of the richest jarl in Kaupangen, for when the two of them were together, the fire demons kept at a distance.

King Olaf hated Inga as much as the warriors did, which naturally only made Tyra all the fonder of her wicked friend. The biggest quarrels in Tyra's and Olaf's marriage were about how Tyra never got pregnant and why Inga was always with her. King Olaf was convinced the two facts were connected and that Inga was poisoning Tyra's mind and body with wickedness. Little did he know that she *had* been pregnant, twice now. Both times, Tyra had packed her bags and prepared to leave the household to protect the new-born from the wrath of its father. The second time she had rowed out of the harbour and gotten halfway through the night before she had felt the pain in her stomach. Olaf had been furious that she had left the household at night, and he had made certain she hadn't been able to leave for two whole weeks. It had provided a good excuse for her tears.

Tyra did want children, but the king was not fit to be a father, certainly not with the fire raging behind his eyes.

She eyed the men as she and Inga skipped across the plain of grass towards the edge of Olaf's lands. The rain didn't bother them. They skipped all the happier because of it, and laughed when Inga nearly slipped on mud as they came to a halt under the half-roof by the tool shed.

'Will you come with me?' asked Inga as their laughs died.

'Not today,' answered Tyra and glanced over her shoulder to ensure the fiery warriors had left.

'I've seen the way they look at you,' Inga whispered. 'They won't hurt you, will they?'

Tyra shook her head. But she was not convinced that they wouldn't. Fire demons were capable of terrible things. Her last husband had burned his men's ships to keep them from fleeing battle. 'They're Olaf's men,' said Tyra. 'They have no reason to harm me.'

Inga didn't seem to find that reassuring. She hated Olaf almost as much as he hated her. 'Well, you're always welcome on the farm,' Inga finally said, and gave Tyra's hands a last squeeze. 'Always.'

Inga was about to slip away, but Tyra caught her hand before she did. There was another reason that Tyra kept this particular company. 'Do you have news of my brother?' she asked.

The laughter and smiles were gone from Inga's face. She shook her head. 'No news of Svend, but your old marriage match has been making alliances.'

'Burisleif?' Tyra asked. At their wedding celebrations, he had not seemed like a man with wild ambitions of conquests.

'He has been gathering up every chief and jarl who keeps the old gods, and there are more than you'd think.'

Burisleif would never have thought to do that on his own. This was Svend's work.

'Takka,' Tyra said and let go of Inga's hand. Again, she smiled, and then Inga skipped off into a run. Tyra laughed at her. Inga was fun company. She acted much younger than her age, and sometimes it felt good to play simple games again and not worry about the fate of the nine worlds.

Tyra headed towards her husband's hall. The rain came down hard around her, but Tyra did not run, for when Inga was not around, she comported herself as a dignified queen, whom the people both loved and feared. As Siv had been, once upon a time.

She swung open the door and entered the hall, not rushing but just loud and hurriedly enough to indicate that she had important news.

Olaf was in deep discussion with his back to the door, and to her. He was standing with his commanders, plotting their next move. Perfect.

Urgently, Tyra hung up her wet coat and stepped towards Olaf and his commanders. 'He is coming for me,' she said.

'What?' Olaf swung around to see her, and although they were standing close, she couldn't see the fire in his eyes. Sometimes, she couldn't tell if it was him or the fire demon who spoke. Perhaps it was always him, and the demon merely made his anger flare.

The commanders also glanced up at Tyra, intrigued, but they knew that they were not allowed to address her unless she addressed them first, and she hadn't.

'My brother is gathering a fleet.'

Olaf scoffed when she said it and shook his head to dismiss it. 'He returned to Jelling at the end of winter. He has his eyes on the west, he won't be coming here.'

'Have you not heard?' Tyra asked, waiting for him to ask what she meant before she spoke again. 'Burisleif has been making alliances. Great chiefs and jarls who still hold the old gods dear.'

'You think Burisleif is coming to claim you as his wife?' Olaf was nearly laughing. 'Well, you did leave him on the wedding eve, so he probably thinks he is entitled to one night, at the very least.'

Tyra had half a hundred remarks ready for that, but chose none of them. Burisleif wasn't important, and Olaf had to know that. 'You knew him in his early days, but I knew him in his later ones. He is done with conquests. He is content where he is. He has achieved what he wanted. He isn't gathering alliances for himself. He is doing my brother's bidding, precisely for this reason. So that you will never suspect what is coming.'

She looked past Olaf then, to his advisers, and to her luck, one of them was brave enough to speak. 'Even in his younger years, Burisleif never relied on those kinds of alliances.'

Olaf was still hesitating, but it was not the first time they had spoken of this possibility. For many moons, Tyra had whispered into his ears of her greatest fear. How she thought that one day her brother would come to kill Olaf and sweep her away. She had prepared his mind for this exact day.

'I know my brother. Better than anyone.' She stared into Olaf's eyes and made certain that he could hear what she was saying. 'He was furious when I left. As soon as you leave to go abroad, he will glide in, and stab you in the back.' She said it as if she believed it. She had become skilled at lying.

Svend would never attack first. She had to force it to happen. Bring the war to Svend, and hope and wish that he had received her bloody dagger, and could finish the deed. Tyra had begun her plotting and whispering back when she had only known of one fire demon in Midgard. Just one king with fire in his eyes. Now there were warriors too, standing tall at his side wherever he went. There was no time to waste. They needed to be eradicated.

'What do you think?' Olaf asked of his advisers, turning away from Tyra.

'Maybe our own coasts are more important,' one of them dared to suggest.

'We should secure our own home first,' another agreed.

The remaining five advisers only dared to nod, but their faces must have been convincing enough for Olaf, for after a glance, his mind was made up. 'We can't go abroad when we're threatened at home.'

Tyra let out a relieved sigh.

Olaf pulled her into a hug and whispered sweet words into her ears. 'I will protect you from your brother.' Sometimes, she truly did think that he loved her, and it was a scary thought.

At least she had managed to convince him that Svend was a threat. So, again, she pleaded.

'Svend knows these lands,' she said when she parted from her husband's hug. 'Perhaps not as well as you, but well enough to surprise.'

Olaf combed his fingers through his itchy beard and looked into Tyra's eyes. She did her best to look convincing. He needed one more push.

'You have to strike now, before his forces grow,' Tyra pleaded. And before Olaf's forces grew, she thought to herself. Svend had loyal people at his side. They were trained and they had been through terrible battles together. They were brothers in arms. His people followed him and stood at his side as they would have supported a friend. Olaf ruled as a king, at a distance. His people had no real connection to him. If he attacked now, Svend could win. As long as it was just Olaf, and not the other eight demons too.

'Tyra's right,' Olaf agreed. 'We can't wait for him here. We need to bring the fight to him. So we can choose favourable ground, and catch him by surprise.'

She had nearly succeeded. Olaf had agreed to everything she had whispered about these past few moons. All she needed to do now was convince him not to take his fire warriors with him. Nine fire demons were too many for Svend to kill on his own, even with Tyra's Ragnarok dagger.

If he met all nine demons in battle, Svend would die, and Tyra dared not put his life in danger. He needed to survive, for as long as possible. Siv had told her as much. He could mend the damage, once the fire demons had been eradicated. Svend *had* to survive.

Tyra needed to ensure that only Olaf would go on the raid. If the king died, his loyal warriors would not be honoured or respected. They would lose their influence. Her husband was the biggest threat to Midgard. He needed to be the first to go. Tyra would take care of the others.

'You don't need to worry about that,' said one of Olaf's older advisers, a man who was much respected, although he himself respected no one. 'We have a bit more experience plotting war than you do, my queen.'

Tyra was not so certain that was true—she had fought when only a child, and since then she had plotted more wars and fights than she could count—but all the same, she retreated. She was no longer wanted in the hall, because now they would discuss war, and the presence of a woman was not welcome. Her advice would no longer be heard. So, she gave her husband a thankful kiss and retreated outside into the rain with her coat slung around her.

Tonight, she would ensure that Olaf had heard the advice and would depart without his fire demon followers. She would whisper names to him and pretend that she felt unsafe if he parted with every skilled warrior. She would do what she needed to do so that only Olaf would go. Anything to give Svend the best possible chance.

As long as he had the dagger, he could kill the fire demon and survive the encounter.

She trusted that Thora had delivered the bloody knife, and that Svend knew what to do with it. He *had* to use the knife. She didn't think a normal sword would do. Her last husband had been struck down as dead as any man, but the fire demon had merely jumped into a new body. It wouldn't die from simple iron. But Tyra's bloody dagger had been plucked from the battlefield on Ida's plain, and no one and nothing survived Ragnarok.

The dagger would do its task, Tyra was certain of it. It was said to lead to the worst of days and to disasters. Tyra wasn't sure it had led her to anything at all that was worse than what she'd had to begin with, but perhaps she had already been living the worst of days when she had received it. One thing was certain: the dagger had never brought Siv back to her.

The rain poured over Tyra. Her hood was soaked. Water trickled through her hair and tickled her scalp. At the corner of her eyes, she spotted the fire demon warriors. They were headed for her. The last time they had caught her alone, she had been saved in the last heartbeat when Inga had arrived, but Inga was gone now, and wouldn't be back until tomorrow.

Tyra rushed through the rain and mud towards the cluster of houses at the outskirts of Olaf's lands. She hoped there would be someone there as there often was: jarls and chiefs with drinks in their hands. She heard laughter from the hall and ran a little faster.

High with hope, she swung open the feast hall doors and slipped inside with her muddy shoes on.

There were no people inside. Only five thralls preparing the tables for a feast. Their laughter stopped as soon as they noticed Tyra, and they stopped their work too, eyes at her feet, waiting for instructions.

'What are you preparing for?' asked Tyra as she turned to dry her muddy shoes and stare out into the rain. The men were marching across the muddy fields, straight towards her. They knew no one was here.

Her heart was beating too loud to hear the thralls' answer to her question. There had to be a way to escape. There had to be people, somewhere.

Voices were coming from the back room. Tyra slammed the door shut and rushed out there. The conversation in here, too, died as soon as the first thrall noticed her. There were a dozen thralls, and still no freemen.

It was too far away to make a run for the next house. The fire demon warriors would be here soon, and there was no one to protect her, and nowhere to escape to.

At least it was a crowd. Tyra hoped it would be enough. There had been five of them outside. They wouldn't be able to kill a dozen thralls before someone screamed and it would be difficult to explain.

Tyra walked to the bewildered thralls' worktable where they were chopping meats for that evening, for whatever feast they were preparing for. Her heart was beating so loud.

'The lamb pieces are too big,' said Tyra, although they were exactly as Olaf liked them. Tyra grabbed a large chopping knife and began to halve the cuts.

She heard the thralls protesting in echo-like voices. It was a task beneath her, they said, and that she would ruin her dress. Tyra didn't mind any of it. She needed a weapon.

Not two rapid heartbeats later, she heard the hall door slam open, and the steps of the men entering. The panicked voices of the thralls inside the main hall. The door to the back room swung open behind her.

'Leave me,' said Tyra, without glancing over her shoulder to look. 'I have work to do.'

'This is a thrall's work,' said one. His voice reminded Tyra of embers.

Knife still in hand, eyes narrowed, Tyra turned around to face them. One of them had stopped in the doorway and the other four were at his back: there was no way for Tyra to push through and escape.

'Are you calling me a thrall?' Tyra asked with as much contempt as she could force into her voice.

'Nej,' the man in the doorframe had to admit. 'But there are better ways to spend your days.'

'So you, a simple warrior, intend to dictate how *I*, your queen, spends her time…?'

'I didn't mean…'

'I gave you an order,' said Tyra. 'Leave.'

They didn't. They did not so much as take a step back into the main hall. They stayed in the doorframe, blocking the way out.

'You're not my commander,' said the warrior.

For a while they stood and stared at each other. Fire blazed in his eyes. He was consumed with rage. He would kill her, right then and there, unless she gave him a very good reason not to. There had to be a way. His hand was reaching for his sword. Tyra's heartbeat sped up and her breath came short and panicked.

'You,' said Tyra, pointing blindly to a thrall. 'My husband is in the war quarters. Go and tell him what's happening here.' She tried not to rush her words, but she knew that she had not spoken with her usual calm.

The thrall left the room in a hurry, through the back door that only thralls used. Off she darted into the rain. Someone who had seen Tyra there and the men too, and had heard the words exchanged. A witness.

Again, Tyra addressed her husband's warriors, lifting the chopping knife to remind all five of them that she was armed and that they would not kill her so easily. 'You'll leave now,' she told them and turned her back to them to resume her chopping. 'Or you won't like what my husband decides to do with you.'

The thrall Tyra had sent off was long gone. It was too late. They knew it as well as her. Even fire demons had to recognise that this was not their time. She heard the door close at her back and their steps in the main hall as they left, and let out a ragged breath.

The thralls were silent, looking at their own feet, pretending not to exist at all as Tyra calmed herself.

'Go catch up with her,' Tyra ordered. 'My husband doesn't need to know.'

The thrall she had sent off might have reached Olaf's hall already, but she doubted that she'd dared to enter. It was no easy task for a thrall to interrupt a king.

A man rushed out of the thrall door after her. The others were still crowded around Tyra, staring at their own feet. She was keeping them from their work. She needed to leave. She would go to Inga's farm tonight, Tyra decided. Some time away to calm herself and strengthen her resolve. Olaf was listening to her advice, she told herself. Soon, it would all be over.

Her mind and heart still racing with the fear of dying, Tyra unclasped her firm grasp from the chopping knife and left the hall through the thrall door.

Rain fell hard over Tyra and the lands. She did not speed up to avoid the downpour, but walked straight through it, headed for the outer gates. The two thralls she had sent off were coming towards her. They hurried to the side to clear the path for her.

Although she did not quite know why, Tyra stopped in front of them. Her heart was still racing.

'I know you,' said Tyra and stared into the strangely familiar face of the thrall she had sent off to save herself.

'I work in the fields. I tend to your husband's cattle and sheep, my queen,' said the thrall. With tasks such as those they were unlikely to have met. The thrall did not meet Tyra's gaze.

Tyra shook her head for that was not what she meant. 'I know you from before,' she said. 'You can leave us,' she told the male thrall, and he did.

She ushered the female thrall away from the downpour and into the cover of the half-roof where she and Inga had said their goodbyes earlier in the day. 'I know you,' Tyra repeated, and suddenly she knew exactly who the thrall was.

The thrall girl's nose had a big round tip like Carlman's had once had, and her hair was the same shade of brown—a little brighter than Tyra's own—and her skin darkened from her work outdoors.

'How are you here?' Tyra asked. She remembered Carlman's daughter. She had been a year younger than Tyra. They had used to play together, such a long time ago. 'Unn,' Tyra said, suddenly remembering the girl's name. She had suppressed her memories from Ash-hill for so long. Slowly, they came back to her. 'You look like your father,' Tyra said. 'How are you here?'

At last, Unn dared to glance up and look at Tyra. The thrall's eyes nearly drowned with tears, then, and she sniffed to keep herself from crying. It had been a long time since they had last lain eyes on each other, but they had used to be friends, as much as a free child and a thrall could be. They had talked about their dreams and run through the fields together. Unn had used to bring Tyra her dinner and keep her company during the long boring days of summer when the warriors were away.

'After Ash-hill bur...' Unn took a deep sigh and tried again. 'We went to Frey's-fiord. All the children and the thralls. We stayed there over winter. It was a good place, but they couldn't afford to keep us. We were sold at the market. I've served many places. King Olaf's trader purchased me last summer.'

Her voice shook as she spoke. 'How are *you* here?' she dared to ask, although no thrall ought to speak first in the presence of a freeman.

'I'm still fighting for Ash-hill,' was all Tyra said, and her heart ached when she looked at Unn's face. She looked so much like her father. Tyra remembered watching him burn on Ragnar's pyre so long ago. Carlman had been a good thrall.

'My parents wanted to free you that summer,' Tyra told Unn. 'For your father's sacrifice.'

'I used to dream about being freed,' Unn said bitterly and looked out over the raining plains.

'Like you used to dream you were a cow.' Tyra smiled at the old memory.

Nervously Unn laughed and nodded.

'Want to?' Tyra asked, serious now. 'Be free?' She pulled up the sleeve of her gown. She had enough gold and silver jewellery to feed a dragon's greed, but she did not wear much. The weight of jewellery had been known to slow greedy men in battle and been their undoing; she would not allow the weight of her own riches to do the same. All Tyra ever wore were her beads, the brooches that held up her outer dress, and a gold arm-ring. She forced the gold ring off her wrist and held it out to Unn. They both knew how much it was worth.

Wide-eyed, Unn stared at the arm-ring, but she didn't take it. She took a step away and shook her head. 'I can't.' She glanced up at Tyra's face as though afraid she'd be angry. 'I'm not smart enough to make my own fortune,' she explained and as if enchanted, shaking her head repeatedly as she stared at the gold arm-ring. 'My father used to say that's why I have a master to care for me. So I wouldn't have to build my own house, and make my own fortune, and farm land or treat sick pigs.' Unn must have thought about this often, what it would be like to be free. And now that Tyra thought about it too, she could see that Unn was right. A freed thrall was just a freeman without a home, or any land, or even cattle. Tyra had always had family and a house to sleep in and rations in winter and warm clothes. She had never had to think about those things before.

Not knowing what else she could do, Tyra continued to hold the arm-ring out to Unn. But the thrall just shook her head. 'Soon it won't be safe here anymore,' Tyra said. 'You should go.'

'It has never been safe here,' Unn said, and she was right. Even for Tyra it had never been safe. She couldn't even imagine the peril of being a thrall in King Olaf's household.

The rain poured so hard that it blurred everything around them. No one would see them standing there under the half-roof, and so, at last, Unn dared to look up at Tyra again, and match her stare. 'I am glad you are alive.' Her voice broke and she hurried to look away again, for a thrall should never stare.

'You might be a thrall, Unn, but you have a fine blood lineage too,' Tyra praised. 'Carlman was your father, and few thralls are as good as Carlman was.'

She put her gold arm-ring back on and placed a reassuring hand on Unn's shoulder.

'I have a favour to ask,' Tyra said. For the first time in many winters, she had hope. 'When I lie on the pyre...'

Unn attempted to cut in, to protest that would be a long time ahead, but Tyra knew what would happen. She had planned everything so well. She knew that she couldn't win against nine fire demons in a world such as this.

'When I lie on the pyre,' Tyra continued, 'sing me to Helheim.'

If no one sang for her, she would never find her way into the afterlife. Certainly not if they doomed her to a Christian burial, which they would. The fire demons knew what they were doing. They couldn't risk allowing someone with Tyra's knowledge to cross into another world, for fear that she would warn the gods, and beg them to save Midgard from the clutches of fire—and she would.

It was no play of chance that both her first husband, possessed by a demon, and her second, similarly afflicted, had turned increasingly eager to eradicate all of Odin's followers, hailing them as enemies of Christianity. The new belief gave justification to purge Odin from these lands. It was no play of chance that the passage graves were being closed all over the north. If the fire demons could expel Odin from Midgard, and close the passages between the worlds, they could have Midgard to themselves. A whole new world to burn to the ground.

Tyra wouldn't let them.

For it was also no play of chance that she had found Thora in a busy marketplace last summer, and a familiar face among thralls she never looked at. The gods were on Tyra's side, and she *would* obey their wishes. The fire demons would not succeed.

No sacrifice was too great to save Midgard, even her own life.

SIV

Chapter One Hundred and Fifty-Six

SOME DIMWIT HAD collapsed the most well-travelled passage graves, so Siv had been forced to take the long way around to the veiled passages from the beginning of time.

Leaving Alfheim had not been a pleasant task, despite Siv's runes and her height. Before she had entered Jotunheim, she had made herself giant-sized, for she no longer needed to hide from anyone. She no longer remembered why she had ever hidden, but she remembered that she had.

None of it mattered now. This was her last hike through the nine worlds.

Wolves were howling. Siv no longer knew which howls belonged to the wind, and which to the beasts around her, for there was always howling in Jotunheim.

The edge of Iron-woods had been harvested for weapons, but the forest still stretched wide and far. As far as Siv could see, and with the snow no longer falling and sunshine poking through the thick clouds, she could see all the way to the last mountain in Jotunheim.

She had marched through all of Jotunheim, a land she had been outlawed from. No giants had dared approach her, not that she had met many. They were preparing for Ragnarok already: they had made their weapons, and were gathering for the last march. Jotunheim lay mostly abandoned this close to the final battle. Surt was assembling giants into battle formation.

Not even the few giants Siv had seen in the distance had approached her.

Siv stared down at herself. She would not have approached herself either. A mere shadow, like a draugr, wearing dark clothes. Soon this burden of life would be over. She took a deep breath and began her last march, into Iron-woods.

The trees were tall, like kinsmen of Yggdrasil. The lower branches had all been broken, and the crowns of the trees were far out of her reach, even in giant form. It still felt strange to her, to walk and live in such a large body. For so long had she lived among short-lived that their size had begun to feel comfortable on her. A giant body such as this had too much room for thought and memories, and the forefathers, too much room for useless things, and Siv did not know how normal giants coped with it and filled their own bodies with thoughts. The forefathers stirred not just with rage but with focus. They too, like Surt, were steering giants to Ragnarok's battlefield. The end was close.

The forest thickened around Siv. Soon the trees surrounded her so completely that when she glanced back, she couldn't see the snowy plains of Jotunheim behind her, only more trees.

She kept having to remind herself of where she was going. Her first-borns were waiting for her. She barely remembered them. Their faces and names were lost in the big jumble of memories that she struggled to hold onto. Perhaps it was easier to fill a giant body with thoughts if one's memories were intact.

Siv had spent so many centuries in Midgard that she struggled, sometimes, to remember the life that had come before. Her time in Jotunheim and in Asgard. She had lived long and passionately before she had lived among short-lived.

In Jotunheim, she had given birth, once. Twins, she remembered, but other than that, all she remembered were flashes of the birth. Clasping onto a warm hand. The pain. The cold of snow falling on her skin afterwards.

'You've returned,' said a husky voice. 'We had stopped waiting.'

A memory stirred at the corner of Siv's mind, but she could not quite grasp it. She stopped, standing tall in the dark of Iron-wood, at the far edge of Jotunheim by the ancient passage into Asgard. She knew where she was, but she could not place the voice that spoke, and she could not see who it was either, but there was *someone*, hiding. Siv could smell the mould forming on moist furs.

Perhaps it was her first-born.

'I have returned,' she said aloud, and felt the tingle of runes around her.

Whoever had spoken, it was no simple valley jotun. Runes were being used to hide. Siv concentrated on her hearing. In the distance, she heard steps on the forest bed, but they were much too far away to belong to the one who had spoken.

'Glumbruck,' whispered the voice of a woman, standing close.

Hearing it, Siv was once more reminded of her own name. It was an easy thing to forget. She had owned so many, but the nine worlds knew her as Glumbruck.

Protective runes were recalled, and Siv felt them being undone, until she could hear the heartbeat of another giant. It throbbed in the same exact beat as Siv's own heart. All hearts of jotnar were steered by the forefathers.

Behind a black tree-trunk something stirred, and out walked a jotun, smaller than Siv, hair hidden by a wolf hide over her head. Despite the cold weather, the giant's arms were bare, and her weapon belt full of sharpened axes and daggers. Nine weapons lined her waist. The pale face once more stirred that memory at the corner of Siv's mind. Once, the two of them had known each other. That crooked nose. A name formed on Siv's lips.

'Hyrrokin,' she muttered, uncertain. The name sounded strange to her, and she could not quite place it. As soon as she uttered it, the name was gone from her mind again, but the expression on the woman's face in front of her told her that whatever name Siv had uttered, it had been the right one.

The giantess caressed the handle of a dagger hanging from her right hip. There were punctures on her hand. They almost looked like the age spots of an elderly short-lived, but they were too evenly spaced. Each one came in a set of two, and instead of being dark brown, they were purple like heather.

Siv had seen those hands before. All the way back in the faint, faraway time that she barely recalled. When she had given birth to her first-borns. 'You held my hand.'

Here, in these woods, Siv had given birth, holding the hand of the giantess in the wolf hide. 'I've come for my first-borns,' she hurried to say, while she still remembered why she was there.

'You gave them up when you left,' came the answer.

'I didn't leave,' said Siv, although truly she could not remember.

They were not alone. Out in the forest was someone else. Her first-borns were there.

'He would have found them,' Siv added. Her tongue seemed to remember more than *she* did. They were not her own memories, nor her own words. They came from somewhere else. The forefathers spoke for her. They knew what had happened, better than Siv did. 'If I had stayed, he would have found us. Killed us.'

'And then we wouldn't be marching to war,' answered the giantess.

'We are all mere tafl pieces to Ragnarok,' said Siv. She vaguely remembered having uttered those words before, a long time ago. Even without her memories, she knew it to be true. No single being, even a giant, could be blamed for Ragnarok.

'Ragnarok calls upon itself,' said the giantess in wolf hide. She did not wear it like gods wore animal skins, becoming the animal itself—merely as a decoration. 'Your son told us you were dead.'

'I was,' replied Siv, and wondered which one of her sons it had been. She had given birth to so many. 'I am.' She was both dead and dying. Life was like a cruel curse that she could not undo.

'Half a forefather,' muttered the giantess in wolf hide.

Siv stared at the heather-coloured punctures on the woman's hands. To look at those hands made her remember so much. She remembered the heather under her feet as she clenched those hands. She remembered snakes and the sorrowful howling of wolves.

Yet, as she remembered, she also felt herself slipping. The dying had begun to take over. The forefathers were strong in her mind. It felt like they were shouting over her thoughts. It felt like they were consuming her and pulling her back into Ragnar's Darkness.

'Hyrrokin,' said Siv, remembering the giantess' name, once more. 'Hyrrokin, Hyrrokin.' She whispered the name over and over to herself so that she might remember, and with the memory, she knew that she had met the woman elsewhere too.

Not merely when she had given birth for the first time. She had been sitting in a hot pit, once, burning up, with the forefathers raging through her. Her trial, so long ago. Hyrrokin had pronounced the sentence, eager to get on with life. Hyrrokin had outlawed her from Jotunheim.

'Do you know where they are?' asked Siv, hardening her stance and safely closing her thoughts off with runes. 'My first-borns.'

'You should have come with me after the trial,' said Hyrrokin whose hands and arms were punctured by snake fangs. 'You should have come with me and watched your sons grow up.'

'If I had, we would all have died at his hand,' Siv said, for she remembered now, why she had been running and hiding for centuries. The Alfather had been so eager for blood and death.

Siv walked past Hyrrokin, deeper into Iron-woods, where she had heard the steps earlier. Someone else was there, and she felt certain in her chest that it was her first-borns. The forefathers' focus heightened her certainty.

A grey wolf stepped out of the darkest part of the forest, and then another. Still, Siv's hope to see the faces of her first-borns kept her heart steady. More wolves walked out of the dark, towards Hyrrokin. They were as tall as the giantess, and some of them growled when Siv came too close.

Unafraid of them, Siv glided past, deeper into the forest. Her first-borns had to be somewhere in this forest. It was where she had given birth to them, and it was where she had told them to remain. If they were still alive, they would be there.

Yet all around her, in the forest, were nothing but more and more grey wolves. Hundreds of them. Hyrrokin had gathered them for Ragnarok. Hundreds and perhaps even thousands of great jotnar wolves were readying to fight in Asgard. Siv rushed through their midst, searching for her blood and love.

At last, her eyes fell upon two familiar faces. Siv stopped with a loud sob. Her sons.

They walked side by side, proud and tall. They were so tall. Taller than any of Hyrrokin's wolves. Taller even than Hyrrokin. Siv smiled at them. They looked like her. They had her eyes, and when they matched her stare, they too stopped, and recognised her for who she was.

They were like the Alfather's own favourite sons. One light and one dark, opposites of each other. And yet when they were together, they were so perfect that they almost shone like the sun and moon.

'Skoll,' she called to her bright-haired son.

'Hati,' she called to the dark-haired one.

Her voice nearly broke. She had not named them herself. Others had given her first-borns their names. Others had raised them. Siv had left to save them. She had erased them from thought to save them, and for once, she had succeeded.

Her first-borns had grown up, alive and safe, because she had been far away.

A harsh wind blew in, and all around Siv and her first-borns, wolves began to howl. Her sons had been safe, but they no longer were. Ragnarok was upon them, and it was time for them to act their role and do what had always been destined of them.

Skoll and Hati ran towards her when she called. They knew why she had left. They had waited for her. She flung her arms around them and held them tight. They had been mere cubs when she had last held them in her arms. They had used to nibble on her toes. They had been so small.

Siv caressed her sons' fur and remembered them anew. Their fur-coats were not as soft as they looked, but rough like the winter weather. Their father had been like that too. Hardened by the weather and the aesir. 'Where is your father?' she asked her wolf sons. 'Where is Fenrir?'

HILDA

Chapter One Hundred and Fifty-Seven

FENRIR HOWLED AT the moon and at the sunrise. Howling so loud and sad that it sent chills of sorrow through Hilda. The ice trembled under her hands. She filled her lungs with air before she was submerged, but the ice held. Fenrir's howls echoed across Lake Pitch-black. The ice was getting thinner the further Hilda crawled. Her knees and hands were numb from the cold.

She couldn't see Fenrir's island yet, but he was out there, calling for Ragnarok. Calling for his sons, Skoll and Hati, to swallow the sun and moon and bathe the nine worlds into darkness. He had to die before anyone heard or acted on his howling. Before Ragnarok.

And Hilda would be the one to kill him. If Fenrir died, the Alfather would live. If she did the deed, she would be the most honoured warrior in Valhalla. In all the nine worlds.

The ice cracked under Hilda's hands. Her snow fox yelped.

Hilda launched herself at her fylgja to silence it, but it was too late. The fox's voice carried over the waters. Not as loudly as that of Fenrir, but loud enough to be heard.

For five heartbeats, Hilda stood frozen, hands at her snow fox's soft neck, listening. That's when it came: the terrible growl of a great wolf. Fenrir knew that she was coming.

The thin ice vibrated under Hilda's hands. She crawled across it as quickly as she could. Her snow fox darted ahead, eager not to fall into the water. It hated water. The sun bathed down over them, peeking through clouds for the first time in three winters. The ice was melting.

Fenrir's growl was followed by yet another howl.

'Kauna, kauna,' Hilda chanted to keep herself warm. The ice cracked under her hands, splintered, and her hand disappeared into the dark waters.

Head first, Hilda plunged into the water. The cold engulfed her. She struggled to hold in air. She swam as fast as she could, below the thin ice which cracked into shards above her.

She heard a muffled bark ahead. Her snow fox was in the water too. Her body felt twice as cold for it. They were one and same, the snow fox and her. They shared each other's heat, and with both of them in the cold black water, there was not much heat left. 'Kauna, kauna, kauna,' Hilda chanted to keep warm. All the rune did was keep her from dying of the cold.

Long black seaweed tried to wrap itself around Hilda's legs. The waters were completely black. She couldn't see ahead. Hilda kicked herself to the surface. Her head bumped against ice and broke through. Sharp ice scraped her cheek. Hilda orientated herself. Her snow fox's white head popped out of the water to her right. The island had to be that way.

Separating her from the fox were stretches of ice, too thin to walk on, but too thick to swim through. Hilda submerged herself in the waters again. She kept her eyes fixed on the ice above her, for a place where it was thin enough for her to break through.

The swim was long. Both for Hilda and the fox.

The third time her head broke through ice, she saw the island: a purple spot in the middle of the black lake. Still far away, but within reach.

The snow fox was ahead of her, and the sun travelled halfway across the blue sky before she reached land. Her face was hot from the heat of the sun while her feet and hands had long lost any feeling in the cold of the lake. Had she been in Midgard, she would have thought that the gods were watching over her, but Hilda knew that no one watched over her anymore. She arrived purely thanks to her own strength.

Exhausted, Hilda hoisted herself onto the island. Her fox waited for her at the bank, its white fur muddied.

Hilda lay down flat and stared up at the sky. The heather prickled her back. Frost was melting off the flowers with the sunlight. Hilda smiled at the purple flowers. She hadn't seen a flower in three years. Even Yggdrasil had lost its leaves. A year in, all the ash trees had lost their leaves and Yggdrasil had stood bare ever since. Like it was dying.

'Is it feeding time already?' came a growl that made all the heather on the island tremble.

Hilda darted to her feet, nearly tripping backwards into Lake Pitch-black. Her right hand drew forth her Ulfberht axe, before she could think to do so. Before she saw the great paw crush the heather where her head had been. The wolf stopped there. A thin chain was tied around its legs, taut at its back.

Hilda's feet splashed into the lake, but she backed away a little further still. So that the wolf was out of her reach, but more importantly so that she was out of *its* reach.

Warm breath washed over Hilda's head. The wolf lowered its head to match Hilda's stare. Its snout was as large as Hilda's entire face. Its mouth hung slightly open as it breathed, and Hilda saw the glint of sharp teeth.

The wolf moved slowly and precisely, examined her so closely that Hilda knew that even if she moved a little finger, the wolf would take notice.

'Why are you here... short-lived?' the wolf finally breathed. Its teeth were sharp and large, like a hundred swords.

Hilda fondled the shaft of her axe. 'I've come to kill you,' she announced.

She stared straight into Fenrir's yellow eyes. She wasn't even half the wolf's size, but she didn't back away. She readied her axe in her hand. She was two paces out into the waters. There was no sand bed, only mud that swallowed her shoes and feet. It would take her several heartbeats to get back into Fenrir's reach. Onto solid ground where she could truly fight, and that whole time she would be up for grabs.

Fenrir tilted its large head to the side and examined Hilda. 'You're not quite big enough to feast on,' said the wolf, and it turned its back to Hilda. 'Neither one of you.'

At that the wolf leapt, and its jaw swept down over the heather. Those great teeth sliced off flowers and leaves and clamped down over white fur. As easily as that, the great wolf lifted Hilda's snow fox off the ground. The fox whimpered and barked, and flailed, helpless in Fenrir's clasp.

The great wolf turned back towards Hilda.

She tightened her grip on the axe and planned her run up to the wolf. If her snow fox died, so did she. She had learned as much on Odin's battlefield. And out here, they would just die, for good. There were no valkyries to revive either one of them.

Every little hair on the snow fox's fur was trembling.

The wolf could swallow her fox faster than Hilda could attack. Relying on her weapon would get her killed. She needed another plan.

'The Alfather sent us,' Hilda said, hoping that Fenrir was as fond of words as the old god was. 'To do what he can't.'

The wolf walked closer to her, Hilda's fox dangling vulnerable from its sharp teeth.

'He sentenced us to death,' she said.

Fenrir let her snow fox go. It fell from the beast's hold and landed on its paws. Barely had it landed when it shot away from Fenrir towards Hilda.

A lock of white fur remained stuck on Fenrir's front tooth.

The fox cast itself into the waters it so hated and cowered behind Hilda's legs.

'Stay back,' Hilda whispered to her snow fox. She took a tentative step towards Fenrir.

The wolf growled. It felt like someone was clawing at Hilda's insides. 'Be on your way,' Fenrir warned. 'Or I *will* eat you.'

Hilda stared back where she had come from. She couldn't see land. Only black waters and ice shards. Yggdrasil was only visible like a faint shadow in the distance that could as well have been a cloud.

'I can't make that swim again,' Hilda said. 'Not so soon.' It was true, though she had no intention of trying, either. Not before Fenrir was dead. 'Not in the dark.'

The sky was already coloured bright red.

Fenrir gave out a forceful sigh that made Hilda's clothes flap around her. 'Sleep, if you dare,' the grand wolf commanded. 'In the morning you leave.'

Hilda stared longingly at the island. She needed sleep. No matter what she did, she needed rest, but the offer was given by the biggest wolf in the nine worlds. The Alfather's bane. Hilda scoffed at the proposal. 'So you can devour me while I sleep?'

'You're the one who didn't want to leave,' Fenrir reminded her.

'Will you promise not to eat me during the night?'

The wolf let out another sigh and turned around. With heavy steps, it walked across the bright heather, inland, away from the coast and away from Hilda. 'I promise,' the wolf eventually answered.

Hilda nodded, though no one saw, and with mud dripping off her shoes and clothes, she splashed through the last of the waters back to the heather island. The mud swallowed her feet. Had she tried to attack Fenrir from that position, earlier, she would have fallen, and she would have failed. She would already have been ground to pieces, warm in the wolf's belly. She had done well to talk instead, as her father would have advised.

Her snow fox was much more reluctant to go back onto the island. She clicked her tongue and tried to speak to it, but it was still shaking like a leaf, and instead of joining Hilda, it turned to Lake Pitch-black, and began the swim back towards Yggdrasil's shade. Even the cold waters were preferable to a night on Fenrir's island.

It would be wise to follow, but Hilda had no intention of giving up her mission. She would slay Fenrir and return to Valhalla a hero.

From the island, she watched the snow fox swim away. It was better if it left. Then she wouldn't have to worry that Fenrir might eat it and kill them both.

Hilda turned away from her snow fox and back to the rest of the island. Fenrir was standing a few paces further inland, watching her. It had promised not to eat her during the night, but Hilda didn't know if she could trust the wolf. Even so, she had no choice.

Hilda lay down on the heather. It was not a soft bed, but it was better than many other places she had slept. Even with the danger of Fenrir looming over her.

She had seen the wolf's past in her visions. She knew it cared about honour. If it gave its word not to attack, Hilda told herself, then it wouldn't.

Trusting that the most dangerous beast in all the nine worlds hadn't changed its principles in the past nine hundred summers, Hilda closed her eyes.

DURING THE NIGHT, she woke. Fenrir was resting at her side. Its nostrils blew warm air over her. It had dried her clothes. Hilda slowly turned to free her left arm to reach for her axe. She stared up at the wolf as she did. The moon was reflected in Fenrir's glossy eyes. The wolf was awake and watching her. Hilda let her hand fall down flat onto the heather and rolled to her side.

Twice more, Hilda fell asleep and woke, with the wolf still awake, and still watching.

When she woke the third time, the sky was still dark. The big wolf had promised not to eat her during the night, but it couldn't be long before night turned to day, and then the promise no longer held.

For a while Hilda lay awake, eyes closed, and thinking. Her best chance of success was to attack the wolf before the night was over. She could reach for her axe and call on the runes. If she made a wind rise so strong that the wolf had to blink, she could strike in that very moment. Strike one eye, then the other. It would take many blows to kill such a large wolf with her small axe, even though it was an Ulfberht. Blinding the wolf would give her an advantage.

Before she could do anything, she had to grab her axe. The trick was to move slowly and randomly, as though she was still asleep. The wolf had watched her all night. It knew how she moved in her sleep. Hilda scratched her neck and then brought her hand down again. By her hip—by her axe. Slowly, she edged her fingers closer to her axe.

The warm air from the wolf's nose ruffled Hilda's hair. Its snout was so close to her head. Hilda moved her hand closer. A little more, and she would have the axe in her grip. A little more and she could attack. She readied her runes. She would use the rune of the traveller. She needed two breaths to get up, swing around and reach the wolf's left eye. The left was the closest, three paces behind her. Taking out the right eye would be more troublesome. The wolf would be aware at that point. But the pain would make it move irrationally. As long as Hilda stayed sharp, she could do it. Once the wolf couldn't see, getting close to it and plunging her axe through its heart would be easier.

Her little finger curled around the axe-handle.

'On your way now.' The wolf's hot breath blew over Hilda. 'You've rested.'

Hilda pushed herself off the ground. Clasped her axe properly and called upon the rune of the traveller. 'Raido!' she yelled, charging.

The rune put strength into her legs. The wolf had noticed her coming, but she was running too fast to stop. Even at this speed, she wouldn't make it all the way. She wouldn't reach its eye. The wolf growled so the earth trembled, and it made Hilda stumble. She threw herself at it, axe first.

The blade sliced through the wolf's wet nose. The growl was replaced by a whimper. The island stopped shaking.

Hilda closed with the wolf again. Its head was high in the air, but Hilda ran under its legs, slicing through the backs of its knees. Fenrir howled, but recovered faster than she had hoped, turning around itself.

Hilda darted through its back legs, swung under its swooping tail, and kept running. Fast, towards the dark lake, to get out of the beast's reach, before it could turn. The names of the runes raced through her mind. She didn't know which one to use.

She would come back. When she had thought it through. When she knew what runes to wield.

The wind blew in with visions, distracting her. Hilda sped up. Two more paces.

She heard a snap at her back. Something slammed into her leg, over her heel, and Hilda plummeted into the dark waters. Her hands dug into the mud. Her left heel was caught. The pain was so great that she couldn't even yell.

Her left leg was lifted off the ground, then her hips. Hilda fumbled for something to hold onto, but in the mud, there was nothing. The wolf lifted her upside down. The pain forced tears into her eyes. She hung three arm-lengths into the air. Dangled by the heel. The wolf's teeth tore through her. Hilda prepared herself to strike and run. If she could.

Then, Fenrir let her go.

She plummeted towards the ground, but never hit it. Fangs

sliced into her leg, and Hilda squealed. Again, she was lifted up before she hit the ground. This time, the wolf had captured her left thigh. A tooth pierced her leg. She was hooked like a fish.

The pain numbed her leg. She tried to wrestle herself free of the tooth, but nothing worked. The wolf shook its head from side to side, and Hilda with it. Blood pounded in her head, and she was filled with nausea.

Hilda took a deep breath and hauled herself upright. The tooth tore deeper through her thigh. Hilda grabbed hold of the tooth and pulled herself closer, keeping her head clear in case the wolf snapped down.

The tooth was too long for her to drag herself off. There was only one thing to do.

Steadying her breathing, Hilda placed her axe at her thigh, just above Fenrir's tooth. Her thigh was thicker than the edge of her axe. She would need at least two blows to cut through, probably three.

She raised the axe.

A shadow descended over her, and Hilda leaned back. The wolf's teeth came down over her. A deep rumble rose from the beast's throat, making her entire body tremble. A new opporunity to escape.

She grabbed an upper tooth with her left hand. It was sharp at the tip, but not as smooth and slippery as it looked. She had a good grip. In her right hand she readied her axe, then swung, slamming it into the wolf's upper lip. The wolf opened its mouth wide. Hilda held on tight.

Her left leg was wrenched off the wolf's tooth. Her grip on both axe and upper tooth were firm. Her left leg dangled helplessly behind her, throbbing. She wouldn't be able to run.

A howl blew over Hilda. She nearly lost her grip on her axe, but held on and then threw herself away, aided by the force of Fenrir's howl.

Hilda's axe slurped out of the wolf's lip, and she plummeted to the ground. The heather bushes broke her fall, but the impact slammed the breath out of her. Hilda desperately gulped for air, until finally her lungs filled. She scrambled up, hopping away on her right leg. Her left was numbed with pain, and blood poured down her lower leg.

The wolf was still howling from pain.

Hilda hopped as far and fast she could to hide under the wolf, out of sight. She crouched under its great belly. Her left leg was dark with blood. It throbbed with pain and bad news.

Hilda slipped her foot out of her left shoe, unwrapped her long sock strip and bound it around her thigh to stop the bleeding. The wolf was still howling, but before Hilda could bend down and force her shoe on again, it stopped.

The wolf turned around itself; Hilda tried to hop out of sight, but she was too slow.

The vast tail slammed into her. Hilda grabbed onto it, not knowing what else to do. Her hands bled, like she had grabbed onto broken glass.

The wolf knew she was there. With a growl it twisted again, chasing its own tail. Every small movement made the wolf's glass-sharp fur dig deeper into Hilda's palms, but she had no choice but to hold on. She brought her legs up and wrapped her thighs tight around the wolf's tail. Hairs like daggers pierced her thighs. Hilda roared in pain, but held on. Tighter she clenched her thighs around the tail. She let go of the fur with her hands and secured her axe at her belt.

The wolf stopped running around itself. It had thought of a new tactic.

Its tail curled up, and Hilda with it, head down, holding on tight. Fenrir growled contentedly and wagged its tail from side to side, faster and faster. Hilda was wrenched to and fro. Her hands were slippery with blood. But she did not give up. Slowly, she clambered down the tail. Her head began to pound, and her vision too. Her face felt warm with blood.

Fenrir seemed to know that its tactic wasn't working. Its tail flapped down, and then up again; Hilda's bloody palms slipped, and she was cast off. Landed on the wolf's back. It felt like she was being stabbed by a hundred daggers. Before the wolf could throw her off its back, she grabbed a thick lock of fur in each bloody hand.

The wolf shook its body from side to side, but Hilda held on. She tasted blood in her mouth. There was blood everywhere. She was drenched in it, but she was on the wolf's back now, and its head, its skull, was right ahead of her.

One hand at a time, Hilda climbed up the wolf's back and neck. All the way to the top of Fenrir's great head, where the fur was slimmer, and she could easily hold on with one hand.

With a bloody smile on her lips, Hilda reached for her axe and struck hard. Her Ulfberht cut through the terrible fur. Again, Hilda raised her weapon and struck.

On the third stroke, her axe hammered through the fur. Blood splattered over Hilda's face. The great wolf staggered, but Hilda held on. The beast's head collapsed to the ground, and Hilda with it. She was cast into the flowering heather. Fenrir's large head was right next to her.

The wolf's eyes were closed, at last. No breath blew from its huge nostrils.

Hilda was smeared black in blood, both hers and that of the wolf. She rolled onto her back, leaving red prints all around her in the heather.

'Hilda Ragnardóttir,' she breathed as she lay there on the heather, staring up at the sunrise, trying to catch her breath. 'Slayer of beasts,' they would call her back in Valhalla. 'Fenrir's bane. Stopper of Ragnarok.'

DARKNESS

DEATH, PAIN, AND fear.

Ragnar came alive in the Darkness once more. His limbs were tired, and his mind even more so. Kill the Alfather, Siv had urged of him.

Stop Ragnarok, stop Ragnarok, Ragnar loudly thought to himself, and as he did, it felt and sounded like a thousand voices were saying "Ragnarok" with him. It felt like the shadow warriors hiding in the dark were whispering it with him. The word "stop" was so faint and weak in comparison. Nothing could stop Ragnarok. Yet, Ragnar had to try everything, even killing the Alfather.

Thinking about the Alfather's youth, Ragnar tapped his distaff. *Tap, tap.*

The shriek of a thousand daggers scraping against glass pierced the silence of the Darkness. The light at the hollow part of Ragnar's distaff shone bright, and out from it stretched a thread that opened a bright veil into another world.

Ragnar walked towards it. The shriek of blades on glass

scraped his ears, but he was reluctant to walk through the veil, because whatever he would find beyond, the Alfather would be there, and Ragnar would have to kill him with his own bare hands.

With a silent sigh, Ragnar stepped through the veil. He stepped onto grass. His distaff pushed the Darkness away, and there, in front of him, was a tall slender man. His hair was not silver-grey, as Ragnar had expected, but long, wavy and brown.

The man was standing there, spear in hand, staring up at something in the distance that Ragnar could not see for Darkness.

Wielding the distaff as a torch, Ragnar walked around the young man, tall and slender, his shoulders confidently pushed back. Two bright eyes stared off into the distance with hunger for knowledge. He had a crooked nose, and a bare chin. The Alfather was so young. He had not yet hung himself, he had not yet sacrificed his eye, he was not yet old, but it *was* him.

His garments were not as elegant as they would be in his later life. He only bore one gold bracteate which carried the image of Yggdrasil.

The Alfather marched ahead, and Ragnar followed.

In his old age, the Alfather used his famous spear as a walking stick, but this young man did not need such a thing, so he carried the spear as the deadly weapon it was. His walk was fast, and Ragnar struggled to keep up, but that was true of the silver-haired Alfather too.

Kauna, Ragnar thought, and his distaff burned away the Darkness so he could see further. They were marching towards a huge branch that drooped over the grass. A branch so thick and large that there was no doubt as to which tree it belonged to: Yggdrasil.

This was the day. The Alfather had come to sacrifice himself. He had come to seek knowledge through sacrifice, and Ragnar would make certain that Odin's sacrifice would lead to death.

The Alfather posed his famed spear against one of Yggdrasil's low hanging branches, so he could focus on climbing up.

Ragnar watched, and although he could not see far, he knew the climb would be long.

He grabbed Odin's spear. His hand went through, but using the runes as Siv had taught him, Ragnar grabbed proper hold. *Mann,* he thought loud. The rune of Midgard and the rune of Man. The spear solidified in his grasp and Ragnar swept it out with a flourish and placed it on the earth, under Yggdrasil's branch, so that the spear stood upright, seemingly on its own.

The Alfather had already climbed a few paces up, but he stared down at his spear, which had sprung to life underneath him. He narrowed his eyes.

Sacrifice, Ragnar thought, carefully placing the word and thought into the Alfather's mind. *Sacrifice.* Ragnar still held onto the spear as he reached for the Alfather's mind and planted this great idea there. *Jump.* The spear-tip was pointed upwards. Its sharp tip glinted in the sunlight. *Jump!*

The Alfather rose to stand on his high branch. 'I offer myself,' he announced, although there was no one but himself, Ragnar and Yggdrasil to hear.

Guided by Ragnar's command, the Alfather dove off the high branch. The spear pierced his chest. Odin slid down the shaft, through Ragnar's arm and to the ground, with a crunch.

Ragnar let go of the spear and stared down at his god. The Alfather had skidded straight through his hands. The spear shaft was red with blood.

The Alfather rummaged. He was not yet dead.

Ragnar knew he ought to grab the spear with runes and stab his god, again and again, until he was dead, and remained dead, but before he could compose himself to do it, Odin had climbed to his knees. His nose was broken from the fall, and the spear dangled halfway through him, as he got to his feet. 'Mann,' he mumbled. The same rune Ragnar had used to move the spear.

In a trance, mumbling the rune over and over, the Alfather approached Yggdrasil's lower branch as if nothing had happened. With the spear dangling far out at his back, Odin resumed his climb.

Ragnar gaped after his god. Old or young, the Alfather would be difficult to kill—he was a god, after all, and a powerful one—but Ragnar could not afford to give up.

Reluctantly, Ragnar grabbed Yggdrasil's low branch and climbed behind the Alfather. Blood from the Alfather's wound dripped over Ragnar, but somewhat into their climb, the blood stopped dripping. The wound had dried up. The light on the branches began to look warmer. Ragnar thought they were nearing sunset, and the Alfather was still climbing, muttering: 'Mann, mann, mann.'

Here is good for a sacrifice, Ragnar ordered through his thoughts. *This is high enough.*

The Alfather stopped the rapid climb, and Ragnar finally managed to catch up. He hung onto a branch under Odin's feet, trying to catch his breath silently, for fear of the shadow warriors in the Darkness.

The Alfather undid the knots on the long, embroidered belt he had wrapped twice around his hip. He hummed a cheerful song Ragnar did not know as he bound new knots. A noose, he made, and the other end of the strong cloth he bound around a branch. He tested the weight of it, before he fastened the noose around his wrist, and readied himself for the sacrifice.

The Alfather grabbed onto the branch around which he had bound his belt. He was still humming, as he pushed off with his feet, and let himself dangle from Yggdrasil's height.

Ragnar crawled up to get closer. *Hagall*, he thought loudly, as Siv had taught him. Shaking, he moved his fingers closer to the Alfather's hands. *Hagall.* Using the rune of disruption, he unwrapped the Alfather's little finger from the branch. Weeping, Ragnar peeled each of the Alfather's fingers off the branch. One hand slipped away. The Alfather stopped humming. He was breathing wildly as he stared up at his hands.

Ragnar reached out and clasped the Alfather's hand, using his runes to stir. The Alfather's eyes were open wide in horror, as Ragnar unwrapped the noose from Odin's hand and slid it over the god's head instead, closing it around the Alfather's neck.

The tears streamed down Ragnar's face as he climbed back up to the branch where the Alfather was still hanging on with his left hand. One finger at a time, he undid the Alfather's hold, until there was only one last finger holding on.

Using both hands, Ragnar uncurled the Alfather's middle finger from the branch. The great Alfather dropped. His hands scrabbled above him for the branch. There was a snap. His head dropped to the side. The embroidered belt hung taut.

The Alfather stopped moving. He was just hanging there, spear through the chest, strangled by his own embroidered belt.

The hanged god.

Ragnar had done it. He had hung the Alfather from Yggdrasil and killed him. He had wounded the Alfather, and he had strangled him with his bare hands.

'Just kill me,' Ragnar cried aloud.

He had killed his own god.

'Take me back to the—'

A spear was cast through his heart with such force that he plummeted off Yggdrasil's high branch. A sword pierced his skull as he fell.

Death, pain, and fear.

EINER

Chapter One Hundred and Fifty-Eight

'I DIDN'T MEAN to kill anyone,' Einer muttered, not for the first time.

Snake venom dripped over him and burned. The fumes in the snake house were getting to him, as they were getting to everyone. Criminals were crawling at his feet, half covered in venom, crying for death and injustice.

Einer too had begun to mutter about the injustice of it all. He wasn't a criminal. He hadn't meant to kill anyone. He had been fleeing. He was with Loki. He knew Loki. They couldn't leave him there to rot with criminals and outlaws.

Einer had found a good place to stand, in the middle of the snake house, far enough from the walls that the snakes couldn't plant their fangs into his skin.

An outlaw clawed at Einer's back, trying to force him off the spot. Einer tackled the man to the venom-covered ground and stood up again. He had to fight constantly to remain where he was, but at least he was much stronger than anyone else in the snake house, and he had not been there for as long as them. His stomach grumbled with hunger and his mind had gone weary, but he was still standing. The gold bracteate hidden under his tunic kept him warm and steady.

Einer watched the corner of the hissing longhouse, as one man pissed into the eager mouth of another. Einer, too, was parched, but he had not yet reached that stage of desperation. They were all famished in the longhouse, and Einer had begun to wonder why they did not eat each other. Perhaps they had tried and failed. Perhaps they had tried and *succeeded*, and were watching him with hungry eyes, because he was next.

A chorus of fresh hissing came from the right side of the longhouse. The snakes in that direction had turned their faces outwards to Corpse-shore. The corpses in the snake house rose to their feet, even the ones who had long given up and lain down in the pooling venom. They all stood erect, their hungry eyes staring at the wall where the snakes' heads had disappeared. The wall came apart. Snakes slithered out of the way for someone to step through. The hot fumes obscured the figure as he did so, but he did not look muddy and dishevelled as everyone else did.

He stood taller even than Einer, with dark and reddish hair. And then the fumes blew out through the opening, clearing the air enough for Einer to see his saviour's face.

'I've come to free you of this house,' said Loki, staring around at the hungry faces. When his eyes finally travelled to the left of the longhouse and fell on Einer's expectant face, he began to laugh wickedly. 'It looks like you have gotten yourself into trouble, Einer,' said Loki in an amused snicker when he had composed himself. He thought it funny that the corpses had decided Einer was a criminal and had outlawed him to Corpse-shore.

The giant reached into a pouch hanging from his belt and pulled out a big pair of metal tongs. Corpses backed away from Loki as he snapped the tongs together.

'I wondered where you'd gone,' Loki said, glancing at Einer, but not paying full attention to him.

Loki had not come to get Einer out. He did not even appear to have known that Einer was there. But he was there nonetheless, so either way Einer was saved.

Loki waved an elderly woman up to him. Her clothes were reduced to strings bound around her body. Her face and all her skin was scorched, her legs only bone. Skewed teeth and dark paint under her eyes made the woman look like she belonged exactly where she was, among the most violent and immoral in the nine worlds.

'Some villagers chased me through Helheim,' Einer explained. 'They thought I was a criminal, because of my long fingernails.'

The old woman presented her slender fingers with their long nails to Loki.

'And you're not?' Loki asked in an amused tone without looking at Einer. He clasped the metal tongs around the woman's middle fingernail.

'Not...?'

'A criminal?' Loki wrenched the tongs back hard. The woman's fingernail ripped off. She let out a shriek, then fell into sobbing as Loki steadied her hand and secured the tongs around the next fingernail.

'I'm not,' Einer said.

Loki tore another fingernail off the sobbing woman's hand. Her fingers were bleeding.

'I would never commit a crime.'

Loki dropped the fingernails into a pouch in his belt. Tapped the woman's hand with a click of the tongue to keep her steady and proceeded to the next fingernail.

'Well...' said Loki as if he didn't quite agree with that, securing the tongs around the third fingernail. 'There *was* the ice mist.' He wrenched off another nail. A piece of flesh came with it. The old woman screamed in agony, but Loki hardly halted before he resumed his work, pulling the last few fingernails off the old woman's right hand.

He worked quickly on her left hand, while Einer searched for words. 'I didn't know about the ice mist,' he insisted.

'It's still a crime,' Loki said as he wrenched off the last fingernail on the woman's left hand. The woman wheezed in relief when it was done and staggered towards the opening behind the giant, but Loki stopped her from leaving. 'Toes too. Lie down.'

She was sobbing so hard her cheeks were bright red as she complied, lowering herself into the venom on the ground to present her wrinkled toes to Loki.

'Isn't this fascinating?' Loki remarked to the woman. 'They didn't cut your fingernails, but they *did* cut your toenails all short. Usually it's the other way around.'

His tongs were too large to wrap around the woman's short toenails, and Einer had time to see her smile at the prospect of leaving the longhouse with her toes intact, but Loki held her ankle prisoner and spoke again.

'Don't worry, I've had a lot of practice.' He brought out a dagger. The woman tried to jerk away from him, without success. 'We just need to scrape a bit of the flesh and meat away,' Loki muttered, loud enough for every corpse in the house to hear.

Loki brought the knife down to the woman's big toe, beginning his work as the woman screamed. He scraped the blade back and forth, parting a nail from the flesh. Blood trickled down the woman's leg.

Einer did not want to look, but it felt even more wrong to look away or close his eyes when someone was suffering in front of him, so he remained steady, and watched as the woman howled and cried and squealed, while Loki scraped off the flesh under her nails and pulled them off, one after the other. Einer still watched as she crawled away, broken and bleeding, out of the snake house.

'Your turn, Einer,' Loki said as he dried the blood on his hands into his trousers.

Einer stared at Loki in disbelief. He couldn't possibly mean to treat Einer like one of the worst criminals in Helheim. Even for the ice mist, Einer had been tried fairly.

'There's nothing fair about jotun trials,' Loki dismissed, and on that they agreed.

A corpse threw himself to his knees in front of Loki, presenting his long fingernails and begging to be next, to escape the dripping snake venom. Even the cold shores of Niflheim to which they were destined seemed favourable to Corpse-shore. Although they had not seen what frozen fate awaited them on Niflheim's shore, and Einer had.

'You can try to leave,' Loki said, glancing at Einer as he pulled the pleading man's fingernails. 'But *they* won't let you until your nails lie in my pocket.' He pointed the bloody tongs to the snakes in the walls, clacking the tongs together with a terrifying smile on his lips.

'But they listen to you,' Einer argued.

'Don't you know that snakes have no ears, Einer? They don't hear the same as you and I. How would I convince them?' He gestured for the man to present his feet. 'Are snakes truly that different in Midgard?'

'Then how will the snakes know if my nails are in your pouch?' Einer asked, his mind weary.

'They have *eyes*,' said Loki. 'Snakes must be very different in Midgard. I only know the Midgard Worm.' He laughed at his own joke as he ripped off another nail.

'But... you control Corpse-shore,' Einer stammered in disbelief. He had expected to be saved when Loki arrived. Instead, he was doomed to the same painful fate as the screaming man lying in venom at his feet, as his nails were torn from his limbs.

Loki shook his head. 'My daughter does.'

Another man presented himself. Unlike the first two corpses, this one did not scream, but his face crumpled with pain as Loki set to work.

'This is my daughter's realm,' said Loki with a pout. 'No one cares what *I* think. But we *have* a shared past, so I'll give you a choice, Einer. You can give me your fingernails, like everyone else, and leave with me. Or give me back the neck-ring and keep your nails. I warn you… the venom won't feel as forgiving then.'

It was not a choice Einer wanted to make. It was not truly a choice either, for he could not remain here all alone through Ragnarok.

'You can't just leave me here,' Einer said. 'You can't treat me like this. I'm not a criminal.' The hunger and weariness were making him desperate. 'I'm Glumbruck's son.'

'Then perhaps, someday, you will act like it.'

It stung like an insult, and Einer was not certain what it meant to act like Glumbruck's son. He had heard so much about his mother, but he still did not know what Loki expected of him.

'You said you would fight with me at Ragnarok,' said Loki between two toenails. 'Did you mean it, or were you merely trying to anger your gods?'

'I mean it,' Einer said. For he did. He had chosen his side at Ragnarok. He chose his bloodline and family. He chose his mother. The mere thought of her made his heart ache. He missed her so.

Loki nodded pensively as he released the man, letting him crawl out of the longhouse. 'Then I have another pair of tongs, if you'd like to help.'

This was a true option to leave the snake longhouse intact. If Einer took the offer and helped Loki, the snakes would see, and know that he was no criminal. Yet he hesitated to take the tongs. He was not certain that he could bear the responsibility.

'They're not leaving here before their fingernails have been pulled,' said Loki as he offered his tongs to Einer. 'Whether you help, or I do it alone. It'll be faster if you help. Besides, you might be kinder.'

Corpses threw themselves at Einer's feet. 'Take me,' they pleaded. 'Me first.' Willingly they offered their fingernails up to him. 'Free me.'

Reluctantly, Einer walked to Loki and accepted the tongs. The giant smiled widely at him, produced another pair of tongs from his belt and continued his task. Corpses were falling over each other to be Einer's first victim.

Einer picked a young woman who had been in the house for far too long judging by her burned skin. Chills rose up his arms and legs as he placed the cold tongs around her first nail. He did not say anything, but looked straight into her eyes and held her gaze as he pulled off her fingernails, one after the other, and he did not look away or offer any excuses. He did his task swiftly, and with as much dignity as he could, but all the same, an unease settled around his heart as he pulled their nails. It felt like a crime.

'It's worse,' Loki said in answer to Einer's thoughts. 'It's war.'

WHEN AT LAST their task was finished and Einer had left the longhouse with Loki, his hands were red with the blood of criminals, and he felt like one himself. His hands had not suffered, but Einer felt like it was his own fingernails that had been ripped out, and he could not help but wonder if it would have been easier on his mind to simply let Loki remove them.

'Nonsense,' Loki declared. 'You'll need your nails on Ragnarok's battlefield. *They* won't, not stuck in the ice.' The giant tapped his full pouch of nails contentedly and led Einer off Corpse-shore, back into Helheim.

Einer did not ask Loki where they were headed, but followed willingly across fields and through forests. They avoided towns and villages, as Einer ought to have done when he had first entered Helheim. They walked for what felt like days: in certain parts of Helheim, day and night were difficult to distinguish from one another.

They slowed as they approached the ocean. Loki kept his hand on his pouch full of human nails as they walked along the waterfront towards a settlement with a port. Many ships were anchored out on the waters.

Loki said nothing, but Einer was sure that the harbour town was their destination. Weary and knowing he would be likely to collapse, Einer grabbed the bracteate and lifted it off. His body seemed to weigh twice as much when he handed the gold neck-ring to Loki. 'Takka,' he said.

It had saved his life, not just in Jotunheim and in Niflheim, but in Helheim too. Einer was well aware that he would not still be alive if Loki had not parted with his bracteate to help Einer escape.

'Keep it, for now,' Loki said, but he looked pleased that Einer had offered it willingly.

Einer was quick to hang the bracteate from his neck again: he ached, his stomach growled with hunger, and he was parched too. His body's needs were difficult to ignore without the bracteate burning at his chest and giving him strength.

'I have a task for you,' Loki said. 'For Ragnarok.'

Einer panted to recover from his few heartbeats without the bracteate.

'There's something I need you to do. Something your mother and I should have done many centuries ago, when we had the chance.' He held a dramatic pause, and for a while they walked in silence, before Loki delivered the task. 'Kill the Alfather.'

'The Fenrir wolf will kill him,' Einer blurted in surprise. Everyone knew that would be the way of it. Every child in Midgard knew how the Alfather would die, in the end.

'Even my son can't kill the Alfather,' Loki said with a sigh. 'But if you work together, he might.'

'It's about the three bracteates, isn't it?'

'Your mother's son indeed,' Loki praised. 'For centuries that piece of gold has kept the old man alive. It needs to come off his neck before he meets my son on the battlefield.'

'And you think I can do it?' Einer asked. That had to be why Loki didn't take the bracteate from him. Only with it hanging from his neck would Einer have a chance of getting close to Odin. 'You want me to go back to Valhalla and steal the bracteate from the Alfather.'

'There is no time left to make that journey,' Loki said.

So, Ragnarok truly was upon them.

In silence, with the burden of Loki's task hanging heavily on Einer, they entered the harbour town. Ship builders were at work, although Einer had convinced himself that it was night. Hammering rang out to sea, and out there, boatswains were busy on the ships. Grand things were happening through the night in this Helheim town.

There were hundreds of ships anchored on the water. A few dozen had been hauled onto land for repairs, and just as many were being built. Too many ships for a town so small.

Suddenly Einer understood why they had come there. This was Loki's fleet for Ragnarok. Corpses from Helheim would crew the ships and sail out of Helheim, past the huge dog the Alfather had once placed at the entry gate as guardian. They would sail to Asgard and join the battle.

Loki marched past the ship-builders' huts, and led Einer into a smith's shed. The smith was seated by the burning furnace, this far into the night.

'Loki,' the smith called brightly when he saw them enter. He stood up and leaned in over his anvil. 'Do you bring me more nails?'

Loki undid the pouch full of nails and dropped it onto the anvil. 'My last delivery.'

'The last one?' the man asked. His stare and voice grew distant. He knew what that meant.

Loki nodded gravely. 'Prepare for it. When the hound howls...'

'The ships will be in the waters.'

'I've come with something else, too,' Loki said. 'Some*one* else.'

Einer stepped further into the hut, out of Loki's shadow.

'I bring you the ship commander who will lead this fleet.' Loki gestured to Einer. 'Einer Vigmerson. He was a ship commander and chieftain in Midgard. He has fought on Ida's plain. He has a good heart and the knowledge required. He will lead you well.'

They were things that Einer had never told Loki, nor even thought about in his presence, and yet somehow Loki knew them.

'I know everything about you, Einer. I've seen your destiny thread. I held it in my hands in the nornir's cave. I even gave it some knots of my own.'

It ought to have been a frightening idea, that a treacherous giant like Loki had seen his destiny and was manipulating him, knowing how his life would look and how it would end, but the revelation did not frighten Einer as it ought to have done. He felt hope at the thought. Because it meant that he was worthy, and that this was his destiny.

The smith examined Einer and finally gave him a nod of approval. 'I'll introduce you to your ship commanders.'

Loki had no time for that. 'Come, Einer, I will show you around before I leave.' He turned to the smith behind them, halted for three entire heartbeats, and then delivered his parting words. 'May we meet on the final battlefield.'

The smith repeated the sentence, but Loki did not wait around to hear the response. He was already out the door.

Einer followed. The gravity of his situation was beginning to dawn on him. The last battle of gods and giants had seemed so distant during the three winters he had spent in Jotunheim, but now it had snuck up on them all. Loki had been busy.

They sped along the waterfront as Loki pointed at this and that ship and named them all and gave instructions about who to trust and who to watch out for, until finally the giant stopped. Ship builders were hammering nails onto a ship on land at their back. Just far enough away not to be able to hear what Loki said next.

'Your friend, Sigismund Karson, will come to collect your bracteate,' said Loki. 'He will be told where you are, and he will come.'

Einer's delight at the thought of seeing his friend again was halted by the terrifying notion of giving up the bracteate before the battlefield.

'Without the bracteate, how can I get close to the Alfather?' he hissed under his breath so that the ship builders would not hear.

'You're Glumbruck's son,' Loki said simply. 'You will find a way. You must, or we will all fight and perish for nothing.'

FINN

Chapter One Hundred and Fifty-Nine

'Is THAT THE one?' asked King Svend.

Their gazes were firm on the horizon. The ships were silent, apart from some whispered talk. The warriors were at their posts, oars at the ready. The commanders had gathered at the aft on Svend's longship to spy the horizon.

Finn rubbed his legs. His muscles were sore. He had not slept well, and his bones ached from the weather. There was good wind today, and the morning had brought rain. By now, the rainclouds had given way to patches of sunshine, but Finn's legs still ached from the weather.

'Nej, I know those colours,' Jarl Eirik finally said. 'That's one of Jarl Sigvald's ships.'

Finn twisted on the helmsman's bench to look over his shoulder, hand still firm on the steering oar. A new ship had come around the island. This one was larger than the last few, and it was understandable why Svend might believe it to be Olaf Tryggvason's ship, but it did not strike Finn as quite impressive enough.

Jarl Eirik was clearly nervous at the prospect of the battle, but the King of Swedes seemed unbothered, and then there was King Svend, who carried such anger in his eyes. His hands were fondling the bleeding dagger arrived to him from hand to hand, with words of his sister. He wanted King Olaf dead, and though everyone understood why, perhaps none did so well as Finn.

Although he had never seen them together, Finn was well aware that Svend did not look at Tyra as most men looked at their sisters, and when she had sailed away on her wedding night, and especially when later rumours had announced that she was marrying abroad, Svend had chosen to blame King Olaf for her leaving. Receiving the bleeding dagger from the hands of a young parent-less girl had made him all the more certain; ever since the dagger had come into his possession, Svend had been set on death and revenge.

'That's the one,' said Svend, with urgency.

Before anyone could confirm, the King of Swedes was running down the ship to join his own fleet and Jarl Eirik muttered curses to himself as he set out for his own longship.

Svend blew his horn. The hollow sound rang around the ships.

Finn glanced over his shoulder. There was a new ship out there, and it seemed to shine, but he could not quite make it out. His eyesight was not as good it had been, once. Thankfully, he knew the oceans and Svend's ship well enough to still be trusted as its helmsman.

Svend was blowing his sad horn when his warriors pushed off from port. Svend's ship, the *Howling Beast*, named for the way the ship sang when the wind came astern, was the first to leave the long island port. They had docked on their starboard side, and under the ship commander's shouted orders, they turned the ship to face King Olaf.

Their fleet was wide and almost made an island of its own. Seventy ships pushed out around the *Howling Beast*. Never before had Finn sailed in such a large fleet. Deep down, although he knew that times had changed, Finn could not help but wonder what would have happened if as many ships had gathered to protect Jutland back when Ash-hill had been burned.

Times were different now, with kings ruling more land than any chief ever had. Every summer, Svend's fleet grew. It had a steady thirty ships now; allied with the King of Swedes and Jarl Eirik they had gathered more ships than anyone had seen sail together in at least a hundred summers.

The sails and yards had been lowered on all seventy-one ships. The masts were up, though, so that they could make a quick escape, if needed. They rowed on half oars, and even so, thousands and thousands of oars splashed in the waters.

The *Howling Beast* turned around swiftly. King Olaf's bright ship had lowered its sail, and so had others out there on the horizon. Finn counted nine ships, but he knew his count was not as accurate as it had once been.

'Eleven ships,' Svend muttered at his side, confirming Finn's suspicions. His eyes had betrayed him again. His raiding career was coming to an end. Sooner or later, his sight would get Finn killed in battle. Perhaps today would be the day, at long last. As long as his corpse did not fall into the sea to Aegir's and Ran's hall. Finn had always sought and been destined for the glory of Valhalla. Nothing less would do.

The rowers fell into a good rhythm. They had taken up a chant. It was not a complicated chant, but they had come up with it themselves and they were proud of it. 'War! War! War!' they chanted with each oar take, and on the fourth they cried, 'Val-hal-la!' Then it was back to: 'War! War! War!'

Finn was glad to be sitting down as they rowed closer to battle. His armour was heavy on his crooked back, and he could use the rest. Svend had drawn his sword and Tyra's dagger was fastened to his weapon belt, bleeding down his trousers. Again.

They were coming close, so close that even Finn could begin to make out the specific ships, and indeed there were eleven.

People on the seventy ships behind them had taken up the simple rowing chant as well, all shouting for war and Valhalla.

Seventy-one ships ready for battle, but their ships were not equal to those of Olaf. The opposing fleet was made up of huge longships. Olaf's own ship was like none Finn had ever seen before, and it *did* shine. It seemed to have been dipped in gold or silver, or some other metal. It had to have at least a hundred and twenty oars. It looked large enough to carry three hundred warriors. At once, Finn understood why they called it the *Long Serpent*. The ship was as long as the Midgard Worm.

Svend's fleet was made of much smaller ships. The *Howling Beast* carried an impressive eighty sailors, but no other ship in their allied fleet came close, and eighty warriors was nothing compared to the *Long Serpent*.

Finn stared at the gold ship as they sailed closer. His mind wandered, and he imagined what it would be like to sail a huge ship like that. He wondered if it wrought in the waters like Svend's ship did, bending and adapting to the waves, or if it was stiff and bumped up and down on waves, and made even old sailors seasick.

It was an impressive looking thing, no matter, but Finn was glad not to sail on it himself. He could not imagine that it sailed well on the sea, and it looked too large to steer up narrow channels and into the fiords of home. It was a ship built not for seafaring, but to impress and terrify.

Terrify it did. Svend's people were all glancing over their shoulders to the gold-dipped serpent as they rowed towards it.

Rowing orders were delivered with sharp commands. The oar-takes steered the ship straight towards the golden *Long Serpent*. Finn merely clenched onto the steering oar in case of emergency, and a little bit for support too.

Finn let out a sigh. Today did not feel like a day for fights.

'Are you good?' asked Svend, concerned as ever.

Since Tyra had left him in Jomsborg, he had been desperate to never lose a comrade again, more and more so with time.

Often, he told Finn to stay behind when he went off to wage war and battles, but on this occasion, Finn's presence had been required: when they won, they would have new ships to sail home, and no one became familiar with new ships quite as quickly as Finn, who had sailed all his life.

'I'm good,' said Finn with another sigh. 'Just weary.'

'Be careful,' Svend instructed. He did not tear his eyes off the *Long Serpent*, and more specifically its aft, where Finn imagined King Olaf was, probably decked out in blues and gold, as Svend's father would have been.

'You too,' Finn warned. Svend had such hatred in his eyes, and nothing killed a man quicker than a hot heart.

'War! War! War!' the rowers were still chanting. The words seemed to give them strength. The ship was thrust ahead with strong oar-takes.

'Oars in! We'll drift the last of the way,' the ship commander yelled.

Startled, Finn looked up straight. He had not expected to be put to work, but it was true that the currents were in their favour, and it was always better to drift the last way to a battle at sea so your boarders were not at their oars when the ships collided. The rowers were already lifting up their own shields and readying their weapons.

Four midship sailors had crawled up the tarred shrouds. A good position with spears and swords, but Finn felt the ship's weight tilt to the port side as they moved about.

'Ballast,' he shouted. Boarders on the starboard side crawled up the shrouds as well, to even the ship's weight and make their sailing smooth. The rowing had given them decent speed, but the movement of the warriors hanging onto the shrouds cost them momentum.

The *Howling Beast* was headed straight for the *Long Serpent*'s gold side. Finn steered them true. Some of Svend's people stood ready with the cloth fenders to take the blow, and others with ropes to tie the ships together. A wall of shields had formed in front. Finn could hardly see where he was steering them, not that he could see much these days anyway. He fixed his gaze on the blurry shape of the *Long Serpent*'s mast and steered at that.

Arrows swished over them. Finn heard yelling from the midship, and saw a warrior fall from the shrouds, but blocked it all out. He trusted Svend to protect him if arrows or spears were thrown directly at him. Eyes fixed on the *Long Serpent*'s mast, Finn took them in.

The ships bumped together.

Boarders jumped from one ship to the other before they had even been bound together.

'Do you have shit in your trousers? Tie the ships up!' Finn yelled after the young ones as he secured the steering oar. He knew that he sounded like a grumpy old man, but that was what he had become.

The *Long Serpent*'s defenders were quick to cut the ropes that Svend's followers tied. The ships began to drift apart. The fighters at the fore of the *Howling Beast* were roaring and Finn saw their blurry shapes and heard the thump of their anchor being thrown onto the *Long Serpent* midship.

Spears were pointed at the warriors on the *Long Serpent* to keep the anchor safe. Meanwhile the aft of the *Howling Beast* was drifting out from the larger ship.

'Don't do anything reckless,' Svend warned Finn with a teasing smile before he darted off to the fore of the ship where his people were jumping from one vessel to the other. In two heartbeats he had disappeared in their midst.

'Ja, ja, ja,' Finn responded, a little late, and dragged himself to his feet. He picked up his shield. Already, his muscles were sore from holding it, and his body needed a good few steps to really get going again.

He picked up his spear, too. In the end, when warriors got old and weary, a spear always became the preferred weapon. In younger days, Finn had fought with swords and axes, and saxes too, but in the end, the spear was better. It did not require nearly as much movement as a sword or axe did. Besides, it doubled as a walking stick. The spear was the old and wise man's choice, which was why the Alfather, too, fought with a spear.

Most older men stopped taking their shield to battle when they switched to spears, to rid themselves of the additional weight, but Finn refused to admit that he was quite *that* old. Even so, Svend continuously tried to convince him that he would move better without it.

A ship bumped into the starboard side of the *Howling Beast*, and Finn stumbled from the force of it. He caught himself with the spear and glared at the new arrival, one of Jarl Eirik's.

The *Howling Beast* drifted back towards the *Long Serpent* from the blow. Older sailors at the aft pushed ahead in another attempt to tie the two ships together.

Clashes of war rang loud around Finn, and young fighters from Jarl Eirik's ship bounded past him. Battlelines had taken form along the edges of the *Howling Beast*. For a heartbeat, Finn stood back and assessed the battle to find a good place for him to join.

Familiar coloured shields were already roaming around the *Long Serpent*. Finn would have bet that Svend was among the first to have jumped ship. He always was, and that was why warriors thought him worthy and wanted to fight under his command.

Battlelines took form at the fore of the *Howling Beast* and on the *Long Serpent*. Finn could not quite make out where Svend's people stopped, and Olaf's started. He would have to get closer.

'O Odin,' Finn sighed, and half sang to an old song as he leaned against his spear for a few good heartbeats, watching the chaos of it all. 'O Alfather. Let me go with honour and serve in your hall.'

Today was the day, Finn decided as he pushed off from his spear. His body ached and he was ready to let go of Midgard and feast and fight with the Alfather until the end of days.

His life had already been long, and Svend had grown up and become a king. His debt to Einer had been paid. His promises had been kept. He was ready to meet the gods.

Determined to make it so, he marched along the *Howling Beast*, lifting his legs high over each rowing thwart, not running on top of them like the younger men. He steadied himself with his spear hand on the edge of the ship.

The newly arrived ship, at the *Howling Beast*'s starboard side, drifted off and left a gap between the two ships. The ropes were coming off.

'Hei! You didn't tie it properly,' Finn shouted after the young folk who had bounded past him earlier, but to no one in particular. He rushed to the edge of the ship and grabbed one of the ropes before it slipped into the waters. Finn placed his shield against the side of the ship, let his spear rest in his embrace and fumbled with the ropes to undo the poor knot and tie it again properly.

He was still grumbling over the hasty young sailors who refused to learn their knots, when more of them came bounding across Jarl Eirik's ship.

Finn ducked under the sweep of an axe. He fumbled to grab his shield, but it was so heavy. By the time Finn had managed to stand with it secure in his left hand, two more warriors had joined the first.

He reached for his spear with his right hand as the man on the right flank twisted his shield to the side and revealed a large sword. Finn's fingers slipped and the spear slid down towards the edge of the ship.

The warriors laughed. The one with the sword smiled and charged. Finn stopped himself from fumbling after the falling spear—his fingers would be cut off, if he tried. Instead, he lifted his foot high, and stepped hard onto the edge of the spear. The tip of it sprang up again. It was heavy.

When Finn looked up at his three foes again, the spear had hooked the charging warrior mid-air. The man must have tried to jump onto the *Howling Beast*. Had Finn not stepped on the spear, he would have succeeded, too.

The other two stood back, startled. Keeping his eyes on them, certain that the sword-swinging warrior was too occupied by the spear through his shoulder to attack, Finn reached for his spear with his right hand, and stepped down from the end of it.

The sword-wielding man slid down. Finn took the weight of the spear shaft with a grunt, and the sharp end sliced out of the warrior's shoulder. The man's feet slipped on the ship's timbers, and he fell between the two ships, into the water with a splash. Finn's spear tip trembled, scraps of cloth and skin stuck to the edge.

'Never underestimate an old warrior,' Finn told the remaining two boys on Jarl Eirik's ship. He too had once been young and foolish, but even he, in his young summers, would not have been foolish enough to die like that. 'Tell yourself that there is a reason he has survived so many summers.'

'Ja,' said one of them, sneering. 'Cowards flee and cowards live.' He leapt up onto the rowing thwarts, lowered his shield to protect his legs, and hopped onto the edge of the ship.

Quick as a hawk, Finn let his spear fall again and grabbed his sailor's knife. He shifted to the side, allowing his flank to be exposed to the third boy for a moment, and thrust the knife into the leaping warrior's foot. The knife went straight through the foot and into wood. Finn let go, then swept up his spear again as the man started screaming. The last warrior didn't seem to know if he should leap ahead, or stay put, or flee.

The second man was still screaming, and was trying to backtrack, but his right foot was stuck on the edge of the *Howling Beast*. Finn lifted his shield and slammed it down over the man's toes. The warrior yelped, and his shield dipped to the side, just enough. Finn thrust his spear straight into the man's face.

'And the over-confident are easily killed,' Finn told the man's corpse. He stepped back and steadied his footing on the deck of the *Howling Beast*.

The third man said nothing. His stance was hesitant. He couldn't decide if he should charge or flee.

Finn sighed. 'So, not today either,' he complained to the Alfather. 'Send me someone worthy next time.'

He retrieved his sailing knife quietly. The third man didn't try to attack. Finn gave the man a long stare. The kid was terrified. Finn sighed, lowered his spear and shield and walked away from him. There had to be worthier opponents elsewhere. So many at war—there had to be someone with the worth to give him a proper fight, and win.

While Finn had rid himself of the two warriors and tied Jarl Eirik's ship securely to the *Howling Beast*, sailors had struggled at his back to heave the ship closer to Olaf's *Long Serpent*. They had somewhat succeeded. Two ropes now joined the ships at the aft oar holes. The gap between the ships was two arm-lengths wide, still much too large for Finn to jump.

The fore part of the *Howling Beast* had turned into a proper battle. Finn couldn't quite tell who fought for who under the shadows of helmets and armour.

'King Svend!' he bellowed to find out.

Those who fought for Svend and his cause roared the name. Finn easily picked out the voices and found his kinsmen. There were more of King Olaf's men on the *Howling Beast* than Svend's own. Something to fight for. A worthy death.

Finn smiled as he raged the last three steps towards the fight. He slammed his spear into the neck of a man who hadn't seen him arrive. The man fell. Finn stepped back over the rowing thwarts. The mast fish was full of perfectly coiled ropes. Finn swept the clue lines down to deck as he backed away over rowing thwarts.

The dead body of the man he had stabbed in the neck was sprawled over two thwarts. The man's shield mates turned towards Finn, roaring for revenge.

Finn lowered his shield with a smirk. He was just an old man who had killed their friend. An old, frail man. They would easily take him.

The first of them stepped forward, shield and sword glistening with blood. His shield-mate, too, approached, with a harsh stare at his dead friend.

They advanced on Finn, their shields together in a slim wall. Finn kept his spear pointed at them, moving the tip to point anywhere they weren't covered. But there were two of them and Finn only had one spear. If one of them could get past his spear-tip, Finn was done for.

The long-bearded man at the port-side, closest to the widening gap between the *Howling Beast* and *Long Serpent*, looked ready to charge. His axe was tight in his hand. Finn tried to redirect his spear, but too late. The warrior leapt onto a rowing thwart and charged.

Finn slid the spear back in his hand and thrust forward, hitting the man on the shin. He kept coming. His friend charged after him.

Finn lifted his shield to protect himself from the first warrior, and guided his spear under the second man's shield, straight at his crotch. The first pushed ahead. Their shields clashed. Sharp pain cut Finn across the back as his spear jolted with a hit. Finn tried to shoulder his shield up and push the first man overboard, but it was too much weight. The man retrieved his axe. Finn felt it sliding out of his back, and a chill went through him.

His legs gave under him, and he rolled to the side between two thwarts. The first man overbalanced and fell forward; he tried to recover, but his back was exposed. Finn got up quickly, reaching for the knife at his weapon belt, and leapt at the bearded man's back. His knife went in deep, and the man collapsed. Finn groaned as he heaved himself up from the man's back.

The other warrior was squirming weakly between two rowing thwarts. Not only had Finn's spear penetrated his crotch, the man had also hit his head on the mast-fish as he had fallen.

A third man was leaping ahead to join them. In his eagerness, he tripped over the ropes Finn had swept aside earlier. Finn clambered to his feet with a sigh, leaving his shield weighed down by the first man. His opponent struggled to unhook his feet from the ropes, as Finn snatched up the fallen warrior's axe and slashed him in the side. Then he hooked the sharp end of his axe around the man's back, and the warrior went down with a groan.

Finn rushed back to his own shield and spear. He pushed the first man aside to recover his shield and struggled to get his long spear free of the second man, and then he stabbed them, all three men, right in the throat to make sure they were dead.

When he was done, he was panting for breath, and had to sit down on a bloodied rowing thwart to regain his composure. The wound on his back ached and itched, but his bones ached more. His left arm hurt. The shield was unusually difficult to hold. He must have strained a muscle trying to push the one man overboard.

The way had cleared to the *Long Serpent* while Finn had fought. The battle had moved that way, onto the huge golden ship. The two ships had drifted further apart, but the *Howling Beast*'s anchor kept the fore of the ship fastened to Olaf's ship.

With a groan, and leaning on his spear, Finn climbed to his feet again. His legs were sore, and he grimaced and grumbled as he moved. There were no more warriors trying to get onto the ship, or paying much attention, so Finn calmly transferred his weighty shield onto the *Long Serpent*'s tarred deck first, and then carefully climbed over.

He plucked up his shield again and found a proper foothold. Olaf's ship rocked on the small waves. There were no permanent rowing thwarts. The deck was higher than on Svend's ship, and it felt like Finn might fall off at any heartbeat. He didn't trust himself not to stumble, so he kept to the middle of the ship. Then, at least, he wouldn't drown if he fell over.

'Where is Olaf?' someone bellowed. The fighting had almost stopped; King Olaf's men were fleeing. If their king was gone or dead, no one was ordering them to war anymore. Finn brushed shoulders with two middle-aged men with long beards as they left the *Long Serpent*.

He walked across corpses. Svend's colours were easy to pick out at the aft. He was standing at the steering oar, staring down at his feet. Finn made his way towards his king and friend. Svend had taken wounds, but none significant. None that seemed to hinder him.

All around them their people searched and yelled to find the coward King Olaf, but he had fled.

Svend was not searching. The anger from before the battle was gone from him. Tyra's bloody dagger hung limp from his hand. Blood dripped slowly off the tip onto the deck.

Finn set aside his spear and put a hand on Svend's armoured shoulder. 'Svend, where is King Olaf?'

'He jumped overboard,' Svend replied, but he was not looking at the sea as he said it, rather at a strange pile of ashes at his feet. 'He's dead.'

BUNTRUGG

Chapter One Hundred and Sixty

FIRE DEMONS HOWLED in pain. Muspelheim's light dimmed. The flames faded around Buntrugg. The pain of burning receded and made his skin itch.

'Sister, sister,' cried the flames. They were mourning.

A fire demon had burned out.

Buntrugg had adjusted to Muspelheim. He had begun to see the different flames and to whom they belonged, and he had begun to feel them, too.

With all the flames in Muspelheim dimmed from their recent loss, Buntrugg could more easily pick out the hottest flames— the ones that belonged to Muspel. He had eyed a blue flame a while back and decided to follow it through the sea of fire.

When Buntrugg had first entered Muspelheim, eight flames had slipped through the veil of the worlds into Midgard, and Buntrugg had not been able to get close enough to catch them before they were gone. He had thought that there was no way to retrieve them without leaving Muspelheim, but he was no longer certain. If the death of a fire demon in another world was felt so profoundly in Muspelheim, then Muspelheim was still somehow connected to flames in the other eight worlds.

Muspel connected all flaming things. So, if Muspel could feel the flames in Midgard, he could call them back too. Finding Muspel's collected flames, and reckoning with the biggest threat in the nine worlds, was Buntrugg's only chance of saving Midgard from eternal flames—of keeping the nine worlds safe, even after Ragnarok.

Surt had left Muspelheim to fight the final battle, and to die. Ragnarok was upon them, but it was not the end of the nine worlds. Buntrugg had been given the task of containing the fire demons for that exact reason. Even when Surt died, and all giants and aesir were dead, the nine worlds would still stand. It fell to Buntrugg to ensure that they would not be turned to ashes.

The little blue flame he followed was becoming brighter, its heat warmer. Buntrugg armed his mind with ice. His face and chest were burning. He wished he had eyelids so he could close his eyes and keep the heat out, but his eyelids had burned off a long time ago. So had the hairs and clothes on his body. He had formed thick skin. The outer layer was darkened to a crust, like Surt's skin.

Every flame, every fire demon, felt a little different. Some tingled, some snapped and many simply burned and burned until there was nothing left. Buntrugg blew hot air on his own Muspel flame. It spread out like a burning shield. Its fire tingled, but Buntrugg had become used to it. He advanced into the deepest part of Muspelheim, where he had never dared approach for fear that he would combust on his way.

The flames were all so bright that he could hardly distinguish them from each other, but there were faint changes in tint. Most of it belonged to Muspel, and Muspel did not tint his flames. His were red and blue and bright.

Eight dimmer flames were arranged in a row. They each had a different tint about them, and they were so dim that they almost looked like holes in Muspel's fire.

Muspel had kept a small flame from each of his sons and daughters who had escaped this world. That was how his demons knew that one of their number had been extinguished. It was why they were so certain, mourning and dimming their lights.

Buntrugg's heart sped up. He reached into the absolute heat and snapped up the eight individual flames. He held them with his own flame. They felt weak and faint in his grip.

'Clever, clever, clever,' snapped fire itself. A voice rang through Buntrugg and made him shiver. In the hottest place in the nine worlds, he shivered with fear.

Buntrugg waited for Muspel's anger to kill him. Surt's anger had nearly killed him before, and Muspel was much more powerful than Surt. Yet the heat that could melt Buntrugg so that even the forefathers could not reject him from the afterlife did not come. Muspel did not attack; almost as if he had waited for Buntrugg to muster up the courage to seek him out. He had lured Buntrugg into the greatest heat in all the nine worlds because he *needed* something from Buntrugg. Like the Alfather had needed something from him, and Surt had needed something, and the nine worlds had needed him.

There was something only Buntrugg could provide, and he knew exactly what it was. Only giant blood could open the passage to leave Muspelheim. Only through the giant-made passage could the demons leave in their full forms, not forced to possess other beings, but free to roam and stretch their fiery limbs.

'You know the premonition,' hissed Muspel. He was whispering so as not to kill Buntrugg with his mere voice. Even a whispered word felt like a slow burn across Buntrugg's face.

Muspel's sons would march behind Surt into the final battle. Together they would burn through the battlefield. That was what the veulve's premonition said of Surt and the fire demons at Ragnarok.

'Surt did not invite you to Ragnarok,' Buntrugg answered. His lips were swollen from burns and his tongue was not familiar with the hiss of fire demons, but Muspel understood.

Buntrugg held his ground. He was still clenching onto the tiny flames of the fire demons who had escaped into short-lived bodies in Midgard. He would pull the escaped demons back into Muspelheim, and he would not open the passage for the fire demons to take over the other eight worlds.

'It is what the nine worlds demand,' said Muspel, not knowing that the nine worlds had already demanded and taken too much.

'I don't care what the nine worlds want. Surt put me here to keep you here.'

'Then he will march to war and die. The aesir will live, their chains never broken. Only we can burn them off.'

Muspel was not wrong. Without fire demons burning through Ida's plain, the aesir were likely to survive the battle. Everything had to go according to the veulve's premonition for giants to be released of their afterlife. Only with the fire demons burning through Asgard would the premonition come true, and the nine worlds be safe from the aesir's reach.

There was no way around it. He needed to release them to fight at Ragnarok, but he also needed to make certain they did not use the opportunity to escape and burn through all the nine worlds. He needed to be able to call them back, somehow.

'Each of you who joins Surt in the final war will surrender a flame to me,' Buntrugg decided, for now he knew. With a single flame, he could call them back. With a single flame left behind, he could regain control.

Muspel cackled with laughter and all the flames in Muspelheim snapped and cackled with victory, their mourning over their sister's death already forgotten.

'Burn Asgard,' Buntrugg said. There was a strange satisfaction at the thought of it. At last, the Alfather would get what he deserved. At last, the nine worlds would be freed from his chains. 'Burn those who call themselves gods!'

DARKNESS

DEATH, PAIN, AND fear.

He had done it. The Alfather was dead. Hanged in the tree of life with a snapped neck. Midgard would never know his name. Fenrir would never be bound up, howling for the end. Never could the wolf call upon Ragnarok. Never would the gods die. The Alfather was dead, but everyone else would live.

The nine worlds would survive. Still, the memory of what he had done—of the Alfather's eyes rolling back as he was hanged—filled Ragnar's mind with nightmares worse than his reality.

The Darkness pressed around him. Ragnar clenched his eyes shut, desperate not to see the Alfather die again, but it was all his imagination could conjure. The Alfather was dead because of him.

Ragnar tapped his distaff. Desperate to escape from his own mind, he thought of his only friend in this Darkness. The thread from his distaff sliced through the dark with a howl.

Ragnar passed through the veiled opening. Steam filled the

bathroom. He let out a silent sigh, for here, in the bathhouse in Alfheim where they met, he always felt his troubles lift.

'Why have you come now?' asked she, as if he had barely left. She stood behind him.

Her dark robes gave her form. Her body was a mere shadow, no more solid than the steam in the alvar bath house.

I did it, Ragnar thought loudly as she had taught him to do. *I killed the Alfather. I stopped Ragnarok.*

Siv glanced around, and then her sight settled on Ragnar, straight on him, as if she could see him. Sometimes he thought that she truly could, and in those moments, he felt less lonely in his Darkness. Although he knew that it was only his use of runes that she could sense. She did not really see him. No one saw Ragnar.

'Wait here,' Siv told him. She swung away from him and glided out of the room. She disappeared into the steam and then she was gone.

He had expected her to ask what he meant. He had expected her to say that the Alfather had been dead for many winters and summers, but she had said nothing of the sort.

Ragnar's heart beat loud with worries and the thought of what he had done. Nausea crawled up his throat. He had killed the Alfather. He had killed Odin. Alone in the thick steam, with the painted shadows on the wall, the thought overwhelmed him.

He kept seeing it, over and over. The Alfather's throat clenched tight by his own embroidered belt. His flailing, in the end. His empty eyes. The Alfather was dead.

When she came back inside, Siv was no longer rushing, and she was not applauding his success either, or telling him how the three-year winter had come to an end thanks to what he had done.

'Whatever you did, it changed nothing for me,' she announced. 'Ragnarok is closing in.'

But I killed him, Ragnar blurted in disbelief. *He was dead. He was dying.*

'Dead and dying are not the same thing, Ragnar. You should know that.'

The Alfather's neck had snapped. There was no doubt about it. Ragnar had seen it.

He was dead, Ragnar insisted. *He was dead.*

'Then even *his* death could not stop the will of the nine worlds.'

Tears streamed down Ragnar's face. He had failed. He could not understand why. He had done it all correctly. He had hung the Alfather. He had seen Odin die. He had strangled his own god, and yet, no matter what he did, Ragnarok was still coming.

'It's time to give up, Ragnar,' said Siv. 'Accept your fate and assume your role. Let the nine worlds have their way. You will never win.'

Even Siv did not believe he could prevent Ragnarok. Even she had given up. There was nothing he could do. Always, Ragnarok was coming. He was incapable of preventing it. Every move had the opposite effect. Everything he did only seemed to *cause* Ragnarok.

'I did it! I killed him!' Ragnar yelled to the Darkness and to the nine worlds. He had done what they had asked. He had done it all. It couldn't still be happening.

Something cold penetrated the back of Ragnar's head.

Death, pain, and fear.

His FACE FELT warm from tears. He had definitely succeeded. He had killed the Alfather, and yet, no matter what Ragnar did, the final battle was always coming.

HILDA

Chapter One Hundred and Sixty-One

THE WIND WAS loud and agitated with visions. Hilda had changed much by killing Fenrir. All the fates in the nine worlds were shaking without the shared future of Ragnarok holding them together.

Hilda had taken the long way around Yggdrasil to avoid its eternal shadow, where she had nearly been lost trying to reach Fenrir. Her snow fox hadn't showed up. Maybe it had taken the shorter way.

With the wolf dead, Hilda had all the time in the nine worlds. The long way brought her out near the ancient passage to Vanaheim, by the seas of summer, past Frey's and Freya's lands, and finally, the nornir's cave.

Even out by the nornir's cave, the snow had melted. The grass was lush green. It felt like summer had arrived in Asgard. Fenrir was dead, Ragnarok had been stopped, and the nine worlds could keep going as they always had.

Content with her achievement, Hilda tapped the sharp wolf fur she had bound into her belt. She had planned to come home to Valhalla, swinging the wolf's head, but even an eye would be too large to carry. She had settled for a lock of sharp fur from its snout: the only part of the wolf that was completely white, not grey or black.

The Alfather knew the wolf. He would know what it meant. She couldn't have cut fur off Fenrir's snout unless the wolf was dead.

Again, the wind blew with whispers and visions. Hilda limped away from Yggdrasil's root and began the steep ascent towards the nornir's cave. Her entire body hurt, but it had hurt for so many days and nights that she hardly noticed. She was so close to the three nornir, and she wanted to see them busily disassembling Ragnarok's threads before she returned to Valhalla.

Her fight with Fenrir had left deep wounds in her ankles and thigh. She could hardly support herself on her left leg any longer. She had bound her wounds, but cuts like these never fully healed. Even Hilda knew that. She would never fight the same. But she had proven her worth. She had stopped Ragnarok and she would have an eternity to learn to fight with a limp.

Her father too had spent most of his days with a limp, Hilda remembered with a bitter smile. He had stopped fighting after he had been wounded. Hilda wouldn't stop. She would learn, as she had learned the runes and as she had learned so much else.

Halfway up the hill, Hilda sat down and let herself rest. She lay on the grasses and stared up at the blue sky above. The wind swept in with visions. Hilda let them come.

A young man stared up at a great ash. Young Yggdrasil, barely tipping above the clouds. He began his climb. The Alfather. Long brown hair and beard. Both his eyes firmly on the top.

The visions settled and stayed. Never had Hilda seen the Alfather so young before. Never had she seen him in a vision, either. She had seen people she didn't know and couldn't recognise, but she had never before seen a god in visions.

The Alfather tested the branch before he let go. One finger at a time, he unclasped from Yggdrasil. He hung so high. A fall would take his life. An embroidered belt was tight around his neck. His gold bracteate twinkled. With two fingers he hung onto the branch above him.

The gust passed and with it the whispers of the vision. Hilda's leg throbbed. She had hobbled far. Still had two days of travel before she reached Valhalla, perhaps four. Her wounds were slowing her.

Bees hummed at her side, searching the bright green grass for flowers. It felt like the beginning of summer. There would be no Ragnarok or blood. The Alfather would live.

Another breeze blew over Hilda. She let its vision take her.

Morning came with frost. The Alfather was hanged from his broken neck. Sacrificed to himself. The hanged god. Dead, waiting for the afterlife to take him. At his neck dangled a large gold pendant.

'Kauna, isa,' Hilda muttered, knowing what came next. From the first runes to all of them. Each came with meaning, and they had all initially been delivered right then, with the Alfather hanging from Yggdrasil. 'Algiz, mann, dagar.' All the runes, Hilda muttered, as she watched the Alfather hang there, in her vision.

His eyes flickered open. He was woken from a dream. From death itself. 'The runes...' muttered the Alfather as his eyes flashed to life. 'Kauna, isa,' he began and through his chapped lips came the names of all the runes. He had learned them. They were his. 'Odin's rune,' he named the last. 'The rune of the messenger. I hear you,' he said. 'I see you,' and for a moment he looked down, straight at Hilda.

Hilda shook herself out of the vision. She had been in it. The Alfather had seen her. He had heard her recite the runes. They had come to him in the same pattern Hilda had recited them. They had been delivered by her thoughts. It was *she* who had delivered his runes, and the Alfather had known that she was there.

Her heartbeat was rapid. Hilda pushed herself up from the grass and struggled up the slope towards the nornir cave. The great doors were open, exactly as Hilda had left them in winter when she had left in favour of Valhalla. There had been so much snow then, but now there was only a little morning dew dripping from the images carved into the wooden door.

Hilda's laboured steps echoed emptily down the hall. Her heartbeat was loud with excitement. In a way it felt like coming home. For three winters she had lived in this cave, but it had looked different then. The snow had been thick. And there had been more threads tied up in the hall.

The nornir had nearly emptied the outer parts of the hall. Threads had been undone and moved into the big tangle called Ragnarok. The works of the final battle looked like a big dark cloud under the high ceiling. It would take the three norn summers and winters to undo it all and restore people's destinies, now that Ragnarok had been prevented.

No one greeted Hilda at the gate. It was not the homecoming she had dreamed of. Not that she was entirely aware that she had been dreaming of one.

Back in Ash-hill, at the end of summer, the warriors used to come home to cheers and smiles and feasts. No one was there to greet Hilda. No one asked her where she had been. Praised her for her courage. No one acknowledged that she had left and was now back. It was as if she had never left. Or as if her presence made no difference, either way.

At last, Hilda saw a shadow move about, deeper into the cave.

'Verthandi,' she called. Her voice echoed through the hall.

The norn's pale face snapped towards Hilda. Verthandi had not seen her arrive. The winds had not warned the nornir. No visions whispered about Hilda's past, present, or future. Destiny was ignorant as to who she was and what she would do.

Alarmed by the unannounced voice in their hall, Skuld and Urd, too, peered out from behind pillars, and their three fylgjur with them, but when they saw that it was her, they merely continued their tasks.

'I know I gave you more work,' Hilda told them. 'But I did save your lives.'

The nornir were too busy with their fates to realise what she had said. Verthandi's seagull flew under the Ragnarok tangle. Skuld's rat scurried into the hall anew and Urd's hedgehog closed its heavy eyes to sleep.

When, finally, the three nornir had restored order to all the fates originally destined for Ragnarok, they would know what she had said, and what it meant. Hilda had done it. She had prevented Ragnarok.

'Have you seen my snow fox?' she asked.

'Your fylgja is like you,' said Urd's motherly voice. 'A stranger to destiny. Always a surprise.'

Hilda smiled. Even the Alfather in her vision had been surprised by her. 'I saw the Alfather, in a vision. He hung himself from Yggdrasil,' Hilda shared. 'I taught him the runes. He said he saw me.'

Those words got Urd's attention. She came out of the dark of the hall as though in a trance, searching the past for the vision. The Alfather hanging himself in Yggdrasil and receiving the runes. She saw it, as Hilda had. She definitely did. All the same, she muttered, 'Impossible,' when her visions receded.

'No one can interfere in past visions,' Verthandi dismissed from further in the hall.

'Well, I did,' Hilda said. No one had told her that she couldn't. Besides, she knew what she had seen and what the Alfather had said. The Alfather had discovered the runes, all those years ago, because Hilda had given them to him.

'You've been busy,' said Urd. She came to a halt in front of Hilda. Her eyes took in everything: the cuts on Hilda's hands, her wounded leg and foot, and the dried blood everywhere. Then she left.

From the back of the hall she produced a stew. It was always stew. For three winters Hilda had eaten stews in this hall, and again, now, as a visitor, all the nornir had to eat were stews.

She swirled the spoon around the stew. It was watered down. No meat and only a few vegetables. Without Hilda hunting and gathering food for them, the nornir's meals had grown even less appetising.

'Ida's plain?' asked the norn as she stood and looked down at Hilda.

Hilda shook her head. 'A fight with Fenrir.' She smiled at the glory of it. She patted the sharp white fur in her belt to make sure it was still there. She didn't want to lose it. She imagined how the hall would go quiet when she returned to Valhalla. Wounded from her fight. Alive and victorious. They would sing songs about her. They would feast in her honour. She, Hilda Ragnardóttir, had saved everyone's Alfather.

Urd simply left her to her thoughts and her stew. The nornir were busy with their threads. With Ragnarok evaded, the threads they had tied together over winter would have to be undone.

For a long while Hilda sat and watched them work as she slurped her stew. It didn't taste of much more than hot water, but it warmed her from the inside and filled her belly. As the nornir worked, Hilda cared for her wounds. Those on her palms and thighs from where she had clenched around Fenrir's fur had crusted; soon they would scar. Her leg would need complete rest when she arrived in Valhalla.

She had tied up all her wounds properly with fresh cloth, before she realised that something was wrong. The nornir were not taking fates down from the large glooming cloud of Ragnarok. They were adding to it.

'Why are you still tying fates to Ragnarok?' asked Hilda.

'We tie what we see,' said the three nornir as one.

So even with Fenrir dead, Ragnarok would come. All it meant was that the Alfather would not end up in the beast's throat. The giants would still come and kill. The fire demons, too. The warriors from Helheim, and the wolves and beasts. Only Fenrir would be absent. The wolf's absence would change the fate of the nine worlds, but Ragnarok was still coming.

'We are nearly done,' said Verthandi.

'Two more days of spinning and then…' Urd's hopeful voice continued.

'An eternity of freedom,' Skuld completed.

'Freedom?' asked Hilda. She had watched them work for Ragnarok, day and night, but they were nornir. Spinning the fates of gods and beasts and short-lived was their duty and task.

'What about all the fates *after* Ragnarok?' asked Hilda.

'There won't be a need for fates after Ragnarok,' said Skuld's distant voice. Her voice came half as an echo and half in the wind.

'You think Loki will win,' Hilda realised. When he had tried to make Hilda join his cause, he had promised a world with no gods, or giants, or afterlives. That had been his promise. No more afterlives, and Hilda supposed that if there were no afterlives to get to, there was no reason for destinies either.

'We don't care who wins,' Skuld said.

'Let *them* decide who wins,' Urd added. She gestured to the dark cloud tied up high in the hall. The threads were bound together so tightly that it looked like a thundercloud, like Thor's hammer might strike at any moment.

'All we do is our part,' Verthandi said.

'Ensuring that they all get to Ida's plain,' said Skuld.

'Our duty was to spin them to Ragnarok,' said Urd.

'And that we will do,' the three nornir whispered together. Their voices were caught in the whispers of the wind and the words were repeated over and over as an echo down the large hall.

'And then what?' asked Hilda. 'What will you do if you won't spin fates?' She couldn't imagine the nornir doing anything else. She had never thought that they might survive past Ragnarok. Had never given any thought to what came after the final battle. She had always known that she would die at Odin's side on that battlefield. What came after had never mattered.

'When our task is done, we are free to travel the nine worlds.'

'Free to decide for ourselves.'

'The same as all other beings in the nine worlds.'

The hope in the nornir's voices almost made Hilda feel hopeful too. She had lived three winters without a destiny thread, and it was comforting to think that she would not be the only one after Ragnarok.

Though the little comfort it gave her quickly transformed into worry. She would still die at Ragnarok, as she had always known she would. She had thought she would have plenty of time before then. Time to heal and time to train with a limp. Time to be celebrated as the slayer of Fenrir. There was no time anymore. In two days the nornir would finish binding all fates to Ragnarok, and the battle would come.

Hilda pushed herself up from the floor. She had to reach Valhalla before Heimdall's horn announced Ragnarok. There was no more time. She had to get home.

UNN

Chapter One Hundred and Sixty-Two

UNN'S HERDING CALL rang around the valley. Down below, in the halls, no one so much as looked up at the pretty sound of the song.

No one ever noticed a thrall, be it in Christian company or in that of Odin's freemen. Unn had always been grateful for that. She didn't like it when freemen looked at her. When freemen noticed her, and when they looked at her, that was what came before the tending of broken bones.

Unn sang her herding call again. The first few cows came rushing out of the woods where they had taken shelter from the rain. She called twice more to lure the cows into the rain so she could bring them down to eat their fodder.

The last half a dozen cows were reluctant, but eventually they followed Olaf's herd into the open where she could count them. Truly, they were Tyra's herd now: King Olaf was dead, and no one could quite decide who was supposed to take over. Until someone else claimed the lands and cows and thralls, Unn supposed that they were hers, in some strange way. She was the one who cared for them.

Unn counted the herd. Thirty-seven. There was only supposed to be thirty-six. Unn tiptoed to see whose cow she had picked up. She knew these cows better even than the thralls she worked with, and when she managed to see across the tall back of Magga, always at the front, she saw the back of one of Sigrid's cows. She knew its back, even if she didn't know its name. She wasn't supposed to talk to thralls from other households, but that cow tried to hide in the midst of Unn's herd so often that she had taken to calling it Thief.

'Thief,' she called and clicked her tongue to make it move. It knew it wasn't supposed to be there, that she was calling it, but it chose to ignore her. She understood what it was thinking. Maybe if it just stayed silent, no one would notice it. Like no one noticed a thrall if they were skilled enough at guarding their tongue and making themselves invisible.

Thief was a slim cow. Its own herd didn't seem to leave space for it at the fodder racks. Maybe that was why it always tried to join Unn's herd, but she didn't particularly want to take the beating for feeding a cow too many.

With a sigh, she marched into the midst of her herd, tapping cows on their bottoms to make them move away with reluctant moos. Thief refused to move, even when she gave the cow a good smack. The cow didn't even moo.

A few of the others had begun to trot away from the rain, back to take cover under a nearby tree. She would have to call them again. But first, she needed Thief out.

Yelling suddenly echoed around the valley. Unn heard the puffs of someone running. A woman was coming up the hillside. She wore a yellow coat, in the rain. Red embroidered edges splashed through the mud. A freewoman came running through cow dung, where no freewomen came.

After her chased three warriors, dressed for battle in helmets and glistening mail that slowed them.

The woman ran determined up the hill, towards the woods where cows and sheep and pigs had taken shelter from the rain. Her wet hood was blown off as she looked back over her shoulder. The woman's long brown hair was undone from its neat braid. She raced like no one Unn had ever seen. And then Unn's eyes fell on the freewoman's face.

It was Tyra.

The men were slowed by their armour. They yelled for Tyra to stop.

This was it. What Tyra had told her about. How they would catch up with her when her husband was gone. How they would try to kill her.

Thief mooed at Unn's back. Quick, before the warriors spotted her, Unn lowered herself amidst the cows. Tyra had made her promise and swear never to intervene. Not that Unn would have wanted to either way. She wasn't brave as her father had been. She didn't want to die, not yet.

The rain splashed around them and dampened the sound of the warriors' yells. No one would hear. No one would think to look up the hill where only thralls and animals grazed. No one would come to help Tyra.

No matter what she had promised, Unn had to act. No matter how scared she was. Her hands shook at the thought of doing something. At the thought of doing nothing, too. She didn't know if she dared. She felt herself freeze up.

All she had to do was sing the herding call of Sigrid's cattle. Thief's entire herd would come rushing, thinking it was their feeding time. Unn knew the call. She had heard it before.

She took a deep breath to calm her racing heart and peered across the backs of her cattle. The men were so close. One of them had stopped running. He held a spear in his hand. The other two were sprinting ahead, one with an axe and the other with a sword. Tyra struggled through the mud and dung. She was halfway towards the woods. Her coat had dragged through cow dung. They were catching up. If Tyra just reached the woods, maybe she could disappear.

All Unn had to do was start the herding song. She took a deep breath, but her voice wouldn't come out. She was shivering at the thought of making herself known. Of the warriors looking at her. Coming for her instead of Tyra. The thought of dying.

She didn't think thralls could go to the Christian afterlife. Once, she had heard the priest say that freemen dined well, but that chicken and dogs and cattle couldn't go. So, thralls certainly couldn't either. Death was the end, unless she made someone sing for her and followed Tyra into the nine worlds in death. It was too late for that, but then, she could have served all eternity in Helheim, or in Thor's household. That thought too was terrifying. Hel was a scary being, and Thor, with his hair drenched with giant blood, was not likely to be a generous master.

Unn didn't want to die.

She was crying at the thought of it, and the thought of Tyra dying if she did nothing. Maybe, if she just slapped Thief and the others to move at the right time, they would cut off the way between Tyra and the men hunting her. Maybe that would be enough. But the cows moved quicker when she did the herding call than when she slapped them.

It was almost too late to do anything.

Unn's breath was ragged as she gathered the necessary courage, and then she slammed her hand onto Thief's bottom. Thief kicked out. Another cow mooed a complaint. More took up the moo and they began to move. Thief and half of the others rushed straight towards Tyra and the warriors, as Unn had hoped. A few went off towards the woods.

In the last moment, Unn put a hand on one of the cow's soft sides and followed it to the woods. She kept low to hide behind the cow and didn't peek despite the men's muffled yelling and the mooing of cows at her back.

At the cover of the tree line, Unn dared to look again. A cow had fallen on its side. Others were standing over it, mooing for it to move. The cow had been tipped by one of the men in a rush. It blocked their path. Tyra was nearly at the tree line.

One of them tried to climb over the cow, but it squealed and kicked and made him fall. The next had less patience. He drove his axe through the cow's skull.

Unn stared wide-eyed at the warriors as they climbed around the cow. More and more cattle mooed, like a funeral song for their friend. Unn couldn't quite see which cow it had been, but from the patched markings on its belly, it looked like Magga.

Unn would be blamed for it. The cows were her responsibility. Or maybe no one would care; King Olaf was dead, after all.

The warriors sped up once they were past the cows. Something was strange about them. Not just because they were chasing Tyra. It was like there was smoke around them. Like their skin was so warm it made steam out of the cold rain.

The man with the spear readied himself to throw it. He had that certain look warriors had sometimes. His posture was confident. He wouldn't miss.

Maybe if Unn yelled at the right moment. Maybe his throw would be off, then. Maybe Tyra would reach the woods. But if she yelled, the other two would come for Unn. They would kill her as easily as Magga, if they found her, and they would. So, shivering at the thought of death, Unn said nothing.

He cast his spear.

Unn followed it through the air. The spear rose and then fell, and with great force, it slammed Tyra to the ground. Face first she splashed into mud and dung. The spear stood upright, through her back.

Tears streamed down Unn's cheeks as she took cover behind the cows and watched Tyra crawl closer to the woods, fighting for safety and for life.

The warriors took their time to march up the last of the hill towards Tyra. Unn struggled to stay quiet and watch. The downpour muffled her sobs.

Tyra still tried to crawl away. She clawed at the muddy ground.

The one who had thrown the spear stepped onto Tyra's back

with one foot and wrenched his spear free. Tyra screamed in pain. One of the other men kneeled next to her. He put his axe away, grabbed her by the hair, lifted her head back and slammed it into the ground. Mud splashed up around him. Again, he lifted her head and slammed it down. This time Unn saw blood splash up his arms with the mud.

He kept at it.

Unn's tears fell so heavily that they blurred her vision, and she was thankful for it. Her attacker kept slamming Tyra's head into the ground, but at least Unn couldn't see the blood and the death. Tyra had to be dead now. No one could survive that.

Finally, he let go of Tyra's head and stood again.

Unn thought they would leave, at last, but they were not yet done. Tyra did not move.

The warriors approached the nearby cattle. Most of the cows had taken shelter in the woods and under lone trees by now. One of them slapped a cow to get it to move. The cow just turned its head away from him, but the man didn't have patience or knowledge of cattle; he grabbed the cow by the ear and dragged it out of the shadows. The cow squealed and kicked and tried to wrestle free, but reluctantly it followed. The cow was panicking.

Another tried to charge and help. The men forced the charging cow back with the point of their weapons. A hand firm on the ear, the cow was forced ahead, towards Tyra.

Unn gasped at the realisation of what they were doing. They wanted the cow to trample Tyra's body to hide the spear wound. They wanted to make it look like she had been trampled to death.

The cow too knew what they were up to. It pulled its head away and tried to get free, but the man held it firm and guided it ahead. The whites of the cow's eyes were showing.

Tyra's corpse was right in front of it. The cow kicked and jumped across. The force of the jump freed it from the spearman's hold, and away ran the cow. Away and away, panicked as if it had seen a snake. Unn would have to go find it, once it was safe to do so. It might try to leave the pasture.

The warriors yelled curses. One of them slapped cows with his sword. They galloped away like horses, but not towards Tyra. Even cattle knew better than to trample a fallen freewoman. Even cattle had more compassion.

All the cows had moved away from the warriors. The three men of steaming heat had begun to curse and spit on Tyra's dead body. They settled for trampling her corpse themselves. Unn watched all the while, tears streaming down her face at the sight. She had seen many vile things in her life, but nothing quite so vile and terrible as this.

It was an ugly death. And what was worse, no one would admit to how it had truly happened. They would make up some lie. She had fallen. She had been mourning her husband. She hadn't been careful. Whatever they said, it would end up being Tyra's own fault.

Unn waited in the shadow of both the woods and her cattle for a good while after the warriors had left the pasture before she headed out. She couldn't even make herself go close to Tyra's corpse. The once yellow dress was dark red and brown from blood and dung. Her face was unrecognisable. Unn didn't dare to approach and see how bad it was.

In any case, Tyra was dead.

Unn walked in a long circle around Tyra. She had to go find the cow the men had scared off. She nearly walked into dead Magga, trying to avoid Tyra's corpse.

The cow wasn't quite dead. Its breaths were ragged. Thief had come and nuzzled Magga's back to keep her company. Magga's eyes were closed. The axe had splashed her brains around, but she was still gasping for breath. Unn grabbed her work knife, stuck into her apron, and placed it at Magga's neck. Without a moment of hesitation, she sliced through.

No cow could survive a wound like that, even one as strong and beautiful as Magga. The blood splattered up Unn's arm, and she caressed Magga's neck. Though terrible, it was a more merciful death than what Tyra had suffered. Unn caressed Magga and stayed with the cow until it no longer breathed and even Thief had gone to seek shelter from the rain.

The rain washed the blood off Unn's hands. She stared back at Tyra as she folded her knife away into her apron again.

She couldn't say anything about what had happened. It was better to pretend that she hadn't seen anything. Not even Tyra's cooling corpse. Let someone else find her and take the blame. Let some other thrall be killed for finding a dead freewoman.

She told herself that it was alright to leave Tyra there, dead in the rain and cow dung. She told herself it was what Tyra would have wanted. There was no use in her dying too. If Unn died as well, then she couldn't keep her promise. She couldn't sing Tyra into the next life.

TYRA

Chapter One Hundred and Sixty-Three

DEATH, PAIN, AND relief.

A single, faint voice called Tyra to the afterlife. It echoed around the Darkness like a herding call. Tyra woke to the sound of the song. Her head rang terribly, as if it was being smashed against the ground. Her entire body hurt and ached.

With open arms,
Hel will cheer:
"Welcome Tyra
Gunnasdóttir."

Gunnasdóttir... Tyra had not been her mother's daughter for many summers and winters. Not since that night of death in Ash-hill. She had been Siv's daughter, and then Siv had left, and since then, all Tyra had been was Harald Bluetan's daughter. Yet, no matter what other names she had borne, the little voice singing her to the afterlife was right—she was Tyra Gunnasdóttir.

Tyra rose to her feet. The Darkness was complete, and she couldn't see anything. Then, a thin strip of light carved itself into existence ahead of her. The song came from out there, leading her ahead.

The Darkness felt strange and cold on her skin. It felt like she had been there before, and yet terrifying at the same time. Tyra dared not even take a breath for fear that she would no longer be able to hear the faint voice calling her to the afterlife. For fear that she would lose her way and be stuck in the Darkness forever.

Through the dark, Tyra stumbled, blindly following the voice towards the tall slit of light.

> *Now your journey*
> *Shall begin.*
> *Greet the gods and*
> *Greet our kin.*

She *did* know the Darkness. Once, so long ago, Siv had hidden her away in an ash tree, and this was how it had been. Then, there had been no song and no slit of light, but the Darkness was certainly the same. Siv had told her not to speak. Siv had taught her so much.

Tyra reached the light. It was an opening, like someone had sliced through the worlds with a dagger. What lay beyond was veiled in white and Tyra couldn't quite see anything, but the singing voice came from beyond.

Tyra stepped through, into her afterlife.

A wind caressed her hands and lifted her hair when she stepped through. This place smelled like wet fur. She had expected the song of birds and green grasses, for that was what she had seen when she had gone to Asgard with Siv, once upon a time, or maybe a meadow like she had seen in Alfheim when she had gone there on her own, after Siv had left. None of that was what she saw.

She stood in the dark and rain of a spruce forest. Tyra stumbled ahead, over the uneven ground and fallen branches until she reached the bright path of a road ahead.

It was a rainy day on the road to Helheim, and Tyra was not the only corpse to find the way. The road to Helheim led up a mountainside with dark spruce trees on either side of the road. Corpses stumbled out of the forest and onto Hel's road, each as confused as the next. Only Tyra knew what lay ahead. She had never been to Helheim, but she had been to other worlds, and she had a good idea of what was there.

Her whole body hurt like she had been kicked awake. Her face more than anything. It felt like it was still asleep—somewhere between life and death. The other dead examined themselves. After observing them for a moment, Tyra too looked down at herself. She had been buried in expensive clothes. Much more so than any of the other corpses she could see. She had gold rings up her arms and gold brooches at her breasts, with colourful beads hanging between them. Her outer dress was red, and the inner was blue. Both had embroidered edges and decorative stitches.

The outer dress was not one that she had owned in life. It had been sewn especially for her funeral. She had been a queen, and buried as such. Almost—she smelled like cow dung. She had died in the pasture, she vaguely remembered. Her hair seemed to have been washed, but whichever thrall had done it, had missed a spot. When the wind came in from the left side, Tyra got a whiff of cow dung.

Tyra hid in the dark of the forest and stared up the road to Helheim. The singing voice that had brought her into her afterlife had reminded her of a time long past. Her parents and sisters. Her life seemed so far away that she could hardly remember their faces and names. Only her mother's name rang loud in her head: Gunna. She remembered her face too. She remembered stumbling over her mother's corpse. An arrow sticking out of her distant face. Tyra had always promised herself to meet them in the afterlife: her mother, and father, and sisters.

None of them had gone to Helheim, and on Ragnarok's battlefield she would never find them. There was something else too. A nagging feeling at the back of Tyra's mind. A reason why she had died, but she couldn't quite grasp it. Pieces of her life came to her in flashes, but she didn't get to choose the details she kept and remembered.

Her heart felt it, though; she wasn't supposed to go to Helheim. If she followed Helheim's road and passed the gate into Hel's realm, she wouldn't get out before Ragnarok, and even then, she had a feeling it would be difficult to prove that she belonged on the ships that would leave Helheim to fight on Ida's plain. She hadn't fought in many summers and winters.

Tyra hid in the dark of the forest and watched corpses join Hel's road. None of them were dressed in as expensive clothes as Tyra. None of them would begin their afterlife with riches.

Men and women marched up Hel's road in the rain. Tyra's eyes caught those of a family, walking together. A couple with two children. They were dressed in ragged clothes. They must have died in a raid somewhere. Been burned without funeral clothes or gifts.

'Help me,' Tyra cried, just loud enough for them to hear and react. 'Help!'

They stopped on the road and looked out to the forest. Tyra was hidden in the shadows, and they narrowed their eyes to see her. The youngest son was tugging on his mother's skirts to keep going.

'I'll give you a gold arm-ring if you help me.' Tyra slipped the ring off her arm and held it out so that it glinted in the daylight.

The husband liked that prospect. He came closer, off Hel's road and into the shadows of the woods. The family stayed behind, wary of Tyra.

The man winced at the sight of her. 'Someone really smashed your face in.'

That explained why her face hurt and why her lips felt swollen. Tyra brought a hand up to her cheeks. They were all strange and swollen and it hurt when she touched her skin. Bones stuck out places they were not supposed to, and her face had a shape she had never known it to have before. She didn't need a mirror to tell her that she looked like a monster.

'My killer had no empathy,' said Tyra and as she said the words, she remembered how she had died. Those warriors had chased her, the warriors with fire in their eyes. The memories came back to her slowly. It felt like trying to remember something distant from her childhood.

That was why she had died, she remembered. To warn the nine worlds that fire demons were loose in Midgard. To save Midgard. She certainly couldn't do that from inside Hel's gates.

'Your killer *did* have riches,' said the man in an envious tone, which made Tyra wary. Her wealth was tempting him to do something he shouldn't. The prospect of entering Helheim with a family to protect and no riches to start a new life was making him consider it. Robbing Tyra of her riches would be easy, and Tyra knew it.

'Indeed, they left me with riches,' Tyra hurried to say before he got any ideas. 'But it's blood sacrifices, and I can't take it. I can't start my life in Helheim with it. I need your help to get rid of these clothes and riches. I don't want them.'

The hungry look in his eyes settled. He looked up from her colourful clothes and into Tyra's eyes to assess her truth. 'Yrsa!' he called.

Yrsa... the name stirred memories. A face smiled at Tyra. A hand petted her head. She knew that name.

The man's wife approached the forest, telling her children to stay on the road, and while her husband convinced her to exchange clothes with Tyra—she did not take a lot of convincing—Tyra searched her memories.

She knew the name Yrsa. She had known it as a child. It was

not her mother's name, but it felt like family. A sister, perhaps. She no longer recalled how many sisters she had.

She was still trying to remember when she pulled on Yrsa's ragged dress. It was significantly colder than her own clothes had been, and she came away shivering.

'Takka,' she told the family, and watched them regain Hel's road. Tyra watched them leave above the hill, before she too headed out of the woods and onto Hel's road. The few others on the road barely acknowledged her. They walked in a daze, as if they could hardly believe that they had died.

At the top of the hillside, Hel's road sloped down towards Hel's gates. The gates were inside the mouth of a cave. Helheim had to be somewhere over this mountain. Corpses gathered in a thick crowd on the other side of the gates. Waiting for their loved ones to arrive, or perhaps looking for a way out.

A bark rang through the rain. The great hound, Garm, lay outside the gates to Helheim. Its mouth was bloodied, and it growled threateningly whenever a corpse inside Helheim came too close to the gates. The gates only opened when there was a large gathering of newly arrived corpses. A short man was in charge of opening and closing the gates. He had strong arms and was almost as wide as he was tall. His face was just as square as his body, lined by a beard.

Tyra walked towards Hel's gates. She stared warily at huge Garm. The hound growled at her, but then its attention shifted to someone else and it barked. Tyra walked to the opposite end of the gate from the hound. She stopped there, outside the gates and outside the cave to Helheim. She turned her eye back to Hel's road. She stood there, silently, until someone asked her why she was there.

Eventually, the short man in charge approached, rubbing his beard. 'It's time to go through,' he told her in a stern voice.

'My master has not arrived,' Tyra said, and she made certain she sounded like she was about to cry. 'I... I would like to serve in Sif's and Thor's household.'

'You're a thrall?' he asked in a bored tone. He did not appear surprised at the revelation, and once more Tyra remembered that her face had been deformed. She could not use her usual tricks. The rules were different now. All people saw when they looked at her was an ugly thrall.

Tyra nodded and said nothing more.

'Name?'

'Unn.'

He was about to walk away to open the gates, satisfied with her answers, when he stopped mid-step and turned back to Tyra. He narrowed his eyes at her suspiciously, like she was guilty of something.

Tyra felt her heart speed up. She wasn't used to people looking at her that way. Freemen used to eye her with envy and desire, never contempt, never hate.

'How did you die?' asked the man.

Tyra took a moment to answer and made sure her voice was trembling when she spoke. 'I tried to protect my master. Men were chasing her. They wanted her dead.'

'And is she?'

'I don't know, but she is not here.'

The guardian grumbled at that. 'You can wait there,' he decided.

Tyra made herself comfortable on the muddy ground, although in the thin clothes she had traded for herself and with the cold wind and rain, it wasn't truly possible to get comfortable. The whole day she waited there, and the following night as well.

Constantly, she had to remind herself that she was a thrall now. Her stomach growled from hunger and her head was weary. She had gathered rainwater in her hands to drink, but the hunger persisted.

As a thrall, she was not allowed to complain or ask anything more of the guardian. She was not allowed to say or do anything that had not been asked of her. She was cattle now.

Appropriately, she caught another whiff of the cow dung in

her hair as she tried to remind herself whom she had chosen to become in her short afterlife, for at least she knew that it would be short. Ragnarok was nearing. Tyra had known that her entire life.

On the night of the third day, someone finally arrived. The short man who opened and closed the gates had been replaced by a stern woman who liked to yell and who had kept Tyra up all night.

A slender woman appeared in front of Tyra. Immediately, she rose to her feet.

'Are you it?' asked the woman. Her skin was rough, and her hair was a tangle of split ends.

'Unn,' Tyra said, looking at the tall woman's feet instead of her face.

'What's that? Unn?'

'My name.'

The woman let out a laugh. 'That's not your name,' she said. 'You have only one name. It's the same as mine. Thrall.'

Tyra swallowed her words. Even though she had owned thralls, becoming one was very different from what she had imagined it would be. Especially in the houses of gods.

'Come,' said the woman, and although Tyra's stomach growled louder than Garm, she trekked through the night with the slender thrall.

They walked far, and for a long time, but all throughout their walk, the woman did not say another word. There were no pleasantries exchanged: no words, no questions. From that Tyra understood that while their names might be the same, this woman was far above her in rank, and she would have to be treated like a master.

At least there was no rain in Asgard, where they walked, and in the far distance, Tyra could see the familiar shape of Yggdrasil, outlined by the moonshine. Fenrir's children, Hati and Skoll, still hadn't swallowed the sun and moon. There was time until Ragnarok, if not a lot of it.

A rooster announced morning when they arrived onto Sif's and Thor's lands. The fields were wide, like none Tyra had ever seen before. They stretched so far that she couldn't see their edges. In the far distance rose the blurry shape of Yggdrasil. There were no forests or mountains to be seen from here. Only Sif's and Thor's fields and their enormous house. The house was shaped like that after which it had been named. Lightning-crack, the house was called in Midgard, and inside it boasted as many as five hundred and forty rooms. No taller structure had ever been built, in all the nine worlds. The building was tall, houses upon houses upon houses. Tyra couldn't see the top of Lightning-crack. It rose way up into the clouds.

The thrall woman who had fetched Tyra still said nothing as they walked through the wide fields towards the impressive residence of gods. Obediently, Tyra followed the woman to the back of the house, where there was a crack with a door that she pushed in.

Together they entered the slim door. So, Tyra would be serving in Thor's house, not in the fields or elsewhere. She wondered where she would sleep. She had seen no thrall dwellings on the way to Lightning-crack. Her question was soon answered, as the master thrall brought her through the long hallway they had entered at the back of Thor's and Sif's home.

Thralls were asleep on the floor. Some had already woken up and were readying themselves, combing fingers through their hair, washing their faces, and straightening the clothes in which they had slept.

The gruff thrall who had fetched Tyra continued walking until they reached some stairs at the far end of the hallway and went up, and up, and up. They passed countless hallways but went down none of them, until finally they did leave the stairs. Tyra's legs were shaking from the ascent and her stomach was so empty that it had stopped growling.

'This is your hallway,' said the gruff thrall, and then she left Tyra and proceeded back down the stairs. No explanations and no instructions. There were a dozen other thralls in the hallway, all ready for something, although no one explained what. No one introduced themselves. No one gave names or lineages. Thralls had neither.

Tyra was not the only thrall with her face bashed in, but their marks seemed more recent. So, Red Thor made a habit of beating his thralls, or perhaps thralls just died more terrible deaths to begin with. Neither guess would surprise Tyra, and she had to remind herself that she was like them now.

Unn the Thrall was her name, and any digressions would be answered with beatings or an execution. She supposed the gods had enough thralls to discard any who didn't do their work properly. Beatings were the way of life. By their afterlife, thralls should already be trained and know better. She didn't imagine that Sif and Thor would keep a disobedient thrall or would hesitate to slice a neck.

A loud voice came from one of the doors leading off the hallway, into the main house where the gods lived. A loud voice accompanied by the stomp of someone coming down steps.

'What do you mean, it isn't here?' Thor thundered. 'Where is it?' The hallway shook with the force of his voice. The thralls, too, were shaking.

There was a sharp sound, and then a wet smack as something fell to the ground.

'Of course it disappears so close to Ragnarok,' he grumbled, and then he bellowed, 'Do you know what my father will say?' His voice reminded Tyra of flames and fire demons chasing her. Fiery eyes meaning to kill her.

'Thrall!' he called in anger.

The thralls ushered Tyra forward towards the door. None of them wanted to go into the room when Red Thor was angry. Even Tyra, who had been a thrall for no longer than a few heartbeats, knew that it smelled of death. Thor was the kind of man who killed for fun and to ease his anger.

Tyra was pushed through the door and into the dwelling of her gods.

A room as large as any longhouse greeted her; inside were pillows on the floor and short tables full of things and anciently carved chests. Tyra knew not to lift her gaze beyond the floor. She saw Thor's feet planted in the middle of the room.

'Clean the bloody house,' ordered Thor.

A male thrall was sprawled out behind Tyra's god. Blood flowed from the thrall's neck onto the floor. Tyra felt faint, but she walked towards the dead man. The thrall was much larger than Tyra, and she wasn't certain that she had the strength to pull the corpse away, but she had no choice.

'Look at me,' Thor ordered in a hiss.

Tyra hesitated. She knew that she shouldn't: a thrall should never look at her master. A thrall should never speak first. But a thrall should also always do what was asked of her.

'Look—at—me.' Each word was spat out in controlled anger.

She would die if she didn't obey. Tyra looked up at Red Thor's face. His beard was not red like she had imagined it, like the beards of men with red hair: it looked like it had been dipped in blood, and his hair too, the colour was so dark.

'Did I ask you to pull your friend away?' His eyes were slim and red, and fixed on Tyra. 'That's not what I said. *You*'—he put clear emphasis on the word—'will find my Yggdrasil neck-ring. You.'

'Will you stop terrorising the thralls?' a voice rang from above. 'They already told you it isn't here.' Someone descended the steps to Tyra's left. Golden-haired Sif. Her arms were strong, intertwined rings flowing up her arms like snakes.

'They're lying,' Red Thor decided. 'I know where I left it.'

Tyra kept her eyes firmly on the ground, trying her best to blend into the wall she had backed up against.

'Then, where did you leave it?' asked Sif.

'Here,' Thor answered immediately. 'At home.'

Sif rolled her eyes at him so obviously that Tyra could see it from the corner of her eyes, although she kept her gaze on the floor where the dead thrall's blood was seeping into the cracks of the wood.

'Find me that pendant.' Thor was about to go, but then he winced as he looked at Tyra again. 'And cover your face. It's disgusting.'

SIGISMUND

Chapter One Hundred and Sixty-Four

THE BRACTEATE HUNG from Sigismund's neck and warmed him despite the rain that hammered over Helheim. It was as if the skies knew they were leaving, as if Helheim was crying at the thought of parting with so many corpses.

'What if there's more than one coming towards me at once?' asked red-haired Aslak, who rode next to Sigismund. He was one of the younger recruits, who had farmed all his life in Midgard and most of his afterlife too.

Sigismund's followers had trained with his weapons and under his command for no more than four winters. They were inexperienced and had never seen true battle, but they were ready to fight for their kinsmen and for justice. They were ready to give up their afterlives for the cause. Their hearts were that of true warriors.

'If more of them charge at you at once, you deal with one at a time,' Sigismund advised. 'You shoulder one of them to the side with your shield, or maybe you can lure them into somewhere narrow where they can't fight side by side, or you make one of

294

them fall so you can deal with the other.'

The young corpse was taking in the information as if it were Odin's own words of wisdom. He nodded so much that his long red hair fell out of its braid. 'And...' he began but then stopped himself and leaned back on his horse, away from Sigismund.

'And?' In Midgard, Sigismund might have dismissed such hesitant questions, but not here in Helheim. This close to the final war, it was crucial that those who were still doubting were allowed to ask their questions. They were headed to certain and final death. They deserved to arrive as prepared as possible.

'What if I meet a... *god*?' Aslak whispered the word, and Sigismund noticed the four men on the cart that rattled in front of them turn to stare at him for an answer.

'Cattle die, kinsmen die,' someone else answered, before Sigismund found the right words. A warrior rode towards them, decked in full armour, chainmail and helmet and furs and gloves.

'We must die likewise,' the corpses muttered in response. They were rightfully terrified at the thought of dying at the hands of their gods.

'Nej,' said the rider. 'Gods too must die.' He turned his horse around to ride next to Sigismund.

The horse was a stubborn thing that cast its head back and forth, but the rider kept steady on its back with his legs clenched firmly around it. He lifted off his helmet.

'Hei, Sigismund,' said Einer with a tired smile. He looked like he had not slept in days, perhaps weeks. His straw-coloured hair was greasy, and his face was flushed.

'Einer,' Sigismund muttered at the sight of his old friend. He had never thought they would meet again. Certainly not on the eve of Ragnarok, and in Helheim. 'I thought you died out on the ice.'

'And I thought you might have drowned on the way here.' Einer smiled. 'You never were that good a swimmer.'

Sigismund laughed and leaned back in his saddle. 'Oh, I nearly did drown. The real question is, how did *you* survive?'

Sigismund was well aware that the bracteate that hung from his neck and warmed him was what had saved his life through the journey.

Einer looked like he had waited for Sigismund to ask. He reached into his belt and pulled out a gold chain. From it hung the same kind of bracteate that hung from Sigismund's neck and kept him warm. The same kind Einer had given Sigismund out on the ice and that Loki had told Sigismund to destroy.

Einer held it out to Sigismund like he knew.

'Loki?' Sigismund asked as he grabbed the neck-ring. Only Loki, and perhaps Hel, knew the task he had been given.

Einer nodded seriously, and they both acknowledged that they would have to speak, alone, when they arrived at the harbour. Sigismund's own bracteate beat hot against his chest and reminded him that he had not succeeded in undoing it.

The worry that he might not find a way to undo them before it was too late made Sigismund bite his lower lip as he dropped Einer's bracteate into his belt pouch.

The red-haired rider next to Sigismund had been gaping at Einer since he had joined them. 'Who are you?' Aslak eventually asked, leaning forward on his horse so far that the poor animal couldn't quite tell if it should go faster or try to shake its rider off.

'Einer. Sigis and I have known each other a lifetime,' he said with an amused glint in his eye.

Red-haired Aslak was stunned back into silence. In life, Einer had always had a gift for impressing young warriors. It was a skill he had not lost in death.

'But here,' Einer added, 'I command Helheim's army.'

Aslak went wide-eyed and Sigismund began to laugh.

Of course Einer was commanding them into battle on Ida's plain. Of course he had found himself in the most unlikely position in the afterlife. Sigismund laughed so his stomach hurt and his horse nearly wrestled him off its back. He had not laughed so much since he had met Loki on the way to Rain-soaked. 'Of course, you are,' Sigismund said, struggling to stop laughing.

He had heard that an Einar would be commanding them to Ida's plain, but so many fallen bore that name that Sigismund had not even thought twice about it. He never would have guessed that the man in charge was his childhood friend, who had killed a white bear in Iceland.

They rode over the hill at the edge of the last field. Below them the large harbour and beach unfolded, full of warriors clad for war and with at least a thousand ships in the waters. Sigismund and the other newly arrived let out one long, unified sigh at the sight of it.

Sigismund dismounted and clapped his horse's neck as he stared out at the beach. There were thousands and thousands of people all the way up and down the bay. Yet no more than half a hundred houses and forges made up the harbour. Never before had Sigismund seen so many fighters assembled in one place. He had arrived with a group of two hundred himself and knew that many more would arrive during the night.

The newly arrived recruits were lined up on the hillside, staring down at the incredible numbers who would become their shield-mates. The rain poured over them, but the warriors on the beach didn't appear to mind. They all looked like they were moving with a purpose. There were commanders training shield-walls, and groups on the harbour receiving instruction in sailing. There were warriors everywhere, but most of them walked in groups, being guided around the harbour and given assignments.

Sigismund let out a stifled laugh. 'And you're commanding all of these warriors?'

'Oh, there are more,' Einer dismissed, matter-of-factly. 'This morning about nine thousand finished their sailing practice. Those who finish take shelter in the first few towns inland. I told them there's no need to stay on the beach. It gets crowded.'

The numbers were so vast that Sigismund could not even understand them. He had thought that the two hundred he arrived with was a big army. In death, Sigismund had trained more warriors than he had in life, and he had thought that in Helheim he was the one who had trained the most. But so *many* had arrived to fight for Helheim.

'We should get moving,' Einer said. 'The group after you will be arriving soon.' He kicked his horse ahead. At his command, the horse carefully stepped out over the side of the hill and onto the sand on the steep slope down to the beach. He forced it halfway down the hill, then stopped and turned in his saddle to shout to Sigismund and the long row of stunned warriors. 'There's a path down there,' he said, pointing towards the settlements. 'You can ride that way and unpack your carts. I'd like your horses and carts back on the road as soon as possible. I suggest that you put on your gear as well and keep it with you. I left mine in a tent yesterday and it took me half the day to find it again.'

The first few riders began to steer their horses and carts down the way Einer had pointed. Sigismund could hardly tear his eyes away from the sea of warriors on the beach.

'Sigis, do you have things on the carts?' Einer asked.

Red-haired Aslak answered before Sigismund could. 'We'll take care of them,' he said, gaining an approving nod from Einer, which made the young corpse's pride swell like only words of praise from a god could.

'Then you can follow me, Sigis. We have things to discuss.'

Sigismund caught himself gaping and closed his mouth. He kicked his reluctant horse after Einer down the sandy side of the beach towards the dense bustle of fighters. Everyone was wearing their full gear, shields too. Einer had no shield with him, but Sigismund supposed a shield was easier to find again than fighting gloves, or a fitting helmet.

'I'm glad you're here, at last,' Einer said with a sigh. 'We were with each other at the beginning. It's only fair of fate to let us die together, in the end.' He had grown calmer and wiser in the short time they had been apart. He had grown older too, which was strange, for the dead did not age in Helheim. Einer had gained wrinkles on his forehead, and creases under his eyes.

'I only wish Leif Ragnarson was with us,' Einer said with a sigh.

'He is,' Sigismund said. 'I keep my promises, Einer.'

To greet Ragnar in Helheim had been Einer's final request before Sigismund had dived into the monstrous waves on Niflheim's coast. The first winter after Sigismund had built dwellings for himself, he had searched for Ragnar and his family.

'Ragnar hadn't found them yet, but Leif will be fighting with us.'

The prospect made Einer smile like a little boy. 'He'll join our secret cause then.'

Sigismund shook his head. Leif would fight for Helheim like so many others, but Sigismund was not convinced he was skilled enough to join their particular cause. 'He is just a boy,' Sigismund revealed. Leif had died young. He had never been given the chance to grow up. 'He hadn't been fighting in the afterlife when I saw him.'

'I trust Leif,' Einer persisted.

Sigismund gave in with an unconvinced smile and a nod. This was why people trusted Einer: because he trusted *them*, unconditionally. It was his greatest strength and Sigismund hoped that it would not be his downfall. Because this close to Ragnarok, Einer's failure could be the failure of their entire army, and the final death of thousands and thousands of corpses.

Sigismund did not envy the responsibilities of commanding such a large army. The demands had to be great, but Einer did not make it show. He had deep dark bags under his eyes, and he had gained wrinkles, but he still smiled and talked in a cheerful tone.

Folk barely parted around them as they rode through the assembled crowd, but everyone had something to tell Einer.

Commanders shouted to him about what their recruits had accomplished, and warriors greeted their high commander. Einer smiled to them all and thanked them for their reports.

He was born for this, Sigismund thought as he watched Einer.

On the way to Magadaborg, Einer had shown an ease with command. He had balanced all aspects of war and made it look easy. He had remembered details and made certain every last warrior felt heard and understood. But this...? This was something else.

There were so many people, yet Einer addressed every commander who reported to him by name. He knew them all, and they knew him.

Sigismund did not know the names of half the people he had travelled with, but Einer seemed to know everyone. Had they been walking and not riding through the crowd, it would have taken them half a day to reach the settlements by the harbour, past all the people seeking Einer's approval.

A little boy came running up to them when he saw them approach the settlement. 'The stables?' he asked, all eager to care for their horses and to do something.

'Just mine,' Einer replied and unmounted. 'My friend's horse belongs to the new recruits.'

The boy gave a sharp nod like he understood, took both Einer's and Sigismund's reins when they had dismounted, clapped their horses, and guided the animals away.

Einer hurried to the door of the first house before anyone else could approach for more praise and words. The door swung open before he reached it, and out came a woman in bearskin. The left side of her face was wounded, and her ear had been cut off.

'Brannar,' Einer said and waited until she looked up at him and smiled. 'Do you know where the others are?' He was smiling like he had just asked her if she wanted to jump a midsummer fire with him, and Brannar smiled back as if she had said ja.

'I saw you arrive. I was just about to get them. Is this him?'

She stared at Sigismund, and there was something about her blue eyes that seemed to see straight into Sigismund's core.

'Ja,' Einer said. 'Sigismund Karson.'

'He's more handsome than you said,' Brannar teased and winked to Sigismund as she walked away, her long brown hair swaying behind her.

'She's quite the girl,' Einer said as he watched her walk away. 'She was a bear hunter in life.'

'Is that how she lost the ear?'

Einer shook his head. 'Some dispute with her father.'

It was strange to see Einer so taken by a girl. In love, almost, and of course not with an ordinary girl from Helheim. Of course, with Einer, it had to be a bear hunter or the like. He had always admired the strong girls.

'A bear-slayer, like you,' Sigismund said, following Einer's gaze.

Einer laughed. 'That was different.' He truly had grown mature. He could laugh about it now. For so many summers and winters the two of them had drifted apart because of that dead white bear that neither one of them dared mention, but now Einer could laugh about it.

He was still staring after Brannar, although she had long disappeared into the crowd. 'She trained in sword and spear fighting her entire afterlife. Amazing.' He sighed, and finally turned back to the open door. 'Are you married?' he asked as they entered the house.

Sigismund nodded and closed the door after himself so no eager warrior would follow them inside. 'I married a few moons after I arrived.'

The house was empty, apart from numerous crates marked as food. Drinks and horns and cups had been set out on top of one of the huge crates.

'Good.' Einer walked straight to the table with drinks. He looked like he needed it. He looked like he needed sleep, too. 'Children?'

'She has a son.'

'Is he here?' Einer asked as he poured them both drinks.

'Not on the beach. His mother wouldn't let him fight,' Sigismund said. 'It was hard enough for her to part with me, but I told her that since she has been married twice, she will find a better man and marry a third time.'

'So, you lied.' Einer understood and laughed. 'I wish I could have married,' he sighed. 'Even if it was just to an ugly jotun girl.' They both chuckled at that. 'My one regret in life.'

Sigismund took the horn Einer offered. 'Your one regret in death,' he corrected.

'Nej,' Einer said and took a drink while Sigismund wondered at the denial. 'You might be,' Einer said at last, finishing his drink and smacking his lips. 'But I'm not yet dead.'

Sigismund's eyes shot up to the wrinkles on Einer's forehead and the wrinkles at the edges of his eyes. He truly had grown older. He was alive and aging.

'Honestly speaking, this is not where I would have ended up in my afterlife,' Einer said. Some might have taken that as an insult, but coming from Einer, Sigismund knew that it was not meant to be.

'Nej, I would have expected to see you feasting in Valhalla's halls,' Sigismund said and took a slurp of his drink. The ale was bitter, but he supposed that so close to the end of gods and giants and corpses, a bitter drink was better than none.

'I was there,' Einer said with the fond smile of an old man looking back on his life. 'I feasted at the high tables in Valhalla. I walked through the halls and fought on the plains. My sword has clashed against Tyr's armour, and I have stared into Thor's red eyes. I dined with giants and swam with the Midgard Worm. I need no afterlife. In life, I did it all.'

'Except marry,' Sigismund said.

'Except marry,' Einer agreed, and they emptied their drinks to that.

The door swung open. Brannar was back, and she was not alone. With her were two large men, one blond and one red-haired, dressed both in chainmail and leather armour. They carried their helmets in their hands and their belts were full of weapons. Behind Brannar and the two men came a tall scrawny boy, who closed the door.

'This is our shield-wall,' Einer announced. 'We're the only ones who know about the neck-rings.'

Then he proceeded to introduce them all to Sigismund. 'Brannar you just met, and then there's Bogi,' he said and pointed to the red-haired warrior. 'Nar.' The blond warrior smiled in greeting. 'And finally, Tassi.' The scrawny boy walked further into the room and rested his back against a wall of chests and crates.

They were not exactly the kind of crew Sigismund had expected. Tassi especially seemed an unlikely addition, but that told him that Einer had a plan.

Sigismund pulled forward the bracteate Einer had given him earlier, and then reached under his tunic and pulled out his own.

'So, they do look the same,' Nar observed.

'And we have two,' Sigismund said. 'We just need to find the last one.'

'*Just,*' Brannar laughed. 'It'll be difficult enough to get close, and then to pull it off his neck.' She shuddered. 'I don't envy you that task, Tassi.'

'Whose neck?' Sigismund asked. They had obviously discussed the plan and knew more than him. All Sigismund truly knew was that he had to undo the three bracteates, somehow, and who they had belonged to, once.

The crew looked at him in confusion, except for Einer, always quick to explain. 'The one I gave you on the ice used to hang around Surt's neck, to protect him against the fires of Muspelheim. The other one belonged to Thor. The last one still hangs from its master's neck.'

Sigismund's heart beat with a fury all the way up into his throat. *From its master's neck.* 'Odin?' he asked, and the faces of the rest of the team told him that his guess was correct.

Loki had said who had created them and owned them, but Sigismund had never thought that they would have to retrieve one from Odin's own neck. All he knew was that he had to undo the bracteates, and that was troublesome enough.

'Nej. Nej. Nej.' Sigismund walked back to some of the crates and leaned against them. He buried his face in his hands to focus. There was no way in the nine worlds that they could steal a neck-ring off the Alfather.

'The gold hangs from his neck,' Einer said as if it was the simplest of things. 'He can only die if we remove it. We have to succeed.'

Sigismund's breaths came short and ragged. Removing the bracteate would be difficult, but it was not just about that. Sigismund had to destroy them too, and that came with entirely different challenges.

'I can't...' Sigismund began. His breaths were so short and his mind raced so much that he struggled to get words out. 'I can't undo them,' he admitted. 'I can't undo the bracteates.'

'What do you mean?' Bogi asked, and had the task at hand not seemed so daunting, his toned, tall figure would have been intimidating.

'I've tried everything,' Sigismund said. 'I've tried to melt it and hammer it and pierce it. I've tried it all, but not so much as a scratch.'

No one else said anything. Even Einer had lost his ability to stay cheerful. 'You... You'll just have to keep trying,' Einer muttered, but his tone was not convincing, and when Sigismund looked up at him, it seemed like his friend had gained new creases on his forehead.

'But you *are* the smith?' asked Tassi. He had a deep voice that did not match his appearance.

'That's what Loki said,' was all the answer Sigismund could give. He had begun to question it, too. Perhaps Loki had been wrong, and Sigismund was not who he had been searching for, or perhaps no one could undo them. They had been forged by dwarves, after all. 'Three Ulfberht blades collected my blood. He said that was the sign.'

'Well, then, it doesn't really change much for us,' Tassi decided, and immediately Sigismund understood why Einer had picked him to be part of the shield-wall.

Einer had too many other obligations on this beach to always see the opportunities and tasks clearly. He needed someone who was not overwhelmed by the seemingly impossible. Someone like Tassi.

'What do you mean?' Brannar hissed.

'We have to steal the bracteate off the Alfather's neck, so he can die. And then give it to *him*.' He pointed to Sigismund. 'If he can't undo them, that's his issue. We just need to ensure that the Alfather dies.'

It *was* his issue, Sigismund thought. Loki had told him the story. Sigismund understood how important it was to undo the bracteates so no one could ever abuse their strength again. He had spent his afterlife with the bracteate around his neck and he knew perfectly well what it could protect against.

'It does somewhat complicate things,' Einer said. His thoughtful consideration had returned after Tassi's observation. 'It means we need a bigger shield-wall.'

'Why?'

'Originally, we just had to protect Sigismund long enough to get the bracteate to him so he could destroy it, but if he can't destroy it...'

'Then he has to survive Ragnarok,' Brannar said. 'By Hel... how are we going to do that?'

'He just wears the bracteates,' said blond Nar. 'They'll protect him.'

'Ja...' Einer said, but there was something about the way he said it and looked at Nar that made Sigismund sweat, because the temptation of life was a lot to walk around with, dangling from his neck, and Nar looked like someone who had a lot to live for. It would be much easier to steal a bracteate off Sigismund's neck than that of the Alfather.

They began to discuss battle plans after that, but all throughout, as Einer explained why they each needed to sail on separate ships so they wouldn't all die if a ship went down, Sigismund kept a wary eye on Nar. When they had tired of discussions of war, and the others had left again and Einer had been called away on duty, so only Brannar and Sigismund sat alone on the floor among crates and crates of food and drink, Brannar leaned in and whispered Sigismund's own thoughts aloud to him.

'You can't trust us,' she whispered. 'You don't know us. You *have* to find a way to destroy the bracteates before the end of the battle.'

Sigismund agreed with a nod. 'We all have to die at Ragnarok.'

VEULVE

Chapter One Hundred and Sixty-Five

VISIONS HAD BEGUN to blend into each other in front of the veulve's star-dotted eyes. Fate had conquered and won its battle against the Alfather. Ragnarok was upon them. At long last. So, the veulve turned her star-dotted eyes towards the present and future.

The past stretched long behind her, with its three-year winter and the cawing of Jotunheim's red rooster in Gallows-woods. The past was long with laughter and battle and plotting, but the future was short, and filled with darkness and blood.

Ragnarok had begun. Those hopeful words had echoed in her mind for the past three winters as she tried to focus her star-dotted eyes on the present. A task not easily accomplished, for her eyes saw everything, all the time. Everything that had been and was and would be.

The future had gained certainty. The veulve no longer saw what might be and what could be, but simply that which would come to be. The three nornir had tied their threads tight. The future was as good as hacked in stone.

A gold rooster will crow from the oak tree, as once Fiallar crowed in Gallows-woods. Its sooty mate crows in Hel's home. The hound howls at corpses by Gnipa-cave. The ship Naglfar *breaks free. East it journeys, across the churned waves of the Midgard Worm's tail splashes. Bounds are broken, at last. Brother will fight brother, and be his slayer.*

The veulve's star-dotted eyes saw all as it would be, and as it was. She felt herself free from that which had bound her destiny to Asgard. Once the final battle had come to pass, she would be free. Her faint hope was being fulfilled.

Dwarves groan at their doors. Heimdall sounds his gold Gjallar-horn. The aesir gather in counsel. Clashes and roars ring throughout Jotunheim. The giants are coming. The skies split in half. Yggdrasil creaks and stands upright. Surt arrives with fire. Giants clash against Asgard's mountain-wall. The barricade keeps the calm of Asgard. Soon, it shall all break.

All of it was happening, or would. So close was the certain future that the veulve could no longer tell what was already happening and what was yet to come, but she kept watching, hungry for more, hungry for the time when all her star-dotted eyes showed her of the present and the future was the dark sky with no sun or moon and the bloodied, rotting corpses on the ground.

EINER

Chapter One Hundred and Sixty-Six

THE SUN ROSE over Helheim. Roosters crowed and warriors awoke. Many had slept in the sand, under tarpaulins and blankets. No one had thought to bring tents to the beach where they gathered.

Einer hadn't slept. All through the night people had come to him with problems and questions, and all through the night he had worked to solve their every issue. He tried to let the hundred senior commanders he had chosen sleep through the night, for he knew that *he* would not have been able to sleep had he tried. It had been weeks since he had last slept.

A group of four people were hissing and arguing on a ship out on the port. Einer let out an exasperated sigh, stepped over the warriors sleeping around him, and pushed through the sand to the port to solve whatever the issue was.

'I don't know what they were thinking last night,' one of them hissed at the others. 'It's so heavy.'

They were gathered on the second largest ship in port, the *Storm Maker*. The one Einer had assigned Sigismund to yesterday morning. At once, he knew what they were arguing over.

He waited until he was close to speak to them. His mere presence startled them into silence. They were new on the beach, but they knew who Einer was.

'Forgive,' one of them said as he approached. 'We'll be quiet.'

Einer kept walking until he stood close enough to whisper so that no one inland would hear what he said.

'The anvil stays,' he whispered. 'I need it, and I need it on this ship.'

'But it's so heavy,' said one of the two on the ship. 'And it takes a lot of room under the deck. We're one crate short of our full count.'

Behind the two on the ship was a crate of food they must have thought fitted nicely at the aft. But some things were more important.

'Then remove some of your ballast stones, or leave the crate,' Einer ordered. 'We need the anvil more than we need the extra food.'

He didn't explain why the anvil was so important, and he could see the confusion on their faces and knew that if he told them nothing, they would talk among themselves, even if he told them not to, and they would wonder, and perhaps one of them might even be stupid enough to try to leave the anvil behind.

'When your weapon clashes against one of Valhalla's gold shields, and the pommel slips off your sword, or your axe head is slammed loose, or your spear-shaft cut in two, you'll be glad that we brought a smith.'

The realisation slowly set in. They had probably never fought in life. They knew that Einer had been a commander and that he had fought on Ida's plain. Wild rumours about his accomplishments had spread across the beach. It meant that the warriors mostly respected that there were certain aspects of war that only Einer knew.

He gave each of the four a look of warning and then he left them there to figure out what to do about the remaining crate of food.

The ships were packed with enough provisions for the force to fight and live for a week. Some would live and fight longer, but for most the end would come as soon as they hopped off the ships. Every warrior had sewn their own food pockets at Einer's instructions, so they would have something to eat during the fight when they were far from the ships. There would not be much time to rush back to the ship for meals. He didn't suppose that anyone would call the fighting to a halt so they could go back to their respective camps to fill their bellies and catch up on sleep. Ragnarok would be ruthless.

Inland, folk were slowly waking up and getting to work. They knew their tasks, and although they were ready to sail out at any moment, there was always more to do. The more training Helheim's corpses got, the better, although Einer had set strict limitations on how much they were allowed to train a day. He could not risk them being sore at the start of battle because they had trained too hard.

As he walked across the beach, his shoes slipping in the sand, and thankful that everyone was too busy packing their personal gear and washing themselves and waking up to demand anything of him, he thought about next week. If they didn't leave within the next two days, they would need to replace their food reserves. They had no more reserves now that the ships had been packed.

Einer was forming his list of whom he should send out to gather food and where to, when someone came to him with more troubles to fix.

'Einer?' a young man called. His voice was high, like that of a child. He *was* a child, thin and without a beard. He must have died young. When Einer looked into the boy's deep blue eyes and stared at his face, his life in Midgard seemed to flood back to him.

'Leif?'

They collided in a hug. Leif was so small and felt fragile. He was not at all the fierce older brother that Einer remembered. His arms were slim and held no strength, not even that of a farmer's hard work, and he was pale, as if he rarely saw sunlight.

They parted from their hug, and where Einer would normally have given his old friend a good slap on the back, he restrained himself, because a good slap on the back might send Leif flying halfway down the beach.

Sigismund was right, Einer knew when he looked at Leif. Perhaps the Leif of his memories had been different. Leif had been older than Einer, and always seemed like a big brother, but he had died so young. In the afterlife, he was just a child.

'It's good to see you, Leif,' Einer said nonetheless, because it was. He had spent a long time missing his childhood friend.

Leif was nothing like Einer remembered him to be. His face was the same. A nose that mirrored Ragnar's, except for the tip, and round cheeks and a square chin, but everything else Einer remembered was not there. The Leif in his memories was steadfast and strong and big, a warrior above all else. When Einer looked at Leif as he was now, and must have been in death, he suddenly understood why Ragnar had been so reluctant to let him fight in the Holmgang. He was so small.

'You too,' Leif said. 'You've truly grown.'

A strange awkwardness installed itself between them. Never had they been awkward with each other in life, as far as Einer recalled, but it had been so long ago, and they had been children back then. The world of children was different.

'Sigismund told me you would join us,' Einer said to say something, anything. 'What crew did you join?'

'I sail on *Hati's Kin*,' said Leif, and for some reason Einer was relieved that Leif and he were on different ships.

'You have a good commander, then,' Einer commented. 'Haskell was a warrior in life.'

'He's a great commander,' Leif agreed, and again, there was that strange distance between them.

Until that moment, Einer had never realised how much he had grown since he was a child, and even just since leaving Midgard. Much had happened since Leif had died.

He was a war commander now, and even though he rarely had any sleep, he *liked* being a commander. He was good at delegating tasks and making decisions and coming up with strategies. He was good at making people work together, and steering them towards a common goal, and he was no longer the young boy who had used to follow Leif around everywhere.

As he looked at skinny Leif, he realised that he no longer wanted to be that young boy, either. 'Forgive, Leif,' he sighed. 'But I have...'

'You have work,' Leif finished for him. The awkwardness lifted. 'Busy life of a commander.'

Einer nodded and hurried away from young Leif. He had thought their meeting would be full of joy and that all would be as it had been back in the days, when they had been children together, but Einer supposed that their roles had changed and neither one of them knew how to adjust to that. Leif had always used to lead when they were kids, and Einer had been content to follow. Leif had been bigger and stronger. Now, Einer was the one to lead and be bigger and stronger and more steadfast. He had looked up to Leif and grown, and in death, Leif had looked up to no one and stayed the same. They were as different as night and day, now.

The strangeness lingered as Einer walked to the shed outside which he and the senior commanders gathered every morning. He had one thousand eight hundred shield-wall commanders and a hundred senior ones. The morning meetings were just with the senior commanders who then spread Einer's word to the shield-wall commanders. The sailing crews were different from the shield-walls: the best sailors were not necessarily the most capable of leading others into battle. So, Einer had engaged a young ship builder to assign the command teams on each ship, and although Einer himself was capable of commanding a ship, he had refused the responsibility.

A few of the senior commanders walked ahead of Einer towards the shed. Einer dragged his feet fast through the wet sand and joined them with the morning's stories of the strangest things he had been asked during the night.

There had been an old man, howling and crying, because he was terrified that they would be chased by white bears when they left the confines of Helheim and sailed along the coast of Niflheim. There had been a hundred spearmen training their grips, but holding their spears in the wrong hands.

The commanders were still laughing at Einer's stories when they reached the shed. More than one insisted that he get some sleep tonight, but Einer knew that he would not. There was too much to worry about.

Once they were out of Helheim, sailing towards Asgard's shores, he would lie down and fall asleep to the roll of the ship. The battle plans for their arrival were clear. But not a moment before. He told them as much, and although he could see that they worried he might not sleep even then, they didn't protest.

'So, what's our final count?' Einer asked to begin their meeting. They found their positions and gathered in a wide circle as if at a Ting.

An old man with grey hair and the strong arms of a fisherman stepped forward. 'We had to count a few times just to make certain we had everyone, but I think the count is nine hundred thousand, four hundred and sixty-three.' He turned to another commander with a frown on his face. 'Did we count Einer?'

The other commander shook his head.

'Sixty-four then. That's your final number.'

Einer nodded at them, barely able to comprehend that they had gathered so many recruits to sail out of Helheim and fight their gods. Nine hundred thousand warriors under his command. Nine hundred thousand warriors to follow him into battle. It was more than he had ever thought he would see in life, and yet, he was painfully aware that it was not good enough.

'That's a lot,' they all agreed.

'More than Valhalla,' a shield-maiden said, one of only five that Einer had selected for senior command. Brannar had recommended her.

'It's not,' Einer revealed in a sigh. He couldn't let them leave for Asgard thinking that they had the advantage of numbers. 'I've fought on Ida's plain, and I know how many heroes the Alfather will have to fight for him, and it's a lot more than what we have.'

The senior commanders' self-praise fell silent.

'How many?' one eventually dared to ask.

'You all know the stories,' Einer said. 'Five hundred and forty doors. Out of each of them eight hundred fighters will march shoulder to shoulder. What the stories don't tell you is how many rows of warriors will march out of each gate. Valhalla has a hundred times more warriors than we do.'

In truth, Valhalla possessed much more than a hundred times as many—perhaps a thousand times—but his senior commanders could never comprehend that, because only Einer had laid eyes on the waste of Ida's plain, and only he could truly comprehend how small their army was in comparison.

The commanders were shocked enough as it was, and when he looked around at their faces, Einer feared that they might lose hope and abandon the cause. They had not been warriors, he reminded himself, neither in life nor in death. They were in Helheim precisely because they did not possess the true hearts of warriors.

The battlefield would prove their strength, but unless Einer was careful, it could be their defeat too.

'Valhalla desperately needs that many warriors,' Einer told them. 'Because they are the only protectors of Asgard. The warriors of Valhalla and the gods. *We* are different. *We* do not fight for glory or honour in death; we already gained that. Anyone can fight for their gods, but to stand up and *oppose* our gods—to strike them when they are wrong—that is true courage, which no corpse in Valhalla possesses.'

A few of the commanders nodded along to that.

'More importantly, we are not alone. The giants will arrive on Ida's plain before us. Fire will burn through the battlefield with us. Beasts will howl at our backs and leap over us into battle. We are merely the ballast on a warship. We keep the scales from tipping. We fight closer to the ground where giants and beasts can't reach. We serve a different role than Valhalla's defenders.'

There were many nods among the senior commanders now, but Einer was not yet finished.

'That is why we must be what Valhalla's warriors will never be. We must be chaos, we must be unexpected. We are not fighters, like them,' he reminded them, for it would be crucial for them to remember on the battlefield. 'But they are no fishermen, or merchants, or farmers, or smiths or ropemakers like us. We know trades they *never* will. We know tricks they could never think up, and that is why nine hundred thousand, four hundred and sixty-four Helheim corpses will be more than enough to overpower Valhalla's golden protectors.'

The commanders roared. Their hope had been restored, along with their will to go to battle and give their afterlives for their families. Speaking to Leif, and seeing that small kid about to head off into battle, and walking around the beach at night, seeing people holding their spears wrong, made Einer realise that his warriors did not need to fight like warriors in Valhalla. Their true strength was that they were *not* warriors.

Their battle strategies would have to change—immediately. At any moment, Ragnarok could begin.

'What they have learned on this beach,' Einer added when his commanders finished their roaring and cheering. 'What we have taught them. The battle strategies and the way of combat... That is how Valhalla's defenders will fight. That is how their opponents will think. But it is not how *we* think or fight. You remind your followers of who they are. Whatever skills they have, they can use. Whatever tools they are familiar with, they can take with them to battle. Teach them tricks. They can hold onto giants' feet and be swept far ahead, into the heat of battle. They can pick up a gold shield and infiltrate Valhalla's protectors. They can cast fishing nets and capture their enemies. Anything they can imagine, they must use. *That* is how we win.'

Again, the senior commanders were cheering. Thick rows of warriors had formed around the commanders' circle, and they, too, had been listening and now they erupted into cheers.

'You've all worked hard,' Einer praised his senior commanders. 'You've taught our corpses everything they need to know. There is only one lesson left. This is it. There are no rules in the heat of battle. So, teach them how to use their trades and tools against Valhalla. To step on feet and tie ropes around ankles. Our commanders must all know, and our warriors, all nine hundred thousand of them. All *must* know this. Whatever they know how to do, they can and *must* use to their advantage in battle.'

Cheers erupted from the warriors surrounding them. This was a battle strategy that they understood and could use. This truly was how they would win.

At that Einer dismissed his senior commanders and saw them rush through the crowds to gather their shield-wall commanders and pass on Einer's instructions. Word of what he had said, and the instructions he had given, were already spreading from ear to ear, and that morning, there was a newfound excitement over the harsh battle to come.

His warriors had hope. At last, and not a day too soon.

For as they began to use their weapons in their own way and gained confidence in their skills, a rooster's livid crowing echoed through Helheim. Not just across the beach or the bay, or the harbour, but across all of Helheim. Hel's black-feathered rooster had woken at last.

Ragnarok was announced.

Panic rushed through the thousands and thousands of people on the beach. Panic grabbed every last corpse in Helheim.

Einer too felt his bones shake at the thought of Ragnarok, but then the fear subsided, and his mind cleared.

'Report to your ship commanders,' he yelled. 'Grab your gear, and report to your commanders!'

His orders were picked up and shouted elsewhere, and to Einer's surprise, his corpses remembered their training and did exactly as they had been instructed to do.

They gathered their things. They put on their fighting gear, lifted their shields and marched into their formations. The first few crews rushed along the port, eager to board their ships.

Einer was about to yell after them not to run and to check their gear twice, but a ship commander beat him to it, and the sailors slowed themselves. The ship commanders had been the perfect picks. Within heartbeats, they had gathered their sailors and calmed them. A handful rushed around, looking for their crews, and then there was only Einer.

The previous night he had left his gear—everything from his shield to his weapon belt—inside the small naust. As the last unprepared warrior, he rushed through the crowds to the ship-builder sheds.

He laughed a little at himself, as Helheim's rooster crowed again. Of course the war commander was the last one to follow his own orders, just as he was the only one who hadn't slept. With a true warrior's calm, Einer slipped on his chainmail and fastened a leather tunic that Loki had gifted him. His helmet came next and the white bearskin at his neck, so that he was completely covered from the back. He strapped on his weapon belt, adjusted it so the weapons were where he needed them to be—his own sword and his father's Ulfberht, as well as the dagger at his back. He had also placed a slim ship-building axe next to the dagger. He was strong enough to carry it, and one could always use an axe: if for nothing else, then to hook onto something.

Last, Einer took the time to crouch down and check his socks and his shoes, before he picked up his shield and walked out of the naust to wait for his own ship crew. He had picked the last ship for himself, so that his crew would be the last to arrive at the beach. They had been sleeping inland. Only their commanders came to the beach for reports.

Einer positioned himself by the port and smiled to all the sailors heading off. He made certain that he saw every single one of them, and that they saw him. He knew what it meant, in large armies, to know one's commander. Not only to know who decided the general movements of the army, which were not always clear to those in the back, but to know that he too was a man, like them, and that he would fight with them.

He slapped Sigismund on the back, and the other members of their secret shield-wall. He stared after Brannar's ship as it pushed out from the port, but above all, Einer remembered his duty, and made certain that everyone felt seen.

Hundreds of thousands of warriors he saw off, in their thousands of ships, before he saw his own crew at the far edge of the beach.

A wail mingled with the wind from inland, and with it arrived a shadow. The shadow glided over the sand, through the thick crowd towards Einer and the ships. Hel had come. Grown men cried and howled from pain and sorrow at the sight of her. Even from out on the ships at sea, the terror echoed.

Einer's heart beat faster and faster as Hel approached. Her coal-feathered rooster crowed for the end of gods and giants. Corpses howled in pain when Hel approached; howled at the mere sight of her.

Half of her had been burned, and was black and crumbling like soot, but the other was bloated and the colour of sunburn. Her robes were like black veils that trailed behind her. She seemed to drain the life out of everyone. The closer she came, the more Einer felt his legs shake at the sight of her.

'Release us,' Hel hissed. Her voice made Einer feel cold as if he was standing in ice, and his head pounded with pain. 'Kill the Alfather, so I may open my gates. Your wives, children, grandchildren... All shall be safe when the Alfather's bones are crushed under my brother's teeth. You *shall* succeed.'

Einer's heart raced with fear as he looked up at Hel's horrid face, and at the same time, it raced with pride. Hel acknowledged their courage, and it had been good for the corpses to see that their ruler would honour their sacrifice. Their families in Helheim would be safe under Hel's command. With the Alfather gone, they would be released to explore the nine worlds as they desired.

One ship after the other pushed off, careful not to make the ships bump against the port as they rowed away. The hulls of the ships were fragile for they were entirely covered in human nails. For hundreds of winters and more, Loki had pulled the nails of Helheim's criminals to cover the ships. The ocean let nothing pass through the blurred veil at the edge of Helheim, only corpses, and no one could swim that far and hope to live. For the ships to pass through the veil, into another world, they had to be disguised as corpses, scaled in nails.

At last, Einer's ship, *Naglfar*, the last ship, set off from port. Einer had a place at the aft. He leaned over the edge of the ship and watched Hel on the beach as *Naglfar* was rowed onto Helheim's ocean. The sail was set, and a fierce wind pushed them forth, a wind that Einer and every other sailor knew had been conjured by Hel herself. Their goddess in death blessed their journey.

He watched her grow smaller and smaller, as they sailed away from Helheim. It felt like he was slowly falling into a trance, or a deep dream.

In front of them, ships disappeared into another of the nine worlds. The veil glinted out on the ocean, and beyond lay another world: Asgard, perhaps. The ocean here was not as wild as the waters by Corpse-shore where Einer had first arrived. They were calm, and perhaps Hel had something to do with that too.

Naglfar approached the edge of Hel's realm. The blurred veil of what lay beyond was straight ahead of them, but there was a ship, there, by the veil. One of the ships hadn't made it through.

A nail must have fallen off and revealed the ship for what it was. Somewhere at the keel of the ship, a nail was missing. Perhaps more than one, and finding the missing nail would not be easy.

'Which ship is it?' Einer asked. 'Which ship?'

'The *Storm Maker*,' someone answered.

That was Sigismund's ship. They needed Sigismund. Anyone else Einer could have told to swim through and onto one of the other ships, or to sail back to harbour and leave through Helheim's gates after the Alfather was dead, but not Sigismund and his crew. They needed Sigismund on the battlefield, and they needed his anvil and tools as well.

'Get us close,' Einer demanded.

'We can't carry them all,' the ship commander said. 'It's too much weight.'

'We won't,' Einer promised. 'I'm going to repair that ship.'

Sailors on the *Storm Maker* were beginning to jump into the waters and swim through the veil into the world beyond, but they had to leave their armour and weapons behind, and that was of no use to anyone.

'Sound the horn.'

Einer's ship commander did as ordered, blowing his horn hard and long. The sailors aboard the *Storm Maker* who were ready to abandon ship, stopped their doing. They gazed out at the *Naglfar* as the ship came up at their rear.

The ship commander had the sail lowered and by oar strokes, he brought them close, though not quite close enough for the ships to bump against each other. 'I don't dare sail any closer,' the ship commander warned. 'If we bump into each other...'

'Our nails may come loose,' Einer finished.

Even getting this close was a risky manoeuvre. Their oars might cause damage on the other ship, or on their own. This would have to do.

'Sail through,' Einer instructed. They could not risk waiting behind, in case the undercurrent knocked a nail off their hull. They had to go through quickly.

'Wait for us on the other side,' he told his ship commander, and steersmen. 'We'll join you, and I'll come back aboard.'

Einer removed his chainmail and helmet and gloves, even his weapon belt. Anything that might sink him. The wind was cold, but he knew that Helheim's waters were a lot more pleasant than they looked. He kept both outer and inner tunic on, along with his seal socks, and then, he dived.

The waters splashed cold against his face, but once all of him was under, it was not nearly as icy as he had feared. Even so, he did not want to stay in the waters for long.

He swam to the *Storm Maker* and dived under the ship. It had been covered in human nails like the scales of a fish. Whoever was in charge of overlaying nails on the *Storm Maker* had not done a sloppy job, as Einer had feared, but a few scales had come undone. Four times, Einer dived under the ship's keel.

'Nine,' he heaved as his head popped out of the water portside from the mid of the ship. 'We're nine nails short.' He was tired and out of breath.

Sigismund peered over the side of the ship at Einer. His long blond curls disappeared and a few heartbeats later, his face popped back again. 'Nej,' Einer puffed, struggling to stay afloat. He knew what Sigismund was about to suggest. If he wore the gold bracteate, it would give him strength and the task would be easier. 'It could fall off my neck, we can't risk it.'

He took a few deep breaths and climbed out of the waters holding onto the tarred shrouds at the middle of the ship. Hands reached down and hoisted him aboard.

'Sigismund,' he called, as he sat on the stacked oars and took a proper breath. He felt colder, outside the water. 'Do you have tongs?'

Any decent smith would have packed not just his anvil and hammers, but tongs too, and Sigismund was both a decent smith and a careful packer. Warily, Sigismund looked at Einer, but he knew better than to question the command.

Einer puffed and did his best to stay awake as he waited for Sigismund to return, although his eyes were closing. More troubles would follow on their voyage to Asgard; the gods would not make their trip easy. But he was so exhausted that his eyes closed on their own.

'Here,' Sigismund said.

Einer blinked himself awake. Sigismund was standing in front of him and held out a pair of tongs. They were larger than Einer would have liked, but they would do.

'You're going to have to pull my nails, friend,' Einer said. 'I can't do it myself.' He held his hand out to Sigismund, presenting his nails. 'We're nine nails short. Pull them.'

'I... I can't do that to you, Einer,' Sigismund said.

'You must. We are nine nails short, and I'm offering mine up.'

'You need your nails.' Sigismund was not wrong. Fighting without nails, with all of his fingers throbbing, would not just be painful but near impossible. But somebody needed to give up their nails if they were to arrive on Ida's plain, and they needed to get Sigismund and his tools all the way to Ragnarok. They *had* to get through the veil. Nothing else mattered in this moment.

'We all need our nails. I'll live without them.' Einer pushed the nail on his middle finger up to Sigismund's tongs, urging his friend to do what was needed. Reluctantly, Sigismund grabbed Einer's hand and secured his tongs around Einer's nail.

'You can have mine too,' a warrior to Einer's left bravely decided.

'And mine,' another added, and more sailors came forward to offer up their nails and courage.

Einer began to cry from their generosity, or perhaps it was because of how tired he was, or how the wind cooled his wet clothes and made him shiver, or from the feel of Sigismund's tongs like ice at the tip of his middle finger, or because he knew what came next.

Sigismund wrenched back hard.

Einer squealed. His nail-less finger throbbed from pain, and it stung in the saltwater dripping from his wet tunic.

Sigismund turned away from Einer to another man, who also offered up his nails. 'Certain?' he asked as he clasped the tongs around the man's nail. The sailor bravely nodded, even as Einer was clenching his wrist and rolling around in pain.

With deep breaths, Einer swallowed his pain, and then he reached for Sigismund, forced open his friend's left hand and grabbed his own bloody nail. He walked to the edge of the ship, preparing himself to dive down and attach it.

A hand grabbed onto his wet tunic. 'What do you think you're doing?' asked Sigismund.

'I need to attach it,' Einer mumbled through tears. He had not even noticed the tears rolling down his cheeks.

'Nej, old friend.' Sigismund pulled Einer back onto deck. He snatched the nail from Einer's hand and forced him to sit. 'You need sleep.' A blanket was thrown at him and sailors half-pulled and half-carried him away. Einer let himself be guided. At his back, warriors were screaming in pain as Sigismund pulled their nails.

'It should be me,' Einer muttered as he was lain down. The tears were pouring down his puffy cheeks. 'My burden.' His eyes closed without his permission. His eyelids were sticky with tears, and he could not quite open them again. He did not have the strength anymore. As soon as his head knocked against deck, Einer fell asleep.

HILDA

Chapter One Hundred and Sixty-Seven

'FENRIR IS DEAD!' Hilda's shout echoed down the length of Valhalla. 'The great wolf has been slain! The Alfather will live!'

Hilda let herself collapse onto a bench near the gates. She had hopped into the hall on one leg. Her thigh had begun to bleed again, and she couldn't put any pressure on her ankle. Her entire body was throbbing with pain. Someone shoved a horn into her hand and Hilda drank. Warm mead flowed down her throat and soothed her insides.

Warriors crowded around her, as she had known they would. Her announcement was still echoing around the large hall. They were yelling about her exploits. They knew how she had been sent from this hall. They had thought the wolf would kill her, but it hadn't. They had thought she would fail. Yet, there she was, victorious, as only Hilda had known she would be.

'Do you know a healer?' Hilda asked the warrior who had given her mead. Her voice was coarse. Even her head had begun to throb from her wounds.

More and more people crowded around her. They lay her flat on the chainmail-covered bench. They were all whispering their questions about how she had done it. How had she killed the great wolf? The first healer arrived quickly and undid Hilda's own bandages to examine the wound.

By the time the Alfather's arrival silenced the questions, Hilda's wounds had been inspected by fifteen healers, who had given her the best care. Her thigh was wrapped so tightly that she could hardly feel her leg and her ankle had become stiff with bandages too.

'I hear rumours,' the great Alfather said with a wicked smile. He stood tall above her, his famous spear in hand and his two ravens on his shoulders. The shadows deepened the wrinkles on his face. 'I hear echoes about a wolf.'

'Fenrir died under my axe-swings,' Hilda said with a wicked smile to match that of the Alfather. She reached for her belt and pulled out the thick lock of sharp wolf fur she had sliced off Fenrir's snout.

Odin eyed her proof. 'Hilda, wolf-slayer,' he muttered.

Her god was pleased with her efforts. 'Fenrir's bane,' Hilda added. During the long trip home to Valhalla, she had thought up a hundred different calling names, and that was her favourite.

Behind Odin came his valkyries. The godly shieldmaidens of Valhalla were dressed for battle in chainmail and shields in hand.

Atop the valkyries' gold shields Hilda was carried between the tables, following the Alfather's elegant robes. She could hear him chuckling, and voices all around whispering her name and her new calling names too. 'Fenrir's Bane, Hilda Wolfslayer.'

The gold shields flowed past above Hilda. The light from the fires in the hall was cast back over her from the gold shields above. People rushed closer to see her. Fenrir's slayer. Blissfully, Hilda smiled. All her wounds had been worth it. Even if she would limp at Ragnarok, it had been worth it. Warriors knew her and feared her.

The Alfather pranced in front of her. She had gained recognition. At last, everyone knew who Hilda was. The nornir had been wrong. She needed no destiny for others to know her.

'Have you seen my snow fox?' Hilda asked one of the valkyries carrying her.

All the answer she got was a sharp shake of the head. She curled herself back onto the shields. Her snow fox was not in Valhalla either. It hadn't been in the nornir's cave, and it hadn't gone to Valhalla either. Her fylgja had run away. Her luck had run out on her, and Hilda feared what it meant to be luckless so soon before Ragnarok.

Being carried through Valhalla felt like a strange sailing trip where the waters were the golden shields above her. Even when they arrived at the high tables, and the valkyries lowered their shields for Hilda to walk and totter the last of the way, she was smiling at the honour.

The warriors at the high tables watched her pass them by. It was not like the first time she had been among them. This time, they acknowledged her accomplishments. They respected her strength.

'She has earned her seat,' the Alfather announced to his followers as Hilda sat down on the bench next to him. At last, she was exactly where she belonged.

The champions at the high table stomped their feet and roared to honour her advancement in their ranks. They lifted their bottomless horns to her and loudly, all together, they said her name: 'To Hilda Wolfslayer!'

Deep they drank, Hilda too, and then they filled their stomach with mead and meats and stories. Even the Alfather listened in silence as Hilda told the story of how she had slain the great beast, and how Fenrir's head had plummeted to the ground. The warriors switched seats and crowded around her to hear her exploits, and all the while, the great Alfather stayed at her side, watching her, and chuckling at her success. He didn't grow tired of listening to her story, even when Hilda grew tired of telling it.

Once in a while, Hilda heard her name echo down the hall in a loud chant. They were making songs about her.

One small thing nagged at the back of Hilda's mind whenever she told her story. The three nornir. They had told her something that had made Hilda wonder. They had told her that their task was to spin everyone to Ragnarok, and yet they had said nothing when Hilda arrived at their gates after having slain one of the biggest pieces on the Ragnarok tafl board. Even if they didn't know that Hilda was the one who had done it, they should have been panicked at the death of Fenrir. Panicked that they couldn't accomplish their task of spinning Ragnarok, but they hadn't been. Busy, but not panicked. Perhaps the three nornir had done something. Like they had tried to do with Hilda when she had first met them, and they had spun a dead destiny thread back to life using Hilda's blood.

Their duty was to spin them all to Ragnarok, they had said. The wind whirled around Hilda with visions, but a new warrior walked to her table and asked to hear the story of Fenrir's death. Hilda dismissed the wind and its whispers and told her story for the hundred and twentieth time.

All those at the high table were feasting to Hilda's success.

The ring of a horn shook through Valhalla. The shields above them whacked against each other. The entire hall trembled. Drinking horns fell out of their holders. Mead and ale flowed over the high table. The horn blow was long and sad.

The Gjallar-horn.

Heimdall was blowing his golden horn. Ragnarok was upon them.

Hilda had thought there would be longer until the battle. Her thigh, ankle and palms were still bandaged from her fight with Fenrir. She couldn't walk far, and she doubted that she could hold her axe properly.

Men and women shot to their feet with panic in their eyes, their feasting long forgotten. They grabbed their weapons, put on their helmets, wrestled their chainmail off their benches and over their heads, and readied for Valhalla's gold-shield roof to fall over them.

'Halt!' Odin bellowed. All the shields on Valhalla's oak tree were shaking, but they did not fall, as they were supposed to at the beginning of each morning battle.

Heimdall's horn was still blowing, but Odin's voice cut through easily. He was a god, after all.

The Alfather spoke with calm, though Hilda, sitting across from him, could see that he was anything but calm. His cheeks and ears had flushed bright red, but his voice was soothing, like the purr of a cat.

'You all heard Heimdall sound the Gjallar-horn. The giants are coming, but they are not here yet. They are not outside our gates. They are on their way,' he told his warriors. 'We have our mountain wall protecting us, and it will take them days to break through it. Golden-comb will crow when they are close. There is no need for us to stand outside, in the rain, and tire our legs, waiting for them. We shall feast, one last, great feast, and then we shall fight. One last, glorious battle.'

A few warriors roared their approval. Slowly more voices joined theirs, hesitant at first. As they roared, they seemed to settle. They picked up their mead horns from the floor, dried their benches and drank anew.

All were toasting to the wisdom of their Alfather. All were toasting to certain victory. Ragnarok *was* coming, but it was not tonight. Besides, the wolf was dead, great Fenrir, and only Hilda wondered why the three nornir had said nothing about it.

Her axe-handle was stained with Fenrir's blood; she had pierced the wolf's skull. But she kept wondering if the nornir had interfered, somehow, as she knew they could.

The Alfather was too flushed at the thought of Ragnarok, and too busy reassuring his people, to listen to Hilda's concern. It would be better if he didn't know. Fenrir had died, Hilda was certain of it, and if the nornir had brought the wolf back, then she would simply have to kill it again. Now she knew that she was capable of it.

A sharp pain in her ankle reminded her that she was not as fit as she had been. So many summers in Midgard spent dreaming of fighting in Valhalla, and of the glory she would gain. Now, her left leg hurt so much that Hilda wondered if she would be able to fight at *all* when the final battle came.

It was too soon.

Throughout the night, the Alfather went from table to table. Hilda watched him from afar, wondering and worrying. Few were those who asked about her exploits now. Ragnarok was upon them, and they had other things to celebrate; centuries of friendships with their bench-mates to remember, and their future deaths to imagine. Hilda kept an eye fixed on the Alfather throughout the night as she twirled the drinking horn in her hands.

Most of those around her had fallen asleep from drinking and feasting, when Hilda noticed the Alfather's robes slip away.

Her legs hurt terribly, but Hilda rose, snatched up a sleeping warrior's spear and used it as a walking stick. It was a terrible thing to steal another warrior's weapon so close to Ragnarok, but Hilda didn't care. She needed a walking stick to catch up with the Alfather.

Odin slipped out of the hall in the slim gap between two pillars, not through one of the large doors.

Though she tried to hop along as quickly as her legs would allow, it took Hilda a long time to reach the wall and find the place between the pillars where the Alfather had slipped through. She forced herself after him.

The Alfather had disappeared into the night by the time Hilda came outside. The rain from earlier had abated to a mere drizzle.

The Alfather had disappeared, but he couldn't hide from her. Hilda knew how to find him. Loki had taught her, three winters ago: "*No matter where you're headed in Asgard, you're always headed towards Yggdrasil, in the end,*" he had said.

Hilda followed the advice, heading in the direction where she knew Yggdrasil was, even though the cloudy sky shielded it from view.

All through the night Hilda walked, until the sun came up. Even then, she walked, across fields and through forests towards Yggdrasil's vast trunk. The enormous boughs crossed the sky over Hilda's head by the time she finally heard something.

People were talking nearby. She had arrived at what she was looking for, wherever it was.

She peered out of the woods. Hundreds of aesir and vanir had gathered under Yggdrasil's bare branches. On the slope of a hillside, several rings of stone benches had been built, overlooking an inner Ting circle. There stood a woman with distant eyes and long red hair. In her hands she held a distaff, carved with runes. Not the kind for wool spinning, the kind for fate spinning, like the nornir used.

Hundreds of gods surrounded the woman. They were all assembled, although Hilda only recognised a few of the ones in the inner circle. The Alfather, of course, and his sons: Thor, Vali, and Vidar. There was the skald, Bragi; the one-handed warrior, Tyr. Heimdall had abandoned his post as outlook, sitting with the great Gjallar-horn. Among the goddesses, Hilda recognised Odin's wife Frigg with grey locks in her hair, golden-haired Sif and young Idun, but there were many whom she could not match to their names and who she had not met that time in the bathhouse.

Hundreds of gods surrounded the inner circle of famed gods. All the gods were assembled, not just the aesir, but the vanir too. Njord, Frey and Freya were no surprise, but at their backs, to the right, were hundreds more. The vanir looked different from the aesir: less purposeful, and more alike. Their fylgjur were docile and calculated, patient cats and watchful birds waiting for their chance to strike.

'How could Fenrir have been killed?' the god Vidar hissed at his father. Odin looked at his youngest son with a bored expression. 'It's not possible. I would know!' A grey wolf sauntered behind, growling with him. The fylgja was larger than Odin's two wolves, but it was feral. The Alfather's two companions barely even acknowledged it.

'It's not how it was foretold,' Bragi agreed. His tongue was visibly coloured with runes.

'And Bragi would know,' Vidar added. He shouldered his wolf hide further up on his back. All his life he must have trained for the part he was foretold to play at Ragnarok. Vidar had been birthed for the fated meeting with Fenrir on Ragnarok's battlefield.

'Fenrir *is* dead!' Hilda stepped out of the shadows. No matter what the nornir had or hadn't said, she knew what she had done. She had the wounds to prove it and the fur from Fenrir's snout. 'The Alfather speaks the truth.'

She looked at him, her god, as she approached. Unlike all the others, who turned in their seats and gasped, Odin didn't seem surprised at her arrival. He must have caught her watching him in Valhalla and known that she would follow.

The gods were all whispering to each other, asking who she was, a question to which no one had an answer. Not even Freya or Frigg or Sif or Idun, with whom Hilda had bathed, once upon a time.

Only Odin and Hilda knew her name, and in all the nine worlds, only Hilda truly knew who she was.

'You didn't see anyone come?' Heimdall hissed at the red-haired woman in an accusing tone. He was eager to be the superior guard, to blame someone else for what his hawk eyes had failed to notice.

'Nej,' the veulve eventually said. Her starry eyes seemed fixed on Hilda. Her hair flowed like blood and her brow wrinkled in confusion. 'I still don't see her.'

'Don't blame her,' Hilda announced, unafraid in the presence of her gods. 'I have no destiny, past, present, or future. She never could and never will see me coming. Just like Fenrir had no chance.' Leaning on the spear she had stolen, Hilda walked all the way to the outer Ting ring, where the gods thronged in rings upon rings.

'No past,' the veulve said, in a trance-like voice. 'No future.'

Hilda descended the steps, past gods of lesser fame and greater fame, to reach the lower stone floor upon which the veulve stood, gazing far away to search for Hilda.

'No present,' the veulve muttered. Freya gasped at the news and stared at Hilda with a fierce hatred in her kohl-ringed eyes. Freya did not remember her. It was as if they had never met.

'That is how I killed Fenrir,' Hilda announced to the large audience of gods. 'In the same way I came here without anyone knowing.'

'Fenrir was mine,' Vidar spat, turning his rage away from his father and straight to Hilda. His wolf fylgja growled at her, too. He was furious that the great honour had been taken from him.

'Then you should have killed Fenrir *before*, rather than wait till he kills your father,' Hilda said. She reached for the sharp white fur she had snipped off Fenrir's face and held it up. 'Fenrir is dead, and this is your proof.'

Vidar was shocked into silence at the sight of the fur from Fenrir's snout. He reached out a hand and cautiously stroked the glassy hairs. His protests died. He sat right back down on the bench next to his brothers. His wolf fylgja whimpered.

'I don't care whether Fenrir lives or dies!' Red Thor's fists were clenched in anger. 'We were supposed to have time before Ragnarok, and now Heimdall is saying that the giants are outside our wall. Ragnarok was never supposed to happen. We were supposed to have time to prepare.'

Hilda gaped at her god in disbelief. His hair and beard and eyes were all the colour of murder, but his words were that of summer. Of someone who hadn't spent three long winters preparing for the end, like the rest of them had.

'Thor,' his golden-haired wife said tenderly, and placed a hand on his clenched fists. 'We *will* find it,' she whispered to him.

'No matter if it was supposed to or not, it *is* happening,' the Alfather said in his smooth voice that soothed all ills and worries. Even Thor unclenched his tight fists at the sound of his father's voice.

The Alfather rose to his feet. Hilda had forgotten how tall he was. In a way, he looked like his famed spear: tall and slender, with a fierce head to stab his enemies. He gained a twinkle in his eye. Using his spear as a walking stick like her, the Alfather took the five strides that separated him from Hilda, clapped her on the shoulder and turned them both to face the audience of gods.

'She slew Fenrir. She can slay all of Loki's beasts. She can defy even destiny!'

There was a newfound interest in the gaze of the many gods. Even at the very top, Hilda saw them sit up straight and focus. Every last god watched her now. Not the Alfather, but *her*.

Freya had stopped frowning. She also saw the potential in Hilda, as she had once. 'She'll slay all the beasts meant to slay us,' the goddess muttered.

'She can save us from Ragnarok,' the Alfather said, laying responsibility for the survival of the gods on Hilda's shoulders. 'But she is a warrior like any other short-lived. She doesn't possess our strength. She might die, too.'

'We need to give her the best chance,' Bragi decided for them all. 'Protect her, and start with the most terrible beasts.'

'Have her fight in our midst,' the Alfather agreed. 'We will make the creatures kneel and she shall deliver the final blows.'

The gods could no longer contain their excitement. They rose from their seats and stomped their feet and roared in victory.

Goosebumps climbed up Hilda's legs and arms. Her gods were roaring for her. She would fight in their midst and be their weapon to victory. She, alone, would save the gods.

In the inner circle of the highest gods, she was offered a seat, among proud aesir and vanir. To her left was watchful Heimdall, and to her right sat the young goddess Idun, who did not remember her. She smelled of apples, and Heimdall of cloves. Sometimes Hilda's shoulders rubbed against Idun's fair skin, and her heart raced at the thought of sitting among her gods.

Idun's squirrel fylgja played with a hare at their feet which had to belong to Idun's husband, Bragi, for Heimdall's companion was sure to be the huge hawk which flew in circles over the assembly. Hilda looked through the tangle of gods and fylgjur, hoping to find her snow fox, but it was not there.

Hilda had always known that she would be seated in Valhalla someday, but among gods, like this, shoulder to shoulder, almost as an equal? Not even in dreams could she have imagined such a day.

The veulve conducted the Ting and had gods of both high and low glory voice their concerns to be resolved before Ragnarok. Since being seated, Hilda had barely heard a word. She was so focused on the gods at her side.

Evening had come again by the time the veulve announced the end of the Ting and gods rose to their feet with laughter, chatting about things normal and familiar—about the last feast, and sailing trips. Hilda stared as her new bench-mates left the inner circle. They nodded at her approvingly before they departed. She belonged among them now. They acknowledged her. Gods and goddesses.

The Alfather cuddled angry Vidar, pulled him close in a fatherly hug. In a lowered voice, he told his son: 'There will be other wolves, my boy. We need you on the battlefield.' Then Odin turned to Hilda, who was still stunned and seated on the stone bench.

'Can you find your way back?' the Alfather asked her.

Hilda gave him a firm nod. With the Alfather and the last of his sons gone, Hilda was left alone at the bottom of the hill. She let out a deep sigh. She was as good as a goddess now.

A hand clasped around Hilda's wrist. 'What makes you think you can live up to their expectations... Fateless?' The veulve was standing right behind Hilda.

So quiet and distant was she that Hilda had entirely forgotten about her.

'I'm a good fighter.' Hilda freed her hand from the veulve's fingers.

'A good fighter...' The veulve's starry eyes were staring into the distance. 'Even with that leg?'

'I can fight,' Hilda insisted, though all that held her up was the spear she had taken with her. Though her snow fox had left her and taken her luck with it. Maybe it was better that way. They were tied, the two of them, and if the snow fox was safe during Ragnarok, then maybe Hilda had a chance of survival. Though she didn't know if her fylgja *was* safe.

'What's the point of fighting and dying?' the veulve asked.

'I can make a difference,' Hilda answered. There was no greater honour than to stand by her gods. Protect them and fight for them. She could be more than a warrior to her gods. She had no destiny thread tied to Ragnarok. She could kill any beast for them. She could save them all.

'At Ragnarok, no warrior will be looking at your destiny when they slice your head off.'

The veulve was right. In Ragnarok, against regular warriors, not having a destiny would be no great virtue. But, against those prophesised to slay the gods, she had a true advantage. They wouldn't expect to meet anyone who could kill them before they had achieved their destinies.

'How do you know that you can kill those whose destinies have been tied to fateful deaths in Ragnarok?'

'I killed Fenrir,' said Hilda. It was definitive proof that she could change that which the nornir had already decided.

The veulve leaned in close so their noses nearly touched, and Hilda looked so deep into the veulve's eyes that she might have been staring up at the night sky.

The veulve took a deep breath. 'Then ask the wind,' she whispered.

As if conjured by the veulve's will, the wind swept around Hilda.

'Ask it about Fenrir's death.'

Reluctantly, Hilda focused on the whipping wind. She couldn't allow the veulve to tarnish her reputation. She had killed the wolf, and the visions in the wind would prove it. But her heart pounded as she demanded through runes and whispers to see Fenrir's death.

The wolf will growl. The night will be dark. Thunder will strike. Fenrir will lunge forth. Its paws will scratch through corpses at its feet. Vidar will let his wolf-hide cloak fall. The wolf will open its jaws wide, and Vidar will slam his shoe over the wolf's lower jaw. He will trap it and hold it down. Will reach his hands up to grab the upper jaw. Fenrir will try to snap its mouth shut. The wolf's teeth will strike through Vidar's hands. Vidar will roar and push his arms above his head. He will tear the wolf's jaw apart. The wolf will no longer growl.

Hilda blinked herself out of the vision. Fenrir's death at Ragnarok. Exactly as foretold. It shouldn't be, not if Hilda had been successful, but the wind never lied. The vision would come to pass. Fenrir would survive until Ragnarok.

'You're right,' Hilda told the veulve, but she was sitting alone in the Ting ring, now. The veulve was gone, and so were all the gods. Only Hilda was left behind. Her head danced with worry. The veulve was right. The gods were wrong to trust her. She hadn't even killed Fenrir.

TYRA

Chapter One Hundred and Sixty-Eight

'THRALL! I NEED MY neck-ring,' Thor thundered through his tall house.

Tyra knew that it was her he was calling, and all the other thralls knew it too. None of them spoke to her or tried to help her, just as none of them had helped her search the house. She had found neck-rings—many of them—but no gold Yggdrasil pendant, like the one murderous Thor demanded of her.

'Thrall,' he yelled again. His voice tore through the house with a fierce thunder.

Tyra tiptoed from the servant's hallway into the main house, ascended one stairwell after another, rushing all she could while Thor raged and yelled for her.

By the time Tyra reached the third floor from the top in the four-hundred-and-twenty-roomed house, she was puffing like a pig.

Thor was trying on battle-gear. He had pulled on a chainmail shirt and was seated on a chest while three thralls rushed around him. Two knelt by his feet to tie armour around his shins and wrap his socks around the armour. Another thrall was braiding his hair in an intricate pattern to lay it flat on his head.

'Give it to me,' Thor ordered without a moment of hesitation when he saw Tyra come up the stairs. 'I need the neck-ring now.'

Tyra stayed back, out of the thunder god's reach. She would have to speak quickly, to say everything before Thor grew angry enough to reach for his deadly hammer.

'I don't have it, but I know where your neck-ring is,' Tyra said, as quickly as she could.

Red Thor fixed her with eyes that seemed capable of killing on their own, without any help from his strong arms.

'It was stolen,' Tyra said in as convincing a tone as she could conjure, although she had no real idea what had happened to the neck-ring. 'Stolen by a giant of the name Glumbruck.'

'What did you say?' Thor kicked a thrall away as he got up. The other two thralls backed away, eyes firmly fixed on the wooden floor where the third one lay clutching his stomach.

Thor walked towards Tyra. Each step felt like a drumbeat and made Tyra's heart race against her will. He stopped right in front of her. Tyra looked down, like any good thrall, and all she saw was Thor's chainmail pushed up against her. 'Say that again,' Thor demanded, towering above Tyra. She was entirely hidden in his shadow.

'The giant, Glumbruck, stole it.' Tyra let no hesitation or doubt enter her voice.

The heartbeat of silence that followed seemed to stretch into all eternity as Thor stood with his belly pressed against Tyra. 'How do you know that name?' he hissed at her from above.

So, Thor *did* know Siv, exactly as Tyra had hoped. Siv had lived in Asgard, after all; maybe with Thor's help, Tyra might finally find her.

'I heard whispers,' Tyra said, and she had, but not about Siv. 'Glumbruck has it,' she maintained.

'Loki,' Thor hissed with such contempt in his voice that Tyra thought the mere sound might have killed a lesser thrall. 'So that was why she was in Asgard. To steal from me.'

At that, he moved away from Tyra. Only a step back, but it was enough for Tyra to breathe again, and catch her breath from her run up the stairs. For a long while they just stood there, Tyra staring at Thor's leather shoes, and Thor shaking with rage.

They were still standing there when Sif came out of one of the bedrooms to the east. She, too, was wearing mail. Behind her ran four thralls with helmets for her to try. Her long gold hair had been braided flat and hung neatly down her back.

'They couldn't find it?' Sif guessed when she saw how angered her husband was. She pointed to one of the helmets, a silver one with a gold nose-guard and rims. The thrall who held it rushed forward to present the great helmet to the goddess.

'Glumbruck stole it,' Thor hissed. 'That's why she was in Asgard.'

Sif stopped the thrall from putting the helmet on her head. She stared at Thor. Tyra swallowed her worries. She was thankful that Thor had told her to cover her face, so no one could see her fear. Sif knew that something was wrong. Perhaps she knew where Siv was, and that Tyra was lying.

The goddess stopped a few paces away and stared down at the floor. 'But Glumbruck's dead.'

'I know!' Thor thundered.

Glumbruck was dead. That was why she hadn't come back to help Tyra. She had died in the nornir's cave. The Alfather had killed her. All those summers and winters in Midgard, Tyra had refused to believe it, but Siv was dead, and wherever giants went in the afterlife, Tyra knew that it wasn't Asgard. Never again would she see her.

'Then where is the neck-ring?' Sif was still staring at the floor, thinking herself elsewhere. 'Loki,' she eventually said. 'He was free by the time her corpse was burned.'

Thor paced around the room in a fierce anger that had him puffing and sighing and growling like a hound. 'I'll never get it back now. The worm will kill me.'

The god seemed more angry than afraid of the Midgard Worm, which was prophesied to take his life at Ragnarok. He reached a hand to his hair, ripping it free of the braid the thralls had laboured over. He shook off the half-attached armour at his calves and sat back down on the chest.

'Get me my shoes,' he ordered.

'Where are you going?' asked Sif.

Thor pulled on the shoes his thralls brought him, and then stormed up the stairs without giving his wife a response.

'Thor,' she yelled after him. 'Where are you going?'

'To see my father,' he thundered in response. 'He will have to give me another bracteate. He can't expect me to go to war without it! Thrall, you come with me.'

All the other thralls in the room looked at Tyra. Thor meant her. Hiding behind her head-cover, Tyra followed Thor up the steps. She had to run to catch up.

'You will tell my father exactly what you told me,' he ordered. 'He'll see. It's all his fault. He should have killed Glumbruck sooner. We should have killed Loki. I told him! I begged him to let me kill that worming jotun.'

They bounded up the last steps, all the way to the very top of the house. They were higher up than Tyra had ever been in life. Thor opened a set of doors that led out to the roof. Dark clouds had gathered around the tall house. Fiercely, the wind swept in and lifted Tyra's itchy skirts. It felt like flying, and Tyra wasn't so certain that she liked that.

Thor whistled. He lifted his hammer and swung it above his head. A white light nearly blinded Tyra, and then came thunder that deafened everything. She cowered back, but Thor was still standing outside, at the edge of the tall roof.

'Come,' he ordered her.

With ragged breaths, Tyra walked to the open doors and the storm outside. The clouds had gathered around the roof so she couldn't see down, and that at least was good, because she knew that she was much further up than she would ever care to know.

The wind tore at her clothes. Outside, in the storm, standing on the roof of the house, were two goats. Their horns were sharp and long, and between them, they pulled Thor's cart.

Thor grumbled a few words Tyra couldn't hear over the rumbling storm. He turned to Tyra, firmly stuck with her feet inside. Easily, he grabbed her waist and lifted her outside. Not just onto the roof, but onto the square carriage hanging on the slanted roof.

Tyra held onto the edge, hoping and wishing that she wouldn't fall. Thor took his place in front of her, and the carriage slid down the side of the roof under the weight. 'Go on,' he commanded. His goats bleated, but then they pulled. The cart glided off the roof. Tyra squealed as they fell towards the ground. The clouds rumbled death, and then Thor's two goats dragged them up again.

Tyra clung on. The goats were hopping on the dark clouds as if they were solid, and the cart bumped after them, threatening to throw her off. The wind blew her hair out in front of her face and ripped at her clothes. She clasped her mouth, so as not to throw up, but then the goats started heading down again, and she thought she might fall off the back of the cart.

She didn't like flying. Not one bit.

Thor was still grumbling loudly, and sometimes he swung his hammer above his head and lightning struck next to them, blinding and deafening Tyra.

At last, the cart bumped onto solid ground. Thor hopped over the edge before his two horned goats even came to a full stop. The goats planted their faces into the grass as Tyra tried to regain her composure. Shaking like a wet dog, she clambered out of the cart after Thor, who had no patience for it. 'Will you *hurry?*' he yelled at her over his shoulder.

The dark clouds that had followed them retreated so quickly that Tyra wondered if she had imagined it all. They were walking towards a large hall with tree-trunk pillars for walls. The sharp gleam of iron tips blinked at the top.

Thor disappeared between two pillars, and Tyra rushed ahead on shaky legs, following him into the hall. They entered a large room that contained nothing more than a single long-table, chairs, and a tall, closed door at the other end of the room. The ceiling was so far up that it was like looking up at a crown of ancient trees, but it glittered with light. The ceiling was made of golden shields, Tyra realised when her dizziness settled.

She was standing in the Alfather's hall. In Valhalla.

Thor had finally stopped grumbling. He paced back and forth behind the dining table, practising a concerned frown and mumbling some words under his breath. Tyra stood with her back to one of the outer pillars.

At last, she had arrived in Valhalla. So long she had dreamt of it. Seeing her parents again, and her sisters. All those she had loved. At last, she was rewarded for her sacrifices in life.

The doors swung open, and in he came: the great Alfather, spear in hand, and long silver hair shining in the bright light of his hall.

She had seen him, once, so long ago in Midgard when he had come for her, but this was different. Back then her room had been dark, and he had been robed in shadows, but here he was bathed in light and all the glory of his hall. His single eye seemed to see more than Tyra's own two did. It seemed to see all there was and ever would be to see.

At the Alfather's back, Tyra heard song, and further into the hall, she saw the glimpse of warriors feasting.

'Loki wants me dead!' Thor said. 'He has been plotting it all. He knew what would happen.'

The Alfather shut the large door, and walked into the room with an incredible calm, as Thor bristled. Odin did not give in to Thor's hasty words or need for approval as he rounded the table. He tapped his son on the shoulder, reassuringly, and his single eye bored into Thor to demand calm and quiet truth.

'It's my neck-ring,' Thor said. In front of his father, Thor's anger seemed to dissipate. His voice became calmer, and Tyra almost thought she heard a hint of fear.

The great thunder god turned to her, then. 'You tell him,' Red Thor ordered her.

The Alfather's eye fixed on Tyra's covered face. He took a deep breath that reminded Tyra of a past when Siv had been alive and shown her the nine worlds, and giants had used to smell her and wonder who she was.

Bravely, Tyra pushed away from the pillar and walked into the great room. She reminded herself that she was supposed to be a thrall, so she looked at the sand-coloured floor as she walked. When she could clearly see the Alfather's pointy shoes, she stopped.

'Your son asked me to find an Yggdrasil neck-ring,' she said. Her voice was shaking, but she did her best to steady it when she continued. 'I searched the entire house, but it was gone. Stolen, by a giant by the name of Glumbruck.'

'Glumbruck,' the grand Alfather repeated, with a certain pleasure.

'It was Loki's doing. Imagine what he might do with it,' Thor said. He was tumbling through his words like a little child in front of his father.

'Ja,' the Alfather mused. His single eye was still fixed on Tyra, and he took another deep breath. His hand fell from his son's shoulder, and he took a step towards Tyra. A single step, but it was enough for Tyra to know that she had not only been heard; she had been seen, too. 'It's you,' he said.

He remembered her, of course he did. A man like the Alfather remembered everything.

'Three winters past.'

Thor was staring at his father, not knowing what to do, and if he could interrupt.

'You're her daughter,' Odin continued.

'I am,' said Tyra. 'More fire demons have escaped into Midgard,' she revealed, for this was her chance. The Alfather was listening to her, and he knew who she was, so he would know that she did not speak lightly, or out of turn. Thor could do to her what he wanted afterwards. All that mattered was saving Midgard—for Svend. 'There were eight fire demons in Midgard when I passed away, and they're set on destroying your name. Your legacy.'

The shock was apparent on the Alfather's face. He knew what it meant. If Ragnarok was upon them, and if he died on that battlefield, then even Midgard would forget him. He needed to eradicate those demons.

Thor was pacing, and grimacing at how his father was distracted by Tyra's presence. 'Go and wait by the cart, thrall,' he ordered, when he had no more patience left in him, and then he returned to pleading with his father. 'It's not fair, I was supposed to live!'

Tyra backed away towards the pillars. The Alfather was still watching her as she slipped through two pillars. 'We shall all die at Ragnarok,' he told his son.

'Not you,' Thor complained. 'Fenrir's dead. You can't expect me to *die* for this. She has to kill the Midgard Worm first.'

Their voices dwindled into silence when Tyra left Valhalla.

Outside, Thor's goats grazed peacefully.

Tyra had wondered if the Darkness would cling to her even in the afterlife. The Alfather's stare made her certain that it had. He had recognised her, despite how deformed her face had become in death. It was the smell of her that he had recognised—and that he feared—and yet he had not killed her, right there on the spot, as Siv had always worried that he would. He had not killed her in Midgard either. He had chosen to let her live, and somehow, Tyra thought that perhaps it was Siv, protecting her even now, from beyond the grave.

The sun had come out, and the breeze brought with it the faint sound of laughter and song. Valhalla's folk were not fighting as they usually did during the day. So close to Ragnarok, they were feasting instead.

This was her chance, Tyra realised.

She set out in a run along Valhalla's outer wall. There had to be a proper gate there, somewhere, leading into the feast hall where her sisters and parents were spending their afterlife.

For so long, she ran, that she had to slow down to catch her breath. Valhalla's gates were far apart, but eventually, Tyra reached the first one. Thor's goats were nothing more than dots in the distance.

Twisted steps led up into the loud hall. Tyra ascended them quickly before Thor returned from the meeting with his father and realised that she was gone.

The hall spread so large that Tyra couldn't see the ends of it. Gaping at the sight, she marched past full tables, searching for familiar faces. They would not be easy to find. Not merely because the hall was so large, but also because people looked different in armour.

Warriors winced at the sight of Tyra as she passed them by.

'Who did *you* meet on the last battlefield?' one of them laughed.

'Apparently, someone very angry,' Tyra said, acutely aware of how swollen her face was, and always would be in the afterlife. 'I think I've lost my way. Do you know where the people of Ash-hill are seated?'

The first warrior she asked didn't know, but another further down the table chimed in that she needed to head west for half a rest to find the fallen of Ash-hill's slaughter. Eagerly, Tyra followed the instructions. She ran until she was out of breath, she skipped and walked as fast as she could westwards down the length of the hall.

A few more times, she asked warriors who stared at her smashed face for directions. They pointed her further into the hall.

At last, she no longer needed directions. From afar, she saw faces from her childhood. There was Ivan with his bald head, and Gudrun with her loud laugh... and then her eyes fell on her mother's face.

Tyra slowed to a halt, though she was still far away. Her mother was not as she had been in life, but as she had been in death. Tyra still remembered stumbling over the corpse in the burning remains of her hometown.

Her mother sat proudly in Valhalla with an arrow wound through the cheek. Her skin had a pale and bluish tint, and there was blood in her hair. Tyra's father was seated at her mother's side, and he too looked different from how Tyra remembered him, and she feared that she would never again remember either one of them as they had been in life.

Her father had scars on his face, but his hair was curly as it had always been, and although he had a scar across his cheek, his smile, at least, was the same as she remembered.

Tyra walked closer, her eyes fixed on her parents. Across from them sat Tyra's sisters. They were somewhat smaller than she remembered them to be, perhaps because Tyra herself had grown since she had last seen them, and they hadn't. They looked so young, just from the glimpses Tyra caught as they laughed and talked.

It felt like she was dreaming as she walked closer, listening to their conversation. She had often had dreams like these as a child, she remembered. Dreams of her parents speaking of her in Valhalla's glorious hall.

'I wish Tyra could have joined us, at least once before the end,' she heard her sister Astrid complain.

Tyra smiled and cried at the thought of finally introducing herself to them, as a grown woman, and to feel her mother's embrace again. She had missed them, but she hadn't quite realised how much.

She took a deep breath, ready to present herself to her family, after so many summers and winters spent apart. So many evenings spent thinking about them, and remembering them, clenching her own aching chest.

'Nej,' Tyra's mother said in a decisive tone. 'I would have liked to see her pretty face, but it's good that she isn't here.'

Tyra paused at that, her smile fading. Her father glanced up at her as she came close, but he didn't seem to recognise her.

'In Helheim she will be safe after Ragnarok,' said Tyra's mother. 'After our fight, when giants and beasts are gone from the nine worlds, she will be safe.'

Her father nodded and lifted his drink to toast. 'We fight for her future.'

'For Tyra,' her mother and sisters agreed, and raised their drinking horns.

Tyra kept her eyes on her family, but passed them by as her parents and sisters toasted to her future. They expected her to be well. Not to live as a beaten thrall in the afterlife.

At a little distance from her family, Tyra sat down on an empty bench so she could see them from afar. She couldn't present herself, with her broken, swollen face. She couldn't take away their reason for fighting at Ragnarok.

They looked happy.

Her sisters were laughing over something her father had said, and Tyra smiled bitterly at the sight of them. Fate had been kind to her. At least she had finally seen her family again, even if they could never know it.

Her family were better off thinking that Tyra was elsewhere, but that left Tyra all alone in the afterlife, having chosen a life as a thrall in Thor's and Sif's household. Sitting in Valhalla, watching her family laugh and smile without her, Tyra remembered, once more, why she had died.

There were fire demons in Midgard. Only the gods could save Svend and every other person in Midgard from the wrath of the fire demons who had killed Tyra, and now she had fulfilled her purpose. She had warned the Alfather. Midgard's fate was in his hands. The Alfather had to act on her warnings. Midgard had to be saved.

Tyra's family were dead. Siv was dead. Everyone else she cared about was dead. But there was still Svend, and only the gods could save him from the demons raging across his lands.

SIV

Chapter One Hundred and Sixty-Nine

THE FOREFATHERS WERE calling Siv. Not by name—they did not allow her such a thing—but they called her, nonetheless. Their afterlife was pleasing. To let herself blend in with them, disappear in their crowd, and follow their motions.

In the afterlife, she was a drop in their ocean, guided and helped by others. And never alone, as she was now. Alone with her thoughts and worries and all of that which she could not remember. She was partly a forefather already, and she wanted to become a forefather through and through.

Siv pulled on the oars again, and the boat drifted further out onto Lake Pitch-black. Her sons had set out on their quests. She tried desperately to hold onto the memory of them. The warmth of their parting hugs. Their fur pressed up against her. Already, she missed them. The memory of them kept her alive. As a forefather, she would have no memories. Her sons would merely be sons; they would no longer be *hers*. She wouldn't remember them.

Siv glanced over her shoulder. The heather island was close.

She had entered Asgard through an old passage her sons had pointed her towards. When she had heard Heimdall's Gjallarhorn announcing the beginning of Ragnarok, she had been walking around Yggdrasil. The aesir had been busy assembling, but she had slipped past, walking through the deep winter green of Asgard. The place where she was told she had died, in life.

In the distance, Yggdrasil was cowering in shame. There were no leaves on its far-reaching branches. It stood bare, for the first time since the making of the nine worlds.

As she rowed across Lake Pitch-black, Siv wondered if Yggdrasil would ever bear green buds again. It looked like the ash tree was being weighed down by the responsibility of the nine worlds.

Her rowboat bumped against land. Her thoughts full of forefathers, Siv pulled in the oars and stepped into the shallow waters. Dragging the rowboat with her, she walked onto the heather island. She left the boat halfway on land, crushing the pretty heather flowers.

There was something about this place. Siv no longer recalled why she had come here, but somewhere within her, forefathers were cheering. Their excitement rose in Siv as she turned to the island and began to remember why she had come.

Amidst the heather was a mass of dark grey fur. It was like that of her first-borns, rough and sharp. Siv glided across the heather and then she saw his face, resting on the flowers, and his chained legs, and although her mind was still searching, her heart remembered.

The grand wolf stared up at her. There was a glint in his yellow eyes that reminded her of times past she knew she was supposed to remember.

She walked closer, hoping with each step that she would remember, but she didn't. The forefathers were so loud in her mind. Loud with whispers and memories of their own. She no longer knew theirs from hers.

Fenrir was his name. The forefathers whispered it over and

over and all agreed that the wolf Siv's heart remembered was Fenrir. His eyes had a sadness about them. His upper lip had a scar, and blood had congealed down the side of his face.

'You're hurt,' she said.

His earth-shaking growl responded, 'You're half a forefather.'

She was more than half now, but she did not correct Fenrir. He stared at her like he could hardly believe it. That she was there—or that she was half gone.

'Can you move?' she asked. His tail wagged slowly, but his head rested firmly on the heather, as if it was stuck there.

He lifted his head painfully from the ground, to show that he could. He groaned as he lowered it again. 'At least the aesir think me dead.'

'Well, then, the nornir were better at reviving *you*... my love.' Vaguely she recalled calling him that once. The forefathers' excitement did not make it easy to remember.

'The nornir had no part in it.' Fenrir's growls sounded like they were reaching for memories. Siv walked closer to him. Memories of a past life stirred nearby, but the forefathers kept getting in the way.

'I was just... playing with her.' Fenrir let out a warm sigh. 'She was not. She was not playing.'

Siv focused on her form, and with runes she made her limbs larger, to match her usual giant proportions. At the top of Fenrir's head was a wound so deep and sharp that it went through his skull.

'She was so weary from her wounds,' Fenrir growled. 'She didn't see my eyes open behind her. She didn't notice the breath I took, and held, as she climbed my snout and sliced off my fur.'

'Why did you let her?' The last blow had pierced his skull. Siv reached out a draugar-like translucent hand. She focused her runes on her hand so she could sweep his fur aside and better see the wound. His skull was cracked.

'I didn't let her hit me, she just did. I couldn't sense her. When my eyes were not on her, I couldn't sense her. She was gone.

She was different. So, I let her believe that she had killed me.'

There was nothing Siv could do. She had learned healing runes, once, but this was beyond any healing she knew runes to conjure. The forefathers hummed in agreement. They were calling on her again, pulling on her strength.

'I'll survive until Ragnarok,' said Fenrir. 'No need to worry.'

She was beginning to remember, despite the forefathers' distraction. Touching Fenrir's fur stirred the murky waters of the past. She remembered being young in Jotunheim. She remembered running through the snow to catch up with Fenrir. Most of all, she remembered laughing. She remembered the way he had looked at her.

'Why didn't you crush her?' asked Siv. She knew he could have. Fenrir could swallow gods and goddesses. It was what his birth had destined him to do.

'The nine worlds didn't want me to. Besides, imagine his terror,' Fenrir growled. 'The great Alfather, believing that his bane-man has died. When I arrive on Ida's plain, he will run from me, like we tried to run from him. I will catch up, like he did. The frightened runner always gets caught. Imagine his screams as I gnaw on his bones and crush *his* skull.'

The Alfather running. She remembered running from him, in life. Falling to her knees in a pool of her own blood. She had died because he had chased her. The forefathers were being pushed back by her memories. They came in waves.

'I know you don't agree,' Fenrir growled. He knew her well. Probably better than she knew herself anymore. 'But the Alfather has to die. We should have killed him back then. If we had, Ragnarok would never need to happen.'

'Back when?'

'Back when there was talk of the Alfather letting his son rule in his stead.'

Aesir smiled and laughed in Siv's faint memories. Goddesses giggled at the sight of Odin's bright son. Smooth words he had uttered in a voice barely out of Siv's reach. They had praised him so. They had seated him in the high chair in Odin's hall and they had said he belonged there. Siv, too, had thought it, once, but she couldn't see it. Fenrir's words stirred something within her, but she didn't have the key to open her memories and see what had been.

'You don't remember?' Fenrir asked in response to Siv's blank stare.

'Nej,' said Siv. Her voice broke, and she couldn't remember her voice ever breaking in life. She tried so desperately to remember, but everything was just out of reach. 'I don't remember anything. Who am I? Who...?'

'Glumbruck,' Fenrir growled. Her name sounded different on his tongue than those of others. It sounded right. 'Your name is Glumbruck.'

'Why did the Alfather chase me all those summers?' she asked, for she remembered being chased. She remembered running. Always watching the skies for the Alfather's black-winged scouts. 'All those winters...'

'Because he thinks you heard,' Fenrir answered.

'Heard what?'

'The words he whispered to his son, Baldur, at his funeral.'

'Baldur.' She remembered. She remembered him, and that time. What life had been like back then, when Baldur had been alive. Odin's perfect son. How they had all loved him. "He will succeed his father," they had said. All the beings in the nine worlds had agreed that Baldur should rule and would do it well. He had been fair to all, even to a giant like Siv.

She remembered his gaze. To be noticed by Baldur felt like being noticed by the nine worlds.

'Baldur was good,' Fenrir agreed. 'He was there when they tied me up.' Siv's eyes floated to the thin chain that bound Fenrir to the heather island. 'Unlike the rest of them, Baldur came back. He came with food, and with you. He was a good friend.'

'Ja,' Siv said in a whisper. She remembered crying at a funeral. She remembered hiding among wolves, looking out at the enormous ship. The biggest ship in the nine worlds, upon which he lay. Her friend, Baldur, Odin's beautiful son. Snakes hissed at her side, and then the Alfather's single eye spotted her, among the beasts.

The memories began to flood her mind and fill her giant body. They came all at once, engulfing her, and she feared they might be gone just as quickly.

She had been staring at the Alfather's shoes, seated in his high hall. "Baldur must die," she remembered being told. A single eye stared at her, and at Loki, and made certain they understood. "Only in death will he be safe to rule after me." The desperate request of a father. The will to save his son. "Your daughter must welcome him, and let him go only when I am dead, and it is safe," the Alfather pleaded with his blood-brother. "Save my son, Loki. Kill him so that he may live."

Siv had not known why she had been called, and why she was there, but then the Alfather turned to her and made his motives clear. "The wolf will kill us. He no longer listens to his father, but he will listen to you." Loki confirmed his blood-brother's words. Guided by her mentor, Siv had found herself agreeing with the Alfather's foresight. He had always been an easy man to trust and believe. Baldur had to die, and Fenrir had to be tied up. Only then could the nine worlds be saved.

'Forgive,' Siv muttered to Fenrir. 'For this.' She stared down at the thin chain that tied Fenrir to the island. While she had lived hundreds of lives in Midgard, Fenrir had lived here, preying on low flying birds and fish. Surviving alone, for centuries, with the sole thought of Ragnarok and revenge sustaining him.

In his youth, he had been a handsome wolf, but he had been put here, and he had never grown up, not like Siv had. He had never matured. For centuries he had wallowed alone in his thoughts.

'Are you not angry with me?' she whispered, for she remembered what they had done, Loki and her. They had plotted murder and they had executed it.

Despite his mother's protests and dire efforts to save him,

they had killed the most beloved creature in the nine worlds. They had brought on Baldur's death. The death of a friend.

Even now, as she searched within herself, Siv felt no regret, for she had known it to be right, and to be needed. The Alfather had foresight like no one else, except perhaps the veulve, and he had merely wanted to save Baldur. His own son. In life, what Siv had wanted more than anything, had been to save her sons, and keep them safe for all eternity, as Odin had done for Baldur. She knew that desire.

'I'm not angry,' Fenrir eventually said. 'Baldur and you explained it. I understood.' He sighed heavily. 'I understand.'

'You know we couldn't have killed the Alfather back then,' Siv said. 'Your father, too, would have died. They are bloodbrothers.'

'Bound in blood, and bound by runes,' Fenrir said, but Siv could hear the truth. No matter what he said, Fenrir was still bitter. He had spent centuries alone with his thoughts, nurturing his bitterness. 'The nine worlds might not have been better off with my father and Odin dead, but *we* would have been.'

'The nine worlds are more important than you, or me,' she reminded him.

The forefathers pushed against her memories, and she felt them fade. Slowly retreating out of her grasp again, as the forefathers flooded her mind.

'He saved me once,' Glumbruck remembered, grasping onto a memory before they were all gone. 'The Alfather.' It had been snowing. A blizzard had risen around her. Her hands had been frozen when she was captured and thrown into the burning pit. In Jotunheim, she had nearly perished. She hadn't seen him, then, but she had known who had helped her escape. 'He owed me, for what I did to you, and Baldur, and he made good on his promise. He had me captured, but he let me go.'

'Why?' Fenrir seemed to think that the Alfather was incapable of helping anyone but himself, and perhaps he was. Perhaps his motives had been selfish then too.

'The Alfather liked the chase,' Siv said as the memory faded from her mind. 'And I think he had begun to like me as well.'

Only with Baldur had the Alfather ever thought of the nine worlds before himself. Knowing that his son would survive in the far away future had been more important to the Alfather than getting to see him grow old.

Even the Alfather acknowledged that Baldur was a worthy ruler.

'Even if he saved you once, he still killed you in the end,' Fenrir said. He was staring at Siv. Her hands and arms had faded further. All of her had. She was no more than a reluctant draugar, now, tied to life by her destiny thread. The forefathers were pulling her back into their Darkness a little more with every breath.

Siv had to fight to stay. She clung onto memories, for they were all that gave her life. Once they were all gone, she would truly die, and disappear into the forefathers' midst.

'I did die at the Alfather's feet,' Siv said, remembering her last moments. Dying and killing were the easiest things to remember in death, but she had killed so many that even that was no easy task to recall. Dying stayed with her on most days. 'I did die because he chased me, but I chose my time and he wept over my corpse.'

Siv leaned down by Fenrir's paws. Her hands reached for the fine, feather-light chain that bound him to this island, but they went straight through. Straight through the chain and Fenrir's fur. She thought of runes and focused all she could on her hands, which grasped the slim chain. She dug her fingers into the knots and tried to undo them, but they were too tight, and even if she tried for a hundred winters, she knew she would never get Fenrir's chains undone that way.

Siv let go of the chain, but kept her eyes fixed on it. She knew she was there to free Fenrir. Her destiny had dragged her here. Freeing Fenrir for Ragnarok was her last task in life, and she was eager to let go and become a forefather.

'The Alfather will die for what he did to you,' said Fenrir, and perhaps it was supposed to be romantic or reassuring, but Siv was too far removed from life to feel any of it.

'Your father will die when you kill Odin,' Siv said.

'He knows,' Fenrir decided, and he was probably right. 'My father wouldn't have started Ragnarok if he wasn't ready to die when I crack open the Alfather's skull.'

Siv sighed. She wished she could remember all that Fenrir could, that she knew what he knew and had his certainty, but that was no longer her reality. Siv lived her last moments only to satisfy the nine worlds, waiting to be released from her destiny and duties. The forefathers pulled on her, demanding her presence among them. Their clamour made her wonder why her destiny had turned out like this.

'What *did* Odin whisper into Baldur's ear?' she asked.

'No one but the Alfather knows, and perhaps you.'

'I don't,' said Siv. Although her memories had retreated in a wave and been replaced by the urgent whispers of forefathers, she was certain of that much. 'I never heard anything.'

'Then he killed you for nothing. And unless I can get out of these chains, and devour him at last, he killed Baldur for nothing too.'

'You *will* get out,' Siv decided. She looked at each and every link in the soft chain, and then she saw the one. A link in the chain that was weaker than the rest, rusted at the edges. Siv brought her ethereal hands to it, and through.

'Not for nothing,' said Siv as she readied her mind with runes to use. 'Out of fear.'

For centuries, everyone's Alfather had ruled in fear. That was why he had chased her all those winters and summers. Afraid, that she knew whatever it was he had whispered into Baldur's ears, and perhaps also because she knew too much. She knew why Baldur had been killed, and if she uttered the words elsewhere, perhaps monsters would hear and decide to eradicate Baldur from the nine worlds before he could emerge from his afterlife and rule, as the Alfather had destined him to do, once he himself was dead.

Siv's hand went straight through the thin chain, by the weak link. She closed her eyes and called forth the rune of disruption, the rune of chaos, and the rune of humanity. Together, she conjured them, and made her hand materialise in the middle of the weak link.

The link broke. The chains loosened. Fenrir let out a surprised howl and hopped up to shake the shackles off his legs. They rattled into the heather at his feet. Fenrir let out a long and happy howl, which echoed across Asgard.

Siv let herself merge into the forefathers, for at last Ragnarok had come. At last, her tasks in the nine worlds were done. At last, they would all die. Soon Baldur would rule, and all would be right with the nine worlds again.

HÖD

Chapter One Hundred and Seventy

CORPSES WERE SINGING, somewhere outside. Höd sat in his favourite chair, listening to their chanting. They were singing about Ragnarok, but their words were distant, mere echoes, and Höd could not hear much more than the names of those who would die on Ida's plain. The names of his family: his father, his mother, his brothers and sisters. His friends.

They had been chanting since Hel's rooster had cawed, six days past. At night the chants died, but in the mornings they resumed. These days in Helheim, there was always someone singing at the thought of Ragnarok.

> *When Odin advances to battle,*
> *The skies darken and demons cackle,*
> *That night, all shall end.*
> *Gods, giants, even you, my friend.*

Humming along to the chant, Höd pushed up from his chair. He walked the three paces to the wall and followed it all the way to the outer door, next to which his coats hung. Before he decided on a coat, he opened the door to check the weather.

A wind was blowing. He heard it whip past, but it didn't feel as cold as he had expected. For a while, Höd stood at the threshold, trying to guess at the weather. Finally, he settled for a light coat, took his walking stick, and left his house. Once he walked out of the cover of his home and the wind whipped, not past him, but around him, pushing him off to the side, he huddled in his thin coat and was thankful for his choice.

The road to Baldur's home was narrow and short, which suited Höd. He felt his way with the walking stick, when he was in doubt, but he knew the road well. Baldur had built a fence along his field, and once Höd reached that, ninety-seven steps from his front door, the rest of the road was easy, even though it bent up and down hills.

Outside, he heard the corpses' chant more clearly.

Then Frigg's second tear will fall and run,
The first was spilled for Odin's fair son,
His bones are broken.
In the wolf's belly rests Odin.

Their sons shall die likewise; none shall wake,
Even Red Thor, poisoned by the snake.
After Ragnarok,
No afterlife, none more shall walk.

The time had come for Höd's brothers and parents to experience death, as they had once forced it upon him. Through many centuries he had carried the knowledge that Ragnarok would come to pass and that they, almost all of those who had condemned him and participated in his murder, would die, perhaps much more painful and terrible deaths than Höd's own.

It no longer gave him comfort, but neither was he sad. Höd had been dead for a long time, but he had never quite gotten over his death. Killed at his own brother's hands. Vali had strangled him, and sometimes, when he was alone or when he was eating, Höd could still feel his brother's strong fingers around his neck, and the cold ground at his back.

His father had demanded he be killed. His brothers had chased him. Höd had tried to explain himself, to say that he hadn't meant to release the arrow that had taken Baldur's life. Loki had guided his hand, and Höd had said that he hadn't known what it would do, although he had. He had known, when Loki had whispered into his ears that Baldur would die, and he had released the arrow knowing what would happen, and what it would mean to the nine worlds.

What he hadn't known was that he would be blamed for it. He had thought they all knew that Baldur had to die for the nine worlds to live. He had to die early so that he may survive, someday, after the final battle. At the very least, he had thought they would blame the giants, Loki or Glumbruck, who both had been whispering, and not their own blind brother.

Yet Höd's father and all of his brothers had blamed *him* for Baldur's death. None of his brothers had known why Baldur had had to die, nor had they cared. His father had known, but even he—even the great Odin—hadn't protected his own son after Baldur's death. Sometimes Höd wondered if he truly was a son of Odin, or if perhaps he had never known his real father, for Odin had certainly never acted the part.

> *When Odin advances to battle,*
> *The skies darken and demons cackle,*
> *That night, all shall end.*
> *Gods, giants, even you, my friend.*

Corpses sang in the distance.

Höd reached the end of the fence between his and Baldur's farmlands. He felt the last post, took aim and set off again. Thirty steps he counted, and then he stopped, reached out a hand and felt the outer wall of Nanna's and Baldur's house. With his walking stick, he tapped the side of the wall, until he found the wooden door. He was only two paces off this time. His aim, and his ability to walk straight, had steadily improved over the last long winter in Helheim.

He smiled as he opened the door and entered the warm house. No one welcomed him with greetings. There was no one in the main part of the large house, but he heard steps from the kitchen.

'Hei, Nanna,' he shouted. He recognised the creaking weight of her steps.

'Hei, Höd,' she answered. Her voice sounded different from usual, like she had been crying. But she tried to sound cheerful, so Höd knew not to ask.

'Where is Baldur?' he asked instead. He didn't take off his coat. They would be off again soon, so there was no real need.

Nanna didn't answer, not right away. People who could see often refused to answer, and without answers Höd could only guess what was happening.

'Nanna, what's happened?'

'Well, you know,' said Nanna, eventually.

'I don't,' Höd answered. Perhaps a seeing person would have known. Sometimes seeing people knew things just by looking at Höd's face. Like they could hear his thoughts. It was a frightening thing never to know what they could see and what they couldn't, and often, they expected him to know and see the same things that they did.

Nanna did not say anything more, but he heard her moving about. Höd felt compelled to guess what she had meant by, "well, you know." Perhaps Baldur was there, and simply didn't say anything or make a sound, but Höd thought that rather unlikely. He had never known Baldur to stay silent around him. Baldur had always been a good brother, even as kids when Höd had struggled to keep up with the others and play strike-him-down. Baldur had used to yell to Höd to tell him which way to go, at his own peril.

'Nanna,' Höd eventually said. He made his way towards the

kitchen, a cautious hand on the wall. 'Why were you crying when I came in?'

'Oh,' she said, and her voice broke anew. 'I was just... It's all those chants. I keep thinking about Forseti. How my son's probably fighting on Ida's plain right now. Perhaps he's already dead.'

'Forseti is smarter than dying on the first day of Ragnarok,' said Höd, but he knew that it was little consolation, for although Nanna's son might survive the first full day, he would perish on Ida's plain before the end.

> When Odin advances to battle,
> The skies darken and demons cackle,
> That night, all shall end.
> Gods, giants, even you, my friend.

The corpses sang on outside, and Höd heard Nanna sob along to the song, although she tried to stay silent. 'Nanna, where is my brother?' asked Höd.

'He's still in bed,' she replied, sniffling.

Höd was about to leave her to her weeping and find Baldur in their bedroom, but he halted for a moment. 'He had a long life, Nanna,' he assured her. 'Even if you and Baldur weren't there for most of it, he lived a good life.'

His words could not provide the comfort Nanna truly needed, but he had to say it, for he knew it to be true. Höd followed the wall to the stairs, and counted all twenty-five steps, as he leapt over them. At the top of the stairs, he stopped for a moment, trying to remember if the bedroom where they slept was to the left or to the right. It had been many winters since he had been upstairs in Nanna's and Baldur's home.

He decided that it had to be the one on the right, because he knew that they had a view of the forest from their room, and not of the farmlands. He walked slowly, down the hall, until he found the door and swung it open.

'Baldur, Baldur, Baldur,' said Höd, as if he was waking up a little kid. 'It's Odin's day. We're supposed to go to the bathhouse.'

'Not today, Höd.'

'Today,' Höd insisted, entering. There was a sharp stench of fart inside the room. So even perfect Baldur knew how to fart, Höd thought. 'It might be our last time.' He knew that was why Baldur didn't want to go, but it was also the reason they couldn't stay at home.

The nine worlds would be injured, but the nine worlds wouldn't end with Ragnarok, and it was time that Baldur accepted that. Their father had saved Baldur by ensuring his death.

'You have to wash before we leave this world,' Höd said. 'Or Yggdrasil might coil away and die from the stench of you.'

Baldur laughed.

'Come on, get ready,' Höd ordered. In moments like these, he was glad to be the older brother, for Baldur listened to him. Höd heard blankets being shuffled aside, and Baldur moving around the room.

He felt around with his walking stick until it hit something. Cautiously Höd approached and felt the edge of a bed. He took a seat with a sigh. It was good that Baldur would come out of his house. Soon they would have to leave all of this behind, when the wolf and the worm were dead, and Loki's third child opened the gates for them to leave her realm.

'Are you not worried about returning to Asgard, and meeting Vali?' Baldur asked suddenly.

The mere mention of Vali's name reminded Höd of his death at his half-brother's hands.

In the afterlife Höd had been gifted with a lot of time alone with his memories. He remembered many things. Although he tried to focus on the sweet moments he had seen in life, there were two things he remembered better than anything: killing and dying.

'You forgave me for killing you,' Höd said. 'I can forgive Vali.'

Few of their kin were destined to survive the final battle, but Höd's murderer was one of them.

'You released the arrow, but you didn't aim for me,' Baldur said. Höd heard him struggle with his belt clasps. 'You thought nothing could harm me.'

Their brothers had all thought it a great game to throw things at Baldur. They would throw rocks at him, and axes. They would attack him at any moment, all the time, and they laughed about it each night, for nothing could harm Baldur. Their mother had made certain that not even a needle could shed his blood. All materials in the nine worlds had promised never to harm Baldur, except for the mistletoe with which Höd had murdered him.

'You didn't intend to kill me,' Baldur said, but he was wrong.

'I did,' Höd admitted, for the first time in all these centuries. Ragnarok was upon them, and he was no longer as afraid as he had been to be left alone in Helheim. 'I did intend it.'

Baldur said nothing. Even the clink of his jewellery stalled. Höd continued to speak.

'I was going to our father, when I heard a conversation in his hall. I stopped between two pillars and listened.'

Baldur had grown so quiet that Höd wondered if he was still there or if he had left the room. 'What did he say?' Baldur eventually asked, and his voice had become all quiet.

'I've never heard him so desperate. He was begging Loki to kill you before the wolf could devour you. If you succeeded him and ruled in our father's stead, the wolf would come for you. It would chew you so there would be nothing left for the afterlife. Only by dying early and being allowed into Helheim could you escape the wolf's ill intentions. That was what he said.'

Höd looked up to his left, where he thought Baldur was standing.

'When Loki placed the bow and arrow in my hand, I knew what it meant. I wanted you to live. I wanted you to survive, somewhere in the nine worlds. So, I released Loki's mistletoe arrow.'

'So, you knew, too,' Baldur said. He released a little laugh, followed by a sigh. Then sat down on the edge of the bed next to Höd, so close that their arms touched each other. 'That is why he made Vali kill you. I always wondered.'

Höd, too, had spent many days and nights in the afterlife wondering why he had been killed by his own brother. His murder had to have been ordered by their father. It probably seemed stranger to Baldur than it did to Höd. Even early in life, their father had always avoided Höd. Never had he truly been a father to him, in anything but blood.

Even to Nanna, Odin had always acted more as a father than he ever had to Höd. He was everyone's father; the great Alfather. Only Höd stood to the side, forgettable and easy to ignore.

Despite his father's disregard for him, Höd had been surprised when Vali had strangled him. Sometimes, still, Höd dreamt about the anger in Vali's voice, and he woke in a sweat.

Baldur seemed to possess an answer to Höd's unanswered question. 'Why did he make Vali kill me?' Höd asked his brother, eager to no longer wonder.

'He had to kill you, because you knew. He must have seen you there, listening.'

'Knew what?'

'Our father's plan.'

'What plan?' Höd still couldn't understand what was so dangerous about knowing that Baldur's early death meant that he would be safe in the afterlife until Hel released him.

Baldur let out another little laugh. 'I suppose he was wrong, then: you didn't know. But I also suppose you knew enough to be a threat.'

He placed a hand around Höd's shoulder. The gesture surprised him. Höd had expected Baldur to be angry with him for having kept the truth to himself during all those centuries they had spent together in Helheim, but somehow he wasn't, and it sounded like Baldur knew more, much more, than Höd ever had.

'Our father was always plotting,' Baldur said with amusement in his voice. Then his tone changed, into something more sinister and bitter. 'He plotted my death,' Baldur said. 'He told Loki and Glumbruck that it was for the future of the nine worlds. That I would survive only if I died, and didn't take his place as leader until he was dead, and Fenrir too.'

So, Baldur had also known the Alfather's plans. The same ones Höd had overheard. Somehow, Höd had always thought that his brother had died thinking that it had been an unfortunate accident, over which almost every being in the nine worlds had shed tears.

'Fenrir would never have killed me,' Baldur said, but truly, he couldn't know. Fenrir was a jotun wolf, and giants were full of chaos. Höd had never been to Jotunheim, but even he knew that. Everyone knew of the unpredictable chaos of giants, and the forefathers that dwelled within their hearts and urged them to do evil deeds.

'When I woke to the afterlife, our father's voice was ringing around me,' Baldur said. His voice was distant, as if he was far away in his own memories. 'Words whispered to my corpse.'

The secret words their father had whispered to Baldur on his funeral pyre. The biggest secret in the nine worlds. Words only their father knew. Baldur, too, had heard them, in his afterlife.

'What did he say to you?' asked Höd. Like all other creatures in the nine worlds, he had always wondered.

During those centuries spent together in Helheim, Baldur had never told him about it, just as Höd had never told Baldur why he had willingly released his arrow, and let himself be guided by Loki's pleasant words. The old saying was right: all truths were revealed before the end.

Baldur let out a sob. 'Father whispered... "Now you'll never take what's mine."'

EINER

Chapter One Hundred and Seventy-One

THE SHIP ROCKED Einer awake. Sailors were yelling. Einer's stomach churned with hunger. He rummaged under his covers.

'Awake at last, Glumbruckson,' said someone that he knew well.

Einer rubbed his eyes and squinted. Above him stood Loki, a hand on the steering oar. His black and red hair flapped around him, and his teeth flashed a smile.

'I never thought I would witness someone sleep that well and soundly on the eve of Ragnarok,' Loki laughed. 'You're a snorer, did you know that?'

'I've been told,' Einer answered, but it came out as a low grumble.

With a sigh, Einer pushed himself up to sit against the side of the ship. The day was so bright that he had to rub his eyes several times before he could clearly see the sailors on the ship. They were sailing at full speed and laughing. A game of hnefatafl had begun at the midship, and many sailors had gathered around to watch. Einer's steersmen and helmsmen were down there too. Einer must have been transferred back to the *Naglfar* while he slept. Smacking his lips, and trying to ignore his stomach rumbling, Einer looked back up at Loki standing tall above him.

'How did you...?' Einer began, but his question ended in a big yawn.

Loki, of course, didn't need to wait for him to finish his yawn to know what Einer wanted to ask, nor to answer. 'They're a nice bunch, the crew,' he said. He was in a good mood and much too talkative for so early in the morning.

'It's evening, Einer,' Loki added, correcting Einer's thoughts. 'You've been sleeping for days. If it wasn't for your snoring, we might have thought you dead.'

Then it was no wonder that Einer's stomach was complaining so much. Einer removed the deck planks at his side, slid out of his blankets and reached below deck to open the food crate stored there. He came back up with a bag of dried meat to chew on.

'You woke up right on time,' Loki said. 'I think you'll enjoy the view.'

Despite how tired he still was, and how cold, Einer wriggled up to look ahead. His breath caught in his throat.

Loki had been right. They were sailing on a broad river, on their thousands of ships. The sun was setting in front of them, behind a stone wall as large as a mountain, and in the distance behind the wall, strengthened by the sunset, were the bare branches of Yggdrasil.

The river would lead them right to the foot of Asgard's outer wall. Einer gaped at it as they came closer, completely forgetting to chew his meat. The last bit of sunlight disappeared in the shadow of the wall, and so did Yggdrasil.

Much taller than any giant Einer had ever seen, much taller than any mountain he had ever hiked, stood Asgard's outer wall. It had to be thick as well. Einer had been so focused on getting them out of Helheim at the call of Ragnarok, on preparing his warriors for what might happen on Ida's plain, that he had long forgotten about the wall.

When he had been inside the confines of the wall, in Valhalla, he hadn't even noticed it. He had seen mountains in the far distance, but never had he thought that those distant mountains were the very wall that defined the Alfather's claimed lands.

'How are we ever going to get through that?' he asked Loki. The sailors were still taken by their game of tafl, and none of them seemed particularly worried. Loki must have reassured them, somehow, that he had a plan.

'I was waiting for you, wall commander, to work it out,' Loki said. 'What *are* we going to do?'

'What are we going to do?' Einer echoed in despair as he stared at the enormous wall ahead of them. There was no way through, and they couldn't climb it either. They were not going to be able to get there. Ragnarok had been announced, loud and clear, but there would be no one for Valhalla's warriors to fight on Ida's plain, because this was an obstacle they could not overcome. They would not get through Asgard's walls.

Loki burst out laughing, and only then did Einer realise that he had been fooled. Of course, Loki had a way through. Of course, there was a reason the sailors were this calm as they sailed in the shadow of the largest wall in the nine worlds.

Loki was cackling with laughter, so loudly and wickedly that it made him sound like a kid, and Einer, too, began to laugh at his foolishness. The laughter made him feel warmer, and awake. So close to the end, it was good to laugh, and Einer knew that the Alfather did not ensure that his people laughed in the way that Loki always did. Their laughter, and their ease—that would carry them far, as soon as they were beyond that mountain-like wall.

'So, you do have a plan?' Einer asked when Loki had managed to control himself. He needed to be certain, because alone, he could not see a way through.

'Ja, Einer,' said Loki, and the way he spoke made Einer feel warm in the chest, because it felt like they were old friends. 'I have a way through. That's why we're sailing.' He had a mischievous glint in his eyes. Whatever way Loki had of getting past the giant wall, Einer was not going to like it.

'They're good sailors,' Loki said, and Einer knew that it was meant as a compliment to him. 'They will be good warriors too.' With a delighted smile, Einer watched his followers laugh over their game of tafl. They were not nervous as they had been. They were ready for war and for final death. Never before had Einer felt as prepared for battle as he felt today. There was only the matter of the wall.

Sigismund's and Brannar's ships flanked the *Naglfar* on either side. Einer hoped that his shield-wall, too, would be ready. Somehow, in the chaos of the war to come, they would need to find Odin and cut the bracteate from his neck.

Einer was fully counting on the help of giants to be lifted far into Valhalla's ranks. He was counting on his warrior reputation from having been seated at the high table, too. A lot had to go exactly as he had planned for them to be able to get close to the Alfather, but in recent winters Einer had realised that he was lucky, and for the first time in his life, he was counting on that luck.

'You're Glumbruck's son.' Once again, Loki had been listening to Einer's thoughts. 'You carry the forefathers within you. Let them—let your mother—lead you in battle.'

The forefathers had been quiet and subdued for so long, since the end of winter, that Einer had almost forgotten that they were there, and that his mother was among them. The thought of her there, watching over him, helped him push his worries aside.

'The only thing you need to worry about is how loud your thoughts are,' Loki said in a snicker.

The wind shifted, suddenly, and Einer rose to his feet, ready for Loki to yell for the sailors to shift the sail so they could go close-hauled, but instead, Loki steered to the side, following the wind. As if he commanded the wind to blow exactly as he wanted.

Other ships slowed behind them, and then Loki steered the *Naglfar* straight towards the wall. He brought them far into the shadow of the wall. It had been built from boulders plucked from Jotunheim's very mountains, as large as those that passage graves were made from. They seemed set to collide. 'Wall!' he heard the outlook yell, and then, and only then, did the wind shift again. Loki brought them so close along the great wall that Einer leaned out over the side of the ship and actually brushed against the rocks.

Their fleet followed, to their starboard side, but further out from the wall than *Naglfar*.

Loki snickered as they sailed ahead. The night was darkening around them. The wall was like a great mass of darkness on their port side.

'Will you take over?' Loki asked Einer. It had been many summers since he had last steered a longship, but he knew the ways, so he took the steering oar. He hardly had to do anything, for the wind was so precise, and right as Einer wished that he could better see, Loki conjured a flame in his hand. It illuminated his wicked face.

He clapped his hands together, and the flame disappeared, but all around them along the ship appeared flames to light their way. Not merely on the *Naglfar*, but on all of Helheim's ships.

During the three winters he had spent in Jotunheim, Einer had seen plenty of runes conjured, but never had he seen one as powerful with runes as Loki, who had come wandering out of the ice winter in summer clothes, and who could conjure flames to light the way for thousands of ships.

His flames twinkled like stars. Instead of following the ships, the flames were steering them. The wall became obscure and difficult to see, but Einer trusted Loki and he followed the burning flames. The wind came in perfectly at the aft and their sail was full.

One of the *Naglfar*'s helmsmen noticed Einer there and came to relieve him from duty. Loki had strolled down amidships at that point, and all the sailors had settled around him, no longer laughing at a game of tafl, but at Loki telling his tales.

'I seduced the stallion who built this wall,' Loki said as Einer came close. He let out a longing sigh. 'He was a handsome stallion, and I was a pretty mare.' The corpses laughed at that. All knew the story about how Loki had slipped on a mare skin and seduced the working stallion to slow the work on the wall so the gods would not have to pay for its construction. All knew how he had succeeded but ended up pregnant with a foal and stuck in his mare skin for many moons until he gave birth to eight-legged Sleipner.

'You laugh,' said Loki. 'But none of you could possibly have matched my beauty back then. Being pregnant gives you a certain... glow.' The sailors laughed louder at the way he said it. 'But Sleipner was not an easy foal to carry. He kicked and kicked with all eight hooves.'

Their laughs rang out over the river, and it spread to other ships too. How terrible it had to be, to sit behind those walls in Valhalla, waiting for the end and hearing nothing other than laughter from the enemy side.

Loki knew how to terrify. Everything was carefully plotted. Every single action he had taken had been planned so precisely that Einer felt a glimmer of hope that he, too, would be successful in his task. Because Loki had chosen him for it.

The night darkened as their ships sailed after Loki's flames. On *Naglfar*, the giant told stories that made their crew clench their stomachs from laughter, and made them sit around and listen like kids, enthralled by the most skilled skald in the nine worlds.

'When I was pregnant,' Loki said, returning to the earlier tale, 'and the work was still ongoing, the giant who built this wall with his handsome stallion was desperate to finish on time.' To hear the famed story told not by a skald, but by one who had been there, made for an entirely new experience. 'He had been promised the sun and the moon, and a wedding, should he succeed. His heart raced at the thought of bedding Freya. So, I gave him a little idea, to complete the work quicker.'

Loki held a pause and looked at every face peering up at him, full of anticipation. His own was changed by shadows: in the dim light, his chin seemed sharper.

'When he reached the first waterfront, the giant built his wall from the bottom of the river all the way to the top, but the work slowed him. So, when he reached the second river, I asked him why he bothered building the wall underwater. I told him that no one swam in the rivers anyway. No one would know. No one but him, and me.'

They would have to swim, of course. Einer had never truly thought about why Loki had been foretold to arrive at the battlefield aboard a ship from Helheim. The stories had always told it so, and he had never questioned it, but Loki never did anything unless there was a reason. He could as well have marched across the rainbow bridge as the giants were foretold to do, but he had chosen to sail to Asgard with the corpses he had gathered in his daughter's realm. Everything had a purpose, and had Loki not been on their ships, they never would have found the way into Asgard.

No sailor or warrior would have thought to swim.

'I hear you, I hear you,' said Loki, although no one had said anything. Their collective thoughts must have been loud. 'You think that means we will have to swim under the wall. Nej, the wall is much too wide. My plan is much better than that, but we *will* have to get wet. Someone will help us get through much faster than we could swim.' Loki rose to his feet and yelled his next words: 'Meet my son!'

Water splashed onto the deck. The ship rocked and Einer lost his footing, falling backwards onto deck. Summoned out of the waters came the Midgard Worm in all its glory. Teeth glistened in the light of Loki's fires. Its green skin was sleek, and water dripped down the length of it. The ship rocked. Sailors squealed and yelled and clung on for life. The Midgard Worm screeched.

Einer clasped his ears, and when at last the screech stopped, and the ship only rocked a little, and Einer lowered his hands, there was blood on his palms. His ears were bleeding from the terror of the Midgard Worm. A sight fit for the worst of nightmares.

Loki laughed at the terrible fright his son had given them all. He was the only one still standing. Everyone else aboard the *Naglfar* had fallen over either from the force of the terrible wave the Midgard Worm had sent their way, or from the sound of its cry.

Einer staggered to his feet, holding a shaking hand on the edge of the ship as he straightened his stance. Seeing the Midgard Worm clearly, out of the water, was different from seeing it in the sea between Jotunheim and Niflheim. It had seemed like a dream, then. Now, the worm was like a nightmare, conjured from Loki's runes and rendered real.

'We're here!' Loki bellowed. 'Prepare to lower the sails!'

Sailors were still staring up at the terrifying vision of the Midgard Worm, but given a command, their bodies began to move, awkwardly, from the surprise of it all. Loki cackled with laughter as he danced aft along the ship. Einer followed to be out of everyone's way.

The night-shift commander was at his post, demanding reports from all parts of the ship. No one heard, they were all still recovering from the Midgard Worm's squeal. Eventually, the sailors moved their trembling legs, and looked away from the Midgard Worm.

The sailors were not as swift as Einer's crew on the *Northern Wrath* had been, but considering that they had only sailed with each other for a few days, they were quick to act and help each other to their posts. 'All ready,' came the mid-shouter's report.

'Lower the yard!'

Clue lines were pulled in fast. The sail curled up under itself, folded close to the yard, as that too was swung down, and tipped.

Sailors were shouting, not in alarm or chaos, but with commands and advice, and then the yard bumped onto the gallows.

'Prepare to lower the mast,' Loki commanded at Einer's back, a command that had the crew whispering. Maybe there was a hole in the wall above the river that they could row through, with the masts lowered, but the wall was still close at their port side, and Einer could see no hole. At least not here, and the way that Loki was humming told him that the plan was entirely different.

On the other ships, the sailors followed the *Naglfar*'s lead and had begun to lower their sails. As far back as Einer could see Loki's conjured flames, sails were being tucked up and yards were being lowered.

The Midgard Worm slithered back into the waters with a quiet slurp, and all Einer could see of it was the subtle waves on the otherwise calm waters, as the worm swam below their ships.

'I hope you've all slept as well as Einer has,' Loki yelled to the sailors. 'It'll be a long night.' His words had them working with laughter and smiles and excitement. They had not trained for as long as Valhalla's warriors had, but these sailors were ready for war.

'They're much brighter than any warriors I could have hoped for. They're almost *too* ready for battle,' Loki said, conversing with Einer's thoughts, as usual. 'We wouldn't want to win.'

'We wouldn't?'

'Nej.' Loki sneered as if the mere idea of it was repulsive to him. 'What terrible failure that would be. Giants surviving Ragnarok and taking over Asgard. What would *we* have to do in Asgard?'

A hand wrapped around Einer's shoulder, then. Loki had walked to stand at his port side, out of the sailors' way as they took their seats around the halyard to lower the mast at their ship commander's orders.

'Nej,' Loki repeated, his hand resting warm on Einer's

shoulder. 'At Ragnarok, we must all die, and most of us must stay dead, too.'

'Most of us?' asked Einer, for there was a certain uncertainty in Loki's voice to which he was not accustomed. Loki never said anything that had not been carefully laid out and prepared.

'Some winters ago,' Loki began in his storytelling voice, 'I laid plans with my blood-brother's captured nornir. The three lovely women. I don't quite remember how that turned out, but sometimes, not remembering is a good thing.' Einer thought that would be the only answer he got, but then Loki seemed to change his mind and speak further. 'While I have planned our death, I suppose that the nornir and Fate itself might have planned our bloodline's survival. Maybe I even gave them a helping hand.' He laughed, then, and grasped Einer's shoulder.

From Loki's laughter Einer understood that the giant which the nornir had plotted to allow to live again had to be none other than Loki, and Einer smiled at the thought. He could think of no one he would rather see live. None was worthier to survive Ragnarok, or to live again, once the battle was over and had been fought, and all had died.

Loki did not correct Einer's thoughts, as they stood there, at the aft of the ship, watching their fighters, and so Einer knew that he was right. Loki had found a way for himself to be revived after Ragnarok and carry on the giant line.

The sailors heaved in the halyard in steady pulls as Loki and Einer stood and watched. Einer lifted a cautious hand, and placed it on Loki's shoulder, and with that simple gesture, they were more like equals than they had ever been, although Loki was above all and equal to none, except perhaps the Alfather.

'Is it the bracteates?' asked Einer, for although Loki had said that he wanted them undone, and that no one should live, Einer could think of no other way for anyone to survive the deadly battle than running from the battlefield, or fighting with one of the three bracteates, and Loki was not likely to flee from anything.

'Nej,' said Loki. He seemed to like having Einer guess, and also to like correcting Einer when he was wrong, which was often. 'If my blood-brother is to die, I too must die. Sacrifices must first be made. All must die, for any to be woken.'

With those words he seemed to acknowledge that he *would* be woken, or at least might be. Loki had planned the end of gods and giants carefully, but as it was with careful and complicated plans, everything had to go right for success to be achieved.

'And if you aren't woken from the afterlife?' asked Einer.

'Then such was the plan of the nine worlds,' Loki said with a sigh. 'And I did my part in their grand scheme, so that Yggdrasil may stand tall above the worlds for all eternity.'

He was not sad at the thought of dying and staying dead. He was not scared, although even Einer felt his heart beat with a certain worry as they drew closer to battle.

With a father's concern and reassurance, Loki clenched Einer's shoulder a little tighter, and gave him strength to endure. 'Death will take us all,' he said as the mast was lowered the rest of the way. 'We have all lived splendid lives. No one needs an afterlife, not even me.' The mast bumped down to rest on the fork at the aft of the ship, and the sailors congratulated themselves for the good work.

Einer knew that Loki was right. He had lived a good and long life, and he had told as much to Sigismund, and anyone else who had asked, but there were still things he would have liked to do in life, that perhaps an afterlife might have given him a chance to accomplish. Marriage and children. For almost as long as he remembered, Einer had wanted and been ready for both, but never had he found a girl he had wanted to have both with, and who had wanted that too. In Midgard, he used to think that even if his life did not provide, the afterlife might have, but it had been a foolish thing to believe.

Loki let go of Einer's shoulder with a few sturdy claps that seemed to say that all would be well, and Einer too let his arm fall to his side.

The final fight was coming no matter what Einer thought, and the end was too near for regrets. All that mattered now was that the end happened the right way. All that mattered was that they reached Ida's plain, and fought, and that the Alfather was relieved of his bracteate so that all could die and stay dead.

'We need to undo all our knots and ropes, and tie everything down, so that nothing will come undone when we pass the wall,' Loki instructed the bewildered crew. 'Tie the mast down. Tie the yard. Tie the sail. Tie the deck planks. Tie everything.'

Einer got to work with the crew. They laboured to untie tarred and untarred ropes. The thick tarred shroud ropes were used to steady the mast and yard to the ship's hull. Einer had taken up the task of tying down the deck planks, and he found that the *Naglfar* was built differently from other ships that he knew. They were not big changes, but there were certain holes for ropes in places that normally made no sense to use a rope, except now that everything needed to be tied. The ship had been built for exactly this purpose, whatever was about to happen. This had always been Loki's plan.

When everything was tied down, and Loki had inspected the entire ship and taken down the weathervane, he instructed them to lie down on the ship, and then he, personally, helped to tie the first sailors to the ship. He made sure they all had a grip somewhere, on a clasp, or the mast fish, or somewhere else. Einer was tied to the top of the mast fish, lying on his stomach with his legs sticking far out over rowing seats. In his hands was a dagger. He was the only one with a dagger in hand, and although nothing was said, Einer knew it was so he could free the others. He was not tied with clue lines, or anchor ropes, but with spare ropes, spliced together during their journey. His restraints would be the easiest to break.

'When you hear my horn, hold your breaths,' Loki told them, and at the corner of his eye, Einer saw the giant hop over the side of the ship and into the cold waters, although there was no splash.

Loki's conjured flames still lit the ship, but the giant was gone. Perhaps to tie down another crew of sailors. He left Einer and the crew of the *Naglfar* to guess what fate awaited them. They lay there for a long time, with the ropes feeling tighter with every breath.

At the fore-ship, the sailors suddenly yelled in terror. Einer twisted in his ropes to better see, but his arms were tied tight around the mast fish, and he couldn't move far.

Cold water splashed over Einer's back, making him gasp. He tilted his head back as far as he could as more of the crew screamed, and out of the corner of his eye, he saw the Midgard Worm twisting its long body around their ship. Before he could get over the shock, or catch his breath, Loki blew his horn.

Einer heard his people inhaling sharply. He held as much breath as he could. The ship groaned and they were taken underwater.

They whipped along, bubbles tickling over Einer's skin. His hair was cast loose from its braid, and he felt a weight in his chest, like it was about to burst from the pressure of the water. The cold settled like a glove around his body.

The Midgard Worm brought them under the thick mountain wall. Einer could see nothing, but the pressure in his chest felt like it might kill him. The ropes tying Einer to the mast-fish pulled hard on his limbs. Einer clenched his arms tight around the mast-fish, to stay onboard, and not be ripped off the ship into the depths of the river.

Cold water snaked into Einer's ears. He was out of breath, but he shut his eyes tight and held on. Suddenly this all seemed like such a bad idea. Loki had pulled them all along with laughter and promises of glory, but they would perish in these waters.

The ship splashed out of the waters. The pressure in Einer's chest lifted, and water trickled off him. He gasped for air and heard others do the same. They had made the journey below the wall, although in the night, and still tied to the ship, it was difficult to be certain.

The ship creaked as the Midgard Worm loosened its grip of them and disappeared. Einer took a few more heavy breaths. With the dagger still in his grasp, he undid the ropes at his wrists, wrestled himself free and untied his feet. Meanwhile, ship commanders around him were demanding full counts. Sailors each announced that they had survived the journey.

Einer peered over the side of the ship. He strained to see without Loki's flames. It seemed that four other ships had been carried under the wall with them.

'Midship number sixteen,' called a ship commander. 'Sixteen.' There was no answer.

'Dead,' one voice shouted. 'His ropes came undone. I saw him float away.' Einer considered himself lucky that he had held on, and that his ropes had been tied tight enough to keep him there.

The sailors were shouting for someone else too, up at the fore of the ship. Sailor number five had not made himself heard, and as soon as Einer was out of his ropes he searched for the man. 'Where was he tied?'

A sailor by the tack pole called out, gesturing to a figure at his feet. The limp body had closed eyes and his face was hidden by his long clammy hair. 'He might be dead,' said the man by the tack pole, quietly so that the entire ship would not panic.

Einer checked the fallen man's pulse. 'Passed out,' he said, and then he freed the sailor who had spoken. Together they freed more.

Before long they were all up, all the sailors, and trying to shake the water out of their hair and beards, and clothes. The sail was dripping wet, worse than if they had sailed through a storm, but Einer supposed that Loki had thought of even that, and probably he knew runes that could dry their sails, the same as he knew runes that could keep him warm in a blizzard.

With a squeal, the Midgard Worm came splashing out of the river. Five more ships, tight in its grip. Its body uncurled from around the ships. Warriors up and down the vessels gasped for breath as the worm quietly disappeared again.

Knowing exactly what they needed to do, Einer's crew worked in the near-complete dark, letting their fingers feel the way, and began to undo all their ropes, and tie up their sail again, and prepare to raise the mast and yard, so that they may proceed.

Again, the Midgard Worm splashed out of the water with another five ships. There were many ships, but the Midgard Worm was fast. By morning, they would all be through. Asgard's horizon was black and silent, on the eve of Ragnarok, but for the occasional splashes of the Midgard Worm and the quiet talk of sailors busy with knots.

Tonight, they prepared for the last stretch towards Ida's plain. Tonight, they readied themselves. Tomorrow, they would be killing gods.

HILDA

Chapter One Hundred and Seventy-Two

HILDA COULDN'T ADMIT to the Alfather that she had failed her task. It was much too late for that. And she couldn't be next to him when he found out, either. She didn't want to die at the hands of her own god. As she feasted at his high table, she wondered how Fenrir had lived. What she had missed. She had struck down the wolf, been drenched in its blood. She had cut the fur off its snout. It hadn't been breathing when she had swum away and washed the blood off her skin.

As she wondered, she shielded her thoughts with runes of protection and deflection, as the nornir had taught her to do. Yet, always, as she wondered, she worried too. About the final battle, fast approaching. If she hadn't killed Fenrir, could she slay the other beasts before her gods died?

The Alfather put a finger to Hilda's forehead in the spot between her eyes. The tension glided out of her at his touch, and all her thoughts too. 'What do you think about so hard, that your forehead crumples like that?' Odin asked as he retrieved his long finger.

In her mind Hilda chanted the rune of protection. It had become habit. He must have wondered why she shielded her mind like that. What thoughts took up her days. She had to admit it to him. She had to admit something.

'I'm not ready to fight,' she whispered, so the others at the high table wouldn't hear and think her weak. 'My leg... I can't fight. It's too soon.' Her heart beat with the truth.

'What you mean is that you can't run to battle,' said Troels, who was seated to her left. He was a good man, and sometimes, the way he smiled reminded her of Einer.

She nodded and stared into the Alfather's single eye. 'I can't fight with this leg,' she announced.

The prospect put the gods in dire circumstances. In a matter of days Hilda had become their hope and weapon. If she couldn't fight, they would die. The Alfather's forehead creased, as her own must have done. But his frown moved, like waves, and as Hilda stared at them, it felt like the problems slowly resolved themselves until his forehead smoothed.

'You won't need to walk or run to fight,' the Alfather said, at last.

He rose from his seat, and warriors at the high tables roared for their god and commander, raising their drinking horns to him. He basked in the glory of their cheers, but then he moved down the length of the hall, and Hilda knew that she was expected to follow. So she did.

This time, she didn't steal a spear. Troels offered his own spear willingly, as Einer would have, had he been there. Hilda winced from pain as she headed off. Starting to move was the most difficult: all her limbs hurt then, not just her legs, and the deep ache filled her body. As she put one foot in front of the other, the pain subsided. Troels' spear held her weight as she hurried down the hall after Odin.

Odin greeted his warriors as he moved past the tables, and Hilda kept enough of a distance to pass without notice in the Alfather's shadow. At the end of the hall, they reached a large door: not one of the open gates that led outside to Ida's plain, but a door to Odin's private rooms.

The Alfather pushed the door open, leaving it ajar for Hilda to follow. She did, struggling to push it shut after herself and balance at the same time. They had entered a large room. Bare apart from a long table, higher and much more formal than the ones in the hall. Individual chairs lined the table instead of benches, but they had not come to sit down. Odin was already halfway through the room, to a door at the other end.

Hoping they did not have much further to go, Hilda followed. They were always walking in Asgard. There was such distance between places. Hilda's thighs hurt terribly, and more and more so as she moved. The Alfather disappeared through the next door before Hilda could catch up.

She thought she heard something from the next room, the whickering of a horse, and when Hilda came close and peered through the door, she realised that she had been right. It hadn't been some distant vision, carried in the wind.

The next room was much larger than the one she had just come from, and although it was inside, it looked like it was outdoors. Only half of the ceiling was covered in gold shields. The other half let a sliver of moonshine through the branches of Valhalla's oak tree.

The hall's sand-coloured floor gave way to grass and hay. An apple tree grew there, inside the room. A normal apple tree, not golden like the apples of youth that the gods ate, and under the tree stood the Alfather's steed. A horse of pure muscle.

Sleipner stamped, marking its place with two front hooves. There were so many legs on that horse, that suddenly Hilda understood how it could go from flying pace, to actually flying.

Odin approached the magnificent horse. It was so large that it reached the Alfather to the shoulder. Its white fur was long and ruffled. Sleipner neighed and cast its head up. It stomped its hooves and then pushed its muzzle against the Alfather's flat hand.

'Hei, Sleipner,' said Odin fondly. 'This is Hilda.'

The horse turned its head towards Hilda. Its eyes were silver, and cold. Its white coat, too, bordered on silver. Hilda took a tentative step towards the strong stallion under the apple tree. In response to her movement, the horse moved out of the tree's shade. Eight legs, Sleipner had, and all eight were moving, and busy.

Hilda leaned against Troels' spear, and waited for the horse to come to her, and for some strange reason she was reminded of her father's funeral so long ago, where they had sacrificed a black stallion on his pyre. Wherever he was now, he would ride to battle on that black stallion. It seemed appropriate somehow, for Hilda to stand here so close to the end and look upon Sleipner's long white coat.

Barely out of Hilda's reach, Sleipner stopped and stamped again. The Alfather grinned under the apple tree. Here was the solution to their troubles. Hilda felt overwhelmed. She had already been honoured so much. At the Alfather's high table, she had been seated. She had spoken in front of the gods. They trusted her with their destinies. And now this.

The worry flooded her then too, and she shielded her mind. This was how much the Alfather trusted that she could save the gods. He entrusted Sleipner to her.

There were no excuses anymore. She had to ride to battle and defeat the monsters. She *had* to save her gods.

Somewhere a rooster crowed, the sound echoing around the large room. Sleipner's ears darted forward. Odin and Hilda both stilled and listened to Valhalla's rooster crow.

The giants were here.

The Alfather rushed across the room to a large door at the opposite side. The shields in the ceiling clattered and shook, about to fall. In five paces, the Alfather had reached the far door and wrenched it open.

'Wait,' Hilda said.

The Alfather stopped at the door. Right as Ragnarok had

been announced, as the shields were banging above them, about to fall into the hands of Valhalla's chosen. Right before certain death, Odin stopped in the door, because Hilda had asked it of him.

The shields above stopped clattering. They fell at the Alfather's command, and he no longer commanded them to fall, for he was waiting for *her*.

There were a hundred and twenty things Hilda wanted and needed to say before the end. What an honour it had been. To sit in his halls and hear his laughter and be brought here, to Sleipner. To be trusted with the fates of gods. She wanted to tell him to take care on the battlefield. That she would do her part, though she didn't know if she could. She ought to tell him that Fenrir was still alive. That the wolf would be coming, and that they would have to fight, the two of them. Exactly as it had always been foretold. There was so much that she ought to say.

Instead, Hilda shielded her mind, and said none of it.

She balanced to stand on her own two feet and held out the spear to the Alfather. 'Troels let me borrow this,' she said. 'He will need it in battle.'

The Alfather neither left, nor walked towards her; he just waited there, in the threshold. Like he too had a hundred and twenty things to say before the end.

Instead, great Odin straightened his back, took a deep breath and said, 'Cast it.'

Hilda lifted Troels' spear. She didn't quite trust her aim, especially on tired legs, but she trusted the Alfather's ability to catch the spear, almost no matter how she threw it, so she did as he asked. The spear carved through the room towards the Alfather.

With runes Odin called it to his hand. He caught it elegantly, like it was some well-practised trick. For a heartbeat longer, he stalled in the doorway. Valhalla's golden-combed rooster crowed again, and then the Alfather left.

The door slammed shut behind him.

Somehow, Hilda didn't fully trust that Troels would ever see that spear again. He would have to steal himself one. At least he was skilled enough to do so. Hilda caressed Sleipner's mane. Though the Alfather had shown her here and given her permission to ride his horse into battle, Sleipner was a horse unlike any other and it might not let her ride it.

The great white horse stood in front of her. Its eyes had gone wild, and its ears were moving in every direction. The shielded ceiling above them began to clatter again.

Hilda looked up, startled, and let out a worried breath. Where she stood with Sleipner there was no ceiling above. The sound of clashing shields thundered, and then, all of a sudden, the shields dropped. They slammed hard around Hilda and Sleipner, clattering against the branches of the apple tree and the walls, and to the grassy ground.

Sleipner neighed in surprise and reared above Hilda. Any rider would have backed away, scared of being hit by one of its many hooves, but Hilda's legs hurt too much to move. Her mind was too weary to react. One of Sleipner's front hooves scraped against her arm. Then the horse fell back onto all eight again, and neighed.

Maybe it was because Hilda had stayed her ground, while no one else would have, except maybe for the Alfather. Maybe it was because she stared straight into the beast's silver eyes. Maybe it knew how she had dealt with Fenrir. Maybe it was for some other reason. But Sleipner settled, then. The horse took the last three steps towards Hilda. It brought its face up close to hers and breathed on her, and so hard and warm was its breath that it reminded Hilda of the great wolf. There was something of Fenrir in Sleipner. Something bestial and wild.

It shouldn't surprise her that they were somewhat alike. They were half-brothers, after all. Both were children of Loki.

'You'll march to war against your kinsmen,' Hilda muttered, as she raised a hand to Sleipner's face. She caressed the soft fur on its nose ridge. 'We will have to slay your brothers, you and I.'

Caressing Sleipner's neck, she limped to the side of the horse. Her fingers ruffled Sleipner's winter coat. Its mane was long. In battle, it would get in the way. Beasts might pull on the horse's mane, or it might flow in front of Sleipner's face to hinder the horse's vision.

Something thundered from inside Valhalla. Asgard's protectors were marching to war. Shields lay in the grass at Sleipner's many hooves. The horse's ears were flicking back and forth, and again it marked its place with two of its four front hooves. It was rightly nervous about the thought of war and final death. Hilda's fingers slipped up to Sleipner's mane and she began to braid it tight.

Caressing Sleipner's soft fur reminded Hilda of her snow fox, and how it had disappeared. She knew it was better that it was safe somewhere off the battlefield, but she worried. She didn't like it when they were apart.

By the time she finished the braid, the hall was louder with stomping and shouting, but Sleipner had calmed. Its ears pointed firmly forward.

'Finally,' Hilda breathed in a sigh. 'To battle.'

She looked around the room. There was no saddle. No bridle either, and that was worse. She didn't know how Odin expected her to ride into battle on a horse without either. She couldn't clench onto Sleipner's neck and still be expected to wield an axe.

Defeated, Hilda looked down at herself. Her weapon belt was too short to be used to hook around Sleipner's neck. At least she wouldn't have to balance her snow fox too.

Her fox. There was her answer, the Ulfberht chain. A long time ago, when Hilda had died, she had unbound her snow fox, and secured its chain around her waist. She'd kept it there ever since, out of habit. She had tied it around her weapon belt for decoration at the beginning of the three-year winter. When she had hunted for the three nornir, she had sometimes used the chain to drag her catch up the mountainside to their cave.

It was still there, wound around her weapon belt, and easy to ignore. Eagerly Hilda unclasped her weapon belt and slipped the Ulfberht chain off. She caressed Sleipner's long coat and approached its head with the Ulfberht chain held up for it to see.

'I'm going to slip this over your neck,' she announced, so the stallion wouldn't startle. She clicked her tongue to get the horse's attention and slung the Ulfberht chain around its neck. At least now she could hold on. Maybe even with one hand, so she could fight as the gods expected of her.

She would have to ride saddle-less, though first, she had to get up on the horse's back. Sleipner was so tall, and it was not a horse that might kneel for her to mount. Neither did she think it would appreciate her tugging at its mane to swing herself onto its back.

Hilda cast her eyes quickly around the room for a solution. There was the apple tree, and there were the many shields on the ground. Hilda limped to a nearby shield and dragged it next to Sleipner. She took another shield and lay it on top, and then another, and another. All the while Sleipner stood and waited, obediently, keen for her to ride it to battle.

Giants and gods, and even Loki's eight-legged son, acknowledged Hilda's worth.

Hilda grabbed one last shield. There was a clasp on it, and she fastened it to her back. Then she climbed up her little tower of shields to reach Sleipner's back.

Her legs were sore as she swung herself up, but then she was seated on Sleipner's strong back, Ulfberht chain in hand, and ready for war.

Sleipner didn't wait a heartbeat longer. As soon as Hilda's legs clenched securely around the horse it broke into a trot, going around the room, over the fallen shields. So steady was it on its eight legs, that even as it clambered across Valhalla's gold shields, it neither slipped not faltered.

It ran in a circle. Hilda pulled back on her chain, hoping Sleipner would stop by the door so she could push it open, and they could ride into the great hall. There was still the loud echo of warriors readying, out there. The distant rumble of stomping feet and yelling voices.

But Sleipner didn't stop, only sped up from trot to gallop to flying pace, and before Hilda knew it, they were not riding at flying pace, but truly flying. Hilda clenched her thighs tighter. Sleipner's hooves pushed off, not from the top of the shields, nor the ground below, but from the air itself. They rode in a circle around the room, rising higher and higher with each lap. Its muscles flexed under Hilda. Every move was precise and practised and perfect.

At last, they reached the top of the tree-trunk walls of Valhalla, and above the wall, and rode through the bare branches of the oak tree. Hilda stared down into the grand hall, where warriors had been feasting earlier. There were long queues now, down the length of Valhalla. Fighters were waiting to get outside to Ida's plain where they would die one final death.

Seen from the air, Valhalla seemed all the more enormous. It was lit by the fires from inside. The shadows soared up the walls and along the long-tables, and the noise of them, so many hundreds of thousands, was deafening from the air.

The wind whipped around Hilda's ears.

Flying felt a little like when she had first heard the Runes clearly, and Hilda smiled at the memory. It was true what the nornir said: in the end of life, there was only the past to remember. The faint whispers of the nornir whisked past her in the wind. Visions, mostly past now.

Hilda thought of her father, and her Runes. Of the fight in Ash-hill, and that in Magadoborg. And as she stared down at the long row of warriors, she wondered if she might see her brother Leif on the battlefield today. She had been so young when he had passed. Would she even recognise him?

Sleipner kept steadily taking them higher into the air, each hoof perfectly synchronised with the other seven. They pushed ahead, faster and faster, higher and higher.

Above Valhalla's leafless oak tree, Odin's two ravens joined Sleipner and Hilda.

'War! War!' croaked the dark-winged birds.

The sun was coming up over the horizon. The sky was brightening. Skoll and Hati still hadn't swallowed the sun and moon, and only when they did would Ragnarok truly be upon them. It couldn't be long now. They had already been called to the battlefield.

Hilda wrenched her eyes off the stirring sight of the Alfather's warriors streaming along the hall, and out the great gates, shoulder to shoulder. She looked up at what Valhalla's rooster must have seen, since it was not the disappearance of the morning sun.

The sky began to brighten. There was enough light to see all the way to the glorious ash tree, and to the mountains in the opposite direction. Yet, Hilda couldn't spot any of the giants that had to be advancing. She saw no great armies, although their arrival had been announced. There was just Asgard, and all its usual morning calm. Until, at last, Hilda looked up.

It had been raining in the night, and now Hilda knew why.

The rainbow bridge had opened. Faint, Bifrost hung above Valhalla, and above Hilda.

A black stream of birds was flying through it. Large birds: eagles and falcons and storks. There were more eagles than any other kind of bird, flying faster on stronger wings, but there were also storks, geese, and even swans.

Once, Hilda too had flown through the bridge into Asgard, robed in Loki's bird skin.

The birds kept coming, in one long, black stream. They didn't screech, as birds usually did. They didn't caw. Silently they flew through the rainbow bridge into this world. They were giants in bird skins. That was why Valhalla's rooster had crowed. The giants were arriving in Asgard.

On Ida's plain, Odin's defenders assembled, staring out into the distance. Thousands of thousands had already arrived from the hall. They were walking across Ida's plain to form their shield-walls, entirely oblivious to the silent rush of giants flying into this world above them. They didn't think to look up at the brightening sky. It was still dark.

'War! War!' cawed Odin's two ravens.

Sleipner was not oblivious. The stallion kept moving up and up. At last Hilda realised why they were still rising, even outside Valhalla's walls: they were riding straight towards the rainbow bridge.

Alone, only accompanied by Odin's two ravens, they were riding to battle.

BUNTRUGG

Chapter One Hundred and Seventy-Three

THROUGH THE BURNING world of fire, Buntrugg led the path back to the lone passageway that opened into the cave and to Jotunheim. The track was long and perilous, and as if to hinder him further, Muspel had gathered all his flames and demons tight around Buntrugg. They were all going to the passageway to be let out. Few were those who had chosen to stay back.

'You must protect them well,' warned Muspel in the tongue of fire and demons. 'All my remaining children.'

Muspel had to know that they were nearing the place where the passage grave stood. The only solid and constant path from any other world, into or out of the world of fire.

As they marched through the world, or rather as Buntrugg marched and Muspel and his many sons and daughters burned across their world after him, Buntrugg wondered why Muspel was so talkative. He was an ancient being, like Surt, and the ancients rarely spoke. But Surt too had recently begun to speak.

'You must protect our remaining flames from dangers,' Muspel ordered. 'From the beasts who want to devour us. From the cold.'

'I won't let you die,' Buntrugg reassured the oldest demon in the nine worlds. Perhaps Muspel was even the oldest being to have ever lived. Fire was one of the first things that had emerged from the Ginnungagap.

'We won't die immediately if our flames are extinguished here,' Muspel told him. 'Not immediately. The rest of us will be burning hot in Asgard, until we burn out.'

Buntrugg struggled to understand what it must be like to *be* fire. To be a demon who lived in heat and fire, burning all in its way.

'Still,' Muspel snapped after a while. 'You must keep our fires burning in Muspelheim.'

'Why?' asked Buntrugg. He knew that it was important. Surt had always protected the fire demons. If he had been made the guardian of Muspelheim's passageway because the demons and their world were merely dangerous and not useful, he might as well have killed them. Surely the Alfather would have led an army into Muspelheim to eradicate all demons if they had no use in the nine worlds.

No one had ever explained what purpose such dangerous beings served, and here at the end of all giants and gods, commanded to stay away from the battle and sacrifice himself to flames instead, Buntrugg *needed* to know why.

'Asgard, Vanaheim, Jotunheim,' Muspel began to recite. His voice clawed at Buntrugg's ears, and the heat of it breathed against his neck. Muspel named all the other eight worlds: 'Niflheim, Alfheim, Svartalfheim, Midgard, Helheim.'

On they walked, until the stone walls that made up Muspelheim's sole passage grave appeared out of flames. Fire crackled around them, and in the fire, Buntrugg could hear the snap of Muspel's tongue, waiting, ready, with the next words.

Buntrugg stopped in front of the passage and looked straight into Muspel's fire, too bright to be looked at, and too warm to resist. His eyeballs felt like they were burning, but he remained there, staring into the flames, waiting for Muspel to reveal why it was so important to protect Muspelheim and its demons.

'It's thanks to us they exist,' Muspel finally snapped. 'It's thanks to Muspelheim their fires burn. Thanks to us, beings all over those eight worlds keep warm at night. Thanks to us, they enjoy the sun in the sky. The shine of the moon at night. It's thanks to us they *survive*.'

Buntrugg felt his heart speed up. It felt like he had been entrusted with the biggest secret in the nine worlds. Finally, so close to the end, he had been deemed worthy of the knowledge of why his life's work was so important. Why Surt had never left Muspelheim's mountain, during all those centuries.

He mattered, Buntrugg realised. The nine worlds had been right. The forefathers had claimed his sister and they had claimed his parents and they had claimed everyone Buntrugg had ever loved, but they had kept him alive, for this. To keep the nine worlds alive.

Without the heat of fire, all beings in the nine worlds would die. Not merely gods and giants, but dwarves and alvar, and svartalvar, and short-lived, and birds and flies. All would perish if there was no sun to warm them, no moon to count days by. No fires to warm their cold skins.

Whatever little lived in Niflheim—white bears and snow foxes and whales and seals—would die first. The ice would spread and capture them. Next it would swallow the rainy world of Helheim. Corpses would perish and never wake. In Midgard, the short-lived would die fast, and their horses and pigs and sheep with them. Dwarves and alvar and valley giants would be next. Aesir, vanir and giants would survive the longest, with runes to warm them for a while, but eventually they too would perish. All would die, if Muspelheim's flames were extinguished.

'Keep them safe,' Muspel pleaded.

That was why he was so talkative, Buntrugg realised. He was scared of leaving. Not of dying. Like all the ancient beings, Muspel only worried about the nine worlds. He was worried that the flames left in Muspelheim would not survive the final battle.

'I will keep them safe,' Buntrugg promised, and he would. He felt it in his heart. Now he knew why his task was so important and why he had survived. He would fulfil his task and keep the fire demons safe, so that the nine worlds may survive after giants and gods and mortals perished on Ida's plain.

Buntrugg placed his burning hand on the passage. Even without a sacrifice of blood, the passage recognised him as a long-lived giant. The stone rolled aside.

Muspel and all his hundreds and hundreds of fire demons cackled with laughter as the stone rolled aside and let fresh air into their fire world.

Although to most people fire demons were merely burning flames, Buntrugg had spent enough of his life around them to be able to distinguish them. Buntrugg pointed to one of Muspel's flames first.

Muspel's flames were spread thin across Muspelheim, but as soon as one of his flames was brought out of Muspelheim into another world, he would appear in full form. Buntrugg suppressed his fears at the thought of it. He had never seen Muspel in his entirety, and he doubted Surt had either.

Buntrugg reached for the flame. It was reluctant, but he forced it towards the open passageway, and thrust it through into the cave in Jotunheim.

The cave filled with flashing light and a thunder of melting rock. Fire roared and flared. Muspel had left Muspelheim. None he met on his path would be safe. Buntrugg reached a hand through the passageway and plucked one of Muspel's flames to drag it back into Muspelheim, keeping a little piece of Muspel and his heat safe and intact.

With Muspel gone, so was the worst of the heat in the world of fire. Buntrugg's skin hissed a little after being freed from Muspel's terrible fire.

Buntrugg indicated another demon, whose flames had a

slight green tint. One by one, he thrust demons into the world beyond. From each he collected a flame, after he had let them escape Muspelheim. Hundreds of small fragments of demons he collected and threw deeper into Muspelheim, away from the passage so that they would not slither through without his knowing.

His fingers were crusted black, and he supposed that most of him was like that now. Like Surt had been.

Finally, the last demon slipped out of the passageway. Cackling, it went, ready for war and battles and to devour all in its path.

With a sigh Buntrugg turned away from the open passage out of Muspelheim. The world of fire felt cooler on his skin with so many demons gone. For the first time since he had entered Muspelheim, Buntrugg felt like he could breathe. His throat didn't rage with heat as he inhaled, and his skin, which had begun to crust at the top like that of Surt, no longer screamed with pain.

Buntrugg heard a growl behind him. Alarmed, he spun around.

The passageway was still open. The rock had begun to roll back, but the growling came quick, and before the passage between Muspelheim and the other eight worlds closed, two wolves jumped through.

The passage shut at their back.

The wolves growled at Buntrugg and the few flames left in Muspelheim. The beasts were like night and day. One had white fur and the other a dark, nearly black, furcoat. Skoll and Hati had come to devour the demons, to erase the sun and moon and cloak the nine worlds in darkness.

Buntrugg rushed at the wolves, but it was too late, and they were too fast. Locked inside the world of fire, Skoll and Hati chased flames out of Buntrugg's reach. The wolves leapt across the burned ground and snapped at the fragments of the demons. The world of fire cooled.

'Kauna, kauna,' Buntrugg called, to give his fire demons strength. The wolves didn't care about Buntrugg. He was a giant and of no concern. They chased only the embers of demons, and they were fast.

Running to catch up with Skoll's bright fur, Buntrugg watched one flame after the other disappear. The wolves swallowed the flames with deadly snaps. Their fur was thick and built for the task. The fire of the demons barely singed them.

Buntrugg stopped running and clenched his fist tight, with his own flame hidden inside. He could not risk the wolves seeing his warm flame and launching themselves after that too.

He would never catch up with them. His runes were not strong enough to fight at a distance. In Jotunheim, against Thor, he had relied on his Muspel flame, but the two wolf brothers were not afraid of fire demons and flames as everyone else in the nine worlds was.

Against wolves such as this, he was powerless. No more than a valley giant, lost to the forefathers.

The forefathers, Buntrugg remembered. He felt for them. He knew their faces, even if their names escaped him. He had seen them. He knew who they were.

Buntrugg closed his eyes to the massacre and thought of the faces of forefathers that he remembered. He thought of their voices and called them to him.

Only once before had he called upon the forefathers' rage. Back then, he had meant to save his sister, but been lost in their fury. This time, he had to save the nine worlds. It didn't matter if he was lost to their frenzy afterwards. No one would care if he became a mad jotun growling in anger until he died. If he could save the fire demons and the nine worlds, none of it mattered.

Anger began to trickle into his mind. Fury climbed up his arm. He even thought that he felt it climb up his severed arm, to his shoulder and his neck. It tightened his muscles and made him growl, as if he too were a wolf.

The forefathers took over with whispers of rage and a hunger for blood. The wolves would die. Buntrugg welcomed the forefathers and their strength.

The two wolves seemed to slow before his eyes as the anger took hold of him. They were no longer a match for him. Within him were thousands and thousands of forefathers. Giants who had been warriors and fishermen and merchants in life. Giants who were angry at the gods and the nine worlds. Giants looking for blood.

With a growl, Buntrugg felt himself launched ahead. The forefathers had complete control over his limbs, and they made him dive straight for Hati's dark fur-coat.

The wolf was devouring a paltry little flame when he reached it. Buntrugg tried to move, but the forefathers had been invited and they had taken over. They lifted Buntrugg's left foot and with ancient strength kicked the wolf. It was cast aside, whimpering. The flame it had been eating flickered and died.

Buntrugg marched towards the cringing wolf. Before it could get up, he punched it in the side with his clenched fist, and then kicked and kicked the wolf in the guts. It stopped whimpering. Just lay helpless at his feet as he kept kicking.

A growl tore through Muspelheim. White fur flashed past him. Skoll bit into his arm.

Buntrugg roared and shook the wolf off.

Muspelheim was dark, so Buntrugg could hardly see Skoll's white fur. A little light escaped from his clenched hand with its Muspel flame. Skoll snapped at Buntrugg's hand, but the forefathers reacted quickly. Buntrugg's tight fist shot through the air; his knuckles smashed into Skoll's jaw.

The white wolf was knocked to the ground, and as he had the brother, Buntrugg kicked the cowering wolf until it no longer moved. The forefathers were still wild with rage. Buntrugg roared through Muspelheim.

All the flames were gone. The wolves had been too fast, and too good.

Hidden away deep in his mind, pushed aside by the forefathers, Buntrugg tried to soothe the rage. He thought of the forefathers' faces. He thought about what they would look like at peace, in death, when Ragnarok came to claim them all. To his best ability, he projected the image through himself so the forefathers may see, and calm.

They did. In Muspelheim's dark, the forefathers began to retreat from Buntrugg's limbs. They slithered out of his mind and trickled down his crusted skin. They left him with only his own anger and sorrow.

Muspelheim was dark. The flames had been devoured.

Buntrugg folded over himself in the cold, lightless world of fire. He let himself fall to the burned ground. The wolves lay dead at his feet in the near complete dark, but he had been too slow. They had swallowed all of Muspelheim's flames. Even Muspel himself had been devoured by the strong wolves. Buntrugg had been too slow. He had failed as a guardian.

He lay shivering from lack of pain. He had been in so much pain for so long, burned by fire demons, that the lack of pain left him feeling like he was dying—and dying he was. Muspel had told him what would happen. All the nine worlds would eventually die from the cold.

Buntrugg clenched his fist tight and felt heat form. His own flame. Buntrugg opened his clenched hand to feel the warmth of the flame, and as he did, he saw, and once more remembered, that his own flame was not all that he kept in his palm.

Eight fire demons roamed in Midgard, and Buntrugg held a part of each in his hands.

He could pull them back from Midgard. He could restore Muspelheim.

He could save the nine worlds.

HILDA

Chapter One Hundred and Seventy-Four

NO ONE ELSE was heading for the rainbow bridge. Sleipner and Hilda made the journey alone. No one but them and Odin's two ravens could fly. Even the Alfather did not join them. Without his eight-legged steed, he was grounded on the plain like his warriors.

They neared Bifrost and the invading giants in bird skins.

Hilda clenched her axe and readied herself. Sleipner was a steady ride. She had about twenty more breaths before they would clash with flapping wings and have to fight.

The sun was coming up over the horizon, casting its light across Asgard. Hilda watched the dawn to calm her heart. It would be easier to fight the giants when they were in eagle and seagull and stork skins, she told herself. It would be easier to strike first.

Five breaths longer.

She would strike the first blow at Ragnarok. Hilda took a deep breath.

The light disappeared. All of a sudden, the sunlight vanished.

All of it. Skoll had swallowed the sun. Asgard was bathed in darkness, with only stars shining above them.

Hilda's eyes didn't adjust in time, but she saw something else happen. Bifrost shattered. A terrible screech tore through the nine worlds.

Sleipner kept going. It was too late to stop. They were so close.

Hilda couldn't see anything, but she heard the beat of wings, up ahead, and the wind swept around her with whispers. Two more breaths. Hilda took another deep one and smiled. She was a norn, and even when there was no light, she could see.

She let visions of present take her.

Wings flap through the dark. An eagle flies in front, crows at each side.

Through the wind, Hilda saw and felt the giants in the present, and let the visions guide her. The giants saw more clearly through the dark than her. But through visions, Hilda saw what they did.

A bird cocks its head to the right. A white mass flies towards it. Three arm-lengths away. A horse, and on its back a girl with black tears down her cheeks.

Hilda smiled, seeing herself in vision.

The bird changes course. Claws first, it darts towards the white horse. Two arm-lengths.

A hawk screeched. Trusting her visions, Hilda struck. Her axe cut through the dark, and in visions she saw it happen. The first blow delivered at Ragnarok.

An axe slices through twig legs. In pain the hawk shrieks. Its wings spread to turn away. Another bird is coming. Their wings collide. The axe strikes again.

Through the vision, she saw not herself but the effects of her attack against the hawk—the giant. This time her axe sliced the edge of its wing, and the bird screeched for more giants to join. In a heartbeat, three birds were on her. Claws scratched her shoulder, and in visions she could see that they were all turning and coming towards her. Hundreds of birds, of giants. Yet Sleipner kept riding straight towards the great mass of them.

Hawks, eagles, even storks. They shriek for each other, and lock onto their target. The eight-legged horse. 'A messenger of Odin sent to destroy,' cries a crow. All of them turn, and glide towards their mark.

Too many giants were coming for her; even in their bird skins, Hilda couldn't defeat that many. Certainly not alone. 'Sleipner,' she hissed, and pulled back on the Ulfberht chain. But the eight-legged horse kept going, running straight into the dark crowd of birds.

Lightning struck above Yggdrasil and lit the night. The dark flutter of wings surrounded Hilda. Birds screeched. Their claws aimed for her face, and Sleipner's too. One heartbeat, and then the lightning was gone, replaced by a loud thunder. Hilda had only her visions to guide her in the dark.

She grunted in pain and struck out. Her axe hit and slowed. Feathers fell around her. Birds screeched louder. One clawed her cheek, others were at her back. She felt them try to settle on the rim of the shield behind her. They nipped at her fingers, which held onto the Ulfberht chain and to Sleipner.

Odin's horse whinnied with pain, faltering in its flight. The birds were targeting Sleipner's head. Hilda leaned forward, swinging her axe to chase them away. 'Sleipner,' she yelled into the horse's ears as she defended them both against the thickening cloud of birds and giants.

Again, Thor cast his hammer somewhere in the distance. Lightning lit the sky full of birds and giants. Claws and open beaks were illuminated with each lightning strike. Sharp slashes aimed for her face. Birds squealed. Hilda slashed her axe through the night.

She screamed for Sleipner to turn around and join Valhalla's warriors. She couldn't see anything, but there were so many birds that she didn't need to reach into visions to know that they were all around Sleipner and her. Hilda targeted necks with her axe strokes. There were so many birds mobbing her that she couldn't see if she hit or missed, though her hands were slick with blood.

Fire arrows lit the sunless day. Her gods had arrived on Ida's battlefield. Delivered by the strength of aesir and vanir and runes, arrows arced up into the air where Hilda was flying on Sleipner's back.

Behind the arrows came something else, too: crows and ravens darting up towards Hilda, spears in their sharp claws. The Alfather's valkyries.

Hilda pulled on the Ulfberht chain to make Sleipner change course. The fire arrows were coming straight at them. Hilda grunted and kept slashing about her. Her axe was slick with blood. A few dark feathers were stuck to the axe-head too.

Sleipner stopped running. All eight legs stopped moving at once, and the horse dove for the ground. Hilda nearly dropped her axe. She cast herself forward and held onto Sleipner's neck. The fire arrows flew above them. Birds were hit, and burning feathers fell with them. Then Sleipner began to gallop again. Hilda felt the horse's muscles move, faster and faster, and then they no longer fell, but were climbing into the air again. Flying.

Above them, the valkyries had joined the fight. Flaming birds and weapons gave Hilda something to see. Another row of fire arrows was launched from the ground.

The valkyries were fearless. They emerged from their raven and crow skins, raised their spears and struck. After each strike, they fell through the air, wrestling with one bird, one giant at a time. Fatal blows delivered, they robed themselves in their skins anew, and flew up to pluck another giant bird out of the flock.

'You better secure your control over that horse,' a valkyrie hissed, as she fell, wrestling a giant in owl skin. As if it was Hilda's fault that Sleipner had launched at the giants in their bird skins.

Sleipner was slow to ascend. The weight of them made it more difficult than it was for the valkyries. Dark wings were already headed towards them, and something worse too.

The giants had learned tricks from the valkyries. Above Hilda and Sleipner circled a stork. Hilda knew what would happen before the horse did. She urged Sleipner to hurry, but eagles were already upon them. Hilda conjured the rune of success as she struck after them. Her axe hit feathers and beaks, but more kept coming, and there was the stork above them.

Hilda glared up, and saw a giant hand reach out of the stomach of the stork. The bird's left wing went limp. Then the other too. Another hand appeared at the opening. The giant was huge, dressed for war, helmet and blood on his head.

He roared as he fell towards Hilda. Birds scattered, but there was nowhere for Hilda to go, and Sleipner was too slow to evade. The giant smashed into them. Hilda forced herself out of the way of the giant's battle-axe, which cut into Sleipner instead. The horse neighed and reared in the skies.

The stork giant was still falling. He grabbed her foot and pulled her away. Hilda slipped off Sleipner's back, and down.

The giant laughed as they fell together. 'I've got you,' he roared in a voice that could shatter mountains. Two of his fingers were curled around her foot and he was trying to grab her with his other hand.

Quick, Hilda folded herself up and struck at his finger, chopping straight through with her axe. The giant howled, and then Hilda was loose.

The giant fell much faster than her.

'Sleipner!' Hilda yelled as she fell, but there was nothing Odin's eight-legged horse could do. She was falling too fast, and although Sleipner was a steady ride, the stallion could not ride fast enough to catch her as she fell.

She tried to turn in the air, reaching for the wind with its whispers and visions.

A giant is falling. Straight towards Odin's steed. Heavy and fast. They collide, the horse and him. Dragging each other to the ground.

The wind whipped past Hilda with the vision. Sleipner was

falling, like her. Names of runes rushed through Hilda's mind, but runes could only amplify or dampen things. They couldn't conjure rescue out of nowhere. Certainly not for Hilda, who was still learning.

Her stomach was in knots as she fell. Lightning struck above. 'Thor!' Hilda yelled. Her last resort. She thought of the messenger's rune, to carry her shout long and far—all the way to the god of thunder. Thor, who was riding his goat cart somewhere out there in the storm. Swinging his hammer. And laughing, as the hammer struck birds and giants and killed all in its way. 'Thor, Thor,' she chanted through the messenger rune as she fell. Her skirts blew around her and the wind whipped past with unhelpful whispers.

More giants were falling. They plummeted towards her, out of their bird skins, laughing. Hilda clutched onto her axe, preparing to grab the first falling giant. There was no way the giants would die by falling. They had to know runes to halt their fall or have some other way of surviving. If she could grip onto a giant somewhere they couldn't grab her and crush her, she might survive the fall.

Something swished beneath Hilda.

'Hagal!' she heard someone yell, and then she smashed onto hard planks. The breath was kicked out of her. Her sides stung. She was thrown to the side and rolled. She heard someone laugh above her.

Thor had heard her call and come for her. He had slowed her impact with runes, but she had still been slammed onto his goat-cart hard enough to break a few bones. Everything hurt; Hilda struggled to work out exactly which bones she had broken. A rib, for certain.

Thunder deafened her, and then lightning struck as Thor threw his hammer again. He laughed as he launched it at the black cloud of giants emerging from their bird skins.

'Glad I found you, little norn,' said Thor and caught his hammer with a loud slam. 'Before the others.'

Hilda struggled to sit up at the back of Thor's cart. More fire arrows lit up the sky, and lightning glinted behind the cart as they rode through his conjured storm. The giants were falling hard to the ground, crushing gold–shielded foes. The giants swelled and shrunk, and the gold shields of Valhalla cast themselves at their huge legs.

Thor steered them away from the chaos. 'Where are we going?' Hilda groaned. There had been too many birds coming at her and Sleipner at once, but now, giants were abandoning their bird skins to fight on the ground. She couldn't see Sleipner. There were too many giants and birds and valkyries. Blood fell like rain. Yet Thor, grand slayer of giants, was riding away from the fight. Away from the giants, and their overpowering laughter.

'You'll take care of my problem,' Thor said. He was so pleased with himself, though they were riding away from battle and glory. 'Like you did for my father.'

Over Valhalla they flew. Hilda peered down into the hall. Most of the fires had gone out, though smoke was still rising from the hall. Veiled in smoke and without its gold-shielded roof, Valhalla looked like it had burned. As once Ash-hill had. Roofs burning and falling, bare walls standing in dark smoke.

Thor swung his hammer above his head and called forth thunder and lightning. His goats bleated until the thunder deafened their calls and Thor's own laughter too. 'You can rest,' he said when the thunder abated. 'It'll be a while before we spot it on the river.'

Hilda shielded her mind. Thor expected her to kill the Midgard Worm for him. They were headed to the waterfront to kill the beast before it arrived on Ragnarok's battlefield. Before it could kill Thor, as the worm was destined to do.

Hilda tried to calm her racing heart, for although she shielded her thoughts, she knew that aesir had sharp ears. Thor might hear her heartbeat and know that something was wrong. Maybe her racing heart was why he told her to rest. Thinking she was tired from the fight, already, though she wasn't. Her heart was speeding for an entirely different reason.

At any moment, Fenrir might appear on the battlefield, alive, howl and announce his survival to all, and here she was with the Alfather's murderous son.

Thor expected her to kill his bane. The Midgard Worm would have to die at Hilda's hands. If she didn't succeed, if she did as she had with Fenrir, Thor would not be as forgiving as the Alfather might have been, had he found out. Not only would Hilda die a terrible death, Thor would dishonour the memory of her too. All who fell on Ragnarok's battlefield would take the knowledge to their graves. Her newly won honours would be tarnished. She would be a dishonour to the nine worlds. All and any who survived would condemn the only memory of her.

Hilda took a few deep breaths. She shielded her mind and cleaned the feathers and blood off her axe-head. There was only one solution.

The Midgard Worm would simply have to die.

FOREFATHERS

Chapter One Hundred and Seventy-Five

WE CALL THEM all forth. All of us shall fight. The one joins us. Her name is still recent on our lips: Glumbruck. She is one of us, now. At last, finally. We no longer see her. She is somewhere within. One of us, steering our hands and voices.

Anger guides us. Tonight, they shall die. Tonight, we shall rest. Long will the night be. As long as the nine worlds are without sun and moon. The battle will last what would once have been days, or weeks, or moons: all one long, angry night, where *we* rule.

At last, we have only one voice again. There was a giant, once. Without, and not within, but already her name is beginning to fade. Her memories are gone. Her shadowed body has faded into the Darkness to become one of us. Truly, this time.

We surge forward, up the arms of all giants in the nine worlds. 'Take us home,' we plead. 'Let us in. Together we shall die.'

When our wolf descendants swallowed the sun and the moon, the nine worlds went dark. As dark as our Darkness has always been. Perhaps in the dark we can slip out. Out of that gaping hole once opened by an Ulberht axe.

We tear at the opening. We make anger rise in the minds of giants. We consume their thoughts and strengthen their kicks, their punches. Through the dark, we hiss, and whisper. The end is near.

'Let us out,' we cry. 'Let us out!'

EINER

Chapter One Hundred and Seventy-Six

THE FOREFATHERS CHANTED within Einer and made his skin pulsate. Not just his heart, but all of him. His skin was trembling to the same drum as his heartbeat. It matched the beat of giant drums in the distance. It matched the chants of the forefathers. Through blood, they were connected on the battlefield. Their hearts were one heart, reinforced by the chanting of giants.

The battle had already begun. The sun had been swallowed. Asgard lay dark, but Loki steered the way through the waters with conjured lights. The wind was steady, and Loki let the helmsmen on the *Naglfar* steer, for once. They were already in their battle gear, and Einer's heart made him feel like he was already in battle. His forefathers were in battle: his kinsmen were fighting, and dying, becoming forefathers in turn and joining the rage.

Even Loki had slipped on battle gear. For all his skills with runes, the giant still required armour in battle. Perhaps he didn't, for his choice of armour was unusual. Loki was a famed giant. He had lived with gods and traded with dwarfs.

For centuries he had prepared for Ragnarok. He could have prepared expensive armour while he had lived in Asgard and stashed it away before he was captured by the aesir, tied up in a cave and sentenced to centuries of punishment for the murder of Baldur. What Loki had instead chosen to wear made even the poorest farmer aboard the *Naglfar* look and feel rich, and perhaps that was why he had chosen his armour. Some final mockery of the gods. Even in padded armour and leather straps, he would survive their attacks and kill them.

'It's all about appearance,' Loki whispered. He sat down on the stack of oars next to Einer, amidships. Those whose forefathers weren't rising within them, who weren't deafened by the drums of battle, were sleeping. Their full armour was out and ready. Most even slept in their armour, this close to battle, but they could still sleep. To them, the battle hadn't yet begun. Only Einer and Loki knew that the first sword clashes had already rung out over Ida's plain and that the Alfather's warriors were already fighting with gold shields in their hands.

'We need to talk about your plan, Einer,' Loki whispered. The night was so dark that Einer could hardly see Loki's lips move, although he could feel the warm breath on his face. 'Your thoughts are going to get you into trouble. The Alfather will hear you halfway across the battlefield and know what you're planning.'

'I know,' Einer sighed, and he did. He had thought about it and he knew that the biggest risk for their shield-wall in facing the Alfather was Einer's own thoughts. They would give their task away. Perhaps the others he had chosen were loud thinkers too.

'You've tried runes?' Loki asked.

'I've got no talent for it,' Einer said. 'And I don't have time to keep trying. It's too close.'

Loki laughed a little, and Einer didn't quite know why. 'Sometimes you talk like your mother. All gloom at the prospect of leaving something imperfect.'

Thinking of his mother, Einer listened a little more carefully to the forefathers' rage and sorrow. They were eager and hopeful, but they were sad as well. They came with thousands of feelings and emotions, and sometimes listening to them became difficult. They gathered around the sound of beating battle drums, and in their frenzy it united them, and Einer struggled to think of his mother as one of them. One of hundreds of thousands of raging forefathers.

'Can you shield my thoughts for me?' asked Einer.

Loki was skilled with runes like no one else he had ever met. Although the Alfather had once hung himself from Yggdrasil to learn the runes, even grand Odin did not strike Einer as being superior to Loki when it came to conjuring runes. If anyone could do it, it had to be Loki.

'Even if I was standing next to you, I fear that some things are simply impossible, Einer,' said the giant, who could conjure thousands of flames and stay warm in summer clothes in Jotunheim's frost. 'I don't think your thoughts want to be silenced.'

'Then what do we do?'

'We use that to our advantage,' Loki said. 'The Alfather also knows how loud your thoughts are. He will find it suspicious if they were to go quiet. He wouldn't trust you, then.'

Earning the Alfather's trust again was not exactly what Einer had planned, and he was about to say so, and tell Loki everything he had planned, but the giant stopped him with a hand on the shoulder, and then he tilted his head to the side and whispered, 'I know. I've been listening, Einer. For days.'

The wind picked up and beat around them, though the sail didn't flap and their course stayed true. Loki had conjured a breeze around them to muffle their whispers so that no half-sleeping sailor with sharp ears would hear.

'You know your plan so well now that it's in your bones. You're a warrior. You've gone over the moves. You've practised them. You've certainly thought about them. You will move by instinct when the opportunity comes. Your body will know what to do. Don't let your thoughts tell you when to act,' Loki advised. 'Instead, let your thoughts wander and search for what else you might do. Use your thoughts to explore other possibilities. Search for openings, and chances to act, but let your body act, not your mind.'

Einer twisted further back on the stack of oars and leaned against the edge of the ship. He had to think about that proposition. Perhaps Loki was right, and his body had memorised the plan, as once it had learned shield-wall manoeuvres so he could move into formation reflexively, without command given. If that was the case, he wouldn't have to think about it. It was embedded in him, and he could focus on other opportunities on the battlefield. It was like taking a decisive step to the right to confuse his opponent before darting the opposite way. A useful move against less practised opponents.

'The Alfather will know,' Einer eventually said. Odin was not a lesser warrior, he was skilled and he knew every move of tafl.

'That's exactly why it'll work.'

Loki leaned in close. The wind whipped his dark hair around in the night, and in that moment, Einer was reminded of something distant. A wind rising. It stirred something familiar within him, or perhaps it was merely the forefathers agreeing with Loki. They drummed through Einer, his fingertips pulsing with their call. They were eager, as if to say that they too would help. They would lead him to a warriors' oblivion. At any moment, he could let them take over his body and drive all thoughts from his mind.

'Last resort,' said Loki, in a rhythm that matched the forefathers' call. 'This will work. The Alfather has met you. He knows the simplicity of your mind. You expect him to be superior to you. My blood-brother too knows that, so he will not expect you to try to deceive him.'

This time, Einer was the one to snicker, for Loki was right. Of course he was right, and in that moment, Einer was gladder than ever to have been given the chance to fight for Loki's cause.

'It'll work,' Einer said, and he actually believed it.

EINER WAS KEPT awake, the rest of the journey, by the call of the forefathers. Their rage grew louder the closer they came to the battlefield. In the distance a storm raged in the night, and lightning struck where Thor rode his goat-carriage.

They were gradually sailing closer to the storm, where the battle had to be happening.

A sailor sat up at Einer's feet. He had been sleeping under a blanket, which he quietly packed away before sitting up on the oars next to Einer, where Loki had sat earlier in the night. 'Is that the sound of the battle drums?' he asked in a whisper.

Einer strained to hear what the man did. He had been so lost in the forefathers calling him that he had thought that was all there was, combined with Thor's rumbling thunder, but then he heard it. The battle drums were without, now, as well as within. They were faint, out on the river, but they were within earshot.

'Ja,' Einer replied. His forefathers and kinsmen must already have been fighting for a while. Einer was eager to join the battle and defend his own. He hoped that they would not arrive too late, to find only dead giants and triumphant gods.

'Can I ask you something?' the man eventually said, after they had been sitting there both staring off at the sky and Thor's distant lightning.

Einer grunted in agreement, and the warrior sat further back on the oars to better see past the sail.

'Do you trust Loki? You know him better than us.'

Einer didn't blame the crew for being wary. For although Loki's charm was easy to fall to, when he was away and out of sight, one always ended up thinking back to those many stories told in Midgard about how Loki always had hidden plans and couldn't be trusted. Einer had been the same, at first.

'Before the three winters, I lay injured in the Alfather's hall,' said Einer. 'I lay there for a long time, perhaps moons, and while I lay there, staring up at the gold shields, the Alfather came to me. Sometimes he simply sat at my side, sometimes he would tell me stories. Other times we spoke. When my wounds were as good as healed, the Alfather seated me at his high table and told me of his plans, and yet I sit here today, on Loki's famed ship, with you and the other corpses.'

The warrior said nothing.

Lightning lit the sky with pretty colours as Einer spoke. The ship cut steadily through the water, and occasionally, they heard the splashing of the Midgard Worm's tail. It seemed, as they sat there, feeling the soft rocking of the ship, that they had all the time in the nine worlds to sit and talk before the deadly lightning would strike at their feet, and they would face their end.

'I trust Loki more than anyone else I've met,' Einer said. 'My mother lied to me in life.' He had often thought about it. In life he had trusted his mother more than anyone, and he still looked up to her, but she had told him nothing of his lineage, or of the anger he carried inside. 'She did it to save me pain, but still, she lied. My father often made questionable decisions.'

Once his father had declared that no one in Ash-hill should pay for mead and ale, and not only had their reserves all been drunk within a week, five warriors had nearly died from it.

'He was good too, but you couldn't always trust his word,' Einer said with a fond smile, remembering. 'The Alfather... The Alfather was grand. Beautiful, even, and standing across from him, I wanted nothing more than to please him, but his tales were robed in shadows, and there was much he never spoke about.'

Once, Einer had expected all his questions to be answered by his gods, and more specifically by the Alfather, but after meeting Odin, Einer had been left with twice as many questions.

'Loki answers my questions, and in all the time I have known him, I don't think he has lied, even once.'

'But the stories,' the warrior said.

'Even in the stories, I don't think he lied. He was always frank, and often got blamed for doing exactly as everyone asked of him.'

The other sailor, too, must have thought of that, for in the faint light from Loki's floating flames Einer saw him nod. 'Even being honest, I don't know. He had Baldur killed, and now the Alfather. Are we sailing on a quest of jealousy?'

This time, Einer was the one to nod slowly, thinking.

He looked down the length of the ship, trying to find Loki, but the giant was gone, as he often was. Loki tended to disappear, and Einer was half-convinced that he was swimming in the river with his son, the Midgard Worm. Nothing seemed below or above Loki, except perhaps lies.

'Nej,' Einer eventually said, after having thought about the question for a good while. *Jealous* was not a word Einer would have thought of to describe Loki. The giant was rash, full of ruse, and trickery. He had a true love for the unexpected and liked to surprise, but he did not strike Einer as a jealous man. 'We are here for many reasons, but Loki being jealous of his blood-brother is not one of them. I doubt jealousy is why he killed Baldur.'

Truly Einer didn't know, neither why Loki had brought on Baldur's death, nor what motivated him to bring about this battle, if it wasn't revenge or jealousy, as this man suggested. Yet, listening to the steady drum of the battle Einer's forefathers were fighting elsewhere in Asgard, and their controlled anger and whispers, he knew that he was right.

'There's an imbalance in the nine worlds,' Einer said, letting the forefathers guide his words. 'We're here to fix that.'

The forefathers were stronger than he had ever felt them before. They made his heart gallop and steadied his breathing. It felt like he was already in a fight. In the battle it would be an advantage to have the forefathers keeping him steady. A taste spread through his mouth, too: iron and blood, like he was already fighting and pushing himself.

The wind disappeared, then. The sail fluttered once, then flopped down uselessly.

'Loki's ships are here,' a voice echoed out over the river. It came from somewhere inland.

'Who is there?' Einer heard the outlook shout, but there was no response.

Naglfar sailed at the head of Helheim's fleet, although now, without wind, it merely drifted forth. Another ship knocked them softly from behind. Sailors at the aft were laughing at the unskilful manoeuvre.

'Lower the sail! Prepare to row,' commanded their steersman.

The shouter at the middle of the ship passed on the order, and sailors wrestled themselves out of their blankets, woken by the loud commands. The man next to Einer helped them pack the blankets under the deck. Einer got up to help, but he did not know where the blankets belonged under deck. What he did know, and thought about, as he cornered aft on the ship, was what would happen once they docked and marched inland. That was Einer's responsibility.

When thousands upon thousands of his people launched themselves into the deadliest battle in the nine worlds, he needed to ensure that they did as had been asked of them. He needed to ensure that none would abandon hope upon seeing the murderous battlefield.

The sailors began to undo the ropes and pull their oars out of the stack Einer had been sitting on. There was a tension in the night air that Einer was certain was not just due to them having to row through dark waters towards a shore they could not see, or due to Loki not being there to guide them.

'No need to tire your arms by rowing,' said the person who had spoken earlier. The ship groaned, twisting sideways through the waters. Sailors gasped and held on so as not to lose their balance. A giant hand had wrapped itself around the fore ship and was dragging them through the river.

The giant was larger than any Einer had seen in Jotunheim.

During his three long winters living among giants, he had learned that not all giants were equal in ability and size. The giants found in the old tales were mountain giants: their skills with the runes were limited, although not as much as that of a valley giant, but valley giants had incredible strength to compensate.

The ship dunked into something on the starboard side.

'Forgive,' said the giant in his slow voice. 'Is everyone alive?'

No one answered but sailors rushed to the side of the ship where the sound had come from. It didn't seem that the ship had been pierced. Einer saw no water flooding in, and no sailor yelled alarm.

Something splashed out of the water to their starboard side. From the depths of the river came the Midgard Worm, with a blood-curdling shriek. Clinging onto its smooth back with seaweed for reins was Loki, laughing and howling. His chin, and the soles of his leather shoes, were lit by his flames. His son stopped its terrible wail that drowned out Thor's thunder.

'Let us ride into battle!' Loki yelled. He was small compared to the mountain giant's hands, but no less frightening for it. Sailors cheered, and the large giant laughed in a deep voice that made the ship planks tremble.

'They are waiting for you inland,' said the giant, whose hand was still tight around their ship. Giants had snuck into Asgard through an old passage, and now waited by the river front for Helheim's ships to arrive. The Midgard Worm gave a parting salute to the sailors of the *Naglfar* by splashing its tail at the waters. The wave rocked the ship and beat against the shore. Water rushed through the oar-holes.

'See you in battle,' shouted Loki to his Helheim army, but already he had moved out of sight from his conjured flames, and all they heard from aboard the ship was the splashing of the Midgard Worm slithering out of the waters, and Loki's happy snickering.

The rest was up to Einer now. They wouldn't see Loki again unless they met on the battlefield.

The mountain giant's hand was still wrapped tight around the *Naglfar*. Sailors had sprung onto land, and through the dark they searched for a place to moor the ship.

Staring at the vast hand that kept them tight, Einer got an idea, and hurried to the part of the ship where he had stored away his helmet, food pack and water sack. He strapped it all on, so he was ready for war; he had decided he would carry no shield in battle. He checked his weapon belt, felt the hilts of both of his swords, content that he had all he would need.

Another ship bumped into them on the port side. The giant's hands were tight around both vessels, as the sailors climbed up to tie the ships together so they wouldn't drift and securing them to land as well. The flames Loki had conjured lit the giant's hands and a part of his lower arms.

Einer took a deep breath. 'I'm the kinsman of Grythak and Fraktir, from the edge of Niflheim,' he announced loud enough for the giant to hear him, if only through his thoughts.

The giant's grip around the *Naglfar* tightened a little, and the ship groaned under the pressure. Something appeared out of the dark of night: a face descending upon them. A round nose nearly struck the mast. Cold eyes narrowed at them, searching through their midst for the one who had spoken.

At last, the giant's eyes fell on Einer and immediately he seemed to know. 'Glumbruck...' he muttered, but even that short speech spilled from him like a howling wind, making both ship and sailors tremble.

'She was my mother,' Einer said. He didn't raise his voice above a whisper, but his thoughts spoke as loud as ever. No matter what any giant thought of his mother, Einer had found that the name gained him respect.

The giant released the *Naglfar*. The ship rocked, and then the giant's hand reached past the rigging and mast. Einer was picked up in the giant hand, as once he had been picked up by Loki, and thrown into Niflheim's cold sea.

The giant clenched Einer's chest, but didn't squeeze as hard as Loki once had. Einer could breathe as he was hauled up through the air. The jotun's face was scarcely outlined by Loki's low hanging flame at the fore-ship. He was an older giant, his face faintly wrinkled, especially around the mouth. His forehead was hidden in the shadow of a wide-brimmed hat. Einer had expected a helmet.

'If Valhalla's spearmen can throw this high, then I'll let them,' the giant whispered, and even his whisper was a roar. 'Their weapons are small like needles anyway.'

'What's your name?' asked Einer.

The giant sighed. Einer struggled to keep his eyes open against the gale the sigh unleashed on him. 'Names don't matter, so close to the end,' said the giant. 'Soon I'll be a forefather. We both will.'

Einer struggled to think of himself as a forefather, with all that rage and no voice of his own, but the giant was right. Nothing else waited for him in the afterlife, and for three entire winters, he had tried to accept that.

Nestled in the giant's grip, Einer tried to find the right words for his request. Truly it was something he should have prepared earlier, because he knew that all his attempts at forming his question were heard as clearly as if he'd uttered them aloud.

'What do you want?' asked the giant, listening to Einer's thoughts like giants always did.

'A ride,' Einer said. He would need the help of giants to get his shield-wall through the worst of the battle, and the taller a giant he could find, the better. This giant was the perfect candidate.

'You're going to get me killed, aren't you?' The giant's breath was so hot and close that it nearly made Einer sweat through his armour.

'You'll die anyway.' Einer put on his widest smile.

'Ha! That's what Loki said.' They both laughed at that, the giant more than Einer, who was shaken in the jotnar's palm like a doll, and was holding onto the giant's little finger, to make sure he wouldn't fall to his death before he set foot on the battlefield.

He knew that was not quite what the giant had meant by getting killed. The warriors of Valhalla had told Einer that after centuries of battle, it was not so much about not dying as it was about the manner in which you died.

Their deaths would be terrible, Einer knew it. Even a death at Thor's hammer would be preferable to what awaited Einer and his shield-wall on their quest, yet there was no worthier way to die either.

Einer looked into the glint of the giant's black eyes, and as loud as he could, he thought about the task Loki had given them. They had to ensure that the Alfather would die, ripped apart by Fenrir's teeth, and no one else could do it.

'Keep dangerous thoughts like that to yourself,' the giant hissed and closed his fingers a little around Einer. 'How many of you?'

'Five.'

The giant considered that. He would say yes, and they both knew it. After what Einer had revealed, there was nothing else for him to do. So, without further word, the giant deposited him on land.

Einer was about to say that he would be at the front of the army when they had all arrived on land and were ready to move out, but the giant spoke first. 'I'll find you, loud thinker. Easily.' And then he was off.

Warriors were already moving food crates and armour and shields onto land. The *Naglfar* had been both anchored and moored; no one would need to make a quick escape. This was not a raid, and there would be no journey home.

The shore was busy with activity. Einer's eyes had begun to adjust to the near complete dark. With no sun or moon, there was so little light coming from the stars that he stumbled through the crowd.

Other giants had arrived to help the ships. He heard the crush of their feet, and hoped that giants could see better than him, and wouldn't accidentally crush someone with a careless step.

Einer positioned himself far into land, where he had told his senior commanders he would be. He found moss and fire strike in a crate a great giant deposited at his feet, but no matter how hard he struck, no fire came, and it wasn't because of the wind, for although Thor's thunder rumbled closer with every heartbeat, there was no wind.

Even without the fire he had promised, the senior commanders found their way to him. They came in small groups, and he gave them the same advice: to remind their warriors of the skills they had acquired in death and life and use those in battle. They went over the list of equipment each person had to carry and Einer reminded them of where the water barrels and food crates would be deposited by giants for warriors to use when their pouches ran out. He wanted everyone to be as prepared as possible, but there was no time to teach them anything more.

Eventually, all the ships docked, and the last three commanders announced that their groups were ready. Einer struggled to get to the front of the crowd where his shield-wall would be waiting for him.

Thor's lightning hit hard. So close was it that Einer had to shield his ears from the terrible thunder that followed, and he heard gasps of mixed wonder and terror around him.

Brannar, robed in full bearskin armour; Sigismund, with the worried frown on his face and his blond curls tied away under his helmet; and Tassi, tall and skinny with nothing but leather armour, all waited for Einer. There was no glorious welcome, only an acknowledgement from each of them, that he was there, alive, and that they were too. Before Einer could ask about Bogi and Nar, the two large warriors burst out of the crowd carrying Sigismund's anvil between them.

'What in all of Helheim are we going to do with this?' Bogi complained when they plopped it down onto the mushy ground at their feet. His red hair was glistening wet with sweat already, and Nar did not look any happier.

'I got us a ride,' Einer said, and he watched their faces settle with relief.

With a thunderous crash, a giant foot smacked down next to Einer. Nar and Sigismund both yelped at the sudden appearance, and Bogi seemed to have gotten hiccups from it all, but Brannar and Tassi merely watched the giant, and neither one of them could have looked more unimpressed with Einer's choice of a ride.

'The anvil too?' asked the giant so the earth trembled under their feet.

Einer nodded. The giant swept the anvil into his belt pouch, and then grabbed all five of them in one hand. Einer was pressed up against Nar's elbow, and Sigismund's foot was hitting his shin, but quickly enough the hand opened around them and deposited them on the giant's shoulder.

Thor's lightning had drawn so close that it lit the plain of giants and corpse-warriors all the way to the ships. Swarms of warriors had begun their march inland.

Storm clouds gathered above them, and somewhere in the distance Einer heard the familiar screech of the Midgard Worm. Again, Thor's lightning struck. They had to be readying for their final fight, out there, Thor and the worm. Soon, hopefully, they would both perish, and none would have to fear dying under the weight of Thor's hammer.

Lightning struck again, flashing across the faces of Helheim's people staring up at Einer and his shield-wall. Thor was coming for them. His thunder already rumbled loud above them. As far as Einer could see, his people looked to him, and in that moment, he was reminded, once more, that they were not truly warriors. Helheim's corpses were here of their own choice, to stand up for their own and for what ought to be right in the nine worlds, but they were not used to war, as he was. Their faces peered up at him, lit by the constant lightning that struck all over the plain, burning giants and trees and fighters.

Einer didn't know what to say. In life, before heading into battle, he had used to tell his comrades that they would meet again in Valhalla, but they wouldn't. Not this time. If they did, it meant that they had failed.

'To glory?' Brannar suggested, feeling Einer's hesitation, but even that felt hollow and worthless before Ragnarok.

Einer looked out towards the battlefield, where he saw giants marching. Out there, somewhere, Loki was riding into battle on his son's back, and suddenly Einer knew exactly what he wanted to say. Mimicking the famed giant's wicked smile, Einer faced his thousands upon thousands of followers. He called upon the forefathers' strength, raised his Ulfberht sword in the air, and bellowed: 'Death to all gods!'

Thousands of merchants and fishers and farmers looked up at him. The words settled into the silence around them, and then, as one, unified as all giants were through the anger of their forefathers, thousands of first-time warriors raised their weapons into the darkness and roared the words back to him.

'DEATH TO ALL GODS!'

DARKNESS

RAGNAR STARED ACROSS the fields of Ragnarok. The Darkness was pushed away through his distaff. Gods were dying, giants were dying. Despite everything Ragnar had done, nothing had changed. Ragnarok was still happening.

'Why is Ragnarok still happening?' Ragnar cried, no longer caring that the shadow warriors would come. 'I killed the Alfather.'

A sword sliced through Ragnar's neck.

Death, pain, and fear.

RAGNAR CAME BACK to his senses in the complete dark. A quick death, for once. Even the shadow warriors in his Darkness were taking pity on him now and finishing him quickly. Ragnar had done so much. He had tried everything, even killed his god. Despite all he had done, Ragnarok was still happening. He couldn't stop it.

Ragnarok. Gods' twilight. Their twilight and their darkness

had come for them. Their end. There was no escaping it. The tears ran hot down Ragnar's cheeks in the Darkness where no one could see. He himself had been named after the gods. Ragnar—gods. To see the end like this, and not be able to stop it... It was too cruel a fate.

Especially for a skald who had used to tell countless stories about the gods in their glory days, before the terrible end he had doomed them to.

Ragnarok. The Darkness of the Gods. Perhaps that was what it meant, more so than the Twilight of the Gods, Ragnar thought. Perhaps it meant that all the gods would come here, in the end, when they died, just like Ragnar had been sentenced to this afterlife. Perhaps his gods, too, would arrive here, after their final deaths.

A daunting thought entered Ragnar's mind, and his tears abruptly stopped.

What if Ragnarok didn't mean the twilight of gods, as everyone in Midgard believed? What if it wasn't the Gods' Darkness either? What if it was simply what it said: Ragnar's Rok? Ragnar's Darkness?

He had made it happen, after all. *He* had ensured the Alfather's death. *He* had freed Loki from the shackles. *He* had made it all happen, stuck in his Darkness.

Ragnar stared through the pitch-black dark that surrounded him with a new fear.

Ragnar's Darkness. That was what Ragnarok was.

He had done this. It was *his* fault, and only his, that the gods were dying on Asgard's green plains.

EINER

Chapter One Hundred and Seventy-Seven

GIANTS SWEPT UP fighters as if they were children plucking grass. At Einer's instructions, their giant was carrying another thirty members of his fleet. Most of their crew had been warriors in life, but had perished away from their battlefields and been denied the glory of Valhalla, despite their worth.

Thor's thunder was loud in the sky. His goat-carriage was up there somewhere. No doubt Thor's red eyes scoured the ground, searching for targets for his hammer.

The giant Einer had enlisted was humming a song that none of them knew, but they were quick to invent words to fit the melody. Three dozen men and women were laughing and singing as they sat on the giant's shoulder, hung from his belt, and dangled in his hair.

> When Thor goes to war,
> Let him try, let him try, let him try,
> He will strike and roar
> Let him cry, let him cry, let him cry.

The song went around, and they took it in turns to add lines, before they all sang it together to the giant's hum. To the hum of all giants and forefathers. Deep within Einer, the melody rose. His fingers throbbed in the same rhythm.

Einer had imagined Ragnarok to be many things, but he had never imagined that he would be laughing and singing as he was carried into battle on the shoulder of a mountain giant.

They finished Brannar's verse. The last one belonged to Einer, and he was left with the great task of finishing their song. With a smile on his lips, he sang loud and clear:

Bitten by the great worm,
Let him cry, let him cry, let him cry.
Thor shall writhe and squirm,
Let him die, let him die, let him die.

The warriors laughed at Thor's terrible end and then they bellowed the verse as loud as they could. They were so pleased with their song that they declared themselves skalds and swore it a shame that none should come to hear it, but of course, before the end many *did* hear, for they sang it more than once.

They were carried far ahead in high spirits as they sang their song, again and again. Their giant began to sing along, and then a giant next to him joined in, and more and more of Helheim's own learned the words and adopted the mocking song of Thor's destined end.

Lightning struck directly ahead of them.

'Someone is angry,' their giant chuckled. The threat of death only made them sing louder, announcing their arrival on the battlefield. They could hear the crashes of war when they weren't singing, and even when they were. Like drums beating along to their songs.

Their singing stopped suddenly. Another lightning strike lit the battlefield, revealing what lay ahead of them. There were aesir on the nearby fields. Weapons were being hurled out in all directions, coming at a speed that not even a giant ought to be able to match. On the side of the gods, only the gods themselves had the ability to conjure runes. They were marching directly towards a god, perhaps several of them.

The Midgard Worm shrieked ahead of them. They were close. They wouldn't get much further on their giant. The others were readying to jump down and fight, but they were not yet close enough to even see Valhalla, and the Alfather would not venture far from his hall.

The giant had not given them the advantage that Einer had hoped.

'Sigis,' Einer called, and leaned in to speak past Brannar, sitting on the giant's shoulder between them. 'We need to get you to Yggdrasil's root so you can set up. We will join the war here.'

He looked at Brannar as well, then. He didn't trust Sigismund to anyone else in their shield-wall, and certainly not to go alone, but they had to split up. It would be too dangerous for Sigismund to head into battle with them. He was the only one who could undo the bracteates. They couldn't risk him dying before the task had been accomplished.

'You two are going to have to go around. I'll ask the giant to take you.'

The giant looked down at them with a knowing smile that said he had heard. He would take Sigismund and Brannar around the battlefield, and all the way to Yggdrasil's outer root so they could set up the anvil and start to undo the two bracteates they already had.

Tassi knew where to meet them. It would be his task to bring the Alfather's bracteate to Sigismund, once they reached the Alfather and Nar, Bogi, and Einer had cut the ring off the god's neck.

'It's time to fight,' Einer yelled to the thirty warriors who had climbed atop the giant with them. 'Ready yourselves!'

The giant took them close to the actual battle, where the gold shields of Valhalla glittered in the light from Thor's lightning.

Something else lit the battlefield, then: fires burning from the south. Huge fires were burning through Asgard. They were far away, but in the utter dark of the nine worlds, they were easy to spot. They advanced fast, spreading through the dense world of gods. They lit the way. Finally, fighters could see what they hit, and giants where they stepped.

'Surt, at last,' their giant grunted.

The ancient giant, Surt, had arrived with fire demons from Muspelheim. Their flames raged through the battlefield and lit the terrified faces of those who fought.

'Stop here,' Einer requested of the giant. He didn't have to shout to be heard. His loud thoughts pierced through the clamour of the battlefield. The giant crouched down and began to pull warriors free of his belt to set them down.

Einer's shield-wall rose to their feet on the giant's shoulder and made ready, wishing each other luck and success on the battlefield. Despite the dark, Einer noticed Sigismund smiling. His old friend hadn't smiled like that since he had admitted that he couldn't undo the bracteates. From afar Sigismund was gazing at the approaching fire. He caught Einer staring.

He cornered around Brannar, still with that wide smile carved across his face. 'The fire demons will melt them,' he announced to Einer in a whisper as they hugged their final goodbyes.

'Stay safe, old friend,' Einer said. Their armour clanged as they embraced each other tight. Einer's chainmail dug into his skin, and he was acutely aware that he was without a bracteate. He was more vulnerable on this battlefield than he had been in years.

'Die well,' Sigismund told him.

They parted from each other's embrace, but their hands held on. Never again would they meet. Einer didn't like the finality of it, but with a nod and a sigh, he accepted that the time had come. Their hands let go of each other, and their destinies parted for the last time.

'I'll keep him safe,' Brannar answered to Einer's unspoken

words, as if she could hear his thoughts as clearly as giants and gods could.

The giant, a caring being, like most giants Einer had met, had waited for them to say their final farewells, and he knew that the time had come. With a warm hand, he plucked Einer off his shoulder, and placed him carefully on the ground. 'Make Glumbruck proud,' his voice rumbled, and then he turned away.

Einer felt the forefathers pulse in him, stronger now than ever before. His mother was among them. Their anger made him growl. Now that battle was mere heartbeats away, the forefathers were shouting.

Einer unsheathed both of his swords. At his side Nar and Bogi had their axes out, hiding behind their large shields, and tall Tassi casually held his spear in one hand and his shield in the other. Slight as he was, Tassi had a calm that Einer had rarely seen. His slim arms were so long that wielding a spear, he far outreached almost every other warrior on the field.

Gold shields were moving fast towards them.

'Bloody shields,' Bogi sighed and raised his own. They were outmanned twenty to one, at least.

Einer took a deep breath, strengthened by the forefathers. He twirled the Ulfberht sword in his hand to secure his grip and brought his own sword out in front of him to use instead of a shield.

'They're only short-lived,' Einer told his small shield-wall, and in that moment, he felt like a true giant, as his uncle and grandparents had promised he would. The forefathers shouted through him. He tasted blood in his mouth, and his breathing was steadied by their constant reminder. Even Odin's gold-shielded defenders were nothing to him. He had fought giants. He had fought gods. It would take more than twenty of Valhalla's best to overman Einer.

Bogi, Nar, and Tassi were less confident, but he had picked them well, and instructed them how to fight on this battlefield. He had even told them to leave ample room around him and

433

announce themselves before they came into sword distance of Einer, in case the forefathers filled his mind and made him incapable of distinguishing kinsman from foe.

The others who had ridden with Einer's group advanced in a shield-wall. They walked, instead of running, as Einer had instructed them to do back on Helheim's beach. Their shield-wall was tight. They were ready.

'Joining your south flank,' Einer yelled to them. Nar, Bogi and Tassi seemed relieved at that prospect. The three of them joined their shields to the wall and Einer strode to the side, unprotected.

He breathed in the rhythm of the forefathers' chant. His forefathers seemed to boil directly under his skin, and their presence gave him strength. They would protect him. The song Einer and his crew had invented was being shouted across the plains. It echoed between the two armies. *'Let him die, let him die, let him die!'*

The advance of fire demons basked the world in both light and shadows. There was enough light for Einer to see not merely his own swords but Valhalla's glinting shields too.

In a roar, Einer launched into a run, as he had taught his Helheim warriors never to do. He was a giant. He was different. Every piece of him hummed with that knowledge. The muscles in his fingers were flexed around his sword hilts. The tip of his fingers pulsed. Even his toes were ready for the fight, hungering for blood. Einer grunted as a spear was thrust after him; he deflected with his sword and kept running. Valhalla's shield-wall stopped advancing. They braced for Einer's blow, and Einer readied himself for theirs.

His armour was tight, chainmail and leather both. Loki had secured the best armour for him. His helmet even had a bump out at the forehead to allow for Einer's arrow stump, which normal helmets screeched against. The sound of the forefathers rang in his head. They steered him ahead.

He took a deep breath and swept his left-hand sword from

bottom to top, diverting an incoming spear. At the same time, he slammed his Ulfberht at the foe directly in front of him.

His sword rattled. The golden shield held, but the warrior stumbled backwards from the blow. Einer shouldered himself against the shield, parried an axe with his Ulfberht, and kicked under the shield. His foot slammed into the other man's shin. The warrior buckled. Einer grabbed onto the edges, wrenched the gold shield out of his enemy's grip and cast it aside. It hit another man trying to corner around at the back, thinking Einer hadn't noticed.

The forefathers heightened every sense. Einer felt the grass and mud through the thick soles of his shoes and smelled the stench of sweat. Their every move seemed so predictable. So easy.

Einer kicked out, avoiding a sword blow aimed at his foot, and kicking another man in the shin. His left hand spun, reversing his sword, and he thrust backwards. He sliced through meat and did not have to move to know that he had killed an enemy. Meanwhile, his right hand parried an axe and two swords, both aimed for his head.

The forefathers did not take over as they had in the past; they merely steered him. Made him aware of what his opponents were planning. It almost felt like he knew what they would do before they did. They only had to *decide* on a move, and the forefathers' keen senses picked up on it.

The two shield-walls clashed. Eager warriors eyed Einer. Something moved at his back. Einer whirled around to see gold shields advancing in a ring around him.

Einer pointed the Ulfberht at the ground, swept it under lesser warriors' shields, and kept it there as he spun. He gritted his teeth in a suppressed roar. Warriors screamed as their toes were sliced off. Einer shouldered an opponent out of the way to find new ground where there was no one at his back.

His sword glistened dark red in the distant flames. First blood had been shed. The smell of blood was strong, and it wasn't just coming from Einer's sword or the wounded. It was coming from the forefathers, too, as if Einer could smell the blood on the battlefield, could taste it in his mouth.

Einer shouldered past his foes. The crowd was tight. No one lifted their weapons free of the wall to strike him in time. Einer kept his weapons low, slicing through shoes and toes and shins as he pushed through. Whatever his swords found.

An axe hacked him across the back. Einer roared and swung around to face his attacker.

The warrior's eyes were wild and shaking; he must have taken berserker caps before launching into battle. Einer ignored the pain in his back and glanced at the man's feet. That was how he had managed to free himself from the crush: one of the warrior's own kinsmen lay buckled over, his shoulder and jaw shattered by the axe. He wasn't dead yet, but soon he would be, trampled to death by his own friends.

Einer let out a forefather's grunt.

The berserker too was grunting, but *his* were different, uncontrollable and desperate. Like a drunk man trying and failing to speak, and furious that no one understood him.

The berserker launched at Einer, but his shield hindered him. The crowd was still too tight. With another wild grunt, he threw down his shield and then launched himself at Einer.

Einer raised his left-hand sword and stabbed through the berserker's stomach, but the man kept coming. The sword was stuck. Einer let go of the hilt and pushed the berserker's arm up. The man managed to hook his axe over Einer's back, again, but this time, it didn't pierce his armour.

Einer kneed the berserker in the groin, but the man merely grunted and attacked again. He had no shield, no weapon, but he had teeth, and he intended to use them. Einer couldn't lift his Ulfberht, and at this close range it would do him no good, so he raised his left hand and grabbed the berserker's shoulder instead. The forefathers hummed loud and filled him with strength. He tightened his grip around the berserker's shoulder until he felt bones break.

Still, the berserker snapped his teeth. The man's shoulder was broken, his arm dangling helplessly, but his teeth were still snapping away. The circle of fighters around them pressed them closer together. Einer stubbed his nail-less finger and howled. He was jostled by shields and weapons on all sides. He wrestled his sword arm up, planted his elbow against the berserker's chest, and punched him in the face with his left hand. Once, twice, three times. His hand was bloody. The berserker dropped at Einer's feet, unconscious or dead.

Warriors pushed in close again before Einer could retrieve his sword. He held onto the Ulfberht and tried to shove his way free of the crowd, but the more he tried, the more stuck he got.

They were not advancing. The crowd was helplessly rummaging, and Einer couldn't get through. He jumped up to look farther, above helmets and swinging weapons and shields, but he could not see Valhalla. Not that he could see much in the night, lit only by lightning and fire.

No matter where Valhalla was, Einer had to get out of this crowd. He peered at the helpless faces of other warriors as he tried to push through. Valhalla's fiercest were as desperate as him to get free and fight. It was like they were caught in a net or surrounded by a tightening rope.

A shadow was cast over their desperate faces. No one had time to react, or do anything but lift their eyes, before the sole of a giant's foot came sailing over them. There was another crash further ahead, and then the foot rose again. Valhalla's champions clung on and were carried into the air. Some fell on friendly weapons and shields, others held on.

Barely had the foot risen before the warriors were forced even closer together, filling the gap the foot had left. Above, escaped fighters laughed, hanging onto the giant's foot.

There was an escape.

Einer was not the only one to think it. They all peered up at the dark sky, hoping to see another approaching giant. A saviour to free them from their sweaty ranks.

Einer let out a frustrated grunt at being stuck. He had lost track of Nar, Bogi and Tassi. He peered over his shoulder but could not see a single warrior from Helheim. Either they were dead, or trapped, or they had moved on, while Einer had fought and become stuck amidst the Alfather's warriors.

Another shadow raced across shields and helmets. Upon Einer, too. Not a giant's foot this time: the shadow was much larger and longer than that.

It fell hard among them, and Einer was cast down amidst the crowd in a tangle of limbs and weapons. His helmet banged against a gold shield. The controlled breath was knocked out of him. Something slimy and slick pressed against his arm and cheek. The Midgard Worm.

Warriors hacked into the worm's skin, and Einer yelled for them to stop. The outer skin was merely slippery, Einer knew, for he had touched it before, but piercing through to the layer beneath would unleash a deadly venom. That was why the waters between Niflheim and Helheim's coasts had been near impossible to swim across, because the Midgard Worm lay out there and bit its own tail short. His grandmother had taught him that.

'Don't strike it!' Einer yelled, but his words were muffled by the Midgard Worm's squealing cries.

As loud as he knew how to do, Einer thought of Loki, and made his presence known to the giant. He was here, crushed by the Midgard Worm! But perhaps there were too many other loud thoughts at the edge of Ragnarok's battlefield, because Loki did not come for him.

The Midgard Worm slithered across Einer. His face was rubbed raw, until the end of the tail rose from his chest.

Einer pushed away those fallen at his feet, climbing up before he was trampled. The warriors who had taken most of the Midgard Worm's weight lay crushed to death at his side. Einer stepped onto their slimy bodies.

He watched warriors screaming above him. Warriors who

had hung onto the worm, axes buried into its skin. Venom was running down their weapons and arms, killing them quicker than they would have died on the ground.

The crowd closed around Einer again. Quickly, he searched for another way out, and then he knew. He sheathed his Ulfberht and ran the three steps that separated him from the next man. Grabbed hold of his shoulders to force him down, then stepped onto the man's back, and then another's shoulders. Further along, a mob had raised their shields over their heads, to better move. Einer smiled and stepped onto their shielded roof.

Looking up at Einer, others tried to follow his lead. They toppled over all around the thick crowd, trying to step on each other, to get up and free. Below Einer, warriors crouched to trip him up, but he moved too quickly across their shields and shoulders.

The Midgard Worm slithered away fast. It was so long that Einer couldn't see which end its head was. Loki would not have heard him, even if his thoughts were the loudest on the entire battlefield.

'He's there!' someone yelled. Einer recognised Tassi's voice and peered over his shoulder. Tassi didn't look like he was stuck in the crowd like Einer; somehow, they had gotten ahead of the mob.

Einer fixed on the direction of his shield-mates and walked across warriors, stepping on helmets and shoulders and shields and anything half-solid. He tumbled over the last shield, then his shoulder bumped against someone's helmet and all of him fell. The muddy ground took the worst of his fall. The forefathers were loud, masking the sharp pain in his shoulder.

A hand reached down, and Einer took it. Bogi lifted him to his feet. They were all there. Unlike him, they had stayed together, and avoided getting caught in the mass of Valhalla's warriors. Einer pulled forth his Ulfberht sword, patted down the empty scabbard where his old sword had been and felt bare for it. But he was free of the thick crowd. There was room to breathe.

Valhalla's warriors had been rounded up, like fish in a net. The outer row of warriors was tied in by simple ropes. Some distance away, Einer saw a giant holding onto the rope, laughing at all the wriggling short-lived he had caught.

He smiled at the sight. Runic ropes and knots kept the Alfather's fighters trapped. He was glad to be out of their midst. He dried the sweat off his forehead. His underarms were slick with sweat. Had it not been for the forefathers' control, he would have been panting for breath.

'Should have stayed with us,' Tassi said in a disapproving tone. Still smiling, Einer nodded.

He had launched ahead, thinking he could cut the way through the crowd for them, but he should have known better than anyone that there was no chaos quite like that of Ragnarok. Getting lost in a crowd was easy, and too dangerous to risk again. 'We stay together, now,' he agreed. 'But first I need a weapon for my left hand.'

A strong stench of piss surrounded them, and when Einer looked down, searching for a shield, or a second weapon to wield, he realised that what he had thought was mud were corpses that had been crushed under a giant's foot. Their shields were broken into pieces, and the corpses, too, ground under the sole of a giant. The shafts of axes and spears were crushed. All of them were useless.

'I'll find something on the way,' Einer decided. Staying put anywhere on this battlefield made them targets, and that was how warriors died.

His three comrades nodded and lifted their shields to form a wall in front of them and Einer. Together they headed off searching for Valhalla, and for the Alfather.

The forefathers chanted loud and reminded him that the end was near. Soon he would join them, for no one survived this battlefield.

As if Ida's plain, too, listened to Einer's thoughts, a light shone straight ahead of them.

It came neither from Thor's thunder nor from fire demons, but from a god's conjured runes. They were coming close to an aesir. It could be Odin, it could be Tyr. It could be any of the gods. They had to head towards the god, whoever it was. Dart into the deadliest part of the battle.

Einer took a deep breath. 'Gods too must die,' he reminded himself, but the words did not calm his worries about what deadly dangers lay ahead of them.

HILDA

Chapter One Hundred and Seventy-Eight

'THERE'S THE VENOMOUS beast.' Thor swung the hammer above his head.

Hilda peered over the edge of the cart. His goats were hopping on clouds. The cart wobbled behind and made it difficult to focus. Even so, the Midgard Worm was impossible to miss. Lightning struck every few heartbeats from the cart's burning hot wheels. The light illuminated the battlefield below. Through the thin layer of clouds, the field looked smoked from the heat of fire demons.

The Midgard Worm was weaving across the battlefield. Gold-shielded warriors hacked at its slick body.

With a roar, Thor launched his short-shafted hammer, which whipped through the clouds. He had aimed straight for the great Midgard Worm, and he was unusually quiet as they watched his hammer fly towards the huge creature. And then it moved—not the hammer, but the worm itself.

As fast as lightning, the worm wriggled. As if it knew. Its tail cast warriors aside. Thor's hammer pounded down and reddened the ground, but it only grazed the Midgard Worm's body. It scraped off a long piece of the worm's slick skin, and then returned. Like an arrow it flew back up through the clouds. Effortlessly, Thor caught it.

He wasn't laughing anymore. His mortal enemy was right there, wriggling out of his reach. He turned to Hilda. 'You know what to do.'

'Dampen my fall with your runes,' she ordered of her god, and then she jumped over the side of his cart. The clouds whipped around her. She fell so fast that it was hard to breathe, but it wasn't like falling off Sleipner's back. This time, she knew, Thor would catch her with runes. She was safe.

She spread her arms and legs out to better steer towards the worm's slick back. It cast its head upwards with a squeal. Its teeth were churning, red with the blood of Valhalla's defenders. Hilda plunged towards helmets and spears, and the terrible worm.

The worm writhed, and Hilda struggled to stay true to her course. She released her axe and readied to strike. At least the Midgard Worm wasn't clad in armour. The landing would be soft. But everything was nearing too fast; Thor still hadn't cast his runes. Hilda's heart clenched at the thought that she would crash and break her neck.

'Ehwaz. Ehwaz. Ehwaz!' Hilda chanted the rune of movement. Her fall slowed. She slammed hard onto the Midgard Worm's slick back and was thrown off again. Her axe hacked into the worm's skin. She hung onto it and wrestled herself onto the worm's back.

Thor hadn't helped her. If she hadn't trusted in her own runes, she wouldn't have survived at all. Her head rang from the crash. Something burned her hands, hurting like her eyes once had, back in Midgard. Hilda groaned and found footing in a wound on the worm's flank so she could loosen her hold on the Ulfberht axe.

Her hands were slick with stinging milk-white stuff. Frantically Hilda dried her palms and the back of her hands on the Midgard Worm's sleek skin. A sharp pain stung her feet. Her left shoe, too, was covered in the liquid. Venom from the Midgard Worm. Her shoe was being undone as she watched it. The venom burned through the leather of her soles. Hilda tried to hold onto the Midgard Worm's slick skin with only her hands, but they kept sliding off. She couldn't throw herself off the worm's back. Spears were pointed upwards and would skewer her. Hilda clenched her teeth and held on to her axe. Her shoes were white with the burning venom and halfway gone already.

'Isa,' Hilda commanded, and watched the white substance freeze thick around her foot. The burning pain receded. Her feet hurt from the cold, but no longer from venom. Venom rushed out of the wound where Hilda's axe was planted and melted the skin right off the back of her left hand.

'Isa,' Hilda hissed through barred teeth. Venom froze on the surface of Hilda's hand and around her axe. It stiffened her grip. The cold nibbled at her fingers, especially at the back of her hand where the skin was lost.

Hilda sighed with relief. The pain of ice was so much better than the pain of venom. Her right hand only ached a little from the venom she had dried off her hands. But now she knew what to do. Hilda planted her right hand into one of the beast's many wounds, barely flinching as the venom cut into her skin.

'Isa.' The frozen venom was thick, but made for good hand rests. It was like wearing gloves.

With ice gloves Hilda wrenched her axe free and shoved her hands and feet into wounds made by other weapons to climb up onto the back of the Midgard Worm. Wherever there were no cuts to hold onto, she made her own.

The great worm kept writhing and slithering. Reaching its back was difficult when it kept moving, but Hilda was so focused that she hardly noticed how long it took her to get there. Finally, atop the worm's back, she hacked holes on each side of the spine and planted her feet into them like stirrups, as if she were riding a horse. Though she wasn't steering. The worm writhed from left to right and Hilda struggled to hold on. In a heartbeat she was knocked from the top of the worm, sliding down its flank. Her feet dug deep into its hide to hold on.

She was numb everywhere from the ice she had enrobed herself in. Hilda lifted her axe and hacked in front of her. Drops of venom landed and burned through her skin. She called on the runes and turned them to shards of ice before they even touched her. They only stung on impact.

Her axe carved a long hole, and she sliced off a layer of skin. Venom flowed like blood in veins beneath the worm's hide, becoming thick and unmoving when she froze it with the runes. Perhaps that was how she could immobilise the Midgard Worm.

A loud blast nearly blew Hilda right off the monster's back. She stared across and saw corpses raining down over Ragnarok's plains. Thor's hammer shot straight through them, leaving hammer holes in their chests and arms and weapons.

The God of Thunder was fighting the Midgard Worm. Now was the time.

If Hilda could conjure enough strength to freeze all the venom, the worm would be petrified. Perhaps long enough for Thor to strike a fatal blow.

Hilda placed a hand close to the milky venom and thought of the rune of ice. 'Isa,' she muttered, and said, and screamed.

The venom solidified at her touch. The worm's skin tightened as the venom froze, but the Midgard Worm was so long, and there was so much venom.

Hilda felt a vein pop out on her forehead. Her eyes strained so much that it looked like everything was trembling. 'Isa!' Hilda demanded.

The worm shrieked, twisting its head back to see what was hurting it. To see Hilda. Its mouth was open, its teeth churning. Teeth larger than Fenrir's—long as swords and as wide as shields.

'Isa,' Hilda called. The wind rose around her, full of runes and whispers. Others on the battlefield were aiding her runes, whispering the command along with her. Hilda's hair whipped loudly around her. 'Isa!'

The Midgard Worm twisted. Its head swung closer. Hilda could smell its breath: the sour venom, mixed with something rotten. Corpses in the worm's belly. The worm saw her, though Hilda didn't know how. It had no eyes that she could see, but its head clearly moved towards her. A few more breaths and it would devour her.

'Isa!' Hilda bellowed one last time.

She couldn't get away. She was stuck in frozen venom. The worm's head swallowed all light around her. Venom poured out of its mouth, around her, and froze with her commands to rain over Hilda.

The worm bit down over its own back to get to her. Hilda was wrapped in ice. All her limbs were frozen in place. The cold stung, she couldn't breathe. Even her face was enrobed in ice.

One of the worm's teeth slammed into Hilda's ice, and then its mouth opened. Venom ran from its mouth and wounds like rivers. Somewhere on the ground, warriors were screaming in pain, and when Hilda looked at them, she didn't see the usual gold shields, the armour and weapons, the blood. All she saw was bones. The worm's venom had etched away everything else. Even the bones were disappearing.

Hilda was nearly out of breath, stuck under the venomous ice, when a familiar thunder made the ice crack. Thor was out there. And then it came: what she had been waiting for. The fatal blow. Something tore through the worm's mouth, left a gashing wound, and kept going. Thor's hammer. It left a gaping hole on either side of the worm's mouth. The worm's head was knocked to the side with a scream, and Hilda with it. She was thrown free of its deadly jaws.

She thought of the rune of protection, right before she slammed into a thick crowd. Ice shattered around her, and she gasped for air. Shards cut into her skin, and then something worse. Axes and swords came at her, before she could get up and find her balance. They slammed over her. Weapons clattered against each other and cut into her arms, and across her helmet.

'I'm with Odin! I'm with Thor!' Hilda yelled.

The blows receded, and Hilda glared up at the eager and terrified warriors. Only then did they see her bloody tears and know their mistake. They knew her face, and they knew her legacy. She was Fenrir's bane.

'Forgive,' one of them piped up.

'Give me your shield,' Hilda ordered. She didn't wait for the warrior to abide, but snatched the shield out of his stunned grasp. Then she turned away from them, back towards the worm.

The Midgard Worm wasn't dead, just angry. Very angry.

Hilda limped along the side of the worm. Her left leg hurt more now than it had, cold from the ice. It groaned with every step, but Hilda carried on. She didn't have time to slow. Least of all on Ragnarok's plains with Thor counting on her.

The Midgard Worm twisted at her side. Warriors were fleeing from the venom that rained over them. Hilda marched ahead, through it all. The venom landed as ice shards around her.

Ahead, the worm screamed at Thor, who swung his great hammer, readying for another strike. His beard was sticky with venom. His carriage was at his back. His goats were poking through the pockets of dead warriors. There were mountains of corpses. There were so few left alive.

Hilda hobbled straight towards Thor. Her heart pounded loudly when she joined him, falling into the rhythm of a song. Giants were singing all around the battlefield. The words were clear, and loud, and they didn't please the god of thunder.

Bitten by the great worm,
Let him cry, let him cry, let him cry.

Thor shall writhe and squirm,
Let him die, let him die, let him die.

Thor roared with rage at the song. His face was so red that it matched the blood in his beard. Hilda wished that they would stop their chant; she didn't want to see Thor angry. He looked like he was losing himself, and she didn't want to see him lost.

She remembered how Einer had once been lost to rage too. A long time ago, in Hammaborg. She had calmed him, but that had been Einer and his white bear of a fylgja. This was Thor, the great god and son of Odin. If he let rage take him, there would be no way to stop him. He would attack everything. Her too. Anyone who came near him would die.

Aware of the dangers, Hilda backed away from her god. 'I'll strike from the air,' she said, and mounted Thor's goat-carriage before he could protest. She threw her new shield onto the cart and hauled herself into it. She wasn't scared of Thor, but she wasn't a fool either.

She whipped the reins, and the goats stopped rummaging through dead bodies and began to hop ahead. The cart rumbled up the mountain of corpses, and then onto clouds conjured by Thor's ride. The wheels rumbled like thunder. The goats led the way, up and up.

Below, the Midgard Worm writhed over mountains of corpses. Warriors and giants ran from the monster and from their god. Thor cast his hammer again. Venom spilled over the god of thunder. His red hair was white from venom. All of him was.

The Midgard Worm's head knocked against the ground. It no longer twisted. Its last squeal died in its throat.

The hammer flew back into Thor's hand. His arm was raised above his head. The Midgard Worm lay dead at his feet. They had succeeded. Laughing, Thor looked to the skies, up to Hilda, turning away from the worm.

The god whistled for his goats to come fetch him, and the cart shot down through the air. Thor walked away from the slain monster, victory clear on his face.

As he took the first step, Hilda remembered her father's stories. She counted Thor's steps. One, two, three. She knew how her god was destined to die on this plain, a mere nine steps away from the great worm. Four, five, six. Thor was sure of his success, but Hilda was not as certain as her god. Seven, eight, nine.

Nine steps from his mortal enemy, and from victory.

At the ninth step, Thor stopped. A shiver went through him, and then he toppled over. Exactly as Hilda's father had told it, more than once, sitting by the winter fire. Thor splashed head-first into mud and venom. Even the back of his head was white from venom. His strong armour was being etched away by it.

Hilda pulled back hard on the reins. The goats bleated in protest, but listened, slowing to a stop. Their loyalty only went so far. Their owner was dead.

Thor was dead.

No one but Hilda had seen his fall. This valley of the battlefield lay deserted. What warriors were still alive had fled. All that was left were the mountains of corpses, which seemed to be moving only because venom was consuming them, leaving a red and milky white slush.

Giants and corpses from Helheim were fighting elsewhere. Their horrid song echoed across corpse mountaintops.

> Thor shall writhe and squirm,
> Let him die, let him die, let him die.

They had killed each other, the worm and him, exactly as it had been foretold. It would have ended the same way had Hilda not been there. Exactly as the nornir had told her. As the veulve had said. She couldn't change what had already been foretold, even if everyone expected her to do so.

Her gods still depended on her.

Relief dripped off Hilda, when she realised that no one else had seen Thor tumble to his death. No one else knew that she had failed to kill the Midgard Worm. Her reputation was intact. No one else would know that she couldn't save the gods as they thought she could.

There was only the matter of Fenrir. His eventual arrival on the battlefield would give her away.

Right then, a call reached Hilda up in her dark clouds: the howl of a great wolf. There were many wolves on this battlefield that were not Fenrir, Hilda told herself, yet she knew that howl. It was different from other wolves, and she had heard it before. This howl belonged to Fenrir.

The veulve had told her, but Hilda hadn't wanted to believe. Now there was no denying the truth that even free of destiny, Hilda could not save her gods, for Fenrir had arrived. And despite what Hilda had told her Alfather, the wolf was very much alive.

EINER

Chapter One Hundred and Seventy-Nine

A WARRIOR EINER recognised flashed past as quick as Thor's lightning. Half a hundred gold shields followed the warrior, roaring, charging at a giant, and overtaking him.

'Discard your shields, and come,' Einer ordered Nar, Bogi, and Tassi. He tossed aside his own shield, feeling bare with only one weapon in this terrible war.

'What?' Nar clung onto his shield as if there was nothing more precious in the nine worlds, and in this battle, up against Valhalla's warriors and gods, there truly was not.

Tassi threw down his own shield with no hesitation. Reluctantly Bogi too did as asked. 'Come on, Nar,' he pleaded. 'We said we would follow orders.'

'Now,' Einer commanded. 'Before they see that our shields aren't golden and strike us down.'

He was already moving after the crowd of warriors. The attacked giant fell, and Valhalla's fighters crowded around it. Within heartbeats the jotun lay dead.

Nar finally cast down his shield, and just in time, as the gold-shielded flock lifted their gazes to search for their next target.

'We're going the wrong way,' Nar complained, when he saw Einer peering back towards the mess they had barely escaped.

'We're not,' Einer told them, and then he set off at a run after the fifty gold shields who had passed them by. The forefathers kept his pace steady and his breathing even. 'Viggo,' he bellowed. 'Viggo!'

Some of the warriors at the back of the large shield-wall turned to Einer. Their eyes narrowed. They knew that Einer and his three shield-mates did not belong in their midst. Within a heartbeat half a hundred weapons were turned on them, but Einer kept coming closer.

'I saw Viggo,' Einer said. 'Is he with you?'

Valhalla's warriors did not answer, but their stares made it clear he had been right. The familiar face had been Viggo's, whom he had been seated with in the Alfather's hall three winters ago. Viggo, who was his half-brother.

A spear was pressed up to Einer's neck, the iron cold against his bare skin.

'We got separated from our bench-mates,' Einer said. 'The fire just raced past.' He made sure to gasp for breath, as though they had barely escaped.

'You were among the demons?' asked a shieldmaiden.

They were let into the cover of the gold-shielded roof. Weapons were lifted. A spear remained cold against Einer's neck, above the collar of his armour. An axe was aimed at his face. Nar, Bogi and Tassi also had weapons holding them back, but still, they were welcomed into the safety of Valhalla's shields.

'Have any of you seen Viggo?' Einer asked. There was no response.

He pointed his Ulfberht sword at the ground to show that he was no threat. As ever, lanky Tassi was quick to follow and plant his spear as a walking stick. Reluctantly Bogi and Nar also lowered their weapons.

'Are you among the Alfather's high shields?' a warrior eventually asked. The man's voice was muffled by a thick beard, and he was hidden in armour.

'Who else did you expect to find ahead of you, on the battlefield?' Einer said with a laugh. 'I'm impressed you all got here so quickly. Where were you seated in the hall?'

'East entrance,' said another warrior. 'We headed out this way as soon as we were free of the hall. Before the sun was swallowed.'

Their weapons lowered, then. Nar, Bogi and Tassi gave relieved sighs, but Einer held his own back, as though he could not have imagined another outcome. Einer was shown further into the shadowed crowd, under arms and shields, and beckoned for his three warriors to follow him so that they would not be separated again.

'Viggo,' a warrior shouted, and then another, and another.

The faces of the fighters were obscured in the gloom under the shields. Einer could hardly see anything. Had it not been for the forefathers' loud chants, his heart would have raced at being shoved into the midst of the enemy like this.

A hand grabbed Einer's arm. A man drew close, so close that Einer could smell the stench of his breath. 'Viggo?' The man drew nearer yet, but he did not recognise Einer. He pushed a hand up and lifted the shield above them enough for the distant firelight to illuminate both their faces. Viggo's armour was golden, and heavy, but his helmet had no nose-guard and revealed his handsome young face, blooded from war.

'You,' said Viggo in delight when he saw Einer.

To stand so close and look at Viggo felt strange, for so much had changed since they had last met in the Alfather's grand hall. Einer knew that they were brothers, the two of them, and the knowledge changed everything. Now that their faces were so close to each other, he recognised Viggo's nose, identical to his mother's, and he recognised the truth that his uncle and Skadi had once spoken. They truly were his brothers. Viggo, and all the other warriors he had been introduced to in the Alfather's hall.

'Einer,' he said, to introduce himself again, for the slight confusion on Viggo's face made it clear that he could not remember Einer's name.

'Einer,' Viggo repeated with a relieved sigh. 'Where were you? The Alfather kept saying you'd come back. I asked. I did.' He might have forgotten the name, but he remembered Einer.

'Well, here I am. Back.'

'What were you doing? Where were you?'

Einer glanced around cautiously, and leaned in to whisper into Viggo's ear. The knowledge of their kinship sang within Einer, echoing with the forefathers' call for blood. Did Viggo also feel their call? 'I was in Helheim,' Einer whispered.

Viggo pulled back to look at his face and saw the truth in it. Einer had never been good at lying. As a child, he had constantly been reminded of it. His mother had seen through him before he had even opened his mouth to lie. He wasn't lying now.

'Why?' Viggo breathed. His hand tightened around his weapon, and Einer did not fail to notice, but he remained calm.

'I've been training spies,' Einer whispered into his half-brother's ear, and that too was the truth. 'My shield-mates...' He beckoned to Nar, Bogi and Tassi at his back. 'They were regular Helheim warriors before I convinced them to join my cause.' Everything he said was the truth.

Viggo smiled wickedly as Einer drew back. He lifted an eyebrow and asked a question that Einer had not expected. 'How far did you get last time?'

Even in the unavoidable end, the Alfather's warriors were eager to bet on their valour and worth. Even now they tried to outdo one another.

'I went far,' Einer bragged like a true warrior of Odin. 'All the way to the giant lines, but then, there was this giantess with red hair.'

Viggo smiled knowingly. 'Ja, there's nothing to do against Skadi,' he said, and as easily as that Einer's worth was acknowledged and Viggo's own, too. They had both managed to fight their way across Ida's plain at least once before.

'You have to help us,' Einer said to Viggo. 'You know everyone. I never had proper time at the high table. I only know you, and Orm and Troels, and…' Einer left a skilful pause that he had learned from watching Loki. 'How are they?' he asked.

'They were good this morning, when we headed out.'

'Was Orm drunk?' Einer asked with a knowing smile. He remembered how much Orm had been drinking during the one feast they had enjoyed together.

'I don't think I've ever seen him sober,' Viggo laughed. They shared something by having been seated at the same high table in the Alfather's hall, and it was easy to confuse with brotherhood. Einer had always wanted a brother, especially after Leif had died.

Einer took a step back from Viggo. His three warriors were at his back. He forced himself into their midst. The shields above them parted a little to leave a hole; dim light shone through and brightened the confused but hopeful faces of Valhalla's faithful.

'Where do you need to go?' asked Viggo, stepping into the light.

'Back to the Alfather,' Einer said. 'It's urgent.'

Viggo rubbed the sweat off his forehead and, in the process, smeared blood all over his cheeks. Back to Valhalla and the Alfather, of all places, now that his group had come so far. Einer too would have thought that was a dire prospect as a shield-wall commander. They had nearly reached the back of the battle and were overpowering giants as easily as they might have shot deer, and here was someone who demanded his help, someone who demanded that he give up everything he had won in the battle and turn back.

'I need you, Viggo,' Einer insisted, for he did. Bogi, Nar, Tassi and Einer would not survive all the way to Valhalla's gates and to the Alfather on their own. They had come far, but the battlefield was so wide. Valhalla had to be much further still.

Viggo was considering it, his brow furrowed with worry. His warriors were pacing, eager to move along, and kill more giants. An impatience travelled over them.

Something crashed over their shields, and Einer was knocked to the ground. A giant hand reached into their midst and lifted a screaming warrior from the crowd. A helmet fell onto the shields. Long red hair floated around the warrior. Einer's eyes widened. He looked to his side and saw who had been taken.

It was Bogi clenched in the giant's grip, one of Einer's own. Bogi screamed, but he was too far out of reach for anyone to do anything but gape up at him, and at the giant. They all watched as Bogi was torn apart in the giant's grip.

Einer allowed them three heartbeats to watch the horror. 'We need to move,' he said, at last. 'Now.'

Thankfully Viggo understood the urgency. 'We head back to Valhalla,' he yelled to his warriors. They were confused. None of them understood the orders. They had come so far, and were so close to the back of the battle; the last thing they could have expected was an order to turn around.

Viggo began to move, shouting at them to get into formation. He was content to leave it at that, but Einer needed the warriors to be focused, to not question leadership. 'We will hit the giants from behind!' he yelled.

Warriors roared and stomped their feet loudly. Their weapons were thrust out past their shields, and they readied to move at Viggo's commands with newfound zeal.

Nar and Tassi were still gaping up at the giant who had torn Bogi out of their midst. Their weapons were ready, and Nar looked like he was about to run forth to claim revenge, but Einer stopped him with a hand on the shoulder. 'Come,' he urged and made his thoughts as loud as he could for the giant above them to hear. *Let us pass, let us pass. I'm Glumbruck's son. Let us pass.*

Einer wiped the sweat off his forehead and let Viggo lead the shield-wall away. The giant watched them scurry away, Bogi's dead remains still tight in his grip. Einer's thoughts had been heard.

As one, they raced ahead, back across the battlefield, towards Valhalla, somewhere out there. In a quiet voice, Einer instructed both Tassi and Nar to keep to the back of the shield-wall. With Sigismund and Brannar elsewhere and Bogi dead, they could no longer afford to take the same risks. Even a well-calculated charge could go wrong. They would have to leave it all to Viggo's warriors and let themselves be pulled across the battlefield. But Einer also knew that they were easy instructions to give, and much more difficult to act upon.

They travelled far, hidden behind Valhalla's shields. They climbed over mountains of corpses. Many had died and were dying, at the hand of this shield-wall and at the hands of their gods and the monsters of the nine worlds. Giants were falling in front of them, hacked down by runes and a golden spear.

The shield-wall slowed. Viggo's warriors were petrified. They even began to back away. Einer wrestled himself to the front line, to see what they saw. There was a god, directly ahead. A fierce fighter in golden armour, wielding a golden spear and no shield. He had only one hand. Tyr, the god of war.

Einer peered out over the tops of the shields, and right then, Tyr twirled around, looking for his next target. His eyes fell on Einer and widened in surprise. They had fought back in Jotunheim's snow, the two of them, after Einer's grandparents had been killed by Thor. They had fought, and then Loki and Einer had fled across the ice.

'He's seen me,' Einer realised aloud. Tyr had recognised him. 'You need to go, before he stops and kills all of us.'

Viggo, Nar and Tassi looked at Einer as if he was crazy, but Tyr's eyes were still fixed on him. As the greatest warrior in the nine worlds, it had to feel like defeat to have let Einer escape with Loki at the end of winter. The god's gaze did not move away from Einer, as he fought his way on. Easily he hacked through corpses and young giants. A duel waited for them, and Einer knew it.

'I've fought him before,' Einer explained to his shield-wall, when they refused to move without him, 'and he has seen me. Now go, before he decides to fight all of you. I'll keep him away.'

Strangely it was Einer's half-brother who was the most reluctant to carry on without him, and Einer's heart tightened at the thought of the bloodline that bound them to one another.

'But the Alfather...' Viggo was aware that the Alfather was unfamiliar with both Nar and Tassi, but he did not know the true nature of their mission. In the end, Viggo, too, would have to die. Einer had doomed his brother by making his shield-wall lead them on. Some things were more important than kinship. Their mother would have agreed.

'The Alfather knows you, and Nar and Tassi know everything that I do. Get them to him.'

Viggo ordered his shield-wall up a corpse mountain to get around Tyr. Fifty golden shields flowed past Einer, and then there were none. He stood alone on the battlefield, without protection, only the Ulfberht sword in his right hand, and the god of war approaching fast.

Einer readied himself. He planted his feet on slippery corpses. His heel slid back onto sticky half-dried vomit. Einer felt his stomach churn, but the forefathers kept him steady and gave him strength.

Tyr flung a bold shieldmaiden aside with a simple tap of the back of his spear. His eyes did not leave Einer, and he seemed angry. Warriors were thrown far out of his path as if struck by Thor's hammer and not the butt of a spear.

'Before I kill you, I shall have your name and lineage!' Tyr bellowed over the loud noise of the battlefield. They were ten arm-lengths away from each other, and the three warriors of Helheim caught between them hurried out of the way when they realised that Tyr was not addressing them.

Had it not been for the forefathers, Einer's heart would have skipped. The greatest honour was reserved him: here, on the battlefield of Ragnarok, the god of war himself wanted to know his name and lineage, so as to kill him with honour.

'Einer Glumbruckson,' he responded, standing tall and throwing his shoulders back.

'Glumbruck,' Tyr repeated with a smile, and it was clear then that the god deemed Einer's lineage worthy of this fight.

In Midgard when he fought and warriors asked for his name and lineage, Einer used to have to specify that his father was a chieftain in a town in northern Jutland, but since he had learned his mother's true name, he never had to specify anything. Everyone seemed to know about Glumbruck, and they respected Einer all the more when he gave her name.

'It shall be my honour to deliver you to your mother,' said Tyr.

The battlefield seemed to slow, warriors running and fighting at the edge of Einer's vision.

Einer raised his father's Ulfberht sword and took in all of Tyr. His gold armour was the same as it had been in the snow of Jotunheim some moons ago. Einer's eyes fell to Tyr's right hip, where he had struck the god, back then, and there was a mark. A chip had been taken out of Tyr's otherwise perfect armour, and it had been Einer's doing.

Neither of them moved, for what felt like an eternity. Ashes fell around them like snow. Ashes from all that which fire demons burned. Corpses and houses and woods burned on the battlefield, and fire demons rose in great flames. Ashes danced between Einer and Tyr.

Einer's stomach clenched at the sight of the grey snow. His body remembered the last time he had seen ash fall from the sky like that. He had been wounded and sitting in the little rowboat on the stream, when he had seen the ashes fall.

His home had been burning. The corpses had lined the streets, and everything had been coloured grey by ashes. Einer's wound had burned as he clawed through the remains. Through corpses, searching for someone. He no longer recalled who.

Then there had been Magadoborg. It had not been ashes, but real snow then, when Einer had come to his senses among the bodies of those he had killed. Even now, so long since, pain shot through Einer's forehead, where his skull had been pierced by an arrow.

All the while, as the ash fell and memories flooded Einer's mind, Tyr and he stood ready, eyes fixed on each other. As a younger man, Einer had sometimes heard warriors talk about a moment in battle where their life flashed before their eyes, as if it were the end for them. Never before had Einer experienced such a moment, and he smiled at the thought that his end had come in this way.

Tyr's spear swished through the air. The god had given no indication that he was about to attack. No tics had warned of his move, and he was still out of reach, but he moved fast with his gold spear.

The forefathers slowed the movement for Einer. He saw the spear come at him, the god charging, and knew that he would slip if he stepped back, so he stepped ahead instead, and half an arm-length to the side. He evaded the blow, and Tyr drew close.

Einer felt like a worthy opponent as he struck with the Ulfberht.

Even hidden below a helmet and beard, Tyr's jaw was square and strong, like that of a true warrior, and it seemed that no one could overpower him, but Einer managed to twist out of the way a second time.

Despite his muscles and size, Tyr evaded Einer's desperate sword blows. The Ulfberht cut through air and landed nowhere. Tyr attacked with both the sharp and dull end of his spear. He wielded it in one hand, and yet he was not any slower for it. He had trained for centuries with a single hand, and he was faster than any other warrior in the nine worlds.

The forefathers rang loud in Einer's head, but even with their help, he struggled to stay on the safe side of Tyr's spear. The god of war hit Einer hard on the hip with the butt, knocking Einer to the side. He landed on hard chainmail. A roar travelled up his throat as he rose to his feet and parried another blow, that would have killed him had the forefathers not directed his hand.

Something took Tyr's attention.

A dog tore through a warrior to Einer's left. The dog was twice Einer's own height, and he knew its furred head and violent growl, for he had sailed right past it mere days ago. Garm, who guarded Helheim's gates, had arrived on Ragnarok's battlefield and found his mortal enemy. Tyr, who had sacrificed his hand to a wolf, was destined to lose his life to a dog.

Einer did not hesitate. Tyr's eyes tore away from him, and as soon as they did, Einer was on his feet again. As the god gaped up at the great dog that would claim his life, Einer saw that this would be his only chance.

Nar and Tassi needed Einer more than he needed a pretty death at the hands of the god of war, and so he fled. He scrambled up the mountain of corpses west of him, pushed warriors down to get away. Slapped them at the back of the knees to make them fall so he could climb over them.

Across the mountain he crawled, and at the top, he spotted the golden shield-wall, moving backwards through the crowd, towards Valhalla. They had gone far, but Einer was alone and slipped right through, hacking his way where he could not evade attacks. Sheer will and a giant's strength and focus brought him to them. Einer twisted through the legs of giants, ducked behind wolves. Loudly, in his thoughts, he told them that he was there to kill the Alfather, and they let him pass. He dodged blows from Valhalla's warriors, for Helheim's own stood back for their high commander, who had instructed them and sailed them out of Hel's realm.

At last Einer's sword slammed against a gold shield, and there they were, Nar and Tassi and Viggo, welcoming him back into their midst. The shield-wall had grown smaller in the short time they had been apart, and Einer did not ask what had happened. Whatever it had been, it had been terrible. Ends that belonged nowhere but at Ragnarok.

Together they moved once more. Einer picked up a golden shield. Many warriors of Valhalla were dead, this far into the battle. Nar and Tassi had also picked up shields. As equals they hacked into giants' heels and roared at wolves larger than any and all of them. They fought, knowing that each heartbeat could be their last, and not caring. That was the only way to survive Ragnarok's terror. Each battle was worse and more perilous than the last, but there was always another, even worse, waiting ahead.

'We're here,' Viggo announced, in a shout that seemed quiet among all the noise around them. He was staring ahead at an enormous mountain of corpses. Somewhere beyond lay Valhalla.

Their feet slipped as they climbed up the side. Spears and arrows were thrown at them, clattering against the gold shields fastened to their backs. Shield mates fell, arrows stuck at their necks, but they kept going, and eventually they were too high up for anyone to launch spears or arrows, although the mountain continued further yet.

They stopped for water and food when they were out of reach. Only Einer, Nar, and Tassi had thought to bring food. All of Helheim's warriors had, under Einer's instructions, and although it was nothing more than dried fish and meat, sitting on the broken corpses of brave warriors, despite the stench of the dead, there was nothing more delicious in the nine worlds.

They were far beyond speaking and joking and laughing. They were exhausted. But they shared their food with Viggo and his warriors. There were only two good mouthfuls for each, but eating, even a little, gave them strength to keep going. Already they had fought for a long time; days, perhaps, for without the sun and moon, time was impossible to tell.

Once more, they climbed up the side of the corpse mountain. The noise from the other side was already deafening. Howling and screaming and squealing erupted around them and came crashing down. The sounds weighed on their shoulders as they climbed.

At last, they reached the top. Fire demons burned through the battle-valley, and there, in their midst, were Valhalla's grand walls. Great weapons stood like tree-trunks in the earth and formed the glorious hall.

Giants were fighting in the valley below. Giants, and fire demons and wolves tore through golden shields. A giant stumbled backwards to Valhalla, almost tripping over its tall walls. Einer's heartbeat matched the giant's every step, and he felt the chant within him rise as the giant grew, right before their eyes. The jotun became taller and bigger. He laughed, but his laughter was swallowed up in the clash of war. He kicked warriors out of his way. He had made himself so large that Valhalla did not even reach his shoulders.

The giant turned to the Alfather's imposing hall. He clasped his large hands around a tree-trunk in the outer wall, wriggled his fingers through, and pulled. Out of the earth he dragged it with all its roots. At the top of the tree was an axe-head. The giant hacked out with his new massive axe. He reached for another tree-trunk, and yanked again, bringing up large chunks of earth with the tree. The giant roared loud and struck around himself.

'Are we sure about this?' Nar leaned in to ask.

'We have to be,' Tassi answered in Einer's stead. 'We can't fail.'

Down there, the crowd was thicker. Five giants swung swords and axes and threw stones. Warriors surrounded them in thick rows. It looked like a raging sea, and the heart of it all, where everything collided, could be none other than the Alfather. Everyone on this battlefield was either eager to kill Odin or to save him.

'I go alone from here on,' Einer reminded them. 'I'll approach him straight on.' They had to surround the Alfather, if they hoped to make him part with his bracteate. 'You can't let me see you,' Einer told Tassi.

'Why not?' asked the tall warrior.

'If I see you, I'll think of our plan, and then the Alfather will know.'

Wolves howled in the long night. Mountains of corpses crashed and fell. Giants roared and toppled over, and fire tore through the field. Somewhere down in that chaos was the Alfather, and the three of them, mere farmers from Helheim, had to ensure the great god's death.

SIGISMUND

Chapter One Hundred and Eighty

FIRE DEMONS BURNED in the distance. Standing on the giant's shoulder, Sigismund could see far above the mountains of corpses. He steadied himself with a hand on a lock of thick hair. They travelled in the dark of night, away from the light of fire demons, hidden by the moonless and sunless sky.

They had journeyed for what felt like days, and Sigismund had already eaten half of the food in his pouch. He had tried to eat it sparingly. He still had water, because the giant had picked up a water barrel and stuffed it into his pocket along with Sigismund's anvil. Brannar was sleeping in the giant's other pocket. It was Sigismund's watch.

Seen at a distance, Ragnarok was almost beautiful. Flashes of light illuminated warriors and painted giants in red. The noise from the battlefield echoed all around Asgard, but here at the edge of Ida's plain, the noise was not overbearing.

Until suddenly, it was. Warriors came tumbling over the top of the nearest corpse mountain. Spears flew through the air towards Sigismund and the giant.

Sigismund hid in the giant's hair, at the nape of his neck.

'You thought you could hide?' one of the attackers hissed loudly.

Sigismund did not move. He pressed himself against the giant's warm skin. And then it happened: he heard the swoosh and smash, and felt the giant dip. Sigismund struggled to hold on, clutching hard onto the hair in his grip. The giant tilted, gently at first, and then they were both sailing through the air, down to the deadly ground. Sigismund lost his foothold to dangle helplessly from the giant's hair.

Then came the heavy crash: first the giant's shoulder, and then all of him. Sigismund fell on the shield he had fastened on his back. The shield boss punched into the middle of his back and broke.

Warriors were yelling and roaring. A dozen weapons loudly hacked into the giant's warm body. The jotun no longer breathed. He was dead. Sigismund crawled into hiding between the giant's shoulder and head. His back ached from the crash.

'What do you think he was doing out here?' a warrior asked.

'Even giants can be cowards,' a woman answered.

Shadows moved around the hair that kept Sigismund hidden. Sigismund held his breath.

'*Especially* giants,' someone else chimed in, from the opposite side of the giant's head. At Sigismund's feet.

Sigismund's heart was racing, making it near impossible to keep his breaths quiet. The shadow in front of him moved away, but still Sigismund held his breath. He listened as the warriors discussed what to do next while cleaning their weapons. They began to march away, but not nearly as quickly as they had arrived, so Sigismund stayed hidden for many heartbeats after he could no longer hear them.

Eventually, after listening long to the distant clashes of war, Sigismund pulled the dead giant's hair aside and wrestled himself out of hiding. Valhalla's warriors had left—or at least, they were far enough away to be hidden in the eternal night.

Sigismund stared up at the large giant who had helped them along. The giant had fallen on his right side, onto the very pocket Brannar had been sleeping in. His heart still pounding, Sigismund approached the giant's pocket. Half of it was stuck under the giant's weight. He let out a ragged breath at the thought of being crushed like that, and then he saw the fabric move. 'Brannar?' he called in a whisper. 'Are you alright?'

'Rusted axes,' she exhaled. The pocket ceased moving. 'I'm stuck.'

At once Sigismund tore at the pocket opening. He peered inside, but Asgard was too dark to see anything. 'I'm here,' he said and reached a hand in as far as he could. He slapped against skin, and Brannar's hand came to find his. He was about to pull back and drag her loose, but then he stopped. 'How much of you is stuck?'

'Just pull,' Brannar groaned.

Sigismund hauled back hard. With all her armour on, Brannar came to twice her normal weight, and she was not a small girl. She slid into view, her teeth clenched in pain. Sigismund grabbed her under her arms and pulled her free of the pocket.

'Takka,' Brannar breathed, leaning back against the dead giant.

Sigismund nodded to her and stared up at the giant's other pocket, inside which his anvil, his tools and the water barrel rested.

He pulled himself onto the giant's arm and began to climb towards his anvil and tools. The pocket was a long way out of reach. He could not get inside and drag the anvil out as he had dragged Brannar free. He could hardly reach the bottom of the pocket.

'Are you out of the way?' Sigismund called down to Brannar. It was too dark to see.

'Ja,' Brannar answered. Her voice did not come from directly below him, so Sigismund carried on. With his sword, he cut into the thick layer of cloth that formed the giant's pocket.

The anvil hammered down. It splashed into mud. His tools clanged on top, and then came the crash of the water barrel.

From high up on the giant's hip Sigismund stared across the dimly lit battlefield with its raging fire demons and mountains of corpses. Following Einer's directions, it looked like they were still far away from Yggdrasil's roots, where they were supposed to meet after Einer and the others secured the Alfather's bracteate.

It was a long way to carry the anvil. On their own, it might take them days. There was no telling how far along Einer and the others were. Days might get them there too late. The battle had already raged for a while.

Sigismund let out a heavy sigh, for he knew what they had to do.

He climbed down from the giant, careful not to slip and fall. Brannar was dragging the anvil out of cover and testing her grip on it.

'Leave it,' Sigismund said as he hopped onto the ground. The anvil would slow them too much and they still had a long way to go.

'We can move it,' Brannar insisted.

'Not that far,' Sigismund said. 'Certainly not with your foot like that.' Although Brannar had only grunted once in pain, he had not failed to notice that her foot had been crushed. She put all her weight on her left one.

'Besides, even with an anvil and my tools, it won't be enough.' He stared at the corpse mountain directly in front of them as he spoke. The bright red clouds flickered with flames. 'We need fire.'

They both sighed at that. Only a fire demon might give enough heat to melt the bracteates. Sigismund had tried everything else, and nothing had worked. There was no fire hotter than that of Muspelheim. If a fire demon's heat could not melt the gold Yggdrasil coins, then nothing could.

'Are you sure?' Brannar asked.

To join Ragnarok this far in would be perilous, and Sigismund supposed that getting close to a fire demon would be even more so, and it would not be easy, either.

'It's our only hope to melt them,' he said. He was certain of himself, for he had tried everything else, and there had to be a way to accomplish the task Loki had given them. He crouched by his tools and packed a hammer and pair of tongs in his weapon belt.

'We should put the neck-rings on,' Brannar suggested. 'We will get further with them. We will survive the trip.'

Sigismund felt the warmth of the two bracteates in the pocket he had sewn inside his tunic, beneath all his chainmail and armour. 'We can't,' Sigismund said. 'No one can know. No one can see.'

'No one would. Under all this armour.'

'We can't.'

'Just until we secure your fire.'

'Nej,' Sigismund decided, and Brannar knew not to challenge him on it again.

She let out a sigh and stared at the corpse mountain ahead of them. Light from the fire demons flickered, lighting up the lowest clouds beyond. 'How – in all of Asgard – are we going to capture a fire demon?' she eventually asked. Her shield was already in her hand. Half of the wood had broken off during their fall, but that did not hinder her. Her axe hung limp in her grip. She reminded him of Thora. He would have liked to grow old with Thora. He would have liked to see her before the end, at the very least. But here they were at the end of all things, and there was no time.

'No need to capture a demon,' Sigismund said. 'We simply ask it for help.'

Brannar nodded thoughtfully at that. 'Fire fights on our side,' she gathered.

Sigismund smiled at her, but did not let on that he thought that fire demons fought for no one but themselves. Besides, he did not think that they spoke Norse.

Side by side, Brannar and Sigismund scaled the enormous pile of corpses. They lay down at a ridge on the top of the first mound and peered down over the chaos roaming beyond. The nearest fire demon was burning through a screaming crowd of Valhalla warriors. The fire burned through everyone and everything.

'They'll burn through us too,' Brannar said, and she was right. 'Sigismund.'

She did not need to say more. Sigismund sheathed his sword and set down his half-broken shield. He unstrapped his weapon belt next and made Brannar hold it so that it would not be lost in the soft mush of the corpses. Next, he removed his helmet, wrestled off his chainmail, and reached in under his tunic to the two gold bracteates. They were warm to the touch and filled his palm.

The image of Yggdrasil had been beautifully carved into them centuries, perhaps millennia, ago and yet they seemed newly made. They showed no sign of Sigismund's desperate hammering to try and undo them back in Helheim. They were as perfect as ever. Sigismund slipped a chain through each of them, so they could hang them from their necks. For a moment longer he looked down at the gold neck-rings. His heart beat with worry and fear and told him not to do it, but there was no other way.

Hoping that he would not regret the decision, Sigismund handed Brannar one of the golden bracteates. She took it in both hands, with full respect. What he handed her was not merely a gold pendant, but life itself. As the gold slipped from his fingers, Sigismund worried that Brannar would not part with it, and as he slipped on his own neck-ring, he worried that he too would prefer to live.

FINN

Chapter One Hundred and Eighty-One

DESPITE THE CHRISTIAN cross that hung from his neck, Svend was a true Jute. Finn had told himself that all winter, and summer, as Svend had allowed Christian churches to be built and priests to preach to his people. To his chiefs and jarls, Svend made the same speeches about how outwardly Christianity could make them look more united, under one king and one belief. A united force to dissuade any foreign armies from repeating the sack of Jutland.

They, like Finn, knew that there were other reasons too. They were rational arguments, but the way Svend sometimes clenched his hands around the cross that hung from his neck, as if he was praying like a Christian, told another story. There was also a reason why it was a cross and not a proud Thor's hammer. In his heart, Svend was still a follower of Odin, but he was angry, and he had been angry for a long time.

The last jarl left the dim longhouse. The tables were wet with spilled ale from the feast they had shared. All the platters had been emptied. Finn and Svend were left alone. The last two men left standing after an evening and a night of drinking. Neither of them had been drinking as much as others, but they both swayed from the ale filling their stomachs.

Even when they were alone, sitting across from each other in the firelit room, Svend did not meet Finn's stare. He was glaring down at the dagger in his hand. The old, ragged blade that had been given to him by a little girl, but originally sent from his sister such a long time ago.

'Are you still bitter over Tyra's end?' asked Finn, quietly, as he turned his empty horn in his hand. He should have asked so long ago, but the question was not easy to get out. The ale, and the late time of the night, helped.

'She left me, Finn,' Svend said, without looking up from the dagger.

'She was murdered,' Finn reminded him.

'She left me. I won't ever see her again.'

'In the afterlife.'

'There is no afterlife anymore,' Svend whispered so quietly that Finn wondered if he had heard right. 'She left me behind.'

Finn's head swayed from the ale, and he tried to steady himself with a firm hand on the table. He tried to steady his thoughts too. His words were muffled. 'What do you mean, there is no afterlife?'

For a long time, Svend said nothing more, just twirled the old dagger in his hand. He had finally managed to clean the blood off its tip, but the blade had begun to rust below the old, clotted blood. It was not pretty, and he had not bothered to sharpen it.

'She knew things,' Svend eventually said, and it was not really an answer. 'She had been to the other worlds.'

Finn stared at the dagger in Svend's hands and tried to figure out if he was telling a story or if he believed it to be true. The other eight worlds. Finn could not even come up with a guess as to how Tyra could have gone there, but Svend's voice was steady, though smoothened by ale.

'It stopped bleeding,' Svend said, and nodded his head once, firmly. 'It stopped bleeding last night.' His voice broke. 'I was too late. She is gone, for good.'

'What do you mean, there is no afterlife?' Finn asked again. It was a cruel thing to tell an old man so close to death and the glory of Valhalla. For summers and summers Finn had fought, hoping death would take him so the Alfather and his valkyries would claim him on the battlefield. All winter he fell asleep smiling at his accomplishments in life, at the thought of waking up to Valhalla's gold-shielded ceiling and a grand feast, in the afterlife.

'She left too soon,' Svend continued, without answering Finn's question. So long since her passing, and he was still taken by grief. 'Too early. I'm not done with life. I wasn't done.'

Finn tried to swallow his old man's anger. *He* was done. For many summers he had been done, and ready for the glory of the afterlife; he was still there, at Svend's side, alive, because Svend, his king, said that he was needed.

'There's still so much to do.'

'Not for me,' Finn grumbled. The words shook as they slipped past his thin lips, aided by the ale that rang in his head, and Svend must have noticed the anger, for his eyes snapped up to look at Finn, and he seemed, in that moment, to realise his error.

'She told me once that this dagger had come from Ragnarok's plains and that it would bleed all the way to Ragnarok,' Svend explained, sensing the need to provide proper answers to Finn's questions. 'It's not bleeding anymore.'

Ragnarok had begun. Finn's carefully planned afterlife—the afterlife he had fought a lifetime to be worthy of—was gone. Finn saw his hands shake with anger. All these winters and summers Svend had kept this knowledge from him, and encouraged Finn to dream of Valhalla, knowing it was a futile dream.

Svend was looking at Finn with a puppy's expectant gaze.

Finn breathed through his mouth to calm his shaking hands. This destroyed everything the two of them had together. All the memories they had spent together. The raids, the sailing trips, the evenings. Svend was like a son to Finn, but he had failed Finn more than anyone else Finn had ever met in life.

'I'm an old man,' Finn hissed. He tried to contain himself. The anger was making his eyes and hands tremble, but he knew that if he yelled and condemned Svend for the betrayal, they would never be close again. Finn had no family of his own, and it was all too late for him. He was too old, too alone. There was only Svend and his closest warriors. If there was no glorious afterlife, no Valhalla and feasts, then he didn't want to spend his last living moments grumpy and alone. 'An old man, waiting to die. Every night I dream of the valkyries finding my body on the next battlefield. How they will whisper in my ears, and bring me to Valhalla, where I belong. You should have told me,' Finn hissed. 'You know what it means to me.'

'Forgive,' was all Svend could say, but some things could not be forgiven.

Finn clenched his teeth tight and turned the empty drinking horn in his hands. A lifetime of expectations robbed in one moment. Had Svend said nothing, Finn might never have known. He would have died blissfully, but never woken. Maybe knowing was better.

'Is there any chance?' Finn asked.

Svend showed off the knife in his hands. 'The dagger isn't dripping anymore. Ragnarok has begun.' He stared up at Finn to see his reaction.

'Begun, but not finished.' Finn rose from the table with his final decision. 'If Ragnarok has begun, then I am long overdue a worthy death.'

Svend stared up at him and Finn could actually see the panic flood the young man's eyes. The king's brows rose and fell as he thought about what Finn had said. Finn held Svend's stare to show that he meant exactly what he had implied, but Svend did not seem to know what to say.

'Have I not been loyal to you all these summers and winters?'

Svend agreed with a nod. He repeated it a few more times, the mead and ale making every movement ripple. Finn had been shocked sober, or as good as. He only swayed a little as he stood and leaned against the table that separated them.

'I implore you, Svend,' Finn slurred. He cleared his voice and resumed, focusing hard not to slur. 'To repay my loyalty and continued sacrifices for you with a sacrifice of your own. Let me fight.' He pushed away from the table and stood up tall to show that even as an old, drunk man, he was capable.

'Now?' Svend asked. His voice was trembling.

'We have both wasted enough time. Ragnarok has begun.' He managed to say it without slurring, and he was becoming better at balancing on his two legs too. He was as good as sober. 'I *will* die a second time on that famed battlefield.'

'Tomorrow,' Svend said. 'When we haven't drunk as much.'

'Tonight,' Finn insisted. 'Ragnarok has begun already. Let me go before it ends.'

Svend clenched the hilt of his dagger. His knuckles went white, and his jaw was tight. 'Then go get your weapons and I will get mine. I will meet you on my grandfather's gravemound.' Svend rose from his seat and stuffed the Ragnarok dagger back into his belt.

Finn stared at him, Svend's words settling in his drink-hazy mind. At last Svend had agreed to let Finn go, and with the end now imminent, a little sliver of fear crept into Finn's mind. Still, the thought of living and never waking up to Valhalla's glory was worse than his fear of death.

'Your grandfather's gravemound,' Finn repeated, and then he turned around and marched away. He reached the door before he realised he was still holding the drinking horn. He turned around, dropped it onto the table and left, for good this time.

The night was cold outside, but beautiful. There were none of the usual clouds. A beautiful night to say goodbye.

The door opened behind him as Svend also exited the longhouse. They each headed into the silent night. Finn stared up at the sky with all its stars, trying to commit it to memory. Even the feel of the cold wind on his bare skin, as he walked through town to the longhouse where he slept when he was in Jelling.

Ida, her husband, his three brothers and the five other warriors who stayed with them were all asleep on a long row on the sleeping bench. Most of them were snorers, although they insisted that Finn was the loudest snorer of them all.

Finn tiptoed inside, cringing as the door loudly slammed behind him. In the dark, he felt his way to his own chest of things, the third sleeping position from the right side. He tried not to wake the others as he stumbled around, looking for his weapons and armour, but the more careful he tried to be, the more noise he made.

His helmet fell from his grasp and clanged loudly against the floor. One of the snorers woke with a snort. Finn stood completely still over his possessions and waited until he heard deep breaths again. He reached for his helmet, but then stopped himself. The plan was to die honourably, not to make it any harder for Svend to kill him. Let it be swift but worthy. Before he was burned on the pyre, Svend would surely dress him in chainmail and battle armour for Finn to take with him into the next life. There was no need for it just now.

He set aside his expensive chainmail and found his weapon belt. He took his sword and his axe, pulled on his worn fighting gloves, and went to the opposite wall to find his shield. In the dark he could not see which one was his, so he took the first one he could find. He tested the grip, and knew that it was not his own, but he doubted that the shield's rightful owner would mind, and if he did, there would be nothing but a corpse to bring his complaints to at the next Ting.

An unfamiliar shield in hand and his weapons nestled in his belt, Finn slipped out of the longhouse and marched through the town again, towards Svend's grandfather's gravemound. He had not realised how long it had taken him to gather his things, until he looked up at the sky, expecting to see stars, but seeing instead a sea of brightening colours. The sun was coming up, and as he stumbled along the road towards the tall gravemound of Svend's grandfather, the roosters were waking the rest of Jelling.

Finn let out a satisfied sigh when he reached the foot of the tall gravemound. It would be a worthy death, and he was ready. His head was blurred with drink—not enough to hinder him in battle, but enough to settle him in his decision.

He took his time climbing up the mound, so as not to tire himself before the last fight of his life. At the top, Svend had lain down on the grass to close his eyes, and although he was not snoring, he looked like he was asleep. He had pulled on both chainmail and helmet, even braided his beard into two strands as was his habit when he went into battle. He was ready for a real fight. For a moment, Finn smiled and sat down next to his son.

Svend had picked the perfect place for their duel. From atop the old gravemound, Finn could see the day's most beautiful sunrise. Perhaps even the most beautiful sunrise Finn had seen his entire life, and he had seen many, out at sea. That he would miss, in his short afterlife—sailing. If Ragnarok had already begun, perhaps the afterlife would be short enough for him not to miss it.

'Svend,' Finn said softly, and shook Svend's thigh to wake him. 'Wake up and see this.'

Svend gasped and sat up fast, pretending that he had not been asleep at all.

'You don't have your armour,' Svend remarked as he rubbed the sleep out of his eyes.

'I'll fight well enough even without it,' Finn assured him. He was still staring at the sunrise. The red sun shimmered above the roofs of Jelling's houses. 'Better, maybe, without the weight.'

Svend followed Finn's gaze to the sunrise. 'It's a good day to die,' he agreed, at last.

Villagers were beginning to wake up from the call of roosters and the sunrise. Wood was put on the nearly burned-out fires in the many longhouses, and dark smoke rose and obscured the perfect red circle of the rising sun.

Finn groaned and pushed off from the ground. Svend was on his feet first; he offered Finn his hand, one last time, and with a smile Finn took it. Svend had grown into such a fine young man, although he was hardly young anymore: there were wrinkles on Svend's forehead, and in the creases by his eyes. Yet when Finn looked at him, he still saw the young curly-haired boy he had met so long ago in Harald's longhouse.

Finn brushed off his trousers and picked up his shield. The shield was that of Ida's husband. Ida who had once delivered that bleeding dagger to Svend, when she had been alittle girl. The shield had appropriately been painted with the bindrune for safe travels. His last journey, to the next world, was upon him, and Finn was ready.

He pulled the sword free from its scabbard. It felt strange for his shoulder to be so light, without chainmail—or even the weight of padded armour—slowing his movements. He almost felt young once more, although the shield hung heavy in his hand. His sword, too, was heavy when he lifted it, but he would rather die with a sword in hand, than a spear.

Svend readied his stance and raised his shield to cover his chest and face. Seeing him standing there reminded Finn of a time in his youth, when he had been standing on a platform in the middle of a river, across from Einer. He had suffered under the outcome of that Holmgang for many winters and summers, but the outcome of *this* fight would instead relieve his suffering.

Finn tapped his sword on his shield. He was ready.

Svend waited a heartbeat, and two, and then he, too, tapped his shield and announced the honourable duel. At once, Svend moved in.

His sword swung for Finn's helmet-less face.

Finn held his ground. He knew Svend's tricks. They had fought side-by-side for so long. He parried the blow with his sword and not his shield, telling himself Svend would not get an opening to strike, but Svend was young and fast. His shield knocked against Finn's helmetless head.

Finn staggered backwards, stunned, and before he could lift his sword again, Svend's sword came under his shield. The sharp tip sliced up the length of his arm. Blood ran down into his fighting gloves.

Lowering his shield, Finn trapped Svend's sword for a heartbeat, and stepped left to get around. He twisted his own shield out of the way before Svend could regain control of his sword, then swung his own blade over Svend's shoulder.

Svend grunted as Finn's blow rattled off his chainmail. Quick, Finn parried the follow-up attack. Svend's shield bashed against his. Finn's shoes slipped over the dew on the grass.

Feeling that he was losing his balance, Finn pulled back his shield and slammed it into Svend's to push ahead and take a step forward. Svend retreated, but he was young and strong, and he only gave away one step.

They matched each other's hard stares. Giving no indication in his expression, Finn swept his sword down at Svend's feet. His sword came back bloody, and Svend toppled. Finn raised his sword again, shifting his shield out of the way.

In the same heartbeat, Svend's sword shot up towards Finn's face. Finn started back. The tip of Svend's weapon pierced Finn's faded tunic, and his skin. He grunted and took a step back. His tunic became warm with blood, but he was not yet dead.

Svend had risen to his feet.

Finn felt his strength ebbing. His chest was bloody, but mostly it was from his arm, which dripped all over his fighting gloves. His fingers were sticky with it.

Svend pushed in close and kicked Finn's shield out of the way. Teeth clenched tight, he drove his sword straight into Finn's chest.

Finn gasped and crumpled to his knees. He looked up at Svend's pained expression. The boy noticed him staring and forced a fond smile.

Finn's shield rolled away, and he fell into the grass. The morning sun beamed hot over his face. His right hand was tight around his sword, drenched in blood. The pain in Finn's chest throbbed. He felt himself shake. His body was both cold and warm at the same time, and so very weary.

With a blissful sigh, Finn closed his eyes for the last time. Death, at last.

HILDA

Chapter One Hundred and Eighty-Two

THOR'S GOATS RACED across the clouds. Hilda held onto the carriage and let them carry her over the battlefield. They didn't listen to her commands as they had listened to those of Thor, but she trusted that they would take her ahead, and stop, eventually.

She peered down through the clouds. Valhalla was close. The flames flickered on the tall iron weapons that marked its outer walls. The goats were taking her home—maybe even to the Alfather. Hilda gulped, imagining how angry Odin would be, if he had heard Fenrir's howl. He would have heard, and he would know what it meant too.

Part of Valhalla's walls were missing, torn from the ground. Giants were fighting, their fingers clasped around axe hilts as wide as ancient tree-trunks. Hilda peered through the crowd. Something white caught her attention. Too large to be her snow fox—her fylgja had long disappeared, anyway—but it *was* fur.

A white bear was fighting. Few animals had taken any part in the battle: there were wolves and there were monsters, but this was the first bear Hilda had seen. The bear roared and slashed, its white fur smeared with blood. A giant swept right through the white bear's head, as if it wasn't there. A living fylgja, in a battlefield upon which all the warriors were dead. There were no other fylgjur fighting on Ragnarok's plains except, maybe, those of the gods, but here a white bear was fighting. Hilda's heart sped up at the sight and thought of it. In life, she had seen many fylgjur, but only one white bear.

Einer.

He was alive. Einer was alive. Hilda grabbed the reins in both hands and tried to force the goats down towards him. To see him. To get close to him.

One of the goats bleated. Neither of them moved even slightly from their course.

The white bear wrestled a gold shield off a warrior and cast it away with a roar lost in the clamour of the battlefield. Einer was fighting for the giants, not for the gods and Valhalla. He had to have his reasons, and despite everything that had happened, Hilda trusted Einer, and his reasons, no matter what they were.

Despite what seat she had gained for herself in Valhalla, she too had once been swayed by Loki's words. She too knew that Ragnarok was so much more than the death of the gods.

Thor's goats took her down, through the clouds. Closer to the ground, but not towards Einer. His white bear disappeared in the tangle of giants and gods and warriors.

Hilda kept her eyes on the part of the battle where he had been. As they passed by, she looked back, staring intently at where she had seen his fylgja. She hoped to catch a glimpse of white fur. Or maybe, a streak of his straw-coloured hair.

Einer. He was alive. But not for long.

The cart wobbled, drawing Hilda's gaze ahead, away from where Einer and his bear had been.

It had to be him. No one else would be alive and fighting on Ragnarok's battlefield. No one else would bring a raging white bear fylgja into battle.

In front of her a thick group of fighters were crowded together. Giants stood in a ring, slapping the same patch of ground. In the middle, amongst hundreds of warriors and giants and beasts, stood the Alfather. His silver hair was hidden by a golden helmet, and he did not move like an old man.

Hilda leaned over the side of the cart to better see him. His chainmail shone, and his spear thrust and swept and was thrown with such precision and speed, that all Hilda could see of it was a blood-red blur.

Thor's goats were taking Hilda to the Alfather. Of all the places on this vast battlefield. Hilda shielded her thoughts with runes. Odin would kill her in rage when he found out that Fenrir was still alive. Unless he already knew.

Although her thoughts were masked, her worries were confirmed immediately. The Alfather thrust his spear through a giant's head, parried blows with jewelled arms of chainmail, and looked up. Through the swinging arms of giants, and straight at Hilda.

He yelled something. His words were lost to the clatter of war, but Hilda didn't need to hear them. The Alfather was roaring her name, and he did not look happy.

Hilda would rather have gone straight in search of Fenrir than dart down there, though her thigh ached at the thought of facing the big wolf again. She would rather have faced even Thor's rage than that of the Alfather. Yet the goats proceeded unforgivingly, straight towards bloodied Odin.

The battle was so loud she could hardly hear anything at all. The noises rang in Hilda's chest. Her heart throbbed with it.

The cart flew close to giants and their rage. She felt like a fly buzzing around them; nothing but an annoyance. A giant caught her gaze, and Hilda hefted her axe, and picked up the shield. The giant was swinging one of Valhalla's huge axes. The axe-head was much larger than Thor's entire cart. He swung the axe at her. Hilda ducked and heard the vast iron head crash through the side of the cart. The goats bleated and kept going.

Down, and down. They hopped from a low-hanging cloud onto the giant's shoulder. He swung around, whirling his axe with him, and narrowly missed them. The goats kept going, jumping onto another giant's arm and then a wolf's back.

The cart wobbled, and Hilda was thrown off. She bumped into a fighter's back, and then fell onto a stinking corpse. Quickly, she grabbed a warrior's arm, and hauled herself to her feet. Her golden shield was no great help here. Most of the warriors had arrived from Helheim.

Hilda could hardly stand, but she had to fight. It was that or immediate death. Hilda hacked her axe through a warrior of Helheim as he turned towards her to assess if she was foe or friend.

The Alfather was a few rows further ahead.

At least the crowd was so thick that she didn't have to balance on her own feet. She plunged ahead, slicing every neck and arm in her way. Blood splashed up on her face until she could hardly see, but she kept swinging her axe and launching herself forwards, at the Alfather.

At last, a fighter fell in front of her, and Hilda saw straight to her god. She tumbled out of the thick crowd, into the Alfather's reach. His famed spear swished over her head. He was standing on a mounting pile of corpses.

Giants and rotting warriors were confused by Hilda's arrival. They didn't seem to know if she was worth the effort to kill, since even the Alfather was yelling at her. He seemed in more distress at Hilda's arrival than before. His voice cut through the chaos. 'You told me Fenrir was dead!'

'And he was! I will just have to kill him again,' Hilda said. She tried to hobble away to find Thor's carriage, but her path was blocked. Besides, the goats had to have flown away by now; staying in this crowd, they would die.

The Alfather fought off attackers over Hilda's head. A wolf kept trying to launch at him from the left, but his spear swished through the dark so quickly that it never got a chance. Its snout and paws were red with blood from trying.

Hilda bent down and crawled closer to the Alfather. Ravens and crows circled above him, keeping him safe, and attacking giants and warriors from above. Odin's valkyries.

'I *will* kill the wolf,' she assured him. Odin had enough to do, what with the hundreds of warriors and giants trying to take the honour from Fenrir.

'When he comes,' the Alfather grunted. He didn't sound in the least breathless, despite how he was darting around. 'You will strike the final blow.'

Hilda watched the Alfather whirl, and readied herself to rise out of his reach. She saw the right moment and stood up, her legs groaning. She parried blows out of habit. She had trained well in life. The blows of the corpse warriors hit hard, but Hilda pushed back, and gave the Alfather a smaller part of the crowd to focus on. The valkyries helped from above, dropping stones and conjuring runes.

Hilda smiled, for that was her advantage, too. She conjured ice and made warriors fall. She conjured luck and struck. She conjured defence and chaos.

As she fought, she searched through the dark, bloodied crowd. Warriors were tired, beasts heaved for breath, but giants still roared. They were restless, and they were angry. So was the Alfather. He held them all back. The crowd began to leave a larger distance to him. They were all done, and ready to die, or at the very least rest. All but the Alfather.

Hilda stared back the way she had come, flying in Thor's carriage, and caught sight of the bear again. The white fur almost shone in the firelight. Many fires had been put out, leaving few demons still alive and little light to see, yet in the dim glow, the bear's white-furred ears were even easier to spot. It was moving closer. He was approaching, heading straight for the Alfather. Straight for Hilda.

'A white bear?' the Alfather yelled to her, over battle-cries and howls and roars.

She had forgotten to shield her thoughts from Odin. At

once, she took to the runes, and called upon them to hide her thoughts.

'A fylgja. There's a living warrior out there,' she told the Alfather, for she had to tell him something, and something that was true.

The white bear cut through the crowd. Warriors fell before him, and giants gave way. And then Hilda saw him. Not the bear, but *him*. He had changed, after so long. His helmet hid most of his face, but she could see his mouth and his cheeks, and it was him.

'Einer,' the Alfather muttered, loud enough for Hilda to hear. He, too, knew him.

Hilda put an additional effort into her runes to shield her mind. Not to give anything away. In case Einer needed her. For he had clearly been fighting with the giants, against Valhalla's warriors, and if he reached the Alfather... He would die.

No one survived Odin's famed spear.

EINER

Chapter One Hundred and Eighty-Three

EINER SPOTTED THE Alfather through the crowd. Alone, he advanced.

He had parted ways with everyone else. Even Viggo.

A wolf blocked his passage, and Einer sliced through the beast's neck. It crashed into warriors of Helheim and Valhalla alike as it died. A necessary sacrifice for Einer to get to Odin and deliver his messages.

Again, he could see the Alfather over warriors and through the legs of giants. He was so nearly there, ready to deliver on his promises and fight on the right side. The Alfather was casting his spear from one giant to the next. To watch him fight was like watching a skilled dancer. Every move looked like it had been practised a thousand times over, yet even the forefathers struggled to predict how the Alfather might move next.

This close to the Alfather, the forefathers were louder and stronger. So many giants had passed on from the battles on Ida's plain already, on their way to becoming forefathers, once their corpses were burned and honoured. If they ever would be.

Valkyries fought by Odin's side. Dark winged birds dropped spears and worse on the warriors below. A valkyrie, out of her bird form and smeared in blood, stood at the Alfather's back. Odin's single eye caught Einer staring.

Einer smiled at the sight of the Alfather, at last. For so long he had been trapped in Helheim, and at last he had returned to where he belonged in death. Although he still was not dead. The Alfather matched Einer's stare, and he, too, smiled, although he did not so much as miss a heartbeat in his ceaseless dance. Warriors continued to rush at him. They came in waves, much too predictable. The giants were falling back, but that was better, for it made it easier for Einer to get close to his god.

Two Helheim warriors turned to look at Einer, and he headbutted the one and knocked the other out with a punch to the jaw. He stepped over their bodies to get to the front. Everyone was eager for the honour of attacking the Alfather. Perhaps they hoped to be the one to bring him down, but none of them could. The Alfather would not die so easily, if at all.

A giant stood next to Einer, stooped over to reach the Alfather. Black wings swarmed his face. Einer turned the Ulfberht sword in his hand and thrust it down into the giant's big toe, yanking it out again as the giant raised his foot with a yell of pain.

Einer rushed under the giant's foot. He ducked under the Alfather's spear and slashed out at a shieldmaiden trying to follow him. The woman continued to pursue. Einer kicked her shield, and sliced off her arm, then ran ahead and crashed into the Alfather, slamming into the valkyrie's shoulder. He pushed himself into their midst so that they became a tiny boar's snout formation; a Swine Array: three warriors, back to back, each handling their side of the never-tiring attackers.

The corpse shieldmaiden who had followed Einer out of the crowd kept coming, even with her left arm and shield gone. She desperately reached out. Einer slammed the woman across the head with the Ulfberht and drove his sword through her face. He struggled to push it through. The Ulfberht was becoming dull at the edges, although he had sharpened it at the top of the last corpse mountain he had journeyed across. He pulled the sword back out.

A giant axe came swinging down towards the three of them. The valkyrie was already on it, conjuring a strong wind to blow the axe off course. She was powerful for her height. Her cheeks were streaked with blood and her head came to Einer's chin, in the same way that Einer's own head reached the Alfather's shoulder.

'Why are you here?' the Alfather asked, with no hint of breathlessness.

The valkyrie, whose left arm brushed against Einer's right, was gasping for breath, and Einer too was panting. His shoulder hurt from the strain of parrying the blows of giants and warriors and beasts.

'You could fight for me anywhere on this battlefield,' the Alfather continued calmly, as if they were sitting down and talking over a hornful of mead, and not in the midst of the deadliest battle in the nine worlds.

Einer struggled to catch his breath long enough to answer. Thankfully, he knew that his thoughts were loud, and he did not have to speak to be heard. He simply had to collect himself enough to be able to clearly think his answer to the Alfather's questions.

There was a reason he was there, and not elsewhere on the battlefield. For he had heard Fenrir howl. The great wolf was coming for the Alfather, and Einer had to be there, nearby, to protect the nine worlds, as best he could. He would give his life, and his afterlife too, to protect the nine worlds against meaningless death.

The faces of giants and warriors around them began to glow. A fire demon approached. It leapt into the air above them, attacking Odin's ravens and crows with its killing flames. Birds squealed and flapped. Fire spread.

Giants and warriors cowered away and lowered themselves.

Amazed, Einer watched the flames bursting and wheeling

above them, and chanced a glance over his shoulder, at the Alfather. All he could see was the Alfather's neck. Odin's jewelled armour rose up high, leaving little space between his armour and helmet. Even a sword would struggle to cut through. Although it looked like the Alfather was only wearing one slight layer of armour, and a blue tunic beneath. A gold neck-ring rested against the rim of the Alfather's armour— armour which must have been smithed by dwarves in Muspel's fires. The things forged by the skilled dwarves often cheated the eyes: even a short-shafted hammer like Thor's own could smash mountains, and light armour could be stronger than stone walls. Einer's eyes once more caught the thick neck-ring, and he sighed with relief.

The light went out as the flames above them died. Ice shards hailed loudly against Einer's helmet.

'I'm well protected,' the Alfather said, when the remains of the frozen demon no longer rained over them, and Einer knew it to be true. The Alfather could not easily be disarmed or killed.

Black winged birds fell out of the sky with iced wings. Some were empty birdskins, still burning. Valkyries landed all around them, spears in hand. Some weaponless. Strong women trampled out the last burning feathers.

A wind rose from directly under Einer's feet, conjured out of nothing by Odin or one of his valkyries. The crows and ravens rode the wind anew, high into the air. Warriors and giants were pushed away. Inside the whirlwind was only Einer, the Alfather, and the bloodied valkyrie at Einer's left side.

Giants roared, struggling to get through the conjured wind. Their voices came from every direction and none at all. Mighty arms tried to reach through, and weapons recoiled from the wind that blurred everything beyond. The light was so dim that it only reflected on the tops of helmets and weapons.

Einer heaved a few deep breaths. The valkyrie to his left, too, took the time to catch her breath, before the next wave, and before Fenrir reached them.

Einer looked down at his sword. It was so drenched in blood that Ulfberht's inscription was gone. He cleaned the sword on his trousers that were also drenched, and then he reached into his pouch. He brought out his whetstone and set to sharpening his sword.

He felt the Alfather watch him over his shoulder, and he tried not to show that it made him uneasy.

'Why would it make you uneasy?' the Alfather asked aloud, and Einer silently cursed his own thoughts for being so loud.

'You're the Alfather,' Einer answered, aloud this time, to not unnecessarily invite anyone to listen to his thoughts. He put his whetstone away, safely in his pouch again, and readied himself. The forefathers hummed loudly and took away some of the pain in his body. He was sore all over, but most of all in his right arm, from wielding his weapon.

Valkyries slipped into their crow skins, those of them whose feathers had not burned off completely. A valkyrie shouldered herself in between Einer and the one with blood tears. He caught sight of the blood-teared valkyrie then, briefly. She was staring at him, an intense stare that felt like she was questioning his motives, like the Alfather was.

Einer stuck his shoulder securely against that of the Alfather so another valkyrie would not try to push herself in between them. There were six of them now, on the ground with the Alfather. The rest of the valkyries were taking to the sky.

The giants had stopped yelling, and Einer felt a calm from the forefathers. Something was wrong.

Barely had the thought formed before the conjured whirlwind around them whipped with flames. A fire demon cackled in something that sounded like laughter.

The tips of Einer's beard caught fire. Frantically he grabbed his face with his gloved left hand. He was blinded by the sudden light. The sweat ran down his arms and forehead. At once the wind died, and with it, most of the fire too.

What remained lit the faces of giants and warriors waiting

to attack the Alfather. Einer stared straight ahead—into Nar's face—and gulped at the worry that his thoughts would give them away.

'Give what away?' the Alfather hissed, before Nar or anyone else had time to attack.

'To your right!' screamed a valkyrie.

The Alfather turned. He parried a shard of conjured ice, and as he did, he twisted around, just enough. Einer saw Tassi's face at the Alfather's back. Nar was rushing the front. He had freed himself from the wider crowd. The blond warrior cornered to the left of the great god, and he got close. Perhaps even close enough to succeed.

This was it. Einer pushed the valkyrie to his left out of the way and turned to the Alfather. He hammered the long end of his sword into his stomach. Odin buckled over in surprise, but recovered quickly, as only a god might. His single eye focused on Einer so it felt like he was burning from within. The Alfather swung his spear at him, right as Einer lifted his sword. Their weapons clashed, but Odin had more strength. Einer stumbled three steps backwards. Something thick and dark flew out in front of him. Valkyries descended on him from the skies.

Einer struck down a bird. A raven's head was sliced off, along with part of its wings. Another was on him before the head of the first hit the ground. And then another. There were three birds all trying to scratch out his eyes. He waved them off with his sword, but they moved too fast for him to hit them.

'Hugin,' a bird squealed and darted down to Einer's feet. Einer tried to see the dead bird he had killed, but valkyries swept down to attack him from every side.

'Hugin,' the bird croaked again. He had killed one of the Alfather's two ravens.

Einer slashed around himself without truly seeing what he hit. He focused on Helheim's warriors, half-hidden behind black wings. He smiled when he saw the back of a helmet. A tall warrior was heading away from the Alfather. Tassi had succeeded.

'Now is the time,' Einer said, and thought, as loud as he could, so all giants and beasts left on the battlefield would know. 'Kill the Alfather!'

Odin's braided beard shook with anger. His single eye went wide, his muscles tense. The Alfather thrust his spear at Einer. It pierced straight through his chainmail and leather armour, straight through all of Einer. Through his ribs, through flesh and blood and lungs, and out through the armour at his back. Odin lifted the spear, and Einer with it.

The forefathers chanted within him. He was cold and warm all over, and he struggled to keep awake.

The Alfather's single eye narrowed in anger and hate. Einer stared down at Odin. The Ulfberht sword fell from his grip. He had no strength left, as he looked at his god. What little he had, he gathered together, to form one final, loud thought. *Cattle die, kinsmen die.* His god was shaking at the betrayal. Odin heaved his weapon to the side.

The spear tore out of Einer's guts. He was hurled off the shaft, and through the crowd. His head banged against something hard: a shield, or perhaps the chainmail of a dead warrior. He gasped for breath, or at least he thought he did, but his lungs were empty.

So, this was death.

HILDA

Chapter One Hundred and Eighty-Four

EINER'S WHITE BEAR stood over his body. It looked down at him and tilted its head.

The Alfather was heaving for breath for the first time since Hilda had joined him. His anger made the earth shake around them. Einer's chainmail clattered against the golden shield he had fallen on. He didn't get up.

The white bear looked up from Einer to Hilda. Its eyes were green like Einer's own. It felt like *he* was watching her, recognising her. Even if it was in death. He was dead. The earth was still trembling, and Einer's body shuddered along with the rest of the battlefield. He did not rise. He did not move at all. The tremors of the Alfather's wrath made Einer's head fall to the side of the golden shield. Hilda stared down at his face.

His eyes were open, but he wasn't looking. Not at her. Not at anything.

His white bear gave a sorrowful roar. It didn't leave, though it was supposed to. Corpses needed no fylgjur. But Hilda supposed that it had nowhere to go. Everywhere she looked there was death and sorrow. Einer was dead before he had truly seen her. Before she had spoken to him, or he to her. He was gone. Before she could tell him that she had missed him. She had. More so now that she looked at him; really saw his blooded face, and the little lock of straw-coloured hair that escaped from his tight helmet. She had missed him, and standing over his dead body, she still did.

Einer's death shocked not just her, but the entire crowd. The Alfather was shaking in anger. Beasts and warriors and giants stood back, afraid. Not only of the Alfather's anger, but of something else.

A wolf growled. Startled, Hilda turned around. Her heart raced with worry that Fenrir had arrived at last. Her thigh wound hurt all the more at the thought.

The growl came, not from Fenrir, or another beast, but from the Alfather himself.

'Traitor,' he growled with such fury that Hilda couldn't look away. His braided, bloodied beard was trembling. Blood splattered off the Alfather's shaking face and off his jewelled chainmail. He looked drowned in blood, and he *had* been. Monsters were keeping their distance on all sides. The Alfather's left hand rose, to show off his jewelled chainmail. He rubbed the blood off his neck. Tapped his blood-red hand all around the edge of his chainmail, at the neck. Almost as if searching for something.

The battlefield had grown quiet. The clash of weapons and shields grew distant, far away from the widening circle around the Alfather.

Around them, giants and wolves and warriors gasped for breath. It sounded, and looked, like they were all taking in the same breath. Their chests rose and fell in the same heartbeat. The sound came in a steady wave. No one attacked.

Weapons were still held high, but they were not used. Shields still protected the faces and hearts of warriors, but their eyes peeked over the edges.

The mountain of corpses they stood on trembled below them all. Maybe Asgard itself trembled in the Alfather's anger. Maybe all the nine worlds, united by Yggdrasil, felt his fury.

A pain had formed in Hilda's heart. It wasn't like her wounds. Not like her thigh that made her limp, or the still-bleeding injuries she had suffered on the battlefield. A pain like an ache. An itch she couldn't reach. It stirred at the Alfather's growling.

'It's *your* fault,' he hissed, and his single eye landed on Hilda. His pupil was shaking. 'You said the wolf was dead! Traitor!'

His left hand quit his neck and darted for Hilda. She ducked out of his reach, but his hand caught her hair and wrenched off a handful. Hilda backed away into a valkyrie. Odin lifted his spear.

Still beasts stood back and watched. Warriors, from Helheim, and from Valhalla, too. Her bench-mates watched, and Einer's white bear. It reached out towards her, as if it wanted to help. As if *he* wanted to help.

No one else would save Hilda from Odin's wrath. She only had herself.

'Fenrir won't kill you,' she blurted before the Alfather could strike. Had he not been so angry, he would have moved faster, and Hilda would already be dead. She knew that, but it was no relief. The Alfather's anger scared her more than death itself. Hilda had died before; death was swift, a pain and then something else. Or nothing at all. A pain, and then it was over.

There was no end to the Alfather's wrath. He looked like he wanted to tear her apart. The wind swept in with unhelpful visions of the past. *Beasts watch the Alfather on Ragnarok's battlefield.* The vision disappeared as quickly as it had arrived, replaced by another. Elsewhere. *The Alfather lifts a warrior by the throat.* Again, the vision was no more than a flash.

At a great feast, all eyes on him, the Alfather tears the wing off a cooked bird. He wrenches off the legs. Hilda blinked and the vision was gone, replaced by another. *The warrior still dangles from the Alfather's grip. He struggles to breathe.* Another. *The*

Alfather brings a dagger to his catch. A deer lies before him. The Alfather's knife is steady as he skins it. Hilda panted for breath. *A dead bird lies on the grass. The Alfather steps on it with muddy boots.*

The visions faded. They had come suddenly, almost as a warning.

Hilda knew enough of visions to know that they had been exactly that, and who had conjured them.

These were the Alfather's intentions. Hilda had no future, and no past, but this was what her future would bring now. Torn apart, limb by limb. Skinned and left alive, to rot as giants marched across her. Her future as it would be, unless she prevented it from happening.

'If I die, your future is as clear as you want mine to be,' Hilda said.

Visions didn't startle her. She had seen horrors in life. She had seen her village burn. Her friends murdered, her father dying. Her uncle, her aunt, her cousins slain by warriors. She had seen children murdered, corpses defiled. She had seen worse things. Pain and death no longer frightened her. The worst pain could do to her, was hurt.

What it would do to the Alfather was much worse. If he hurt her, he was doomed. He would die, as he was destined to do. Never to wake. Unless...

'You can prevent this,' he seemed to realise, then. Hilda was no longer shielding her thoughts from him. She had meant for him to hear.

'Only if I can reach the nornir's cave in time,' Hilda said aloud.

At that news, the petrified warriors and beasts and giants decided to move, all in the same heartbeat. They launched at her. Kill Hilda, and they might kill the Alfather.

Odin was faster than them all. He knocked Hilda to the ground. Not to kill her; he was protecting her, now. For only she could wake him from death. Hilda pushed herself up. She limped towards the Alfather, and he pushed her behind himself. The Alfather and four of his valkyries formed a small circle of protection. The corpses at their feet had stopped trembling. The Alfather was no longer angry.

Once more, Hilda chanted her runes silently in her mind, to shield her thoughts from her god. So that she could think freely.

The white bear still stood over Einer's corpse. She could see it under the Alfather's arm, through the crowd of agitated warriors lunging for her.

The bear refused to leave Einer. She supposed her own snow fox had been the same. Even after Hilda had passed on, her snow fox had chosen to stay. It had followed her even without a chain tying them. Together they had travelled through Asgard. Now, it was gone, but it had stayed with her for much longer than any fylgja should stay.

Maybe that was different. Hilda and her fox had been tied together by more than destiny: by blood and by runes. They were both the same, always tied. Einer's white bear stayed out of choice. They were not bound by anything other than experiences.

'Give her your skin,' the Alfather hissed to the air. Hilda looked up. Crows and ravens were fighting above. Against eagles, and hawks, and mostly giants. They swarmed around giants, scratching out their eyes and shrieking into their ears.

A crow folded up its wings and shot straight down. Hilda protected her face with her arms. The crow landed right there, on her arm, its claws folding softly around her wrist. And she felt the weight of it. It grew larger, pushed her arm down, and then it went limp. An empty bird skin hung from her wrist, and she felt someone press up against her back. Leather armour rubbed against her chainmail.

The valkyrie who had come out of the bird skin pushed away, to fight with her bench-mates, and her god. Hilda cradled the precious crow skin in her hands. The feathers on the left wing had burned, and it was slick with sweat, inside and out.

Protected by Odin and his valkyries, Hilda set her axe away. She knew exactly what to do and how to do it. Once before, she had put on a bird skin in a hurry. The problem was getting out of it again, once she had put it on, but she hadn't known the runes then, and she knew them now. She wasn't worried about getting out this time. If Freya had been able to free her from the skin, then a norn like Hilda would certainly be able to do the same.

Hilda slid her left foot into the sweaty skin. It was warm on the inside. She got her right toes inside as well and forced the opening on the back to become wider. She wrestled it up her legs, coming closer and closer to the ground as she pulled herself into the skin. At the hips, she gently tipped her Ulfberht axe into it, to make sure that it didn't get stuck outside. At the waist, she stopped and inserted her left hand. She pushed the skin all the way up, so it rested at her armpit. Then, she forced her head inside. Her helmet was smooth with blood, and she struggled to keep it on. It kept sliding to the side so she could hardly see out one eye. With a frustrated grunt, she pulled off the helmet and forced herself inside without it. Right arm and head at the same time.

The valkyrie who owned the skin must have eaten onions at the last feast before Ragnarok. The skin stank sourly of sweat. Hilda pushed her head all the way in and wriggled her nose until she could feel her beak. The stench of sweat wasn't nearly as bad, smelled through the beak. It was subtle, and almost pleasant.

Hilda flapped her wings and stretched her long-clawed toes. The thigh of the corpse beneath her felt soft at the touch of her claws. She tested the beak and let out a little shriek, and then she flapped her wings, slowly at first, and then with all the strength she had in her.

Her slick black body rose into the air. Harder, she flapped her wings. They took her up fast. Hilda let out a longing sigh. She loved flying. The skies were black, and so were the wings of the valkyries and Odin's surviving raven. They were so fast, she couldn't follow.

She kept flying up. In a straight line.

A giant hand swept in over her. Hilda made a sharp turn. She collided with another bird. They both tumbled down and tried to flap away. Their wings kept hitting each other. Again, the giant's hand reached for them. Hilda hacked out after the giant with her sharp beak. One of her claws slid into his skin. She was swept through the dark air, but unhooked herself and flapped to get away. She brought herself up fast, and high, out of the giant's wide reach.

For five more heartbeats she rose straight into the air. At last, she stopped struggling and let her wings keep her afloat. She glided over the battlefield.

Seen from above, there was something beautiful about it. Three flame demons raged through the crowd in a valley between huge corpse mountains. They shone in the near dark. Faces of horrors were illuminated around them. Shadows were cast on the rest of the fighting crowd. Everything was moving at once. She had always thought that Ragnarok was chaos, but there was a certain order to it, seen from high above, and from far away.

At last, Hilda caught sight of the white fur she was searching for. She stared down at Einer's white bear. Watched it mourning Einer's death. The crowd parted around the bear, leaving it alone and exposed, and Einer's body too.

At the bear's back someone advanced. One of the hundreds of wolves, but not just any wolf: it was Fenrir himself, at long last.

Hilda no longer knew if she should be fearful at the thought of the Alfather dying, or happy. He had hissed at her in the end. At least Loki had never treated her like that. She had never imagined that she would see the Alfather spit in anger. Other gods, perhaps—certainly Thor—but not the grand Alfather. He was always composed. At least, he had been, before the fear of dying had reached him.

The crowd parted for the great wolf, leaving a direct path from Fenrir to the Alfather. Soon, Odin would be dead. Unless Hilda did something, and the Alfather was right: she hadn't lied to him. She *could* do something.

Three winters ago, Loki had delivered her to the nornir. There, she had been taught how to revive a dead giant. She knew the way, and Hilda was certain that a god, still alive, would be much simpler to save.

SIGISMUND

Chapter One Hundred and Eighty-Five

'WHAT DO WE do now?' Brannar hissed to Sigismund.

They had fought their way past warriors of Valhalla and out of the way of a goddess who was terrorising the entire valley. They had not come close enough to her to find out who it had been, but a rumour travelled across the battlefield that it was the golden-haired goddess, Sif, furious over her husband's death.

Sigismund tried to catch his breath from their last run. The fire demon they were headed for was close. It burned through warriors from Valhalla and Helheim with ease. Everyone was trying to flee the demon.

Only Brannar and Sigismund were moving *towards* it.

'I need your bracteate,' he said.

Brannar snapped around to glare at him.

'We're never going to convince a fire demon to help us,' Sigismund said. 'I can't even tell who they're truly fighting for.'

She knew that he was right, but she did not want to part with the bracteate. Sigismund could not blame her for it. He was just as reluctant to let go of his, for once their deed was done, they would need to travel out through the fighting crowd again and find Yggdrasil's outer root to meet Tassi and get the last of the three bracteates. Assuming Einer and his shield-wall had succeeded.

Reluctantly, Sigismund drew the neck-ring over his head. The gold bracteate twinkled prettily in the distant light from the demon. The image of Yggdrasil had been hammered so precisely and beautifully. To destroy it seemed a deed worthy of outlawry. Even death seemed too simple a penalty for destroying such beauty. Yet such was Sigismund's task, and he knew that he would die for it. In the end, they would all die on this battlefield. Sigismund had to destroy the three bracteates before he let death take him. No one else in the nine worlds could do it.

'Bracteate,' he said and put his hand out to Brannar. Her teeth were clenched together, but she reached into the neck of her armour and brought out the neck-ring with the large gold coin attached.

Sigismund took it and tried to juggle them both with his sword and shield, holding the bracteates together in his shield hand. He gave up with a deep sigh and sheathed his sword. Despite himself, he prayed to his gods. He knew that most of them lay dead on this battlefield, and those who did not would be unable to help. Still, he called upon their strength.

At least his warriors had drowned. In life, he had never thought that drowning would be the preferable fate, but Ragnarok was grim, and Sigismund was glad that Frey-fiord's warriors were safe in Ran's and Aegir's hall beneath the sea. He hoped that Thora was too.

His fighting glove was too thick for fine work, so he pulled it off with his teeth and stuffed it into the neck of his armour—his belt was too full of weapons and hammers and other tools. He transferred the bracteates to his now-bare right hand. For a heartbeat longer, he stared down at them, laying innocently in his palm. He hoped this would work. If they couldn't be melted by a fire demon's touch, he did not know what else to do.

'If we can't reason with it, then what's the plan?' Brannar wanted to know.

'We approach. We lure it towards us. I drop the bracteates. It walks over them. Hopefully that will be enough to deliver my hammer blow.'

'Drop them?' Brannar whispered. The plan made Sigismund as uneasy as it made her, but he had no other ideas as to how they might stick the bracteates into a fire demon's flames without dying in the process. And they couldn't die yet; there was still the Alfather's bracteate to destroy.

'Clear the way for me to get close. I'll drop them, and when the demon comes, we'll retreat.'

Before Brannar could protest, Sigismund walked down the corpse mountain. A sheildmaiden came running up at him, and he knocked her helmet with the edge of his shield. The woman stumbled back, and Sigismund heard Brannar deliver a fatal blow.

Two heartbeats later and she was in front of him, clearing the way. No longer worrying about the battlefield, Sigismund stared at the approaching fire demon. Ashes fell around them like snow. The demon was burning through corpses. The fire snapped loudly. It burned across the plain after a group of warriors that were running away with all their might.

Brannar cut down one more warrior, and then they were alone. First in line to be burned by fire. Sigismund let go of the two bracteates. They tumbled at his feet, onto the bloodied belly of a giant. A beast had torn out the jotun's guts to feast.

'Back,' Brannar yelled into Sigismund's ear, shoving him. He looked up. The fire demon rushed at them, burning fiercely. Sigismund turned and ran all he could, to get away. Brannar raced at his side, not quite as fast as him. But then she stopped, and so did Sigismund. The air was no longer as foul at his back.

He pulled out the hammer from his belt and turned to see if their plan had worked.

The fire demon had stopped chasing them. It had stopped

chasing everyone. The fire burned steadily without moving. Right on top of the dead giant. The two bracteates Sigismund had dropped shone in the demon's hottest fire.

The fire demon bent over the bracteates. It had noticed the golden rings. Its long slender fingers reached down, as if to pick them up.

'It can't,' Brannar breathed, but it could.

Its fiery fingers clasped around the bracteates and lifted them from the corpse-coated ground. They hung awkwardly from the demon's fingers and the chain burned away, but the bracteates merely shone bright.

They were shining. The metal was hot enough for Sigismund to deliver his hammer strokes. He had been right. But he had not thought that a demon could pick up the bracteates or would even notice them.

Sigismund clenched the hammer tight in his hand. His heart raced at the thought of what might happen next. Nothing ever went according to plan. Certainly not at Ragnarok.

The fire demon swayed from side to side. Its feet burned the corpses beneath it, but the demon itself was focused on the two flat coins. They were deep inside the demon's core. Inside its chest, where they shone as brightly and strongly as its flames.

Sigismund launched himself at the deadly fire. No demon would get the bracteate and live forever to burn Asgard bare. He ran towards it as fast as he could.

The fire demon was too taken by the bracteates to notice or care.

Even before Sigismund's skin touched the outer flames, it felt like hot needles were stabbing his skin. His shield began to burn, but not as hot as the demon, so it still protected him. The hairs on his left arm flamed. His tunic, too. His chainmail was bright and hot. His layers were melting.

Sigismund pushed ahead, through the pain. The skin on his hand dripped away. He swung his right arm back and delivered the hammer blow.

His aim was precise, though he could hardly see through the smoke of his own skin cooking. His hammer clanged against the two bracteates and forced them onto the ground and into the dead giant's soft stomach. Both bracteates and hammer went straight through. The bracteates burned themselves down through flesh and meat.

Sigismund heard Brannar's shout off to his left. He stared down at the bracteates as he removed his hammer. The heat on his face receded. Brannar had captured the fire demon's attention.

Sigismund's skin bubbled with burns. The pain went all the way through to his bones, to the deepest core of him. His head was light from the pain, and he thought he might pass out, but the will to stay alert was stronger even than the worst pain in the nine worlds.

Beneath the hammer was a flat coin. Completely flat.

The image of Yggdrasil's root had been hammered out of the top bracteate. Sigismund let his hammer fall and reached for his tongs. He picked up the flat gold coin to see the second one. The two of them were stuck together. Sigismund lifted them both out of the dead giant and turned them around. Both sides were flat. The image had been undone. The strength was gone from them. That was why the fire demon had abandoned them, too: they were just coins now.

Sigismund released a relieved sigh, and with the knowledge that he had succeeded, the pain returned. His skin bubbled loudly. Pain etched deep into his left arm. His arm had taken most of the blow. His beard had burned off. His chin was hot, with a prickling pain.

Sigismund swirled around to find Brannar and tell her all, but he had no strength. He fell. The pain took over. It screamed through him. It felt like he was still burning, although the fire had gone out. His chainmail remained hot.

Sigismund struggled to push himself up to sit. There was still the third bracteate. They needed to get to Yggdrasil's root, to meet Tassi and get the Alfather's bracteate, and undo it. So that Ragnarok would not have been fought in vain. Sacrificing himself, coming here to undo the two bracteates, even Ragnarok itself. All of it would be meaningless if Sigismund did not undo the last one.

His face was hot. He felt himself turn red and blue. He could not breathe. His heart had slowed so much that he could hardly think. Yet his body struggled and struggled until the end, for all of him knew what he had to do. Undo the bracteate, save the nine worlds from the Alfather's rule.

Sigismund's eyes closed, and his thoughts stalled. He had no strength left to struggle. This was his end. He had failed. The Alfather would live. They had all died in vain.

TYRA

Chapter One Hundred and Eighty-Six

FINDING HER WAY to the battle in the complete dark had not been easy. Tyra had followed her ears, but the screams of war rang out all over Asgard. Sometimes, it was hard to tell if they came from east or west, and even harder to tell which *way* was east and which west.

Something was calling her. Not towards the battle, as she had initially thought, but somewhere else. The call was distant, and there were no words, just an unspoken pull. A feeling that Tyra didn't want to ignore.

She remembered, once, being pulled towards a place in this way. Back in Midgard, when she had been a child in Jelling. The dark of a passage grave had pulled her close. It had called her, all the time, when she was close. The call was the same, now.

Tyra answered the call. She let the pull guide her through Asgard, through the dark of a forest. She stumbled past trees, feeling them as she went. Once, she had walked in a dark place like this, along one of Yggdrasil's roots, with Siv. She had been a little girl then, ignorant of much. Of how their time in Asgard would end, with Glumbruck's death at the Alfather's hands. She had been scared even before she had known how it would end. She had been right to be.

Asgard was a scary place. Tyra had travelled much, not only in Midgard, but in the other worlds, too, with her bloody dagger. She had seen much and met many beings, but there was nowhere in the nine worlds that she knew of that carried as much terror as Asgard.

Especially tonight.

She no longer stumbled as much as she had. After days in the dark, Tyra had begun to adjust to it. Ahead, she could see lights reflected on smoke and clouds in the sky. Ragnarok's battlefield was near, and this close to the last battle, Tyra could more or less see the ground where she walked. At least, she could see a good step ahead. Large tree-roots and trunks no longer popped out at her unannounced. As long as she walked slowly enough, she no longer tripped.

The forest stopped, and Tyra travelled onto a plain. Clouds flashed with light in the distance.

Tyra nearly stumbled over something on the ground. At the last moment, she spotted the tree-trunk and hopped over it, only to realise that it was not a tree-trunk as she had thought, but a tall man. She rocked him with her foot, but he did not move. Her first Ragnarok corpse.

He lay alone in the near dark. A little light escaped over the top of a nearby mountain. It was not as far away as she had thought. At last, she was close to the battlefield.

She crouched down by the dead man to better see him. His forehead was furrowed, and he only held onto his spear with one hand. His left was clutched around something else, which he held to his chest.

Tyra crouched down at his side and reached for his clenched hand. She could hardly see, but between his clammy fingers was a metal coin. She wrenched it out of his death grip and held it up to the light.

It was a large metal coin. Gold or silver, perhaps. A bracteate meant to be worn in a neck-ring. Tyra slid her fingers over the cold metal. An image had been hammered into the coin on both sides. Tyra twisted it in her hand to see it in the little light that escaped across the nearby mountain.

The image on the coin was Yggdrasil, with all its twisted branches and roots.

Tyra let out a little laugh. There it was. The bracteate Thor had sent her to look for before the battle. It had found its way to her, as sometimes happened with people and the things they desperately searched for. The coin necklace had made its way to her much too late to save her from Thor's rage, but she still held onto the gold coin as she rose from the corpse's side.

Thunder rumbled above. Tyra stared up at the flashing light in the skies. The battlefield was being fought out there. A nagging feeling made Tyra look away from the mountain, which was all that separated her from the battlefield. She stared into the dark, back the way she had come. Back towards Yggdrasil.

That strange feeling which had guided her this far called her that way. It had brought her across plains in the complete dark, and through forests too. It felt familiar, like home, and even now it was calling for her, as once the dark of a passage grave had called for her.

Tyra rubbed her finger across the image of Yggdrasil. Even the bracteate seemed to want her to go back towards the great ash. So, she listened to the will of the nine worlds, as she imagined Siv would have done, and set out the way she had come.

Across the plain she marched, letting the pull guide her through the near-complete dark. She could see the outlines of tree-trunks as she came close, and then something else. One of Yggdrasil's great roots snaked out behind a much smaller tree. Tyra walked to it and placed her left hand on it. In her right she still held onto the Yggdrasil bracteate. Rubbing the image on it made it easier to ignore the distant screams from the battlefield.

The pull dragged Tyra ahead, along the great root. She almost felt like she could hear a voice calling her closer. Almost.

Her fingers slipped over something, and Tyra felt a sting in her heart. Like an old memory trying to push through. Carefully, she brushed her fingers back over the side of Yggdrasil's ragged root. There was a hole in the root.

She strained to see it in the light reflected from the flashing clouds above.

The eternal night of Ragnarok was dark, but nothing like the hole in Yggdrasil's root. That was different. It called to her— that Darkness. It was the same that resided within all ash trees. The great Ginnungagap where Siv had once hidden Tyra away to save her from the slaughter in Ash-hill.

Tyra reached her left hand into the deep dark darkness that had called her there. A cold clammy hand clasped onto hers. There was someone in there. Inside Yggdrasil's root. Inside the Darkness.

DARKNESS

It all made sense to Ragnar. Why he had been sent here in the afterlife. Why it was him, and not someone else. Ragnar had told stories all his life. He knew all there was to know about the gods. Only he could connect the stories and spin destinies so that Ragnarok would happen. That was why Ragnarok bore his name: Ragnar's Darkness.

This was what Siv had tried to tell him, once. It was why he had woken up to the Darkness in the afterlife, and not to Helheim's bliss. No one but him could ensure that all went as it was supposed to. Only he could influence the minds of gods with the runes Siv had taught him, and only he knew what needed to happen for Odin and Thor and all the gods to die on Ragnarok's plain, exactly as it had been foretold. Ragnar had to ensure their fates. Siv had told him that he was fate itself, ensuring the destinies of all gods and giants and Midgard folk. All the beings who had destinies for him to decide over. It was often difficult to believe.

Even his own destiny, he had ensured. Or so Siv had told him.

Ragnar stared out through the Darkness. It was so dark, although somewhere out there was a hole out of the Darkness. Not nearly wide enough to escape through, but wide enough to look out. Maybe even to push a finger through. The shadow warriors had crowded around it. They still had to be crowded around it, for it was out of sight—hidden by shadowy figures dreaming of escape.

Ragnar, too, had once dreamed of escaping. He no longer carried such hope. This was his fate, and as Siv had told him he would do someday, he would fate himself to this afterlife.

Thinking of his own end, and the funeral song he had heard when he had first woken up in this place, Ragnar tapped his distaff silently in the complete dark.

His distaff pushed the Darkness away. A white thread formed and shot into the dark. With the screech of hundreds of knives sharpening against glass, it tore a long, veiled opening into the Darkness. A veil which led to a sunny day somewhere out in the nine worlds.

Ragnar stepped through with his eyes closed. Birds were singing and flies were buzzing. The sun beamed warm over his face, and after so long spent in Darkness, it felt good to be warmed by the sun's touch again. Uneven grass poked into the soles of his thin leather shoes. This was Midgard. Home, at last.

Now your journey
Shall begin.

People sang. Ragnar opened his eyes, knowing exactly what he would see.

Fire blazed in front of him. He had opened a veil to his last moments in Midgard. His funeral, after his death, when the villagers had sung him into the next life. A grand pyre was burning in front of him as villagers sang.

The funeral pyre was tall, and Ragnar was thankful for its height, for he could hardly see himself lying on top. Only his own pale hand and the yellow sleeve of his tunic were visible from down here. But there was something else too. A bundle of a man was bent over Ragnar at the top of the funeral pyre.

So long he had spent in Darkness that he had forgotten how he had first arrived there, but there had been song. This very song. And he had not been walking; he had been riding on a black stallion. His loyal thrall in life had been walking at his side.

The villagers had sacrificed much for Ragnar's funeral. Not merely wealth, but a horse and a thrall, too. The singing villagers stood in a large circle around Ragnar's funeral pyre. He turned away from the fire to look at them all. Two people stood closer to the burning pyre than the rest, right behind Ragnar. A young woman and man.

Immediately, Ragnar recognised the chieftain's son, Einer, but the woman was a stranger, or perhaps he had merely been dead for too long to recall who she had been.

She had a strong jaw and square chin that made her look as tough as any warrior, and she felt somewhat familiar. A distant memory of his wife laughing made Ragnar smile, and he could almost see Signe stand before him, although, of course, she had passed away long before he had. Her life had been short. The young woman at his funeral looked a little like Signe. Perhaps she was one of his wife's cousins. Ragnar could not quite remember how they had all looked. It had been many winters, and lifetimes, since he had met them.

Einer he recognised, although he looked different from how Ragnar had expected him to look. His memories had changed after the many deaths he had suffered in this Darkness. Life itself, in Ash-hill and Midgard, seemed so distant. Nothing more than a dream.

As inconsequential as a dream, as well.

A bright cold coin hung from Einer's neck. Like the one Ragnar had often noticed hanging from the Alfather's neck. Ragnar stared at it.

Greet the gods and
Greet our kin.

Siv stood behind her son, watching him, and in that moment, Ragnar understood how Siv had known that Ragnar had doomed himself to this life. The bracteate did not belong in Midgard, but to another world. Siv had gifted it to her son, and it had strength. It could accomplish this, and more, perhaps.

At once, Ragnar knew where to plant his thoughts, and where to use his influence. With runes, he reached out to Einer.

Ragnar does not belong in Helheim, he thought, and meant it. He sharpened his hearing with runes and watched as Einer mouthed something to the funerary fire.

'Goodbye Ragnar, skald of Ash-hill, son of Erik Ivarson,' Einer said. 'I hope you'll never have to go to Hel.'

And like that, it was done. Ragnar's will had been made, and his destiny decided. Ragnar looked past Einer, to his mother. Siv had been right. She was always right.

He had doomed himself to this dire fate.

In death.
In death, we shall meet.

He owed Siv a final visit in Alfheim.

Ragnar sighed loudly, calling Siv's forefathers to himself, so that they could bring him back into Darkness, through death.

Something smashed into Ragnar's face. His nose broke. He was kicked down. Staring up at the blazing fires of his own funeral. An axe hammered into Ragnar's chest. Slowly, death took him, as it had many times before, and would many times more. The Darkness claimed him.

Death, pain, and fear.

HILDA

Chapter One Hundred and Eighty-Seven

HILDA KICKED IN the blooded door. Visions had guided her through the eternal night, all the way to the blood-painted house in the blackest corner of Asgard.

The house smelled of rot and decay. It smelled like no one had opened that door since the beginning of the three-year winter. It was quiet inside.

Hilda kept the axe in her hand. The valkyrie crow skin was nestled in her belt. Tied around twice, so she wouldn't lose it. The house was dark, but the wind guided her.

Her visions had become sharp with practice. She conjured visions of the past of this house to see where she should walk. She had found the house in the same way. Flying, above clouds and in the complete dark. Visions showed her what had once lain below and what still did.

The battle had spread from Ida's plain out through Asgard. The loss of the sun and moon cloaked all the lands in darkness. Fire demons had escaped from the battlefield and burned through forests and fields. Some of them were still burning, and the skies were thick with smoke.

The floorboards creaked under Hilda's weight. Her shoes felt glued to the floor. It was sticky with blood, like the rest of the house. A night breeze blew in at Hilda's back, bringing with it the refreshing smell of smoke from outside.

Even smoke was preferable to the stench of rot inside this house. She had seen it in her visions. Every plank was sticky with blood and wrinkled with runes. The strength of all those runes tingled on Hilda's skin. Runes that had been chanted, carved and coloured in worthy blood. They were stronger than others. Stronger than the ones in the Runemistress's hut back in Midgard.

'Why are *you* here?' asked the rusty voice that belonged to the veulve. She sounded like she had lived for centuries, and she had. 'I thought you would be off fighting the Midgard Worm... Or Fenrir, again.'

There was no doubt that the veulve knew who had intruded into her blood-dripping home.

'How did you know it was me?' Hilda asked. The visions never showed Hilda. The nornir could never find her in their visions. Hilda's lips formed a smile on their own. 'Because you can't see me,' she said, answering her own question in the same heartbeat.

There was only one person in the nine worlds whom even the veulve could not see coming, and that was Hilda.

Her sudden arrival must still have startled the Veulve, as she had wanted it to.

'I need your help,' Hilda said into the empty room. She expected to hear an echo, but her voice was swallowed by the blood-dripping walls and ceiling. 'That is why I am here, and not on the battlefield.'

The veulve did not deem her request worthy of an answer. The house was dead quiet. So much so that had the veulve not spoken, and had Hilda not been guided here by visions, she might have thought there was no one inside.

Yet, the veulve *was* there. She had heard Hilda's request and chose not to answer it. Hiding in silence inside this empty room.

Hilda focused straight ahead, where she knew from visions that a fireplace was. If she could see the veulve and the veulve could see her, there would be nowhere to hide.

'Kauna,' Hilda whispered. She focused on the rune of fire. Thought of flames and fire and demons. All that burned and warmed.

The house remained bathed in darkness. For all her skill with the runes, Hilda still had not mastered the rune of fire. No matter how much she tried, she couldn't conjure enough heat out of nothing to produce a flame.

'You need a norn.'

'Ja,' said Hilda, wondering how the veulve knew.

She had kept her mind clear of any unnecessary thoughts and shielded her mind with runes, too. But a trick that might misdirect gods, and the Alfather, was likely not enough to guard her thoughts from the veulve. No one was more powerful with runes. Not Freya. Not Loki. Not even the Alfather.

Of course, the veulve knew everything.

'You want to save him from certain death,' the veulve correctly guessed. 'That is why you need a norn. To spin a fate. To slow the end of a life.'

Perhaps she was watching the past *around* Hilda, and that was how she knew. Perhaps she saw what the Alfather had said on the battlefield, earlier in the night, even if she couldn't see Hilda in visions. Perhaps she could guess where she had been. If anyone could find a trace of Hilda in the destiny of the nine worlds, it was the veulve.

'How do you know?' Hilda asked. It felt strange to ask such things, when gods and giants were dying on the blooded plains outside. When so many were already dead. When fire demons burned through Asgard, and burned out. When the cold of the eternal night had begun to settle so that even Hilda struggled to keep warm.

The wind brought the sound of the dying with it. The stench of the dead, too, and the smoke that rose from Asgard's ground. The end was here.

Yet standing in the veulve's home, listening to the quiet drip of blood from the ceiling, the nine worlds seemed to have stalled.

'How do you know so much?' Hilda asked. For there would be no other time to ask.

The end was upon them all. Those who did not die at Ragnarok would die from the cold of this eternal night. Only the Alfather could save them from the dire end. Perhaps. If he survived.

'That was the price to pay for my star-dotted eyes,' said the veulve. 'Do you want to know more, or what?' She used the exact same words as the old stories Hilda's father had used to tell. Every verse about the veulve had always ended with that question.

Hilda nodded in the dark. She didn't think that she needed to say anything for the veulve to know her answer to the question.

The wind rushed in with whispers. Like they had used to do, back in Midgard. Not merely full of Loki's whispers, as they had used to be. Visions conjured by the veulve to grant Hilda answers to her questions.

Her star-dotted eyes stared up at the blue sky. They were glossy, but did not reflect the sky. They reflected what she saw. Visions of war. Blood and terror. Kisses and words whispered in bedrooms. The images flashed past. The veulve's forehead wrinkled with pain and confusion as the visions streamed by.

'There was a time,' said the veulve, as the vision of her past flashed before Hilda's eyes and made her feel what it was like to be a veulve.

Visions from all corners of the nine worlds were within the veulve's grasp. They pushed against her starry eyes and demanded to be seen. Just as the visions conjured by the veulve nagged in Hilda's wind and demanded to be acknowledged.

A young woman sat in front of a small tree, once. Ash leaves blew softly in the wind. Another vision replaced it. *The tree had grown. The woman still sat in front of it. Her red hair was longer, halfway down her back. The tree was taller than her, now. Brown leaves fell in the wind.*

The visions were all past, but once they had been past, present and future. 'A time before time. Before places and before destinies. I cannot show you that time. All I can show you is what followed. After time came into existence, after Yggdrasil's deepest roots were planted.'

The ash tree was thick. Its trunk wrinkled. The girl still sat by it. Her head was tilted back to look up at the crown of the tree. Her eyes came into view. They were distant, black as the sky.

'I lived through visions,' the veulve said. 'After the tree was planted. I watched it grow, not with my own eyes, but with those of others. Do you want to know more, or what?'

'You were blind,' Hilda realised.

'Before time, there was no use for eyes. No use for any of it. We were flowing, feeling our way. Surt burned next to me. Even then, his mind was always warm. When we gained form, his skin was still burning. We didn't adjust as well as others, he and I. Do you want to know more, or what?'

The visions still rushed past. Yggdrasil grew in front of Hilda's very eyes, and the veulve too was getting older. *Red hair spread out over the grass at Yggdrasil's growing roots. The tree was tall above the veulve. The grass was burned behind her.* Surt. Hilda was watching Surt's memories of the early days of the nine worlds. The visions came fast after that realisation. Bright flashes. Few of them stayed long enough for Hilda to truly grasp them.

The visions had left their marks on the veulve's black eyes. A white dot had appeared in the middle of her left eye. Visions flashed past, always. Another took Hilda. *Her eyes looked like stars now. Yggdrasil was huge at her back. The trunk was so thick and wide that one could see nothing else.*

Hilda came out of the visions breathless. The veulve had no choice. The visions came and kept coming. Hilda could ignore the whispers in the wind; the visions only came when someone conjured them for her, or when she did so herself. The veulve had no choice. All destinies were shown to her. Resisting them hurt.

'Always, I see what the story-maker decides,' the veulve said. 'The three nornir tie up the fates, as he dictates them to me. To all my children.'

'Your children?' Hilda breathed.

'I had many children, and they had many more. Do you want to know more, or what?'

A woman screamed. A new-born wailed in blood and slime. The veulve grunted. Her face was red and wet with sweat. Another new-born blinked its eyes. A hundred births and a hundred new-borns the veulve shared with Hilda.

Finally, the visions receded and left space for the utter dark of Ragnarok to settle again. The dark felt soothing after so many flashes. The veulve's visions were more potent than the ones Hilda conjured for herself. She could feel a pain in her lower belly, as if she remembered the pain of giving birth, although she never had. The nornir were all children of the veulve.

'Am I...?' Hilda barely dared to ask. Freya and the three nornir had told her that she had norn blood. A birth gift from her father's lineage.

'No one else hears the whispers in the wind,' the veulve whispered.

Ragnarok's crashes and roars echoed comfortably in the distance. Just enough to remind Hilda that the veulve and she were not alone in the nine worlds.

So, she was a descendant of the veulve. They were kin, the two of them.

'The whispers...' It felt like the veulve controlled all the whispers in the wind. Perhaps she did. Her voice was close and present. She was not far away into visions, as Hilda had expected her to be. Like the three nornir had often been.

'The visions. They bind us together,' the veulve said. 'All my descendants. All my skilled kinsmen. Do you want to know more, or what?'

A memory popped up in Hilda's mind. Not a conjured vision, but a memory from her own afterlife. Words said to her, words that had guided her across plains and through forests. All the way to the nornir's cave at Siv's funeral.

"We ask the Darkness whom it hides," Loki had whispered to her, once. Not in the wind, but in person. Someone, hiding in the dark, had freed Loki from his chains before Hilda had reached the cave of punishment. Before she had even known that the whispers belonged to Loki.

With those words Loki had lured Hilda to the nornir's cave. He had presented her with a mystery. Find out who had freed him, who was hiding in the dark. And Hilda had followed. She had never been able to resist a quest.

Hilda took a ragged breath. The veulve knew more than she could ever have imagined.

'Who hides in the dark?' Hilda dared to ask. She needed to know that her sacrifice had not been in vain. She needed to know the truth, before the end. Before it was too late to ever ask. 'Who freed Loki from his chains?'

'The story-maker,' answered the veulve. 'The story-maker changes what he wishes. Hiding in his dark. He, too, is one of mine. Only one of my descendants could have such ease with runes as to steer the Ginnungagap, and step into visions. Do you want to know more, or what?'

It felt like Hilda was being told an old story by her father. It felt like he was standing in the room with them. He had used to speak like this, when he had made up stories. He had used to stress the exact same words when he had recited the veulve's poems. It felt like the veulve was speaking in his voice, or perhaps like he, too, had heard whispers in the wind. Maybe that was why his stories had always been so vivid.

'Even now my words are steered by him. His whispers reach out of the Darkness of Yggdrasil's root. His stories guide me. Do you want to know more, or what?'

The Ulfberht axe suddenly felt heavy in Hilda's grip. It had sliced into Yggdrasil's root, once. The bark had peeled off to reveal a blackened place within. It had felt like someone was looking out at her. Someone that she knew. The story-maker. Her kinsman.

Never had Hilda expected that her questions would lead her here. She had not come to ask questions, she had come to spin a fate, but faced with the veulve and the end of the nine worlds, she had not been able to resist. She hadn't known the questions mattered until she had asked, and now she almost wished that she hadn't.

Now, every vision and every word the veulve spoke in reply gave Hilda more questions.

She had never given much thought to where her father had ended up in the afterlife. She had known it wasn't Valhalla, so it had to be Helheim, like her mother and brother. She had never doubted that, until now.

For to listen to the veulve was like listening to her father. She had long forgotten his voice, but hearing the veulve speak, she heard it now. His tone, the way he paused between certain words. The way his voice always felt like a close whisper, even when he was shouting his story to a hundred raucous freemen.

Now, she saw the reason his stories had been so compelling. He, like her, was a skilled descendant of the veulve, and perhaps more than that. She remembered what it had felt like to look into the Darkness of Yggdrasil's root.

Hilda licked her lips. She was breathing so deeply that she could hear her own breath as she readied to speak. Patiently, the veulve waited for Hilda to calm her own racing heart and thoughts. It couldn't be, she told herself before she asked the last, nagging question.

'Where does Ragnar Erikson spend his afterlife?' Hilda whispered it.

It felt like a secret. To know, and even to ask.

'In the Darkness,' the veulve replied. 'Twisting fates.'

TYRA

Chapter One Hundred and Eighty-Eight

TYRA REACHED FAR into Yggdrasil's Darkness, and a clammy hand grabbed hers. She gasped in shock and snatched her hand back, but the hand held on. As if it wanted to pull her into the Darkness—or for her to pull it out.

A crash echoed at Tyra's back, and the earth rumbled. Light shone bright behind her. She could clearly see her own shadow against Yggdrasil's tall root. Her hand was stuck in the Darkness inside the root.

Another crash echoed around Asgard. Tyra looked over her shoulder. Someone had set fire to the forest she had walked through. It burned high and wide, jumping from tree to tree under Yggdrasil's wide-reaching branches.

Tyra tried to wrench herself free of Yggdrasil's root, but the clammy hand held on. She couldn't see it, or anything else in the dark hole.

'Let go,' Tyra hissed, but the hand did not listen. The Darkness was still calling her closer, and demanding that she stay, as fire consumed the forest at her back. Her heart was yielding to the call. She felt like she had to stay. The thought of leaving hurt.

She belonged to the Darkness, for Siv had hidden her away in it, so long ago, when she had been a child in Midgard. She had known there would be a price to pay. The dark had been calling her ever since, and now it had her.

The clammy hand tugged on Tyra's arm again. She placed a foot on the root and yanked back with all her strength. Her hand came out of the Darkness, and something else came with it.

A shadow of a hand, the hand of a draugar. She tried to let go, but the shadow hand would not release her. The Darkness still whispered to her. Tyra grabbed onto the shadow arm and pulled again, and a draugar's arm was hauled out of the dark. Yggdrasil's dead spirit wore an expensive tunic, embroidered not just at the edge, but all the way up the sleeve. A wealthy man must have been buried there, under Yggdrasil's root.

Tyra pulled back with all her might, and although the hole had been so small, it seemed to grow as she hauled, until finally the face of a man surfaced. His wild eyes found her immediately. Tyra tried to get free of his grasp again, but he held on. His hair was braided neatly back in the ancient style, exactly like Siv's hair had always been braided.

He did not attack Tyra. He just held onto her and waited.

His intent was clear, and Tyra knew that she would not get free from his grasp unless she abided by his wishes, so she pulled him further out. She dropped the gold bracteate onto the grass and reached for him with her right hand too.

His torso was wrapped in leather armour. He was a warrior. Tyra tore him out so the weapons belt at his hips hung free, and then the warrior let go of her, and crawled out the last of the way himself.

Tyra stepped back and stared at him. He was much taller than her, and as she stood and gaped, he grew taller yet. As tall as a giant. The burning forest at her back illuminated his smoked face. He was nothing but a shadow. A dead giant.

The draugar rose to his feet and just stood there, staring

down at her, and then he turned to look back at the dark hole in Yggdrasil's root. Tyra nodded with understanding. The draugar was not alone.

Unafraid, now that she knew what to expect, Tyra reached into the hole again. Fingers groped her arm, and then they clasped around her. Tyra, too, held on, and then she stretched back.

The second shadow arrived with more ease than the first. This one was a woman. They were both tall, and they were growing, now that they were no longer in Darkness. Their weapons were inlaid in an ancient style that Tyra had only seen on her mother's heirlooms. The woman's hair was braided back in the same way. Like Siv had kept her hair, like Tyra too had braided her hair, before she had become Thor's thrall in the afterlife.

The two draugar did not leave, even though they were both free. In the same heartbeat, as if they were one and the same, they both turned to look back into the dark hole from which Tyra had pulled them.

There were more of them.

Tyra reached into the deep dark a third time. Again, a draugar grabbed onto her. A gloved hand grasped her arm at the elbow. The third was a man, and this one wore a helmet.

The first two headed off as Tyra pulled the third one free. They ran along Yggdrasil's root, straight towards the forest fires, and Ragnarok's battlefield beyond.

The third man held a spear in his left hand. It took him and Tyra a little work to get the spear through with him. She had expected him to head off after the first two once he was free, but as the first draugar had done, he just stood there, and watched her for a moment, and then he pointed back to the Darkness.

There were more. Always more. Tyra pulled free another man, and then another. After that came three women, and still they insisted that there were more behind them, waiting to be pulled free.

They were all dressed as warriors. They had no shields with them, but they carried all sorts of weapons: axes, spears, some swords, and even bows on their backs and daggers in their belts.

Dozens of warriors she pulled out of Yggdrasil's root, and then the count was over a hundred. Every time she thought that there could not possibly be any more draugar, another grasped her hand when she reached in through the hole.

After a while, the fires stopped raging as threateningly at Tyra's back, and she was certain that the shadowed warriors who had set off towards the battlefield had dimmed the fires to keep her safe, so that their kinsmen could be pulled through.

Hundreds of warriors Tyra pulled free from the dark. Soon, she no longer knew how many times she had wrenched a warrior free. All Tyra truly had to do was pull a warrior far enough out for the shadowed giant to grab each side of the small hole, and then they could wrench themselves through on their own.

It felt like days and nights passed as Tyra pulled warriors free of Yggdrasil's dark. The fires which had raged through the forest at her back still burned at the tops of some trees, but most of it had been extinguished. The flames no longer spread. The clashes of war from Ragnarok, beyond the mountains, also seemed further away, and smaller.

Tyra watched another shadow warrior climb out of the dark hole. She had pulled free hundreds and thousands, perhaps hundreds of thousands of people. Most of them were clearly warriors, and all of them were armed.

This one carried a spear. He was old. His beard and hair were both white, and he moved slowly. He was large, like the others. There was no doubt for Tyra anymore: they were all giants.

The warrior looked at her, like the others had. None of them seemed to quite understand how she had been able to pull them free of Yggdrasil. Tyra too did not quite understand, but she supposed that it was because the Darkness knew her. It had known her ever since the battle in Ash-hill when Siv had hidden her away inside the ash tree.

The old shadowed warrior leaned against his spear.

Tyra rose from the grass and readied to pull yet another free. The old giant draugar watched her approach the slim hole.

'One more,' he said.

Tyra stalled and stared up at him. She wasn't sure what she had heard. He couldn't have spoken. None of the other shadows had spoken to her.

The warrior seemed surprised at the sound of his own rusty voice. With a confused look on his face, he walked away. Along Yggdrasil's root, towards the final battle.

Tyra stared into the hole. One last giant to free, and then she too would head into battle. At last.

Smiling, she reached into the deep dark. A soft hand grabbed hers. This giant's hand was slender. That of a woman, not much larger than Tyra. The hand followed willingly as Tyra pulled it far enough out for the giantess to free herself.

She stood back and watched the last giant grab onto the edges of the slim hole and pull herself through. Gold-coloured hair surfaced. This giant too had braided her hair in the old style. Her hands did not hold onto weapons as the others had. Her gown sparkled and shone in the dimming flames. The giantess wrenched herself free, and at last placed both feet onto the grass, and looked up at Tyra. Exactly as hundreds and thousands of warriors had done before.

Tyra gaped up at the giantess, and before she could truly comprehend what had happened, or how, tears were streaming down her face, and she felt like a little girl again.

'Siv,' Tyra whispered through her tears.

Siv's wide shadow looked down at her. It cocked its head to the side as it examined Tyra. As if Siv couldn't quite recognise Tyra and tried to remember who she had been.

Tyra brushed the tears off her swollen cheeks, and only then did she remember. She had not just grown older since they had last seen each other. Death had not been kind to Tyra. Her cheeks were permanently swollen. In the afterlife, she did not look as she had alive. Her face had been smashed when she had died. Her jaw and nose were broken.

'Who?' asked Siv's draugar in a distant whisper. Her voice sounded exactly as it used to, so long ago. Suddenly, it felt like no time at all had passed since they had parted ways in the nornir's cave.

'Glumbruck,' Tyra whispered. It truly was Siv. She could hardly believe that they were standing in front of each other again. After so many winters and summers spent searching. At last, they were reunited. Right before the end. 'You said you would find me in the afterlife,' Tyra blurted her thoughts aloud. 'You promised, and here…' Siv had never made promises that she couldn't keep. Even in the end, everything she promised came true.

Siv's draugar was still staring at her, with narrowed eyes.

Tyra sniffed to stop her tears and brushed the last of them off her face to look at least a little more presentable. 'I'm your daughter, Glumbruck,' she said. 'Your only daughter. Tyra.'

Siv blinked her eyes furiously as she looked at Tyra, and took her in. Under Siv's questioning stare, Tyra suddenly felt how much she had changed. She was much taller than she had been, although Siv, too, was taller. She had taken on the full size of a giant.

'Tyra,' Siv repeated, and her face melted into a smile. 'Tyra.'

Siv reached out a hand to Tyra. All Tyra truly wanted was to bury herself in Siv's embrace and tell her how much she had missed her and how long she had searched, but all Siv offered was a hand. Tyra took a deep breath and stretched to take it.

Siv's hand had been cold when Tyra had reached into the Darkness to pull her out, but now it was warm. Siv clenched Tyra's hand. Such a small gesture, but it felt like a warm hug. Like at last, after all those winters of searching, she had finally come home.

'Tyra,' Siv said, again. Her voice sounded like a whisper, and her lips hardly parted. Instead, they clenched into a smile. 'Glumbruck,' she said, too.

She was still staring at Tyra as she said it, as if she thought that too was Tyra's name. As if the sound of her own name had become unfamiliar to her, and she no longer knew who she was.

'My daughter,' Siv added. The worry melted out of Tyra. Siv *did* know who she was. Her smile widened. 'I am your forefather.'

Siv clutched harder onto Tyra's hand. So much so that it almost hurt, and then it did.

Tyra snapped her attention down to her hand to free herself from Siv's hardening grip. Siv's shadow fingers no longer clasped Tyra's hand. They had gone through Tyra's skin. She was reaching inside her.

Siv stepped closer. Their arms began to merge. Siv's shadow was disappearing into Tyra. Even as a shadow, Siv's stare was piercing, and it petrified Tyra. She didn't dare to move. Beneath the surface of her arm, something warm moved, and Tyra felt stronger for it. It felt like Siv was giving her strength, the sort that Tyra had spent a lifetime trying to imitate after having watched Siv.

Tyra took a deep breath, and then Siv was gone. All of her shadowed self had disappeared. For a heartbeat, Tyra thought she had imagined it all. Exhausted from the long night, she must have fallen into a waking dream. Yet it had felt so real.

The warm feeling was still inside Tyra's arm. It spread up from her fist, to her shoulder, and then coursed through her body. It had not been a dream.

A calm settled over Tyra. Someone's reassuring thoughts whispered through her. Siv was with her. At last, they were together again. Closer than they had ever been. Strength that begged to be used made Tyra clench her hands into fists. Nothing could stand in her way. No warrior or giant. Not even gods were a match for her.

So, this was what it felt like to be as strong as Siv.

Hundreds of muscles flexed through her body with every tiny move. Siv's strength flowed through her and made her feel acutely aware of her own body, and of the strength that she had always possessed.

Tyra crouched down in the grass. She couldn't quite tell if it was her moving, or Siv. It felt a little like it was both of them. The thought to crouch had not come from Tyra herself, but the command did. They both decided it, together.

Tyra picked up the Yggdrasil bracteate. No one had to tell her what to do. Not even Siv had to steer her hand, for Tyra felt what the nine worlds wanted of her. The Darkness had called her here to pull Siv and the other giants free of the ash.

The bracteate itself seemed to yearn for the dark. Holding it in an outstretched hand, Tyra approached the dark hole into Yggdrasil's huge root. She cast the gold coin inside, and with a smile she turned away.

It felt like her life finally had meaning. All those winters and summers had shifted something within Tyra, and at last her lifelong sacrifice was being rewarded.

The nine worlds acknowledged her.

Force sailed through Tyra as she set off towards Ragnarok's battlefield. Siv's strength coursed through her, settled her heart so that nothing felt like a threat. Even death was nothing to be feared.

Tyra smiled as Siv's motherly voice whispered, guiding her to the final death.

FOREFATHERS

Chapter One Hundred and Eighty-Nine

At last, our weapons clash against others. At last, our voices have meaning. We are apart, but we have been one for so long, that even apart, out of the constraints of giant bodies, we think as one.

Our descendants roar in confusion. They are used to our voices within them, demanding to be heard and calling for blood. Without us, they stumble. They fall. We rush to their rescue, and to show them. We have not disappeared. We are not yet dead, but we are ready to be done.

We charge at gold-clad warriors. Arrows are shot. A kinsman is injured. We used to feel it, every injury and every death. Now our number no longer grows. We are one. We always have been. Soon, there will be none of us. We shall die here. Fighting the very battle we have spent centuries craving and calling for.

At last, we are free from our afterlife. At last, we may fight and die for good.

The Alfather no longer binds us to Yggdrasil. When we die,

we will be undone. At last. Returned to the nine worlds. As we were always meant to be.

With our help, many more shall be undone in this battle. Our weapons taste blood. We bite out necks and roar in freedom. Laughing, we kill. Smiling, we die.

FINN

Chapter One Hundred and Ninety

FINN WOKE HAZILY to his afterlife. All was dark around him, but there were voices nearby. Finn walked towards them. A song guided him ahead, to a tall slit of light in the dark. He could not quite make out the singers' words, but he heard Svend's voice, and he trusted his son to lead him into the afterlife.

With a longing sigh, Finn passed through the veil, into the light, and into his long-awaited afterlife.

The light dimmed around him as soon as he was through. The song disappeared. All that lit the room beyond was a low, guttering fire. A far wall had burned and was still flaming, just enough for the light to reach down a long hallway, glinting on the polished stones that made up the floor. There were huge gates at either side of the hallway, and when Finn tipped his head back and looked above, he saw no ceiling, only the glimmer of the hall's dying fire against some branches above.

Finn went straight to the nearest gate and pushed it open. His steps echoed far away. There was no light on the other side, but the fire from down the hallway lit the opening of an enormous room. In front of him were benches and long-tables. Half-full drinking horns had been tossed aside atop the tables and lay undisturbed among rotting meat.

Valhalla lay abandoned.

Finn backed away into the hallway again. The warriors were all gone. Finn stopped and listened carefully. He could hear more than the constant snap of fire at his back. A distant rumble and roaring voices, from outside.

Svend had been right. Tyra had known.

Ragnarok had begun, and Finn had arrived right on time. Before the end, as Valhalla's warriors had been called to battle to protect the great Alfather and all their gods.

Finn examined himself. Everything hurt from his death, but he had been burned on his funeral pyre with chainmail and worthy weapons. His own sword and a new axe with a nicer grip than his own worn-down one hung from his belt. Svend had done him great honour in death. His tunic was the bright red ceremonial one Svend had gifted him two winters past, and gold rings hung on his arms and fingers.

Finn grabbed the axe in his left hand. He held it around the axe-head. He also took out his sword, in his right hand, and went searching for a shield to use. At least he was equipped with a helmet.

Down the hall to his left was a bloody mass of something.

Cautiously, ready to strike, Finn approached.

The bloodied limbs of a warrior lay scattered across the hallway. First Finn encountered a torso in a chainmail that looked like it had been made from jewels. The arms and legs had all been torn off, but he could only see one broken piece of a leg, which lay across from a hip bone, sucked clean, next to the man's halved head.

The man's once-grey, almost white hair had been coloured light red, like Finn's tunic. The face had been split in half. The jaw had been torn off with the long beard. It lay several steps further down the hallway, by the top of the old man's head. His skull had been crushed and his brains torn out. It looked like someone had taken a bite out of his brains.

Finn gagged at the sight of it. He had seen many deaths in his long life, but never one quite as vile as this.

The warrior's long spear had been cracked in half and lay next to the half-eaten mass of brains. The spear was crooked, looking as much like a walking stick as a spear. Runes had been carved along the shaft. Never before had Finn seen a warrior torn apart like this and left to rot.

A gory trail of pieces of guts and bloody paw prints showed the way to a broken gate at the end of the hallway. The blood trail led all the way to the broken gate, and outside, into a night full of screams.

Finn's bones groaned as he walked towards the broken gate. It looked like the gate had been torn open by a huge beast.

Finn was not scared of anything. Only a draugar could make his skin prickle with goosebumps, but this... this was something he could never have imagined. He stared back over his shoulder to the old man who had been torn apart and half eaten.

A huge beast. The beautiful, broken spear at the old man's side. His perfectly combed beard. The jewelled pieces of chainmail. Finn stared back at the top part of the man's head. There was the final clue: a single open eye, staring out in terror.

The Alfather's corpse.

Finn's stomach convulsed. Vomit filled his mouth, and Finn coughed it out. That torn up corpse was his god. The bile kept coming at the mere thought. It spilled out of his mouth and ran from his nose. Finn managed to keep down the next surge.

He spat out a last scrap. Something got stuck at the top of his nose and made him gag again. He coughed. The bitter smell of it lingered, as he looked up from his final chewed dinner in life, at the bloody remains of his god.

Finn wiped his mouth with the back of his hand and stumbled away from the gory pieces of the Alfather's corpse. He was too late. Ragnarok was over and done. His gods were dead.

Beasts howled outside, in the impenetrable darkness of Ragnarok. They had killed the Alfather, but they would pay with their life, Finn decided. His head was spinning—and now that his stomach was empty, he felt weary and weak, too—but he was still a warrior of Valhalla.

Late or not, he had woken up in the Alfather's hall. That made him one of Odin's proud warriors. Even with the end upon them, he could not give up, or give in.

The axe head was firm in Finn's left grip, and he raised his sword properly. He walked all the way to the broken gate. The noise outside was deafening: screaming and hissing and roars all around. Careful of splinters, Finn walked over the broken planks and outside.

The fire from down the hallway lit the first few arm-lengths. Beyond that, the battlefield was loud, but dark.

Finn took a deep breath and readied for the confusion that would follow. He was too old to rush. He took another deep breath and set out.

The ground was littered with cold, rotting corpses. Finn had barely walked across two of them, relying on the light from the hallway to see, when his first opponent on Ragnarok's battlefield appeared before him.

A tall man, perhaps a half-giant, stood above him, but the light from the hallway went straight through him. He was nothing but an eerie shadow. A draugar.

A yelp burst out of Finn before he could hold it back. His reflexes acted first. He lashed out at the draugar, swinging his sword with all his might so he nearly tumbled over from the blow, but it went straight through the shadowed warrior's stomach. As if there was no one there.

The tall draugar smiled down at Finn and delivered its blow. An axe as tall as Finn's head hammered down towards him. It hacked straight through his helmet and opened his skull.

BUNTRUGG

Chapter One Hundred and Ninety-One

MUSPELHEIM FELT SO lonely and dark. Skoll and Hati had devoured thousands of flames; the few remaining had left this world to devour the plains of Ragnarok, and Buntrugg knew that they would not be back. He had counted on the fragments that each demon had left behind when they had gone to war, but they had been consumed by the two wolves.

Even the forefathers were gone. There was silence inside Buntrugg, like he had only experienced that once, in a passage grave with a dwarf. When the forefathers had left, and he had seen their faces. Now they were gone from within him. And they weren't laughing in Midgard, either. They were simply gone. To fight and die at Ragnarok, like all other giants.

There was nothing left of the fire demons who had gone to Asgard either, but there were still a few faint flames left in Muspelheim.

Nestled inside Buntrugg's closed fist were the last nine flames in all of Muspelheim. He had kept them warm in the palm of his hand.

Buntrugg unfolded his burned fingers from around them. Nine distinct flames lit the scorched world of Muspelheim around him. Each small flame had a slightly different tint from one another.

One was Buntrugg's own, that he had captured long ago to scare the svartalvar into helping him, but the other eight were not entirely his. They were demons who had left Muspelheim to feed upon fires in one of the other eight worlds. They had left before Muspel and the rest of them had gone to fight at Ragnarok.

The eight flames in Buntrugg's palm were pieces of fire demons who had escaped into Midgard. They raged across the lands of the short-lived with their eager fires.

For a long time Buntrugg had lain in the dark of Muspelheim, recovering from his wounds and gathering the strength to pull these eight demons back into the world of fire. Only with fire demons burning hot in Muspelheim did the other eight worlds have a chance of surviving past Ragnarok.

Buntrugg set down one of the flames in his palm.

'Raido.' He called upon the traveller's rune, and then he combined it with another. 'Othila.' The rune of home and family.

In his mind he imagined their combined bindrune as he repeated the names of the two runes, again and again. He chanted the runes, loudly and clearly, so that no matter where in Midgard the rest of the fire demon was, it would hear his call, and know to return home.

His chant gained in intensity, out of his desperation to save the nine worlds. At last, a sharp sound cut through, and a veil opened between this world, and that of the short-lived. Buntrugg kept calling with the runes.

He reached through the veil, and wrenched a fire demon back home, into Muspelheim. The demon cackled nervously at the sight of Buntrugg and its empty home.

Buntrugg did not have time to halt his work. He set down yet another small flame and began to chant the runes again. Seven more fire demons Buntrugg wrenched out of Midgard, back to their homeland, so that all that was left in his palm was his own Muspel flame, and then he released even that one.

This world needed all the fire and heat it could get, if flames were to spread anew and suns were ever to rise over the horizon of the nine worlds.

Nine fire demons danced across the vast lands of Muspelheim. Given time and care, they would spread. Once more the sun would rise in the nine worlds. Those who survived Ragnarok would be safe. They would not die from cold, in darkness. Light would greet them after the last battle, and warm their skins.

The night was over. The sun would rise over Midgard's innocent grave mounds. In Helheim it would push away the rainy clouds. It would once more set over Svartalfheim's desert and shine through the glass ceilings of Alfheim's halls. Vanaheim's fields would grow again. Home in Jotunheim, the snow would melt, and rivers would flow into the valleys, and in Asgard the sun would warm Yggdrasil's proud leaves. Even in Niflheim, the light would dance through the pillars of ice, while here in Muspelheim, the flames would spread, and once more, fire would consume.

No one else would perish from Buntrugg's mistakes. With a satisfied sigh, Buntrugg lay flat on Muspelheim's ash-covered ground, and this time, he knew for certain, he would never again rise.

DARKNESS

AT LAST, RAGNAR felt ready to say his final goodbyes. Silently, he tapped his distaff, which pushed away the Darkness. With a shriek, a white thread surged out from the hollow tip and tore a veiled opening out of the dark.

Ragnar stepped through. He arrived in the familiar alvar bathhouse, where Siv lived the last three winters before Ragnarok. This was the final time he would come. She had taught him the runes, and she had taught him how to survive in the Darkness. She had even taught him why he was there. He had doomed himself to this fate, and no longer did he wonder what his role was and why the gods had destined him for this afterlife. He had destined himself to it.

'What have you come to discuss today, Ragnar?' asked Siv as she entered.

I have come to say goodbye, Ragnar replied through his thoughts, and with runes.

'Have you found a way to leave the Darkness?' she asked, and coming from Siv it did not feel like a taunt. She was merely asking, and although there was that tiny hole out of which Ragnar could sometimes see, there was no way to exit the Darkness.

I was foolish to ever think I could leave, answered Ragnar through his thoughts. *You were right, after all. I doomed myself to this fate. To be fate itself.*

'Perhaps it wasn't so much you, as it was the nine worlds,' Siv suggested.

Ragnar did not quite know what to say to that. It was a somewhat consoling thought.

'You were destined for this life, at birth,' said Siv. 'Your bloodline marked you for it, as it marks us all. You can only do so much to escape the pull of your bloodline, for without the blood in your veins, you wouldn't be alive, not even in the afterlife.'

She was right. As ever, Siv told him exactly what he needed to hear to continue his journey in the dark. He would miss her, but they had already spent so long together. Learning runes and practising them. Seeing her like this, elegantly seated on the far bench in the bathhouse, with her long golden hair braided perfectly to the side, and her calm stare, it was easier to say goodbye.

'I'm ready to return,' Ragnar said aloud to the Darkness.

He waited for the shadowed warriors to attack and kill him. None did. No one came for him. But he still needed to die in order to move out of the veiled vision, and back into the Darkness.

Knowing what he needed to do, Ragnar let out a ragged breath and lifted his distaff in both hands. The end of it was made of a long, twisted narwhale tooth. Ragnar gulped. He knew that there was only one way to leave this place. So, he placed the distaff over his heart, and gathered all the bravery he had in him. Even all of that he had never known he possessed.

Hard, he forced the distaff into his chest. Blood splashed over his fingers. Pain surged through him, and Ragnar screamed.

Death, pain, and fear.

* * *

RAGNAR TREMBLED FROM terror. He was returned to the Darkness. Hundreds of deaths he had suffered in this place, but never had one hurt as much. The mere memory of it made him sweat. He held the distaff loosely in his hand and tried not to remember what he had done with it, and to focus on something else.

The Darkness felt different, somehow. Colder, if such a thing was even possible.

Ragnar did not immediately tap his runic distaff to seek refuge beyond the veil, in another world. He still vividly remembered his own funeral. Seeing his own corpse burn on the pyre and dooming himself to this Darkness.

The dot had returned. The hole out of the Darkness. Something wild like fire glimmered beyond. Needing a moment to himself, Ragnar marched towards it. Through the dark, and straight towards the hole, until he stood right in front of it.

He had expected the shadow warriors to still be crowded around it, as they had been for so long, but they were not there.

Shields had been abandoned below the little hole out of the Darkness, as if the shadowed warriors had left, and at the very top, above hundreds of shields, lay a perfect gold neck-ring. It shone in the little light that entered the Darkness through the hole. Ragnar took the gold bracteate.

There were so many abandoned shields at his feet. The shadowed warriors who had killed him over and over did not seem like the kind to set down their shields.

Ragnar turned the bracteate in his hand and narrowed his eyes at it. It was exactly like the one Einer had worn at his funeral. The one Ragnar had used to doom himself to a lifetime in this dark. It was identical to the one Odin had worn when Ragnar had hung the god from Yggdrasil.

Ragnar lifted the bracteate and slipped on the neck-ring. It felt comfortable and warm on his chest, like it belonged there, and he felt a certain strength from wearing it.

Bravely, Ragnar looked into the deep dark, and after many lifetimes and many deaths, he dared, once more, to speak. 'Hei,' he shouted into the Darkness.

Great drums were beating, and they approached, closer and closer. Ragnar flinched with the sound, certain that a hammer would split his skull, or a sword would hack off his hands, or a spear would pierce his chest. Yet nothing happened.

The beating sound came closer and closer. It matched Ragnar's speeding heartbeat, and then it stopped. It sounded like the drummer was standing right in front of him.

'Ragnar?' asked a voice. It wasn't Siv, but a man. One of the shadowed warriors had spoken.

Kauna, Ragnar thought, demanding that his distaff push the Darkness away so that he could see who it had been. To his left, a large stallion pranced.

Ragnar held out a hand to its muzzle, and the horse pushed softly against him. He knew that horse.

'We've looked everywhere for you,' said the voice, and it wasn't the horse speaking, and it wasn't a shadow warrior either. The voice came from above. Ragnar tilted his head back and looked up. He forced his distaff to push the dark further back.

On the horse sat a middle-aged man with short brown hair. He was dressed in a ragged brown tunic. A thrall's clothing. On Ragnar's own funeral pyre, his thrall had been wearing the exact same tunic.

'Carlman?' Ragnar whispered.

Carlman smiled down at him and dismounted the horse. He held the reins out to Ragnar, to offer him the honour. Ragnar just stood and watched, clenching onto his runic distaff. There was his loyal thrall, in Ragnar's Darkness. A friend in a time of need.

Ragnar threw his arms around Carlman and hugged him so tight that he thought he might break his own bones. It felt good to hold someone again. He had forgotten what it felt like. After such a long time in the Darkness, he had forgotten. What it was like to live, and be alive.

'I've missed you, my friend,' Ragnar cried into Carlman's shoulder. 'I should have known. I should have known.'

The horse neighed impatiently, but Ragnar did not let go of his loyal thrall.

When he had first woken up in the afterlife, he had been riding the stallion through the dark, and Carlman had been walking at his side, but it all seemed so long ago, and since that first death, he had forgotten all about it. For what felt like centuries, he had been stuck in this nightmare, all alone, never knowing that a friend had been there with him, all along.

At last, Ragnar knew. He was no longer alone in the Darkness.

HILDA

Chapter One Hundred and Ninety-Two

'Who is Ragnar Erikson to you?' the veulve asked Hilda. The one thing the veulve couldn't see, despite her endless stream of visions. No one truly saw Hilda's past. 'How do you know Ragnar?'

'He's my kinsman,' said Hilda. All those with norn blood were her kin, she knew now. Even Loki, and the veulve. Perhaps the Alfather, too. He had conjured visions for her on the battlefield. 'The same as he is to you,' Hilda said. 'The story-maker.'

'He is fate,' the veulve added. 'Destiny.'

'I have no destiny,' Hilda said. Saying those words made her realise that she had no father either. He could not remember her. For even fate had forgotten to spin her future. If her father was fate itself, then he, too, had forgotten all about her. Like the veulve, the Alfather, and everyone else.

No one knew who Hilda was and had been but herself, and perhaps Einer's white bear. It had recognised her and looked at her and roared to her. In the end. After he had died.

'Do you want to know more, or what?' the veulve asked in the exact same tone as Hilda's father had done, when he had used to tell the old stories. She missed him. She missed how things used to be. Before her father had died and Ash-hill had burned.

Late summer days they used to gather around bonfires at the beach. All the young villagers, and some of the older ones, too. Her father had rarely ever joined, but sometimes Hilda's uncle and aunt had used to sit around and sing songs with them.

In the winter, she and Einer used to do a hundred things. Each day they had left to train together, but by the end of the day, when they came home again, and her father had asked what they had done, they had been up to so much, that all Hilda had known to say was: "nothing". Even on the rainy days, and there had been many of those, Hilda had been outside in the woods all day, and come home with some firewood, to look useful, and her dresses muddy all the way up to the hips. The days had been packed with adventures. There had been no real threats.

She had always had a home, at the end of the day, wherein a fire burned. In the evenings her father always used to tell stories, sitting around the fire and cooking dinner. Sometimes it had only been Hilda and her cousins listening, sometimes it had been half the village. There was a certain comfort to knowing that even in his afterlife, her father was still spinning tales and stories.

Hilda let out a ragged breath. She, too, had come here to spin. A life needed to be preserved. For the sake of the nine worlds, and a little for Hilda's sake, too.

'When destinies are spun, does it matter where they are tied up?' Hilda asked.

'As long as they are spun, the story-maker takes care of them,' the veulve answered. 'Do you want to know more, or what?'

'Nej,' Hilda said. She had all the answers that mattered. She knew what needed to be done. Loki had shown her how to revive a giant, expecting Hilda to do the same for him after Ragnarok. For three long winters, she had watched the nornir work with destinies. She knew how to undo deaths.

Hilda opened her eyes to the dark, except the dark was not as complete as it had been. The veulve's pale face was half an arm-length away from Hilda's own. Her starry eyes looked beyond, at the visions. Light came into the hut at Hilda's back. The horizon was brightening; morning was near. The morning after Ragnarok, which meant that the Alfather was dead already.

There was no time to waste.

The veulve didn't seem to have noticed that the final night of Ragnarok had come to an end. She held a runic distaff in both hands, like the kind the three nornir had used to spin destinies. A spindle was fastened into her belt, like the ones the three nornir used to spin fates. The veulve's tall distaff went all the way to the ground like a walking staff.

Hilda kicked the runic distaff, and the veulve crashed onto the floor. Hilda bent and wrenched the runic distaff from the veulve's grip. She snatched the spindle from the veulve's belt. The time had come to spin one last destiny.

She had come here knowing that to spin a destiny, three things were needed. A norn to spin the thread, a runic distaff and spindle to do the spinning, and another norn's blood to spin with.

Hilda planted the sharp end of the distaff at the veulve's stomach.

This time, Hilda would not be the one whose name and lineage and destiny was taken. For three winters, she had watched the nornir spin destinies. It couldn't possibly be that difficult. This time, Hilda would be the one to do the spinning.

Now she knew for certain that the veulve was her kin. Her blood would make a beautiful thread. The blood of an ancient being like her had to be more powerful than Hilda's own. Hilda stared down hard at the helpless woman at her feet.

The veulve didn't squirm away, even with the sharp end of her own distaff pointing at her guts. She had to know what came next, yet she offered herself up willingly. Hilda didn't like that. It didn't feel right. As if the veulve knew something that

Hilda didn't. As if she could see some future with her starry eyes that meant she didn't have to fight.

Hilda glanced over her shoulder and out of the house. The sky was brightening. Smoke and clouds dotted the sky, coloured purple. It wouldn't be long before the sun was up. The field outside was bare. It had burned down. No one was coming to save the veulve. Yet she just lay there, accepting that Hilda would drain her blood and take away every memory of her from the nine worlds.

As if she had known this would happen.

'If you knew what I intended, then why?' Hilda asked. The veulve could have left. She still could. At the very least, she could fight back, with runes, even with force.

'I die free from my shackles,' the veulve responded. She sat up a little more erect, but made no move to fight Hilda for the distaff. 'It's all I have ever wanted. To die and be returned to the nine worlds.'

'You won't die,' Hilda said, for she had been there, on the other side of the distaff, and she thought she knew. 'Probably,' she added, as once Loki and the three nornir had assured her.

The veulve smiled bitterly. Clearly, she disagreed, and she was not just a norn, like Hilda. She was *the veulve*. The most powerful of all the nornir. She knew the future, all of it. She knew her fate.

The veulve grabbed the end of the distaff and placed it over her own heart. She didn't want to survive. She didn't want to be remembered.

'They always chased my words. They all wanted to know what my eyes saw,' the veulve said. 'I won't gain true freedom until they no longer remember. I will always be captured, in the past and in the future. Unless they forget. Unless all of you forget.'

Hilda tried to retrieve the distaff. This wasn't how it was supposed to go. The veulve wasn't supposed to let herself be sacrificed. It wasn't even supposed to be her, at the other end of the distaff. Except, she had revealed that the two of them were kin, and if Hilda's blood worked, the veulve's had to as well.

Even so, it wasn't meant to be like this.

Hilda thought she heard her snow fox yelp. She snapped her head around, stared out into the field at her back. Her snow fox wasn't there. When Hilda looked back down at the veulve, she expected her to be gone, but she wasn't. The woman still lay there, waiting for Hilda to strike the fatal blow. To spin one last destiny from her blood.

'All I want is to be free to die,' the veulve pleaded. 'Allow me to be dead. In the future, in the present, and in the past. Let me perish. Allow my Asgard-bound corpse to rot. Let my knowledge flow into Yggdrasil's dark, again. Let me be nothing. Let me be whole.'

Hilda clenched her teeth in resolution. Even the veulve wanted it to be this way. The sun was coming up outside. She could see the veulve's face clearly. All that fear of death. Her quivering lips, and the resolution to stay seated.

Hilda took a deep breath. She had to do it now, or it may be too late.

With a grunt Hilda thrust the distaff deep into the veulve's chest. The veulve screamed from pain. Hilda pushed harder into the woman's heart. The scream died instantly—and the veulve, too. She fell flat onto the blood-sticky ground. Hilda held the sharp end of the distaff steadily against the veulve's heart. The hollow edge of the distaff began to fill with blood.

For a heartbeat longer, Hilda hesitated to begin her work. The Alfather had sent her off to revive him after the battle, but she didn't have to. She could revive Loki instead of the Alfather and change the fate of the nine worlds. She could tip the scales in the favour of giants, as Loki had wanted. But as she plunged the distaff deeper into the veulve's heart, only one name brushed against her lips.

Einer. Einer. Einer.

She began to hum, as once the three nornir had done, when it had been Hilda lying on the floor in a pool of her own blood. She didn't know where the song came from, but as she thought of Einer, it was as if the wind and the runes themselves hummed along with her. The song of his life. The song that had led him to death.

She would slow his song. Stretch his life longer.

Her singing voice was husky, and not practised like that of the three nornir. Her spinning was rough. Einer's thread was the first she had ever truly spun. The last time she had spun anything at all, she had been a child, back in Ash-Hill, and Einer had been spinning at her side. They had been laughing over how even his thread was prettier than Hilda's masterwork.

Einer's blooded destiny began to stretch as Hilda spun. She held her tongue between her lips to focus. His destiny had to be perfect. Not like the few threads she had spun as a child. It had to be as perfect as Einer would have made it. So, Hilda took her time.

Never before had she taken her time with anything. Never before had she thought she would slow down. Einer's song was comfortable to hum. It slowed Hilda's heartbeat and forced her breathing to become deeper and calmer.

The tune was cheerful, reminding her of so many old memories. Like that week when the entire town had thought she and Einer had run away from home, but really, they had just been hiding on the warships and played raiders all week. Hilda had been eight, and she remembered that she had been the one to insist that it would be fun. When they had been found out, she had told the chief that Einer had suggested it. Einer had been too shocked to contradict her.

Einer had never said no to any game Hilda had suggested. Even the death swim that had nearly killed them both. Or the barrel run where Hilda and five other kids had stuffed Einer into a mostly empty mead barrel and—accidentally—pushed him down the hill. Hilda had run off to tell Einer's mother, and pretended she had nothing to do with it. Einer had been rescued, mostly in good health. He had rolled out of the barrel, drunk on mead, and with a broken ankle and a swollen eye.

She had spent all winter apologising. She had even promised to never ever hurt him again, though that promise hadn't lasted long. At the end of summer, Einer had fallen off the roof, and this time he was sent to the village healer with a broken wrist.

Einer's destiny thread stretched out of Hilda's spindle, as she hummed and thought of the old days. She had so many good memories featuring Einer. Soon they would be sharing them again and laughing over them.

She missed his dumb farmer smile. How droopy his eyes would get, and how goofy he sounded when he was really laughing. She imagined he would smile and laugh like that when he saw her on the cooling battlefield and recognised her.

Even among the thousands and thousands of corpses, he would be easy to find. There wouldn't be many other survivors, and with the huge white bear fylgja at his back, Einer would be easy to spot. She was certain the bear wouldn't have left him. It hadn't left when he had died. It had even looked at Hilda, as if it knew what she would do. Before she herself had known.

Einer's thread began to shine in the sunlight. It looked like silver, dipped in blood. It was rolled into a long bundle on the floor, and Hilda kept spinning. She turned the distaff into the heart of the woman who lay at her feet and spun the spindle with care.

The life song that she hummed had slowed. His life would be long.

Finally, the spindle stopped turning, and when she looked up at the runic distaff, Hilda saw that she had used all the blood it had sucked up. Her song ended.

She let go of the distaff and dropped the spindle. In her hands she took Einer's life thread. Watched the perfect thread as it lay prettily in her palms. Even the three nornir couldn't have made a better thread. They had been right. She was a norn, like them, and she had talent.

A woman lay at Hilda's feet. She was soaked in blood. Her heart had been pierced by a weapon. Hilda stared up from Einer's perfect thread to the woman. Her face was pale. She was dead, and Hilda knew that it was her who had done it. She had intended to kill someone, but she couldn't remember who, and she didn't know why the woman lay there. Who she even was. Whoever she had been, she didn't matter.

Hilda coiled up Einer's perfect blood thread. She didn't want to stuff it carelessly into her belt and risk breaking it, so she spent a few heartbeats coiling it in her palm.

It looked so fragile, but she knew it was strong. Perfect, even. All it needed now was to be hung up in the nornir's cave. She would bind it up high in the nornir's hall for safe keeping.

Hilda smiled down at her creation. At last, she was no longer alone in the nine worlds. Einer was out there, with his white bear fylgja. The white bear had looked at her, above the heads of thousands of warriors. It remembered. Einer knew who she was. Somewhere out there, he was waking from death. A lone warrior waking after Ragnarok.

Loki, the Alfather. They had both thought that it would be them. They had both tried to trick Hilda into reviving them after the end, so they could rule over the nine worlds. But what the nine worlds needed wasn't more cunning.

The sun was coming up. It shone through the open door and warmed Hilda's back. Gods and giants were dead. The nine worlds needed nothing more.

For winters and summers, the nine worlds had done nothing but take, from Hilda and from everyone she loved. They had taken and never given back. The time had come for that to change. For all of Hilda's sacrifices to be rewarded.

Her father had always said that sacrifices were rewarded. He owed her. The story-maker, destiny itself, owed her this. At the very least. After everything he had allowed to be taken from his own daughter, he owed her this much. What use had her father's life been, if he couldn't even reward his own daughter's sacrifices in death?

Hilda had finally found something that *she* needed. A home. She needed Einer.

MUNIN

Chapter One Hundred and Ninety-Three

My radiant home has been burned and ruined. My wings are spread wide as I glide across mountains and valleys of corpses. Rivers of blood spill out over Asgard's fertile fields. Crops have been drowned in blood. I would fear for our survival, but there are so few of us left that even if all that Asgard leaves us is a single field to live upon, we shall live.

'*To begin with, the beginning had not begun,*' I croak to remember.

We had thought the sun lost, and the moon, too. We had thought that we would die of cold before we would perish from hunger. But the sun rises anew, and my heart beats with a pure certainty that even the moon shall be revived. We will have to make new lives for ourselves.

My beak lets out an aching caw. There is no more *we*. The thought makes my feathers shake.

My brother is somewhere down there, dead at the dirty hands of Glumbruck's son. My master, too, has been taken from me. My mind is empty without them here. We used to always be connected. I used to always know when they were near, and now all I feel is that they *aren't*, and never will be.

I fear that I shall never learn to think for myself. I fear that they shall always be in my thoughts, and I shall always seek to fill that great void that they leave behind. My chest feels empty, and my heart feels like its bleeding, but I have checked, more than once, and I am not wounded.

My slick wings have taken me far. Beyond Asgard's enormous wall, to the real, far-away mountains of this world. Not those made of the corpses of my friends and kinsmen, and of my deepest enemies, but mountains that my Alfather made once upon a time, using teeth from Ymir's frozen corpse. The great mountains whose ancient passages open into the other eight worlds.

My brother and I used to fly through those passages when we left on our Alfather's missions. I have flown across my world without thinking, and my wings brought me here, where nothing seems to have changed.

Except that something is moving down there.

I fold up my wings, eager to discover something worthy of a report.

There are corpses outside the gates of Asgard.

Hel has kept her promises. Her gates stand open, and Helheim's corpses are walking into Asgard, soon to find their gods and kinsmen dead. All of them dead, along with mine.

And though I have finally found news to report, there is no one to tell it to. My Alfather is not waiting for my return, eager to hear my whispers. My brother no longer urges me to fly faster, so we can get home.

That life was mine for many centuries, but it shall never be so again.

I remember, for I always do, as the Alfather tasked me to do. Once in Valhalla, there was a giant in the back room. I remember how large he was and how his arms and face and all his skin was burned and wrinkled with scars. He spoke to me, once. To me—not to Hugin and not to our Alfather. Just to me.

I let the memory flood me, as I have often done, and remember once more what the terrible giant said to me.

"*He is you and you are him. What you see, he sees. What you hear, he hears. You are him, but you are also you. A servant for now, but not forever.*"

I shall learn to survive, for I was warned. Eventually, I shall learn to live, too. For my brother is gone, my master is dead, and neither one of them shall ever rise again, but my black wings still taste Asgard's winds. The nine worlds unfold beneath me, and there is still much to see.

'*Because change changes and does not change back*,' I sing from up in the skies.

Although I am alone, my name is Munin—memory—and I shall remember for the nine worlds. I witnessed the final battle. I know who died, and I know why. She thinks I don't remember her, but I remember *everything*. Even that which has been robbed from other minds. I know it all, and I shall remember, until my wings tire and I can no longer glide across the skies. I shall tell their stories.

'*And, in the end, the ending will not come to an end.*'

EINER

Chapter One Hundred and Ninety-Four

EINER BLINKED HIMSELF awake. He was dead. Every bone in his body confirmed that he had died. His stomach ached more than anywhere else, where the Alfather had stabbed him with the runic spear. Everything stung, and the pain worsened the longer he lay still, staring up. There was light somewhere out there, but something pressed on his chest, and something else had been laid across his face so he couldn't see. Einer had no strength to try to move. At least, not yet.

His heart beat uneasily; no forefathers steadied him. So, this was the afterlife. Without the support of the forefathers within him, Einer felt bare. No one steered his hand and focused him. There was no chant and no strength to pull from. The pain was deafening. Einer could hardly hear his own thoughts, and his chest felt tight from whatever had fallen on top of him. He needed to get free so he could breathe again.

For a few good heartbeats he lay and steadied his breathing, gathering his forces and trying to convince all his limbs to help him move. He tried to push himself up, but whatever had been slung across his chest was too heavy to lift far. Einer tried to knock off whatever lay over his face, and his fist clanged against a metal shield. He forced the shield away and pulled himself up and out. A giant's leg was draped across his chest.

Einer slung himself under it, groaning from how much his limbs hurt as he moved.

When at last his legs were free, and his Ulfberht sword, too, he let out a heavy sigh. He had not expected to wake up to an afterlife, and as Einer looked far off into the distance at the sun hanging low in the horizon, he saw the mountains of corpses beneath and knew that this was not an afterlife. This was where he had fought and died.

He had woken up to Asgard. To life, and not to death.

Corpses of giants and warriors and monsters were mingled on the battlefield under Einer, and all around him. The sun beamed over them, and no one was moving. The battle had to be over, although it couldn't be, because Einer was still alive, or alive again. If this was the afterlife, that meant they had failed. The Alfather must have survived, for the afterlives to not have been abolished as they were meant to be.

Yet, the forefathers were gone. That should have been his afterlife, too: an angry forefather, raging for blood and revenge. They were all gone. All the dead giants who had steadied Einer's breaths.

Without them, his breathing was ragged and the pain in his limbs was difficult to ignore. Einer looked around at the neverending piles of the dead around him, and something moved. It wasn't one of the corpses, but a living being.

A woman stood at a distance, looking at him. She was entirely covered in blood, as if she had been dipped in it. Her braided hair had been blonde, but was coloured red by the blood. Her dress and her chainmail, her arms and legs and even her face, were all smeared in red. Her raised eyebrows and sharp jawline made her stare feel as deadly as the spear that had cut into Einer's guts and killed him.

'Hei,' she said.

'Hei,' he replied.

For many heartbeats that was all either of them said.

At last, she moved closer. Slowly, she balanced from one body to the next, down towards Einer. He took a few rapid breaths and forced himself to stand up. His legs hurt, but standing up helped, and moving did too. The pain was more bearable when he moved. Einer was relieved: in that case, the wounds would heal nicely, given time and care. The Ulfberht sword hung loosely in his grip.

The woman stared straight at him as she approached. Although she moved slowly, with a limp, there was a certainty to her steps. There was caution in her, but no hesitation.

Einer kept the Ulfberht in his grip, and readied to defend himself.

The woman held nothing in her hands, but a short axe hung from her belt behind some dark feathers. A dead crow had been stuffed into her belt, or perhaps only a skin. She came into his reach; if Einer wanted to, he could strike her with his Ulfberht, but he did not, and she did not draw her own weapon, merely came closer.

She came so close that a sole arm-length separated them.

'Hei,' she whispered this time and smiled at him.

She looked at him as if she was waiting for something, but Einer didn't know what. The square chin and those deep blue eyes seemed so familiar, although her features were obscured by the blood that she was drenched in.

'I know you,' he finally whispered back.

Something happened behind her eyes as he said it, and her lips wrenched into a smile that made Einer forget what he was about to say.

She was beautiful when she smiled, even more so for the blood she was drenched in. Even her teeth were bloody as she smiled. Her smile reached every part of her face. Her cheeks shot up and her eyes narrowed, wrinkling at the corners. She radiated when she smiled, and before Einer knew it, he was smiling foolishly at the sight of her.

'I knew you would remember,' she said. She cackled, wickedly.

Einer searched through his memories. He had definitely seen her before. He knew her. Suddenly, as if the thought had been put there by someone else, he remembered exactly where he knew her from.

'The valkyrie with the blood tears,' he said. There was much more blood on her now than there had been. She looked like she had been swimming in a red river. 'You were fighting at the Alfather's side.'

'And you were with the giants,' said she, unimpressed. The revelation that they had fought on opposing sides did not particularly seem to bother her.

Einer's grip on his Ulfberht sword relaxed. She stared at him and glanced down to his sword. Immediately, he slid it into a belt clasp. His scabbard had fallen off at some point during the battle, or perhaps after he had died.

By the time the sword was secure, the woman had walked straight past him, and was climbing the steep side of a corpse mountain.

'Are you coming?' she stopped to ask, a few paces further along.

'Where to?'

She wriggled her sharp nose as she looked around at the mountains of corpses. 'Away. It reeks here.'

Einer laughed, and so did she. It felt good to laugh.

Because that was the truth, here at the end of it all, atop the corpses of friends and gods. Once it was all over, they were all just rotting meat, with a horrid stench. Einer forced himself to move. He balanced on top of bodies with difficulty and tried to brush his tunic clean. He did not quite know why he bothered. Blood, his own and that of others, had long dried into the fabric and stiffened it.

He tried to break into a run, but his limbs were all too tired to allow it, so he merely walked after her as fast as he could. They both struggled up the steep slope of the corpse mountain. Despite her limp, the woman was a little faster to reach the top than Einer.

'Hurry up,' she called down to him. 'The view isn't so bad.'

Einer pushed himself ahead the last of the way. She was right. The sun bathed Asgard and Yggdrasil in gold. The ash tree's branches cast beautiful snaking shadows over the corpse valleys. All over, golden shields twinkled in the morning light.

The woman was smiling as she looked across the bloodied plains.

'So, you're a valkyrie?' Einer asked at last.

Her beautiful smile faded at his question, and Einer's heart sank. He felt like he had done something terrible, although he did not know what.

'Nej,' she answered, quite simply. In a steady pace that Einer could not quite follow, she began to walk down the mountain of the dead.

'I was dead,' he explained, waddling inelegantly across corpses to catch up with her. 'I died.'

The revelation did not impress her. 'As did we all, at some point,' she wisely said without addressing his implied question. Had it been she who had woken him from death?

Einer tilted his head to the side. He had most definitely died. He checked his chest, and his heart beat true, and his chest was comfortable to the touch, not burning hot as it had been when his gold bracteate had saved him in the past. It had been something else this time; some other circumstance.

'Is everyone else…?'

'Dead,' she confirmed. She was still walking ahead of him, but she had slowed her walk to allow him to catch up. 'Everyone on this battlefield.'

Nothing moved across the long rows of mountains. No one else was travelling across Ida's plain. There were not even any birds in the sky. It was still too early for the flies to find the battlefield.

'Who won?' Einer asked, staring out at the dead fighters. In death, wolves, giants, gods and short-lived all looked alike.

'Ragnarok won,' answered the woman. 'The nine worlds got their way.'

Loki had been successful, then, Einer thought, and he wondered if somewhere else on this battlefield, the crafty giant was waking up to the afterlife, like him. Loki must have hidden a norn away to spin him alive, that must have been his plan, or maybe it was a valkyrie he had swayed to wake him. But the battlefield seemed entirely dead. No one was alive, apart from the two of them.

'Did you survive the battle?' Einer didn't quite know what else to ask.

'I suppose I did.'

'How?' She looked like the kind of warrior who would be the last one standing, almost like she had taken the last swing and killed the final fighter on this battlefield.

'The nornir forgot to spin a destiny for me, so there was nothing to cut at Ragnarok.' She chuckled at her own words. 'It seems like fate was kind to me, in the end.' She smiled mysteriously as if that meant something more to her than it did to him. 'I suppose fate was kind to you, too.'

He matched her smile and stared at her. When he had first seen her standing on the rotting hill, he had expected that she would come swinging an axe and kill him. She was certainly capable of it, but she had not done that, and Einer could not quite comprehend why, or how she was even there, alive. How he himself was alive.

Her stare turned intense. Einer realised that he had been gaping at her. He closed his mouth and tried to remember what he had been about to say.

'I'm Einer Vigmerson,' he said, in a hurry to introduce himself properly to her, but then he corrected himself. 'Einer Glumbruckson.'

'Glumbruckson,' the girl repeated, and the name made her smile.

'Did you know her, too?' Everyone in the nine worlds seemed to react at the mention of his mother's name. They all seemed to know who she had been, and often he thought that they knew more about her than he had himself.

'Know who?' asked the sharp girl.

'Glumbruck was my mother's name,' Einer explained. 'I'm told she was famous in Asgard.'

The girl nodded slowly at that, as if she had to think about it, before she answered his question.

'I don't know of any Glumbruck,' she finally decided, but there was something about the way in which she phrased it, and how she had looked at him, expectantly, when Einer had first opened his eyes to the afterlife, that made him doubt.

She had been there when he had woken up to the afterlife, and clawed himself free of corpses, as if she knew that he had survived and had known exactly where he would wake.

'Do you know me?' he asked.

She took a moment to answer.

Her deep blue eyes studied his face, and matched his stare, and she seemed to look far into the depths of him, in search of something, or waiting for something to happen.

At last, she diverted her eyes. 'Nej,' she declared, and walked on again. 'I'm Hilda.' She turned to smile at him, as she introduced herself. 'Hilda Ragnardóttir.'

'I knew a Ragnar, once,' Einer told her, although he didn't quite know why. 'He was a storyteller.'

'So was my father,' said Hilda.

'The best—' they both said in the same heartbeat, and then they were laughing, and it felt like Einer hadn't laughed that way in winters and summers. It felt silly to walk across corpses of gods and giants and laugh like that, but it felt good too. It felt like even at the end of all things, some things began too.

'You sort of look like him,' said Einer. 'My Ragnar.' As he said it, Einer realised exactly how true it was. Her eyes had that rare shade of blue that he had only seen in the eyes of

Ragnar and Leif, and there was something about how sharp her jawline was, too, and her square chin.

'I look like my Ragnar, too,' said Hilda, and again they were laughing at how silly it all was.

'I should hope so,' Einer laughed. 'Or your mother owes your father some explanations.'

Even as they walked on across the next corpse valley, Einer could not stop smiling. The past three winters had been dire, even when Loki had appeared with his funny tales, and Einer could not quite remember the last time he had walked like this and just enjoyed someone else's company.

'Where are we going?' he asked again, for Hilda seemed like she was heading somewhere.

'Into our future,' she said with a smile. 'Where no story-maker gets to say what we should do.'

Einer nodded at her answer. She had good answers to all his questions. The kind of answers he could not quite predict. It felt a little bit like talking to Loki, or the Alfather, or both of them.

'No matter what my destiny says, I could use a bath,' Einer eventually said, and he looked at her, all drenched in blood. She stank of iron. 'So could you,' he added and laughed.

Hilda did not quite laugh, but he did catch a brief smile on her lips.

A strong wind swept in at their backs. For two long breaths Hilda stood still, closed her eyes and seemed to just enjoy the feel of the wind teasing her hair from its braid.

'The bathhouse is west of here,' she said when she opened her eyes again, and then she pointed the way and they set off in that direction.

Now that they knew exactly where they were headed, they walked with more purpose.

The sun indicated midday, and it beamed down hot over them. Einer's stomach grumbled loudly, but they could not even see a corpse-less plain yet, if there even were any. Yggdrasil was coming closer, but much too slowly for Einer's liking.

Hilda was no longer walking at his side. She had stopped short and was staring down at some corpses.

'What is it?' asked Einer and walked to her so he could see what she did.

'That arm,' she said, pointing to a severed limb among the corpses. 'It's the Alfather's arm.'

He stared down at it, but all Einer saw was a bloodied arm with age spots, a gold ring attached around the wrist, and half of a broken shoulder bone. 'How do you know?' he asked. Although he had met Odin on the battlefield, and in his magnificient hall some winters ago too, it did not look like an arm that could belong to the great Alfather.

'Einer,' she said, in a loving tone like only his mother or an old friend might have used. 'I was fighting at his side. I rode Sleipner into battle. I *knew* Odin.'

She crouched down by the corpses and reached for the arm. She lifted it, cautiously as one might lift a baby, and then she squeezed the elbow tight with one hand and reached for a gold arm-ring with the other. She slid the gold ring over the wrinkled wrist, threw the Alfather's broken arm carelessly down onto the corpses again, and spun the bloodied arm-ring in her hands.

At the end of all things, here was this girl, who not only knew the Alfather well enough to recognise his torn arm on the widest battlefield in the nine worlds, but then saw fit to loot his body.

Einer smiled at it all. Loki would have loved that. He imagined the old giant would have been cackling all the way home at the thought of that, and that even final death, if that had been his fate, would have felt lighter.

'Why?' asked Einer. The ring was pretty, twisted and smithed in an ancient style, but here at the end of everything, it seemed like a luxury that no one needed. He did not understand why she bothered to steal it.

'It's the ring,' said Hilda. 'The famous one. Every nine nights, it sheds another eight, identical.'

'And you need another eight, identical?' he asked with a smile, finding it all unbelievable; the fact that they were here, alive, standing over a piece of the Alfather's corpse, discussing if they should steal from the old man or not.

'I will need many more than eight,' said Hilda. '*You* might have been rich all your life,' she commented as if it was written in runes across Einer's tunic that he had been a chieftain's son— and perhaps it was, his war clothes were clearly expensive. 'But any riches we had in life are gone now, and *I* know that in order to survive in the nine worlds, you need gold. And here it is, a never-ending flood of it.'

Einer began to laugh and looked around at the mountains of corpses that surrounded them. Dead people were heaped and littered across the plains of Asgard, yet here she was talking about trade, as if there was anyone left to trade with anymore. 'And who is going to demand gold from you?'

'Do you see any dwarf corpses?' she asked. 'I've traded with dwarfs, and I see none on this battlefield. No alvar. No svartalvar. There are more beings out there. This is only the end of gods and giants.'

'And afterlives,' said Einer. 'One life, we get. That's why us giants went to war.'

'You're a giant?' she asked, as if that was the important piece of information.

He nodded. Hilda looked at him and thought for a moment, and then she spoke again. 'Your mother,' she said, nodding to herself. She seemed certain of herself as in everything she did or said. 'Glumbruck. That's a giant name. She was a giant.'

Again, Einer nodded, just staring at her as she walked ahead, following their original path again.

Whatever he had expected to find after Ragnarok, he could never have imagined that a girl like this would be marching across Ragnarok's plains, robbing the Alfather, certain of every limping step.

Einer shook his head in disbelief and followed her.

His friends were somewhere there, among the corpses. Everyone Einer had known in life lay dead at his feet. His friends and family, his father, perhaps even his mother. They all had to be lying there somewhere.

The last thing he could have imagined, when he had sent all those thousands of warriors of Helheim into war, was that he would be walking across their remains, when the battle was over. He had not expected to die, and he had not intended to survive.

Hilda's limp was obviously bothering her. It reminded Einer of Ragnar, again.

'Are you wounded?' he asked, although it was obvious that she was. He did not quite know what else to ask, but he wanted to keep talking and keep asking—something—anything. She seemed to have all the answers in the nine worlds, and besides, she was just comfortable to walk next to. Like an old friend. Except that he had a lot more questions for her than for an old friend.

'The limp?' she asked. 'It's not fresh. That was before Ragnarok.' She smiled bitterly. 'An unfated encounter with Fenrir.' When she stopped, she balanced entirely on her right leg, and when she walked, she hardly ever put pressure on her left one. It was more like hopping than walking.

'Do you need a hand?'

'A shoulder would be welcome,' she said, although she did not look like the kind of girl who accepted help from just anyone.

Einer crouched so that she could reach across his shoulder. Somehow it felt like a privilege to be allowed to support her weight, to help her walk across the bloodied wreckage of Ragnarok.

They matched their steps easily. Everything felt easy now, after what they had been through. Even though Einer's wounds hurt, the pain merely reminded him that he was different from the corpses at his feet, because he was alive.

'No afterlives,' Hilda repeated after a while. She must have been thinking about it while they had walked across the mounded dead. 'I think... that most people, when they die, aren't undone. They live on in the hearts and memories of those who survive,' she said.

Einer smiled bitterly at that. It sounded like the forefathers he had always carried within him, without knowing what they truly were. Once he had known what they were, there had been something consoling about knowing that his mother was always with him, but she was gone now. There was no call within him anymore, no anger or urge to kill, and Einer knew that he would never again meet anyone who had died.

'I like to believe that someone will remember them,' Hilda said. 'I can think of nothing worse than to be forgotten for all eternity. So, I like to imagine that they will be remembered.' She stared blankly down at the corpses at their feet. 'All those who died here. Someone in Helheim, someone in Midgard will remember them. Until they too die, and someone else is left to remember.'

'I like that,' Einer said, thinking about the forefathers and the comfort they had given him in life, at least in the end, during the last three winters. 'I don't believe it's true anymore, but I like it.'

They smiled at each other, and something felt right inside. Not just because they could talk about things such as this— Einer had held conversations like this with Loki, once upon a time—but because they could disagree, and both be happy with that. Perhaps it was because they could discover each other through disagreeing, and that felt both like a beginning, and an acknowledgement of something old.

Einer shook his head again. He had never imagined that he would have a conversation like this with a stranger, but he supposed that they had exchanged lineages and so they were more than mere strangers. Besides, something invisible bound the two of them together. They were the last survivors of Ragnarok, after all.

They walked across the mountains of corpses with their arms slung across each other's shoulders. It was the first time, he realised, in as long as he could remember, that he was not staring down at the faces of the fallen and searching for a familiar face. For the first time in what felt like forever, Einer was no longer chasing *anything*, or anyone.

'What?' the girl asked, seeing his thoughtful expression.

Einer let out a relieved sigh at the thought that, finally, no one was listening to his thoughts. The responsibilities he had held during these rough winters melted off his shoulders in that moment.

'What?' she prompted again.

'Nothing,' he responded at once, but as quickly as he had said the word, he regretted it, and changed his mind. 'I'm glad I met you,' he said instead. 'Here at the end of all things.'

Hilda smiled at him, a warm smile that felt like home.

'I'm glad I met you too, Einer.'

HÖD

Chapter One Hundred and Ninety-Five

THE SUN WARMED Höd's face, and despite how even the wind stank of death, it felt good to be home in Asgard after so many centuries stuck in Hel's realm.

'You two go on,' said Nanna, with urgency in her voice. She was not looking at them as she spoke, Höd could tell. Her voice came from another direction. 'I want to check on our house.' She sighed with frustration. 'They better not have burned it.'

Höd and Baldur stood there for many heartbeats, holding each other's shoulders.

'What does it look like?' Höd asked. His brother had always been the best at describing things. He could describe the sea so that even Höd could see every wave and scrap of foam.

'Like home,' Baldur said, and the word made Höd melt into a smile. In death, he had missed Asgard, always longing for the day when they would return home, even if it meant that their other brothers and father and most of their kinsmen were dead.

'Corpses everywhere I look. All of them are red and their blood still flows. Down over other corpses, like ice melting on a mountain. I can see the Midgard Worm,' Baldur said. His descriptions were not nearly as sharp as usual. He was still taking it all in and trying to make sense of how their home had changed. 'Its long tail spreads through the valleys.'

Valleys, he said, though this part of Asgard had never had any.

'It almost looks like Ymir himself is lying across our homeland. The first being. That great giant slain by our father, in the time before time existed. This, too, was our father's doing. More corpses than I can count, or even see.'

Höd imagined corpses laid out on top of each other to form bundles. He imagined that the warriors who had stacked them up must have been dripping with blood too.

'Torn arms and legs. Heads.' Baldur broke into an empty laugh. 'That's a lung, right there. Torn out of someone's chest.'

Höd's neat imagination was shattered by Baldur's description.

'Pieces of people, Höd. We might not even recognise our own brothers in this mess, or our father. If we could ever *find* any of them.' He did not say who else they might not find. Baldur's own son, dead on this battlefield. If it truly was as bloody and horrid as it sounded, then perhaps it was better not to find him.

Baldur stifled a laugh at something. 'There's a snow fox down there,' he said, suddenly. 'Its fur is still white.' He sounded amazed. 'Well, almost. It's pushing its snout through the corpses,' he observed. 'At least someone has plenty of food. What a feast for a scavenger.'

"*At least someone,*" Baldur had said. Höd placed importance on words, for they were how he saw the nine worlds and how the nine worlds saw him, so he had not missed Baldur's phrasing. 'Will there be enough food for us?' asked Höd.

He did not mean just himself and Baldur and Nanna. There had been more survivors from Helheim, and although most of them would likely live outside Asgard's walls, there were no crops planted that far out, and the past three winters had been tough on Helheim's crops. Most of the reserves had been spent on this war.

'Plenty,' said Baldur and then he continued to describe what he saw for Höd. 'Corpses litter Asgard's plains from here to Valhalla, and probably far beyond, but our homeland is wide, Höd, and when I look out west, I see the river that curls around to Yggdrasil's western roots. It runs red, now, but it flows as steadily as ever. Snow melts from the tips of the far mountains and once the blood runs out, the river will become clear again. There are fish to live on, and the land is green on the other side of the river, where no fire demons have reached. Forests span all the way down to the river front. Frey's farmlands will be out there, and I suspect that even at the apparoach of Ragnarok, he would have made certain that they were well tended to. There is much land to live on, and we have fewer people to feed,' Baldur reassured him. 'Much fewer,' he added in a trembling voice.

Again, Höd was reminded of the unspoken facts. Baldur's son, too, lay somewhere out there on the battlefield. Dead at the hands of a giant, or a beast, or perhaps even another warrior. From Baldur's description, they might never find his body, but they did not need to see it to know that he had perished, and that it had been a proud death, like all others on this battlefield.

'Despite all the death,' Baldur eventually said, 'our home is more beautiful than I remember it, Höd.' He clenched Höd's shoulder tight. 'I wish you could see it, too.'

'All of it is yours to rule now,' Höd told his brother.

'Nej,' Baldur answered.

There was a long pause after that, and Höd waited. It had sounded as if Baldur had more to say. Perhaps he was watching something. Seeing people were always watching things when Höd least expected it. They could drift off in the middle of a sentence and share a sigh over something beautiful while Höd was left waiting, hanging on for their next words.

'No one person should rule all of this,' Baldur said. 'It's why our father died; he wanted to rule it all by himself. He wanted to be the only god to the short-lived in Midgard. He always wanted to decide, but no one person can, or should, decide over all of this.'

'But someone needs to unite us, or we will live in the chaos of giants,' Höd said. He had heard of the chaos of giants, and it did not sound pleasant.

'Someone does unite us and binds us to these lands, and to each other,' Baldur said, and he sighed. 'Branched above us.'

It was a simple riddle, and this was one that Höd too knew. Only one thing could be branched above them, in reality and in ability as well. 'Yggdrasil.'

Baldur let out a hum of agreement. 'Yggdrasil stands tall above us, and I do believe that those are green buds on her far-reaching branches.'

YGGDRASIL

Chapter One Hundred and Ninety-Six

WHEN WINTER RETREATS and spring buds, when the obscurity of night gets swallowed by a morning's light, when old things rot away and births that which is new. Through it all, Yggdrasil protects the nine worlds and all their bustling life.

Across the nine worlds her ash children stand against snow and hail and frost. Her kinsmen—her oaks, her spruces, and her beeches—spread into wide forests and make her proud. Moss grows up her trunk, and she lets it. Squirrels gnaw at her bark, and she lets them. Deer nibble on her leaves and she leans down so they may reach.

She was there before the beginning, and she will be there long beyond the end.

ACKNOWLEDGEMENTS

HERE, AT THE end of all things, few words remain unspoken. Solemnly, horns in hand, let us remember those who sacrificed time and effort to bring us across Ragnarok's battlefield.

First, to my closest kinsmen.

To my father, Lars, who was the only other person in the nine worlds who knew which way we were headed across Ida's corpse-ridden plain. You kept me on the path when I faltered. Also to my mother, Helen, the shieldmaiden whose strengths and battles inspired the women in this tale. Always as capable as Siv, as hopeful as Tyra, as impressive as the goddesses.

To small Sif too, the goddess of a golden tomorrow under Yggdrasil's fresh leaves. May your days be long and bright and filled with love. Likewise for those of Ane and Lau who showed pride at my small successes and continue to believe in the big ones. Thank you for the belief.

Next, let us drink a hornful in the honour of my shield-mates. Those who willingly stand at my armoured side in battle.

To my agent, Jamie Cowen, who opened the first passage grave into the other nine worlds for me and trusted in my abilities as surely as Surt trusted in Buntrugg. You secured the ending for me; ensured that the nine worlds would prevail. Thanks to you the story now lays complete in the hands of readers across Midgard.

To my editor, David Moore, and the team at Rebellion, who exerted every effort to arrange a safe passage across Ragnarok's perilous battlefield. Thank you for believing enough in my story to invest in it, and thank you for improving the prose and getting it into all corners of the nine worlds.

I would also like to raise a hornful of mead to the friends I gained and lost along the way. To those who stayed up to chat late into the night, who provided distractions and who accepted my disappearances whenever writing and editing took over my life.

To the little sisters too. To Tora who fell asleep in the bed next to me on our eleventh floor in Seoul as I typed away into the early mornings to complete this grim tale. Your next step into the nine worlds will be grand, do not doubt it. Also to Vilma, launching fast into the nine worlds. Trust in your own abilities and aim for those stars. And to the both of you: know that you will always have a safe place here.

As the hall slowly empties out and quiets down, I ask of you, dear readers—dear warriors—to please rise from your seats, make a ruckus to be heard across all the nine worlds and raise your horns to Hilda, the shieldmaiden with bloody tears. To Einer, the lone white bear. To Ragnar, the bane of gods. To Finn, who gained everything he wished, but not in the way he wanted. To Siv who finally obtained the freedom she chased for so many centuries. And to Tyra who grew into a proud daughter of Glumbruck. Let us gulp down one bottomless hornful to each of these brave warriors who allowed me—some more reluctantly than others—to write their sorrowful tales.

And while you're standing, allow me to praise your contribution as well. This tale could not exist and continue to spread across the nine worlds if there were not readers who loved it and championed it, showed it to their friends and family, and talked about it. Thank you, truly. Your time and interest in this tale have been invaluable to me.

At last, here at the true end of everything, let us raise one last hornful to the Forefathers whom we mourn. As I wrote my way across Ida's plains their wishes and memory echoed through me as clearly as they did for Einer. To my grandfather, Arthur, who told tales of grand sailing trips in his youth. Thanks to you I discovered the joys of the sea which I had always shunned. To my grandmother, Else, who always wished for me to find a meaningful connection to my Danish beginnings. Thanks to you I dug deeper into the Vikings and they brought me here. Both of you left deep imprints into the eternal snow at my feet. This last hornful is for you, dear Forefathers. May our memories of you never fade.

ABOUT THE AUTHOR

Thilde Kold Holdt is a Viking, traveller and a polyglot fluent in Danish, French, English and Korean. As a writer, she is an avid researcher. This is how she first came to row for hours upon hours on a Viking warship. She loved the experience so much that she has sailed with the Viking ship the *Sea Stallion* ever since. Another research trip brought her to all corners of South Korea where she also learnt the art of traditional Korean archery. Born in Denmark, Thilde has lived in many places and countries, taking a bit of each culture with her. This is why she regards herself as simply being from planet Earth, as she has yet to set foot on Mars…

Thilde is currently based in Southern France where she writes full-time.

FIND US ONLINE!

www.rebellionpublishing.com

/rebellionpub   /rebellionpublishing   /rebellionpublishing

SIGN UP TO OUR NEWSLETTER!

rebellionpublishing.com/newsletter

YOUR REVIEWS MATTER!

Enjoy this book? Got something to say?

Leave a review on Amazon, GoodReads or with your
favourite bookseller and let the world know!

THE KNAVE OF
SECRETS

ALEX LIVINGSTON

'Drama, mystery, bloodshed, grim humour abound'

STARBURST

INFERNAL

THE CHRONICLES OF STRATUS BOOK ONE

MARK DE JAGER

⊙ SOLARISBOOKS.COM

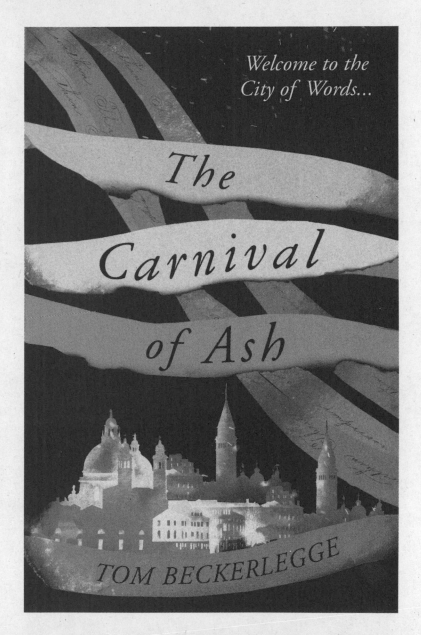

Welcome to the
City of Words...

The
Carnival
of Ash

TOM BECKERLEGGE